THREE DAYS AND TWO KNIGHTS

An Amusing Arthurian Adventure

Scott Davis Howard

Merry Christmas!

Scott Howard

11/25/17

THREE DAYS AND TWO KNIGHTS

An Amusing Arthurian Adventure

Scott Davis Howard

PJPF Press

The Piedmont Journal of Poetry & Fiction

www.piedmontjpf.com

This story is a work of fiction. Names, characters, businesses, places, events and incidents are the products of the author's imagination, from European history, mythology, and are used in a fictitious manner. Any resemblance to actual persons, living or dead, or actual events is coincidental.

ISBN - 13: 978-0692755273

ISBN - 10: 0692755276

Cover design by Kyle Pratt at www.kyleavpratt.com
Map design by Scott Howard and Heather Kaehler
Author photo by Keyyatta Bonds

To Eric, with whom I have shared unnumbered adventures, the most recent of which being when he flew down to Virginia to donate a kidney to my wife—a sacrifice that shows both the bonds of brotherhood and the quality of his generous soul. May he find one more adventure in these pages.

Donate Life: www.kidney.org

AUTHOR'S PREFACE

For those unfamiliar with Arthurian romance, a few words may be helpful before reading this book. The tales of King Arthur are legendary and reputed to have taken place in the waning days of Roman rule in Britannia, roughly around the year 500 AD. However, they were recorded primarily in the 14th and 15th centuries, a time of chivalry, full plate armor, and medieval feudalism. Because of this, they have always taken place in an anachronistic paradox, occurring simultaneously in the 5th and 14th centuries—by this I mean that the knights are equipped as and behave as ideal chivalrous vassals of about the year 1350, but the physical setting is assumed to be long, long in the past, about the year 500. It would be analogous to retelling the story of William the Conqueror using actors equipped with modern military technology and openly referencing any historical event between 1066 and today whenever it was pertinent to the theme or plot. I have exerted every effort to maintain this paradox that is foundational to the genre.

And with that, I ask you to draw your swords, consult your maps, and let your imagination lead you where it will.

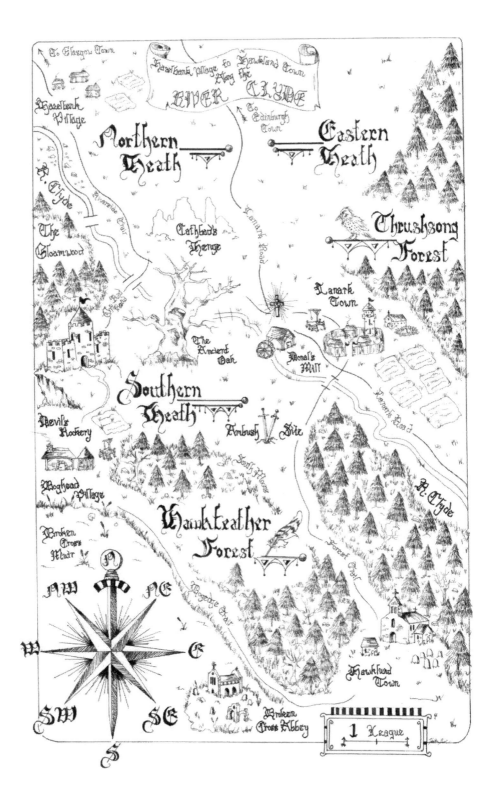

Prologue

Few tales tell of heroes and dragons, kings and giants, magic, miracles, a banshee, and the undead. Fewer still are those told with the skill to evoke tears of sorrow and induce those of laughter. I, Aelfric the Entertainer, glorious, immortal, and peerless—author among authors!—bring to your armchairs just such a tale, learned from the ancient writings of those heroes who were involved—at least, those who survived. It is a tale that began during a bleak time in our great nation of England.

King Arthur, of whom you have certainly heard, was betrayed by that incomparable (and insufferable) Frenchman, Lancelot, and his own promiscuous queen, Guinevere. Bereft of both love and friendship, Arthur took solace in hunting, which, though it may seem strange today, was entirely natural at the time—it appears that all knights and kings loved hunting almost as much as (and indeed, in no small number of cases, more than) their wives and kingdoms. In any case, a 'small' party including only Arthur, his dogs, and a few select retainers (who of course brought their own retainers) decided to hunt the moors of Scotland for a monstrous boar named by the locals "Unghtoosk."

The boar, nearly as old as the king himself, was big as a bear, gray-backed, covered in thick bristling hair, and possessed a pair of terrible yellow-white tusks that it sharpened daily on rocks within the shadow of its cave. It had bright yellow eyes and when it snorted in the early morning of early autumn, breath curled out of its nostrils like smoke from an ancient dragon.

Unfortunately, Arthur never managed to set an eye upon Unghtoosk (rather, a young knight of Celtic descent named Clyde undertook the slaying of the boar, a matter of another tale entirely), for before he ventured far into the moors of Scotland, Arthur himself became the hunted . . .

Unbeknownst to the king, a secret alliance had been gathering against him. For those unfamiliar with the story, Arthur himself was, as so many 'great' rulers are, more or less a pawn of his intelligent and powerful advisor, Merlin, whose untimely disappearance left a large gap that could not be filled. Ultimately, only through the prowess of his military—namely in the person of Sir Lancelot—did Arthur maintain control over his kingdom. Now, without the brains or the brawn, so to speak, Arthur began to amass rivals.

The most famous members of the 'secret' alliance against Arthur were Mordred, Arthur's son *and* nephew (you don't want to know) and the sorceress, Morgana le Fay, Arthur's half-sister and Mordred's aunt[1], both of whom had allies across the moors of the North. Mordred had the sworn allegiance of a minor lord named Malestair and of an aspiring warlock who called himself Rabordath, while Morgana le Fay had done a favor for the local banshee, who haunted the area with her legion of skeletal minions—literally a legion, the remnants of two cohorts of a Roman army from the time of Hadrian. This alliance decided to take advantage of Arthur's exposed position and capture him on the hunt.

Perhaps before I get to the battle and Arthur's hopeless stand on the foggy moors, a bit of information on these three local figures would be in order:

Malestair, the bastard son of Sir Maleagant, was one of the more competent and ambitious servants of Mordred. Tall, swart, and skeletal, possessing a type of physical strength that can only be termed 'sinewy,' and a type of canine cunning that is best labeled 'lethal,' he had, if anything, an inflated idea of his importance. When drunk or possessing time for self-indulgence, he wrapped himself in wolf skins, smiled vaingloriously, stroked his long blonde moustache, and dwelled upon the events of his life, thinking of himself (not entirely incorrectly) as a powerful villain in some troubadour's romance—one whose arrival in the song is always heralded by a few menacing and low notes of the viol.

Arthur granted Malestair lands in the North because of his capability to crush the constant rebellions of the local population—combat and tactics being two of the skills at which Malestair excelled. (If Arthur had a gift, it was in delegating authority to people of

---

[1] It was Morgana who instigated Arthur's incestuous relations with his half-sister, Morgause, and Mordred was the ensuing offspring (to be fair, I did warn you that you didn't want to know).

ability—a valuable trait in a ruler, but almost completely negated by the king's utter failure as a judge of character. All he ever succeeded in doing was appointing enemies to the positions for which they were most suited and from which they could do him the most harm).

In any case, Malestair ruled a forlorn and fenny strip of land, populated not only by howling, drunk, full-bearded Scotsman and blue-painted Woden-worshipping Picts, but also by deformed goblins that skulked in the dark places of the woods, hulking stupid-eyed ogres that lurked among the boulders, wagonloads of wandering gypsies and Jews, and (to the medieval mindset) other like manner of creatures that had been exterminated from lower Britannia by Arthur's God-fearing knights. Malestair dispensed his 'justice'—such as it was—from his seat of power, a creaking black armchair within the ground level of a damp stone keep that squatted upon a stumpy hill. The keep became known as "the Devil's Rookery" because it was home to many purple-headed ravens, whose cackling cries could be heard in all corners of the marshland. Malestair built a wooden palisade around the keep, complete with four towers and a gate. Aside from a handful of splendidly dressed knights, his men sallied forth from this strongpoint, wearing no coats of arms, bearing no flags, and abiding no laws, save those which could be enforced at the tip of a sword.

The second member of this tripartite group, Rabordath, was slight, middle-aged, and walked with a chronic limp—a condition for which he carried a cane of witch-hazel topped with an iron sphere and footed with an iron spike. He was one of those wizards whose ambition far outstripped his actual ability. Fond of illusory charms, he mastered a spell that turned his hair and beard into a conflagration of red-orange flame. For years Rabordath could only maintain this magical effect for moments at a time and saved it to add effect to his frequent (and often carefully scripted) eruptions of rage, but during the previous winter he'd managed to cast a permanence charm on it, rendering his hair and beard into undying flame.

Thankfully for him, this illusion was only of the visual kind, and produced neither heat, sound, nor genuine light. While not a particularly practical or useful magic, one can imagine the effect of his infernal countenance on the impressionable with whom he came in contact. They all supposed his powers to be much greater than they actually were. That is not to say that Rabordath was without some efficacy as a magician. He could, in a pinch, produce open flame within a ten foot radius, cause a stiff wind to blow inside a closed room, briefly turn any stick of about three feet in length into a (poisonless) snake, make writing on parchment emit an eerie scarlet glow, and other parlor tricks of that kind.

However, the main area in which Rabordath claimed a degree of excellence was his knowledge of dragons. His eyes devoured every tome about dragon-lore on which he could lay his black-nailed and calloused hands. Indeed, in his deeply nasal baritone (a paradox that even I cannot explain—suffice it to say that he had a large and long nose and forehead, and his voice reverberated almost to echo within it), he could recite the last thousand lines of *Beowulf*, and the early parts of the *Volsung Saga* by heart, and he often would do so when he thought that no one was listening. He even made up lyrically perfect alternate endings to each in which the dragons emerged victorious. For example, I believe that in an ironic twist of fate (or fatal twist, if you prefer), Beowulf's dragon wrenched the hero's arm from its socket and used it to club him senseless.

In his mania to know all about these beasts, he'd sought out druids and tortured their ancient knowledge from them. In fact, Rabordath once traveled all the way to Munich to hear the words of a magus who was said to have seen a dragon, though in reality the magus had only unearthed a dragon skull—a five foot monstrosity full of teeth and so heavy that it seemed to be made of stone.

Finally (and I have gone on so long that I will try to keep this brief) we come to the banshee, Asacael. Little is known of her, except that she was dead, had been for a long time, and hated the living with a kind of stark raving insanity. The story goes that as a beautiful young woman, she fell madly (and I mean this literally) in love with a brawny and handsome hero. He, in his turn, lusted irresistibly for her, and during their brief 'courtship,' he mentioned words that sounded to her like 'eternal love,' or some such expression. They shared a brief intimate closeness, but he began to realize that she was, for lack of a more delicate term, insane.

Her lunacy was alternately obsessive, manic, narcissistic, and monogamously nymphomaniacal. These traits benefited the romance for about a month, and then the warrior, being a hero and possessed with an innate knowledge of the world, realized that she was really a bit of a monster. Therefore, he took her to a 'romantic' spot beside a peat bog, where, as he told her, he planned to ravish her. He tied her arms and legs to heavy rocks (this excited her), and then instead of ravishing her, composedly lifted her, rocks and all, with a feat of superhuman strength, and plopped the whole bundle into a deep pool of thick brown peat.

There, while her undying hatred kept her soul alive, she waited, thrashing occasionally, for the acid of the bog to eat through the thick hemp, which happened gradually over about a thousand years. After her escape, she wandered the moors by night, frequently overcome by anguish, and screeching her keening lament, a demon woman bewailing the loss of her lover in agony and wrath. She came to exist as a composite of hate, rage, and sorrow. Her one momentary joy (like the joy of smashing something fragile in a fit of fury—complete with the almost instantaneous regret) was to slay the living.

Enough of that. Although it might seem difficult to accomplish, the ambush and capture of King Arthur by these three was a short and bloody affair. The king and his retainers had little chance.

A deep, moist vapor descended on the moors, severing Arthur from his advance guard (namely his nephew, Sir Gawain, who scouted the road ahead). Six leashed hounds led the hunting party, which tracked north along a disused path through the brown and purple heather. As the group wound their careful way down a rocky hill and into a swampy hollow, they came across a scene that seemed from another world. There, strewn across the valley floor, barely discernible through the curling and clumping mist (in fact, only momently revealed as the playful wind gusted), was the rotting remains of an ancient massacre. Contorted skeletal forms lay scattered on the ground, still encased in rusting ring-woven armor and open faced helms, bone-white fingers still grasping swords, spears, and shields (these, curiously well preserved). Their skulls gaped empty-eyed at the trespassers.

Clustered among the rocks in the center of the hollow, where it seemed that they'd fought a desperate last stand, twenty armored skeletons lay piled around a bowed staff. Driven deep into the muddy ground, it stood there, topped with a tarnished gold eagle, marked with the numerals

VIIII[2], and hung with rotting crimson cloth. Dew dripped from the banner onto the stones beneath.

The knights drew near, reined in, and dismounted to examine the scene, remarking on the eerie chill and boggish stench in the air. From the central point, they fanned out to inspect the battlefield in more detail, each as his inclination led him. A few minutes after Arthur's party split, a horse neighed from somewhere deep in the fog, and the king called out (in his classic oratory style):

"To me, lads! Gather here, for I fear that foul magic is afoot on the moors of the North!"

Punctuating his shout, several swords simultaneously slid from scabbards, sounding to all like the menacing hiss of a hydra. A bitter breeze blew up from nowhere, peeling the fog away and exposing Arthur and his few dismounted knights. Across the flat, not a hundred yards distant and without a word of direction, a line of forty mounted warriors spurred toward them, naked blades clasped in mailed fists.

Hooves thundered and the ground shook. Swords clashed, bones cracked, and men screamed and died.

About fifteen of Arthur's party survived the initial charge, including Arthur, his Seneschal, Sir Kay, and his nephew, Sir Agravain, each towering over the others by a whole head. Excalibur had sliced through the torso of an attacker, and his horse fled, still mounted by a pair of armored legs.

"To me!" Arthur bellowed again, and the remaining knights gathered around the rocks, forming an overlapping shield-wall beneath the ancient Roman eagle.

At that very moment, the skeletal legionnaires began to writhe, rising from the low-clinging mist that re-formed on the swampy ground and brandishing their weapons before them. They came at Arthur's party from all sides, and the sound of clashing iron and steel echoed across the dell. The riders galloped in a wild charge, and after a brief bloody stand, only the king, Kay, Agravain, and one heavy-set

---

[2] Interestingly, the famed Ninth Legion used the numerals "VIIII" on its ensign and equipment while stationed in Britannia. This was, of course, before the entire legion infamously "vanished" during a march across the moors of Scotland. When the legion was later reformed in Belgium, it took the more standard IX as its numeric symbol.

serving woman remained of Arthur's party.

A horseman scooped up the woman, her fists flying and legs flailing, but the three knights fought on. Their skill saved them, standing with their backs toward each other, swords flashing, cleaving the helms, armor, and shields of all who came near. Of the forty horsemen, twelve remained unwounded. They reined in and watched for a moment as the skeletal legion smashed hopelessly against the three legendary knights like the sea upon a formation of stone. Then, as if on cue, the riders turned their mounts and galloped away, leaving the king and his knights to their fate. As one, the mounted assailants disappeared down the valley into the resurgent mist.

The wind died and the temperature fell. Undead legionaries stepped back, hollow sockets staring expressionlessly from helmed heads. They locked their oval shields in a perfect circle around the three knights. Frost crept down Excalibur's gleaming blade.

Agravain lifted his visor to utter a boast, but as he did so a raven fell, lifeless, to slap the mud near his feet. He looked down, then back up, and he saw her. His ears buzzed, his mind tumbled down a deep tunnel into darkness, and his vision—indeed, his very eyes—seemed somehow at a greater and greater distance from his internal consciousness.

Her damp skin shown rust-brown, the balls of her eyes were russet and half eaten away, her hair was bleached to an orange-red, and her emaciated body hung like a sack around her bones. She stumbled forward, rather than walking, and the prune-like bag of her naked chest expanded and contracted unevenly, as if she were breathing.

A small songbird dropped, *plop*, onto the moor between them, and then the withered woman's chest expanded, groaning and creaking like aged leather, straining almost to the bursting point. Her mouth opened, a ragged circle of sable shadow, and an otherworldly scream—a keening, moaning, wailing, trailing, blast of sound—swept across the hollow.

Day One

1

NIGHTFALL, THE DEVIL'S ROOKERY

Heather sat painfully upright on a bench beside a rough-hewn plank table in the dank smoky hall of Malestair's tower, enduring his sly glances as his lanky but well-muscled form stalked from one end of the room to the other and turned to shadow against the backlight of the crackling pinewood fire. Tall, broad-shouldered, and uncommonly long of limb, weathered skin stretched tight across his skull, which was set with sunken brown eyes. He was balding. A triangular island of short-cropped blonde hair sprouted from atop his lined forehead. His insufferable gloating wore on her nerves.

"You see, my dear," Malestair sneered from under a well-groomed flax-yellow moustache, "I am in a unique position to take advantage of you." He came around to her side of the table, picking up a lamb bone with long large-knuckled fingers and flicking it to the oversized wolfhound in the corner. It caught the bone with a smooth motion and snapped it between powerful jaws. "Mordred wants only Arthur. He said nothing of you, so I assume from his silence that I am free to do whatever I please." He chuckled pointedly.

Heather shuddered inside at the staginess of Malestair's melodramatic performance—he was obviously playing the part of a ballad-monger's villain—but she remained perfectly still in her seat. He ran a cold, dry finger across her plump shoulders and through her red-brown hair.

"I often wonder," he scoffed, "how I ever existed under Arthur's ridiculous code of chivalry. Thankfully there are other men of equal vision and power... and I serve one." He sniffed her hair and whispered in an artificially husky voice, "You smell like fear." He inhaled, adding, "and you are neither as young, nor as foolish as most of Arthur's mistresses."

"I am *not* his mistress," Heather answered icily, breaking her silence. "And I'm not afraid, either," she added to herself.

"Then tell me what I am to believe." Malestair dropped the lock of hair and stalked around the table again to face her. "Am I to believe that Arthur, with an extremely small and *loyal* bodyguard, and one lone woman, of uncommon," his eyes darted down the length of her upper body, "beauty . . . were riding through the Northern Marches for some other reason?" He leaned close. "Your presence alone among the party confounds me."

Heather was just shy of her twenty-third birthday. Her auburn hair curled naturally, but those curls twisted to ringlets in the damp climate. She had almond-brown eyes, flecked with gold, and she wore somewhat humble clothing, designed for travel: a loose-fitting cream colored tunic and a thick brown woolen skirt that was cut at the ankle. A heavy hooded cloak of Lincoln green felted cloth draped down from her shoulders. Despite her unassuming attire, Malestair was quite correct. Heather was extraordinarily beautiful by the standards of the day, which means that she had wide hips, broad shoulders, a broad bosom, but a comparatively trim waist. Her limbs were hefty and she was tall—perfect for bearing a beefy warrior lord's beefy warrior sons.

As for those of more modern sensibilities, most would call her skin a little too pale, her mouth a little too small, her eyes a little too close together, her forehead a little too tall, and her thin nose a little too long, but to a man of Arthur's day, her traits made her simply irresistible.

Indeed, I fancy that even now she would make resistance difficult, for an inexplicable force, as of gravity, drew one toward her eye, and a calm confidence resided in her voice. Added to this was the fact that she owned more than her fair share of both wit and courage, commodities which were in short demand in the shallow, often Byzantinely political world of the female court.

Her backstory was not as complex as her character. She was the illegitimate daughter of a sometimes-renegade knight and lord who called himself King Pellinore. He eventually bent the knee to Arthur and served him more or less loyally for the remainder of his years. In the meantime, the Lady Elaine[3] fostered Heather in a small castle on an

---

[3] Lady Elaine, as many of you may know, was wed to Sir Lancelot (what a failed marriage that was). He consented to the match against his will and inclination, and only did so on

island off the west coast of Scotland, where she had a pleasantly uneventful childhood. She was serving maid to that lady and would remain so until she married, an inevitable event which she'd already forestalled many times, and which, due to her loyalty and excellent service, Elaine did not encourage.

As might be expected, when Heather came of age, she became Elaine's confidant, and Elaine sent her to Camelot to keep an eye on the wayward Lancelot. So it came about that Heather found herself at the center of the scandal and for a brief time an important person at court. She was, in fact, the real reason for the king's 'hunting' expedition to the North. She could procure access to Lady Elaine for Arthur. It was the king's idea of a covert attempt to broker a peace with Lancelot. He thought that perhaps Lancelot's wife might appeal to his sense of honor and shame him into submission. Often a word from a wife to a husband outweighs a royal decree.

Whether the gambit would have been a success or not, we can only guess—I, personally, fancy that it was destined to fail. Whatever small power of guilt Elaine once held over Lancelot, she'd used up long ago. Oh, self-reproach certainly stung him, but it is one of the most ironic paradoxes of the male temperament that the more shame a man feels, the less likely he is to be persuaded to repent by the person whom he has wronged, especially when she uses guilt as a motive. Like most men, Lancelot lashed out in anger when his shame was too much to bear, thus amplifying his guilt, rather than ameliorating it. It is an all too common downward spiral with men who cherish their honor but act dishonorably.

In the tower, however, Heather set her chin and studied the waving patterns of woodgrain in the crumb-littered pinewood table.

"Believe whatever you want," she replied. "If it suits your

---

the direct orders of the queen, who wished with all her heart to be his lover, but foolishly thought that the wedding would remove it from the realm of possibility. Yet—as is often the case with such things—the more impossible it became, the more desirable it seemed. The marriage gave Lancelot an air of moral respectability, but it was poisonous. Though it gained him outward respect, it smashed his self-respect. As for poor Elaine, she began the romance awed by Lancelot's prowess in battle, reputation, and good looks, and ended it awed by his egotism, indifference, and betrayal. If not for the birth of Galahad, it would have been a total failure, but I digress.

vanity to think that you might force yourself upon a woman who has slept with the king, then by all means, loose your imagination. However, that is all it is—imagination."

Malestair picked up an errant piece of copper cutlery, removing it from Heather's reach and testing the dull blade on his thumb. "*I*," he emphasized, "have not the least interest in your feminine charms, though I do not doubt that someone—or more than one—in this tower *will* enjoy those charms before the week is out, possibly even on my orders." He paused for effect, and then continued with the kind of careful choreography that only comes from rehearsal: "Arthur's hypocrisy has gone too far. The king catches his best friend and his *wife*—the Queen—in bed and he disavows the law—*his own law that he made*—and allows both to live. And now he breaks his own code of chivalry by taking up with a mistress, *married* though he is." He paced, putting on a grand show of being agitated and disapproving, then he slammed the knife down into a crack in the table, rattling the greasy platter and dirty tin plates. He left it there, sticking up like the sword in the stone. "We are back to the ancient problem—one law for the king and another for everyone else—hardly a fair arrangement, and hardly one that creates loyalty among followers, which is why many of us have chosen to side with Sir Mordred, who has pledged to uphold every law he creates."

She scoffed. "It is only because of Arthur's laws that he didn't have *Sir* Mordred and his kind killed. Kings before him wouldn't have needed evidence to execute those they knew to be adversaries."

A grin creased Malestair's face. "A pity, to be sure, but back to the matter at hand. If Mordred chooses to let Arthur live through this, which—by the way—I doubt, I will be sure to spread word of his impropriety far and wide. There are many lords and knights who waver still between Arthur and Mordred. A well substantiated scandal such as this, added to the recent debacle with Lancelot and Guinevere, is bound to have its effect." He paused, then added, "Unless you can provide me with some other reason for your little excursion."

"We were hunting wild boar," she said at last. "Obviously, that is the reason that we had bows and spears and dogs."

"You're lying," Malestair responded. "Boars live in the forest— you were crossing the moors, and *no one* takes a lady on a boar hunt."

She leveled a stare at him. "Do you really think that Mordred will reward you for this?" she asked. "Like as not, he'll accuse you of the king's murder and then behead you to cast himself as a righteous hero. Even if he does reward you today, he'll mark you as a future threat, and you'll find yourself disgraced or dead soon enough. Tyrants reign insecure on their thrones and cannot afford to allow competence in a subordinate—it's too dangerous a trait. You must know that."

Malestair's eyebrows rose. "My lady," he said, a sudden respect underlying his tone. "I see now that you are more than you appear to be—a pretty face *and* a keen mind." He snorted, curling one side of his mouth. "Fear not that I have planned for *every* eventuality. I am, as you say, competent. I have won each and every contest in which I have had tactical command. Planning, you see, careful planning, is my forte."

"Plan all you want," Heather responded. "All I know is that the king's knights will catch up with you eventually, and when they do, I especially will enjoy the spectacle of you abasing yourself before them in an attempt to save your life."

Malestair shrugged off his melodramatic acting and stood suddenly tall, square shouldered, comfortable, and genuinely powerful for the first time since he entered the room. The change was unmistakable; the air seemed to chill.

"I am man enough to face any of Arthur's knights, and warrior enough to best all but two or three from the Table-Round," he said with the kind of offhand confidence in his ability that only comes through skill. He rubbed a long-fingered hand across his close-cropped blonde hair. "However, we aren't talking about my life here, or even yours." Malestair turned toward the fire, warming his hands. A pine log popped, sending skittering sparks across the floor. "We are talking about your future treatment in this tower, and whether I choose to show you proper hospitality, or choose to have my men show you their ... *hospitality*." Sudden harshness hardened his tone. "I ask again: why are you here?"

"It won't work, you know." Heather replied conversationally, ignoring the threat.

"Oh it won't, will it?" Malestair stepped back toward Heather with long strides.

"No," she answered, returning to her previous topic, "begging for mercy never works on Arthur's knights—not when you're guilty.

My only question for you is what manner of execution you prefer: burning alive, hanging, the headman—"

Malestair interrupted, his voice serpentine. "I am awaiting an answer to *my* question, *mistress*."

She sat upright, smoothing a wrinkle out of her brown dress with pale hands. "And I am awaiting one to *mine*." His eyes narrowed and then without warning, he slapped her full across the face. She recoiled and her chair began to tip backward. He caught it, righting her. "I will deal with you soon," he whispered. "Insolence only arouses in me an interest in digging to the truth… I will have one of my best men pay you a visit." Slowly, passionlessly, he touched his dry lips to her forehead and inhaled, his nose pressed against her hair. His flaxen moustache scratched her skin. She leaned back, turning her head in genuine disgust. "Young women always smell so much finer than the air here—" he whispered "—wedged as I am between the moors and a stagnant swamp. And, in my varied experience, I've found that the perspiration of different emotions produces distinctly different scents. Apprehension is, by far, my favorite. Thank you."

He turned from her, footsteps echoing on slate flagstones as he crossed the hall, ascended two steps, and sank into a black creaking armchair."Guards!" he shouted, "Take the *fair* mistress to my room, stand by the door, and call Gurth Stoneface up from the dungeon. Have him bring his… tools. I will arrive presently."

Two men at arms crossed the keep's greathall toward Heather.

"In the meantime," Malestair continued, now done with Heather, "I have a letter to dictate. Fetch my scribe, best rider, and fastest horse."

2

LANARK TOWN

To Lord Ghent, written by the hand of Alanbart, your grace's loyal servant and knight, always.

My Liege, in due course of time my travels have taken me north to the most remote and pagan parts of the isle. Here, the beating drums of Druidism still echo in the forests. Disdain for our Lord is muttered by goblins in every grove, witches in every seaside shanty, and ogres atop every knoll. It is indeed a clear hiding spot for the Cup of Kings. Whoever hid it here was wise as Solomon, for who would look for such an artifact among pagans? The Grail is an elusive charge—rumors of its existence abound in all four corners of the world. And it is only though a discerning intellect that I have traced its whereabouts to an isolated island monastery.

It is on this matter that I must beseech your grace's aid. I have arrived here with an empty purse, and the locals, being either loyal to their pagan wise-men or to Arthur Pendragon, are refusing me food and shelter. If you wish to obtain the Holy Grail before the knights of Arthur's court, it will be necessary for me to hire boats and boatmen, and to rally the local population to our cause through the use of that ever-effective tool of persuasion: gold. Please dispatch some to me forthwith. I am currently lodged in the house of Donal the miller outside of Lanark town.

I humbly remind your grace that once I present you with the Grail, all of Britannia will flock to the banner of Lord Ghent, rightful ruler and High King, and neither this upstart Arthur, nor his rival, Mordred. I await your charity.

Sincerely and earnestly (as always), your faithful and courageous servant,

Alanbart of the Outer Isles, son of Alardane.

Alanbart ended with a flourish on the final letter, lowered his quill, and blew on the paper to dry the ink. He folded it and sealed the paper with beeswax from the candle that burned beside him. His signet ring pressed the stamp of house Alardane into the yellow wax—a cockatrice in fighting stance, wings outstretched, neck and beak forward, lizard tail curling under its legs.

The letter was neither poetical nor allegorical, but it would do the trick nicely, he thought. He wasn't quite as destitute as his writing indicated, but he was a man of taste and wouldn't last more than another month on his current budget. Besides, he needed to hire some local muscle before he could raid the island monasteries in search of 'the Holy Grail.' Whatever non-grail artifacts he happened to keep for himself or sell, well, that was no one's business but his own. He hoped there would be books; this northern existence was dreadfully dull.

Sir Alanbart was of an average height and weight, though somewhat fleshy, especially around the waist and under the chin. He had pale skin, ice blue eyes, and receding nut-brown hair. Scruff shadowed his square jaw. He looked older than his twenty-eight years, seeming to be nearing middle age at first impression. His mother used to mock him, saying that he'd been born wrinkled and never smoothed out. Perhaps she spoke true. He'd had lines on his forehead, under his eyes, and at the corners of his mouth for as long as he could remember. The crow's feet that furrowed the skin outside of his eyes, however, were a new development, but he fancied that they added some sincerity to his smiles and some gravity to his demeanor.

The only child of a poor but loyal knight, Alanbart didn't exactly take to his birthright as he should have. While he could not be described as frail, he wasn't stout, and his aptitude for swordplay, and indeed everything that required hand-eye coordination, was well below average. In fact, he had inherited many more of his sickly, scheming mother's characteristics than those of his father: bad circulation, cold hands, a touch of anemia, a quick mind, and a penchant for dishonesty…oh, and a love of money. About all he got from his father was tendency to drink—heavily, well, heavily for a man of his unimpressive physique and stature.

He paced over to his straw-filled mattress and collapsed with a groan. He didn't like the North. It was a cold, damp place without much in the way of beauty—at least, in regards to the women.

Alanbart sighed and pried the cork out of a bottle of cheap white wine with his dagger. He was about to put it to his lips when he heard a commotion outside. A child cried, a dog barked, and he heard a number of male voices talking excitedly. The sounds came closer in what seemed to be a collision course with his door. Alanbart winced.

"Damn," he muttered and took a quick swig (which spilled down his chin) before he re-corked the bottle. He sat up, pulled out his sword, and arranged himself so that it might seem like he'd been sharpening it all evening. Just as he got into position, a loud knock rang through the thin door to his room.

"Come," he answered and wiped the dribbled wine off his chin and tunic.

A swarthy collection of penniless peasants poured into the room, led by old Donal the miller himself. They appeared threatening in the flickering candlelight, the playing shadows of which detailed the topography of their gaunt and pock-marked faces. The largest and ugliest of the trespassers shoved forward a thin, straw-haired boy of about twelve years of age.

"Tell him, young Andrew," he muttered.

A muddy sheepdog circled nervously around the boy's feet.

"It's my sister, Lord," the boy said rather self-consciously. "We were out herding my father's sheep, like every day, when a giant came up out of the valley and took her. Just like that, he did." The boy finished with a motion that indicated clubbing and stuffing something in a sack.

Alanbart sighed and stood up. "You say a giant?" he asked, dropping his voice an octave.

Young Andrew nodded.

"How tall?"

"He was twenty feet if he was a foot."

"And he carried a club?"

A nod.

"And he took your sister?"

A nod again.

"And did he take any sheep?"

The boy shook his head.

Alanbart smiled without his eyes.

"Well, no harm done then. I doubt the giant will treat her any worse than her husband would have at marriageable age. In fact he has saved your father a dowry and the cost of a wedding." He clapped the boy on the shoulder. Dirt fell to the ground, and Alanbart filled with revulsion to see a louse crawl up his wrist. He flailed his hand, trying to remove it, and continued abstractedly, "and you have all your sheep—indeed even the company of an old sheepdog, which is far superior, as I'm sure you will agree, to the company of a sister." He bent down to scratch the dog's head, but drew his hand back as he imagined the lice—and fleas—upon such a hairy mutt.

It obliged him by sitting up tall on its front legs and scratching earnestly behind its left ear with a rear paw. Alanbart stood and herded the boy toward the door. He waved dismissively at the rest of his uninvited guests.

"Can any of you gentlemen think of any other reason for bothering me at this late hour?" Not giving them time to answer, he continued, "If not, then, I suggest," he motioned to the cracked and unpainted plank door, "that you all go find your homes, bottles, or gutters, and leave the knightly decision making to a knight."

At this the boy broke into tears. A high pitched whine began deep in his chest.

The burliest of the crowd leveled a calloused finger at Alanbart and shouted, "If you are a knight like you say you are, and a knight of the Round Table and King Arthur, then you'd best find that giant and young Andrew's sister or you may find this land a sight less friendly than you did before!"

"And I thought you knights always helped people," came a voice from the back.

"Especially women and girls!"

"And aren't you supposed to be hungering for glory like killing a giant?"

Alanbart sighed. He knew where this line of questioning led. His grin faltered and he closed his eyes for the count of two seconds to regain his composure. When he opened them, he was positively cheerful. Dropping his voice yet another octave, he explained, "Well of course I'll help, if that is what you are asking. I was just endeavoring to find the most equitable solution for all involved—but it appears that this boy genuinely *likes* his sister, and that being the case—and the giant endangering the town, I see no choice, and indeed, my liege, King Arthur, would see no choice but to slay this giant and save you all!" A rumble of approval and a couple of "hear-hears" came from the crowd.

"There is, however, no point in doing anything tonight. It is too dark to track even a giant, and besides, I must take time to ready myself for travel and battle," Alanbart said. 'And escape,' he thought. "I will emerge to track this giant on the morrow. You need fear nothing."

After the crowd left, Alanbart uncorked his bottle for a second time. He took a swig and swished the vinegary liquid around in his mouth before swallowing. He made a disgusted face and then followed it with a couple of big gulps. 'Well,' he mused, 'my time in this town is over.' He started packing his things and glanced over at his armor. At least he could make a show of it, he thought, polishing the tarnish off of its corners.

As he shined his inherited and resized armor, he imagined the scene that he would make in the morning. He'd get up and leave town in a grand show of bravado—the brave hero, off to fight the giant—never to be seen again. He could ride north to a new town, modify his letter to Ghent and await his gold there. That was the sensible thing.

There was likely no giant anyway—the boy was obviously lying. Why would his father send two of them to watch the sheep when one boy and a dog would do the job alone? And why would the boy run to town instead of straight home? And why would he leave his sheep— especially if the giant didn't take any of them? He stood to lose too much to poachers or wolves if he did that—particularly in the night. He would have at least left the dog to watch the flock. Yes, there was no giant and no sister, just a glory-hungry, story-happy shepherd boy, who instead of crying wolf was crying giant.

After telling himself this, Alanbart felt much better. He fluffed the sulfur-yellow plume in his helmet and set it back on the floor. For now, he would drink more wine and get an adequate night's sleep.

3

THE DEVIL'S ROOKERY

Heather scanned Malestair's quarters. The tower itself was Spartan, but this room seemed to have many of the comforts of home. A mildewed tapestry depicting a scene of knights and ladies hawking hung on the wall. A large roughly hewn oak-framed bed graced the leftmost corner of the room, and a number of thick black and gray wolf pelts covered the gritty flagstone floor. A dying fire flickered in the fireplace, almost collapsed to embers. Across the room, a stunted archway led onto a small balcony. Beyond that loomed a thirty foot drop to the damp gravel and a twelve foot climb to the top of the palisade. She wondered if a watchman stood guard atop the tower. Probably. Malestair was a militarily minded man, after all.

There was no moat. That made things more difficult. She couldn't jump and expect to survive, and she couldn't wait here for Stonefaced Gurth—whoever he might be—and Malestair to arrive. She shuddered at the thought of his cold lips and bit back on a feeling of nausea as she recalled his snuffling inhalation. Of course, she assumed that most of it had been an act intended to scare her, and so melodramatically carried off, she thought, that the whole episode and Malestair himself would be laughable if he wasn't deadly competent with a blade and if he wasn't the lord of this place.

'There must be a way out,' she thought as she scanned the room. The idea might have been a bit overdone, but her first thought was to use the tapestry, bedding, and pelts to make a rope and climb down. Malestair, however, had a fondness for dogs—indeed, even his coat of arms was a gray wolfhound—and, no doubt, they could track her and catch her before she got a message to anyone. She thought a bit more and came up with nothing.

What if she faked a rope escape from the tower and hid under the bed? They might go off searching for her, and three or four hours later she might make her way down to the stables and escape with a horse and at least a chance to get to the nearest village. She could think of nothing else on such short notice. In any case, she reasoned, things couldn't realistically get worse.

She set about making a rope. She needed to work quickly, for she had no idea when the master of the tower would arrive, and she needed to work quietly because a guard waited outside the door. It was simple work, though, and she made good time. She tied one bed-sheet to another, to the tapestry, to her cloak, to a pelt, and so on until she'd convinced herself that the length was adequate to climb down. She did doubt whether it would hold her weight, but that didn't matter. She tied it to the bedpost and threw it from the window. It stopped about a dozen feet from the base of the tower, but it was more than enough to look the part. Slinking back into the room, she wedged herself under the squat bed to await the arrival of Malestair and prayed that he was neither as smart nor observant as he pretended to be.

She didn't have to wait long. About three minutes after she hid, the door opened and two pair of boots tromped in, halted, and then ran to the window.

"Gurth," she heard Malestair say with urgent calm, "get down to the base and scour the area—she can't have gone far. Assemble hunting parties with hounds, if necessary. And send for Rabordath. I may have a use for him."

One set of boots left. She watched the other stand at the window for a few minutes until another form arrived at the door. This second visitor wore soft shoes, but they couldn't be seen under a flowing crimson cloak that enwrapped his whole body. A red-dyed wolf fur lining ringed the lower hem and was turning gray from exposure to dust and dirt. The iron tip of his cane tapped the floor between every silent step.

"Rabordath," Malestair said.

"I came as quickly as I could, my lord," a deeply nasal, unctuous voice responded. "What service might I render?"

"Arthur's attractive maiden," Malestair described her with contained venom, "has escaped down this rope"—he tossed it onto the floor—"I trust that you have a spell with which we can track her."

"I do," the newcomer replied, "But I need something of her—a hair or two, perhaps—to make the spell function, and it will take a few hours to prepare. I hope that your men find her before that."

"They will." Malestair sat on the bed. The wood slats bowed and a few loose straws fell to the floor. "You may save your spell, for we will have her sooner than it would be ready. However, I must inquire, how are the preparations going?"

"Well," Rabordath answered, smugly, "quite well indeed. I need only wait for the blue moon to take Arthur's blood with his own blade. That gives us just two days before we can conjure the monster."

"Then I will dispatch our rider to Mordred at once, and we will greet him with a proper welcome." Malestair laughed. "What fortune to capture Arthur, here—in my own realm—instead of having to track him and steal him from Camelot. It troubles me though; why did he come here? What possible purpose could be served in his coming north?"

"I don't know," Rabordath replied, "but it's lucky for us that he came. With the royal blood we should be able to conjure quite a creature, certainly a far more powerful beast than we could have made with the blood of that paltry and self-important Thane of Glamis who has been languishing in your dungeon for half a year. And I need not point out to you that we must recapture the girl as well. The conjuration requires the blood of a king and the blood of a virgin, cut with a silver knife that has never before tasted blood. The more highly born the virgin, the more powerful the creature conjured—it is a fairly simple calculation. *And,*" he laid unusual emphasis on this word, "she must retain her virginity until the conjuring."

"Yes, yes," Malestair dismissed his concerns. "And when we summon it, the beast will be under our complete control?"

"It will be at first," Rabordath answered. He seemed to hesitate a moment before continuing. "But it will grow phenomenally hard to manipulate, and, by my calculations, after about a year, it will have strengthened enough to be near invincible and will care little for the whims of its conjurers."

"So we can use it and then dispose of it? That is acceptable— once Arthur and Mordred's armies are annihilated and we have left most of Britannia in flames, they will call me king and we can slay the beast ourselves."

"I…" Rabordath faltered. "I somehow doubt that we would be able to defeat the monster after that time—dragons are notoriously resistant to both weapons and magic. I think it best to give the thing to the North. It couldn't keep a territory larger than that anyway, and this area is nearly a wasteland already. And," he added in a sly voice, "this realm is always in revolt against any king, besides. Why not obliterate it entirely?"

Malestair sounded jubilant. "Why not? The smell of it nauseates me—stagnant fens and rancid rock coasts, croaking ravens and screeching gulls—why have I spent my life holding lands like these? I will be well rid of this place."

Rabordath chuckled.

"Yes," Malestair continued, "I am quite agreeable to that plan, quite agreeable indeed." He crossed to the window. "In the meantime, I will find the girl and you will continue preparations for the summoning. I want it ready at the first opportunity. If the girl isn't found, we may have visitors. Brush up on your incendiary magics, because if Knights of the Round Table come, we may be overwhelmed here, and if Mordred comes uninvited, he may very well bring Morgana with him, and then we would see once and for all if your boasting has merit."

Rabordath replied, "Yes, my lord," and swooped from the room, tapping his stick and trailing his crimson cloak behind him. Malestair relaxed on the bed and sighed deeply. Heather lay silent beneath the mattress, focusing on a few stray blonde hairs curled near the bed's leg, holding her breath, and waiting for her opportunity to escape.

Day Two

4

MORNING, LANARK TOWN

Ducking under the low arch of the miller's door, Alanbart winced in the dazzling sunshine. 'Of all the mornings for this dreary land to be bright, why this one?' He gave up on shading his eyes and lowered his helmet's visor. He'd drunk too much again before falling asleep, and his head throbbed.

He stepped in something slick. Soft green manure covered his newly polished metal boot. Grumbling, he shook it from his foot, but bits remained between the articulations. He took a breath, rolled his eyes into his head, forced down a bitter laugh and the desire to vomit, and set his course for the stable.

He must have looked quite the sight, he thought, as he strode across the street. People gathered to stare in small bunches, which made him feel more hopeful. Though he was no Percival—his armor was dented, worn, and outdated—these people rarely had the chance to see a knight, so they would still be duly impressed, especially with the sunshine glinting off its polished surface. He gritted his teeth inside his helmet, but gave the gathering crowd a flamboyant (and squeaky) wave as he entered the stable.

Taffy, Alanbart's stout cream-colored Welsh charger, was well past his prime. Someone must have told the stable master of Alanbart's imminent departure, because as the knight entered the building, a stable hand led his horse to him, saddled, readied for a journey, and shining with a careful grooming. He took the reins with neither a word nor penny of thanks, then led Taffy into the sunshine.

The crowd cheered as Alanbart rode out of town. His sulfur-yellow plume tossed and pennant snapped in the northern wind, and he felt, as he often did on these occasions, quite knightly. 'At least,' he thought, 'this must be how a knight who has talent with a blade or lance and prowess on the field of battle must feel during a moment such as this.' Even Alanbart could get lost in that illusion for a while. Unconsciously, his mind sought out a suitable verse:

> *Fearless Roland   rushed to that fray,*
> *'Lone and last   to die that day,*
> *Yet how he gleamed   in golden sun.*
> *His mind it dwelt   on battles won.*
> *His mail was hard   and bright and new.*
> *His blade was bold   and strong and true.*
> *His lance was long   and straight and thick.*

"Heh, thick," he chuckled at the innuendo, and then returned to the lines.

> *The wrathful wind   his pennant whipped.*
> *He laughed at the   oncoming hordes,*
> *Disdaining yet   to blow his horn.*
> *Though through that fight   he could not last,*
> *Yet never was   his fame surpassed.*

'Roland,' he thought, 'now there was a famous fool who martyred himself for pride. A fine famous fool—beloved, admired, and dead, just like Bheorhtnoth, Beowulf, Sigmund, Caesar, Leonidas, Achilles, Hector, and every other idiot who ever put values before life. He ducked to ride under the gate of the town wall, 'Alanbart, take a lesson from history: love yourself and stay alive.'

A loose clutch of boys and dogs trailed behind him some distance from town, but he knew that they would tire of the journey and head back to their hearths for a meal and a safe bed. As he expected, in groups of two and three, they all did just that, until about one league[4] out only one boy and his haggard dog remained. About a hundred yards later, the boy spoke. "The giant's that way." He gestured to the west.

Alanbart lifted his visor—and swore out loud. It was the same straw-haired boy who'd told him the story last night, young . . . Andrew, was it? If he left, the whole countryside would know that he was a sham. He closed his eyes again, frustration threatening to overtake him. 'Of course,' he thought, 'if the boy doesn't make it back to town, who would be the wiser?' He considered this, but as logical as that course of action might be, he had the vice of cowardice and a notoriously weak stomach for blood and gore. No, he couldn't eliminate the boy, which left one option. "Andrew, is it? You look like a brave and trustworthy lad. How would you like to be my squire?" Alanbart asked. "I've been in need of a squire to lead my horse, sharpen my sword and cook my meals—what about it, lad? Are you up for helping a knight?"

The boy blinked at him.

"Of course you'd have to leave this life behind and follow me wherever I go. And our first stop will have to be—"

"No, milord, I'm happy with my father and sister." The boy answered. "I'll be twelve years old in a fortnight and we're going to roast a fat haunch of lamb." He smacked his lips, patted his belly, and thumbed his hand southwest. "The giant's this way," he said, and headed into the hills. "Come on."

Alanbart opened his mouth for a moment and then closed it. It seemed that nothing remained for him to do but follow the child. The journey would buy him time to think of another plan. In any case, he needed time to walk Taffy. The charger was getting older and Alanbart could never be sure when he'd need the horse's speed and stamina to beat a hasty retreat, even if, he told himself again, there was no giant.

He sighed, dismounted, and led his horse off the trail, swishing into deep grass and through low-clinging purple heather flowers after the boy. Beads of moisture and clumps of grass seed collected on the legs of his polished armor. Soon the beads formed droplets and the

---

[4] A league, for those who don't know, is a general measurement of how long a person can walk in an hour at a good pace, roughly three miles by modern calculations.

droplets ran together in tiny rivulets down into his boots, which already began to soak though.

"Damn," Alanbart swore.

5

THE HEATH

Heather hurried through a wet pasture. Untended sheep grazed to the north. The sun peeked over the hills and began to warm her, but dew had soaked her dress and she'd parted with her cloak back in the tower when she'd tied it into the makeshift rope. Her plan to steal a horse had been thwarted by a well-placed guard, but she'd managed to escape through the front gate and traveled in the direction that she thought lay inland—toward the faint indigo and then bright lapis of the soon-to-be rising sun.

She ran into Malestair's men once in the night. As two of them returned to the castle, one stopped to relieve his bladder. She lay still under a clump of briars and avoided his notice, but the outmost hem of her dress got the worst of the encounter.

Now the sun shone, and she needed to find a cottage or shepherd to give her directions. She hadn't thought it through from there. Perhaps a wandering knight might help her. Unlikely. Perhaps she could find Sir Gawain. Her heartbeat quickened at the thought and her chest swelled with hope. Gawain had been riding forward as advance guard when Malestair ambushed Arthur's party, and as far as she knew, he'd missed the battle. The possibility of meeting him, though, was not good. She knew that her best option would be to steal some peasant's clothing and make her way south along the road until she came to Arthur's kingdom. Perhaps—

Heather froze in mid-thought. A muted, but clear bark sounded a few miles back. She could only assume that Malestair's men were on her trail, using hounds to run her to ground. Forcing control over an eddying stream of panic, she picked up her pace, hiked up her skirts, and jogged up the hill through the grass, collecting yet more beggar ticks and bits of thistle in her hose.

6

ELSEWHERE, IN THE HEATH

Alanbart slowed and let the boy stay about twenty yards ahead of him while he discussed his options with Taffy. He was one of a class of human beings who thought more clearly and creatively while in conversation—even pseudo-conversation with an animal—than he did in silence.

"What are we to do with this boy?" he asked the horse. "We can't kill him. Unless," he added slyly, "you did it, you know, by 'accident,' a stomping or a kick to the head… perhaps if something got stuck in your shoe that only little fingers could get out…"

As if in response, Taffy whinnied and pulled the reins.

"Well," Alanbart added defensively, "it was just an idea. After all, it is the most logical solution. What if we just tied him up?" He winced and added in a hopeful tone, "He might escape."

Taffy whinnied again.

"You're right of course; the boy has a dog and it would go get help—they invariably do, it seems. So my reputation will be ruined."

Taffy stopped to chew some grass; Alanbart continued walking two steps before the reins pulled him to a halt.

"Fine!" he exclaimed. "I admit it; I have no reputation. Are you happy now?"

The horse bobbed his head and blew humid breath between his lips. They resumed walking.

"What then, if you have all the answers, should I do?" Alanbart asked and scanned the rolling hilly landscape ahead.

The boy stopped and stood, fidgeting, next to a small grove of saplings surrounding a squat and exceedingly broad oak tree.

"What do you see?!" Alanbart hollered in his direction.

"Here's one of his giant footprints!"

"We'll see about that," Alanbart mumbled, walking up to find the boy inspecting a mark on the ground. Sure enough, in a splash of mud beneath the trees was a huge print at least three feet across and a foot wide. "Well I'll be a son of a…" Alanbart began, but trailed off. "I don't believe it."

"I told you," the boy said smugly. "That footprint must be five times the size of yours."

"Must be." Alanbart's head ached with the implications of a footprint this big—there was indeed a giant out here somewhere. He stood up straight, drew his sword, and gave the area a quick scan. He felt like he was being watched, yet he saw no giant. It would not be able to hide in this open landscape.

"How many of your feet across is't?" the boy persisted.

"I'm not sure," Alanbart answered, still thinking rather than actually listening. He needed to find some prompt solution to this problem. He set his foot into the giant's heel and started pacing forward to discover how big the print was. At least this way he could extrapolate how tall the giant must—

Halfway across (on his third pace), Alanbart was snapped into the air upside down. His armor shrieked with the change in position, and then settled down about three inches, almost covering his mouth. By the time he recovered his senses enough to get his bearings, he was swaying in a lazy figure eight with his head directly above the footprint. The rope snare went up and into the gnarled gray and lichen-splotched limbs of the ancient oak. The boy giggled. Alanbart's visor fell open as a figure strode out of a grove of elderberry bushes surrounding the trunk.

The man seemed like something straight out of druidic legend. He wore woven pants of brightly dyed green and yellow leather, no shirt, and had brilliantly orange hair. His athletic body, broad chest, and narrow face were plastered with blue pigment. He'd obviously thickened his flaming hair with grease, or some such substance to make it stand up in all directions. It looked, by all impressions, like a midnight star. A long nose dominated his horse-like face, framed by a pair of oval eyes and oversized ears. He carried an enormous two handed sword, balanced with the flat on his shoulder. He grinned, baring large square teeth, and his peridot eyes glimmered as he handed the boy a silver coin. Alanbart open his mouth , "But—"

"Run along home," the painted man interrupted. "I'll take care of matters here. And remember," he added as the boy headed away into the grass, "if anyone asks what happened to Arthur's knight, it was the Bandit King that killed him, and not a giant!" He turned to Alanbart. "You've got yourself in quite a spot, haven't you?"

Alanbart waved his sword in the direction of his assailant. "There was no giant," he said, more as a point of fact. "You used me." The motion of talking loosened his helmet, which clattered to the ground, splattering the thin layer of clayish mud.

"To be perfectly clear," the painted man responded, his eyes watching the helmet, "there is a giant in these parts, but yes, the story that the boy told you was a lie. I was just waiting for my chance to defeat a knight."

"So you're going to try to kill me?" Alanbart swung slightly on his rope. It had ensnared his left foot, throwing his whole body off-balance. He shifted his grip on his sword to both hands.

"Try? I am fairly certain that I will kill you. You may have noticed that you're hanging helpless, dangling down, and tied to a tree."

"Ah yes," Alanbart countered with his best show of bravado, "I had noticed that… but I am wearing armor and you are not, so that shifts the balance distinctly in my favor."

"Perhaps," the bandit answered with a wink, "but as a student of the old ways, I shun armor as a device of the weak, so there's nothing for it. However, I have been sharpening my sword since sunup, and I assure you that it is both heavy enough and pointed enough to make short-work of your metal skin. I do believe the advantage still lies with me."

"Maybe, but I am a trained knight of Arthur's Round Table, and as such have had extensive experience in all situations of mortal peril, while you, a simple bandit, have not had that experience at all which puts the advantage in my corner again." He studied the crude hemp rope around his ankle. Strands stuck out at angles hair from a blonde beard.

The bandit opened his mouth to speak, then closed it, sat down cross legged, and pulled thoughtfully at his ear. "You may be right," he nodded. "I'll wait here while the blood rushes to your head. When you feel addled enough that we would be an even match, please tell me so that we can fight. But make sure it is when we are evenly matched—I don't want an unfair advantage."

'I don't want an unfair advantage' Alanbart mimed as he spun slowly in a wide arc. The silence got awkward. The bandit broke a stick in two and to pass the time, began tracing Alanbart's coat of arms in the reddish mud with the sharp end.

"What is your name, Sir Knight?" the painted man asked abruptly. "I have been trying to guess from the stories, but you don't look big enough to be Gawain or any of his kin. I know Galahad, Percival, and Bohrs to be on a grail quest, and Lancelot to be in France. You are not old enough to be Bedivere or Lucan, and I do not recognize your heraldic device—a crimson chicken on a yellow field is it?—so I am at a loss as to your name."

"It is a *Cockatrice*, not a chicken!" Alanbart cried in exasperation. "Can't you see that it has a lizard tail and bat wings? It can turn you to stone with a glance." He gestured lamely at his surcoat and sighed—why was he saddled with this ambiguous coat of arms? He continued, "Alanbart is my name. My stories have been..." He paused, thinking of the proper phrasing, "less widespread," he finished, then added with just the right touch of meekness, "but that suits my humility. What is your name, oh painted one?"

"Scot," the bandit answered.

"That's not a very Pictish sounding name for such a meticulously painted face."

"That's why I go by 'The Bandit King!' but I'm giving up banditry for bigger and better things."

"Such as?"

"I am bringing back the old and honorable ways of my proud people—Woden's ways."

"And what is honorable about war paint?" Alanbart asked.

"Well, it's the tradition," Scot replied. He paused to think. "By wearing paint instead of armor, I am saying that I am man enough to stand up to anyone without the fruits of ill-begotten wealth to protect me. It would be just me and my enemy—face to face. If I was a knight, I could spend more than you on armor and win that way."

"I see," Alanbart answered, "so you are arguing that we use money to gain advantage in combat?"

"Yes, certainly."

"But if you had money you would use it to marshal more warriors to your cause?"

Scot, scratched behind his ear. "Well, if I had money, I suppose I would, yes."

"And isn't that an unfair advantage, setting up unequal sides based on monetary influence?"

Scot jabbed his stick deep into the mud. "Maybe, but that's not the point! The point is that my ways are more honorable than your ways. That's all."

Alanbart cocked an eyebrow. "And why else are they more admirable? I assume you have another reason?"

"Because you and your kind are destroying this land!" Scot stood and started to pace. "You claim to be protecting the people and taxing them so that you can continue with your protection, but all you do is live off of us and feud with each other. There is famine and strife and all of it exists simply to allow you to continue to lie in the lap of luxury with your armor and your painted ladies."

"And you propose to paint the men instead?" Alanbart asked with a smirk. A gust of wind ruffled the oak leaves and rippled across the heather.

Scot's eyes widened, "AND" he continued, cutting Alanbart off, "when there is a battle, both sides arm knights and peasants—the knights, on *both* sides, line up against the peasants and charge. All the peasants die and the champion of the day is the knight who killed the largest number of them. That's how my brothers died—may the stone preserve their spirits."

Because Scot picked up his sword, Alanbart decided that it might be best to remain silent on this point.

"The old ways were so much better," Scot continued doggedly. "The farmers farmed and Woden's warrior caste protected the land[5].

---

[5] In case you are wondering, 'Woden' in the Old English language is supposed by most historians to be synonymous with 'Odin' in the Old Norse. He is the all-knowing one-

We fought monsters and dragons—and the Romans."

"And lost," Alanbart interrupted. He cursed himself for egging on the bandit like this, but he couldn't help it—sarcasm was in his nature.

"And we had plenty for all—and there was none of this foppish chivalry. It was all about honor."

"And aside from painting yourself and putting …whatever that is… in your hair, what exactly is the difference between then and now?" Alanbart asked. "Warrior caste? What do you think we are? Surely you can't be angry because we exterminated most of the monsters and dragons. Perhaps that is just an indication that we do our job better than you."

Scot stopped pacing. He lowered his sword a bit and sighed. "I just don't explain it well. You should talk to Cathbad. He can explain it better." He smoothed an eyebrow with his middle finger. "Unfortunately, that won't ever happen because in order to bring fame and recognition to my cause, I have to kill one of Arthur's knights and send his charred skull back with a note. Then I do the same to the next one he sends to avenge him and so on… until people once again see the power of the old ways." He shifted his grip on his sword, got into a combat stance, then cocked his head to the side. "Oh, and that's grease and lime that I put in my hair—you know, to keep it stiff. I'm using mutton grease, but I've used goat grease and fish grease before. That fish grease stank to Asgard, though—I'll never do that again. How's that head feeling?"

"Still clear as a bell," Alanbart lied. It felt like his eyes might burst. "Though, before you kill me I have a confession to make."

"And what is that," Scot asked, starting to circle Alanbart, and occasionally tapping his armor with the tip of his sword.

"I'm not actually one of Arthur's knights."

Scot stood still; his jaw dropped open. "What?"

---

eyed father of the gods of Asgard in pagan Germanic mythology, and he factors into a number of English place names, is the original forefather listed on many genealogies of kings and royal families, and is responsible for the ridiculous way that we spell Wednesday (Woden's day) which, as a matter of course, is directly followed by Thursday (Thor's day).

"In reality, I serve Lord Ghent, a nobleman who rules a large part of Kent."

"Who?"

"Lord Ghent," Alanbart sighed. "It's not surprising that you've never heard of him. He doesn't have very much power at all—in truth he is under the delusion that if he can find the Holy Grail before Arthur, then he can be made King of Britannia." Alanbart chuckled. "Which is how I came to be in his service. I am his quester—I go around 'looking' for the 'Grail' for him. As it turns out, you and I aren't much different—we both steal money from the rich to keep up our lifestyles. I, too, am a bit of a bandit.

"You see," Alanbart continued, buying time by launching into a languid autobiography. "I was born into a family of noble birth but base wealth. We had no money and no means to keep up our station. My father, Alardane, died in a duel of honor with one of Arthur's more famous knights. I was very young… As a result, my mother and I wandered as exiles from court to court, always scheming for a way to make enough money to live. I didn't get much training in any aspect of knightliness because we couldn't afford it, and I grew up to be a shabby sort of a knight—and scheming like my mother.

"So now I pretend that I'm on a Grail quest for Lord Ghent and he pretends to pay me money for it, and in the meantime I masquerade as one of Arthur's knights so that the local peasants will put me up and feed me for free—I figure Arthur owes me that much for depriving me of a father." He exhaled noisily. "And now if you are going to kill me, I suggest you do it—though I must warn you that I am of below-average skill with the blade and my head is pounding so hard that I can clearly see two of you. However, I do feel for the first time in my life that I could make an honorable end, so please attack before I lose either my nerve or the contents of my bladder."

A dog barked somewhere nearby, punctuating Alanbart's request. Scot raised his eyes to the clear blue heavens in exasperation, then drove his sword into the ground. "Damnit!" he exclaimed, "you aren't even Arthur's knight—and you can't fight me anyway?" He rubbed a hand down his face, smearing the paint. "This is just my luck, you know. I never get the luck. I ask you, have you ever heard of 'The Bandit King'?"

Another dog barked, closer this time.

"No." Alanbart answered. "But I haven't been in the North for very long."

"No one knows me because every time I set up an ambush to rob someone, I get the wrong man. I've meant to rob a magistrate, a bishop, a merchant, and one of Arthur's knights. And I've caught a perverse miller, a gluttonous monk, a haughty haberdasher (that's where I got these fantastic pants), and now you, a false knight. You see, I am an unlucky bandit—though I can fight—a pity you couldn't see firsthand."

Behind Scot the barking intensified; the leaves of the saplings rustled. Alanbart craned his neck to try and see past the bandit, and Scot turned around just in time to find a woman with wild red-brown hair entangled with sticks and twigs come bursting out of the undergrowth.

"They're after me!" she screamed. Her forehead and arms bore bloody scratches.

"Who's after you?" Alanbart and Scot asked simultaneously.

The woman ran behind Alanbart, grabbed his armor, and spun him toward the small grove of oak saplings. She pointed at the wood just as a rangy, storm-gray wolfhound and five men burst into the open[6].

"They are!"

All but one of the men wore black leather armor with rusted metal studs. The other, who stood a bit taller, donned a suit of well-oiled chainmail with a dark-plumed open-faced helmet. His oddly gray face bore no expression. They all carried sharp swords but stopped when they saw Alanbart and Scot.

Taking advantage of the moment, Scot turned his painted head toward the woman and asked, "Whom do I have the honor of

---

[6] I always find it amusing how wolfhounds share little resemblance wolves. Anyone who makes that mistake is confusing the animal with the purpose of its breeding. Wolfhounds were reared to hunt wolves and were so effective that they totally eradicated the species from the British Isles. A wolfhound is tall, trim, and fast. About four feet at the shoulder and weighing as much as a man, it runs like a greyhound and fights like a mastiff. Bands of Celtic warriors leading these hounds into battle so terrified the invading Romans and left such an indelible impression upon the mind of Julius Caesar that he wrote about them in his account of the wars.

defending on this fine sunny morning?"

"Heather," she answered simply.

"Ahh, a lovely Celtic name, that. I would be proud to—"

"Close your mouth and focus!" Alanbart interrupted. "We are surrounded by brigands intent on taking our lives—we need a plan—what are our resources?"

The dark armored men fanned out in a line.

"You," the gray-faced one croaked in a throaty voice, gesturing to the three men on his right, "Take care of the Pict. And you," he gestured to the man with the dog, "get the girl. I'll take the knight." They continued to spread out, circling the small bunch and closing on their targets.

"Resources? Plan? Are you daft?" Heather interrupted. "You—painted one—" she ordered Scot, "take the three on the left. We'll improvise."

"Improvise!" Alanbart exclaimed, "that's your *whole* plan?"

"I'm refining it now!" Heather steered him toward the advancing warrior.

The chain-clad attacker advanced; the subtle clinking of his armor filled Alanbart with dread. There was no escape. They had no plan, and he was snared, hanging upside down with a blinding headache, no fighting ability, no helmet, and no shield.

"I'll keep you facing him," Heather yelled. "Get your blade up and defend yourself!"

Alanbart raised his sword and started clumsily fending off the armored warrior's feints. Out of the corner of his eye he saw the dog's master unleash it and order it to attack. The hound bounded across the field.

"Heather! Dog!" was all Alanbart could get out, as his assailant swung his sword. Alanbart couldn't parry in time and a loud clunk resounded as the sword connected, slashed through his surcoat, and bit into his breastplate. Heather let go, causing him to sway and start spinning.

She turned to the dog, pointed at it, and with considerable authority yelled, "SIT!"

The dog stopped in its tracks and sat. It raised an eyebrow, cocked its head, and lifted its ears. She followed her command with, "STAY!"

Clang! The attacking knight connected with Alanbart's armor again, sending him spinning farther to the left, where the battle between Scot and the three other warriors came into view. Scot amazed Alanbart by parrying all of their attacks and actually forcing them back. Suddenly with a burst of inspired motion, he cut all three of them down in as many strokes. He turned to face Alanbart and shrugged his shoulders as if to say, '*See,* I told you that I can fight.'

Heather spun Alanbart back toward the warrior, and again his reaction time was sorely tested as he deflected a blow aimed at his head.

"Hey, painted man!" he heard Heather yell "Go get that other guy—we'll hold off this one."

"We'll do what?" Alanbart exclaimed. His voice cracked as he deflected another swipe. "I don't know if you noticed, but I'm *losing*!"

"Then I suggest you *think* of something!" Heather responded.

Alanbart focused on finding a weakness or a flaw in his enemy's strategy, but they arced around so that he got distracted by everything he saw in the background. Alanbart got a good upside-down look at the hound, now lying in the grass with his head on his paws and his watery eyes still staring at Heather. Behind the hound, Taffy, his horse, had been grazing placidly, but now backed himself into the tall grass, and began doing his best to fertilize a raised tussock. The dog's master streaked across his vision running straight at the horse and shrieking. Scot chased after him, screaming like a banshee and brandishing his gore spattered blade above his head, two handed. The warrior managed to rip Alanbart's yellow shield off the horse just in time to use it to block Scot's first attack, at which point they swung out of view.

The parry and thrust continued between Alanbart and his assailant for a few seconds more as the dark warrior tried to gain advantage. Alanbart could still hear loud cries and banging of metal on metal behind him.

"I've got an idea," Heather hissed in his ear. "I think he is underestimating you because you haven't even tried to strike him yet. When I say go, you thrust your sword straight forward as hard as you can, and I think we'll finish him."

Alanbart parried again. The crashing and shrieking fell to an abrupt silence behind him. The dark armored knight glanced nervously that way, and Heather screamed: "NOW!"

Alanbart closed his eyes, let out a bellow, and thrust his sword forward with all his might. At the same moment, Heather shoved forward with her legs and lifted herself onto Alanbart's back, adding her weight to his momentum. They swung hard, crashing into the enemy warrior. Alanbart's blade pierced deep into his side. The dark soldier fell with a cry, grievously wounded. Alanbart opened his eyes to find him writhing on the ground, his gray face frightened. Heather and Alanbart swung back and forth, both gasping as their adrenalin drained. Then, at the third swing through the central point of the arc, the rope snapped. They collapsed in a heap of shrieking metal, rustling fabric, and splattering mud.

Scot dispatched the dying warrior and offered Heather his hand. Alanbart struggled to his feet, dirty and dripping. He then bent to retrieve his soiled helmet, wobbled as the blood left his head, and leaned on Scot for support. Taffy paced over, passed Alanbart, and nuzzled Heather. Alanbart furrowed his forehead. "I'm glad you're so concerned for my well-being."

Taffy snorted in response.

Scot handed Alanbart his battered and staved-in shield. Alanbart assessed the damage to his property. His plume was ruined, his surcoat slashed, his armor dented and scratched, his sword chinked, and his shield broken. He sighed. "See? This is why I hate combat. It's so damned expensive. I cannot possibly replace or repair all of this on my current budget."

"Sorry," Scot replied, then smiled broadly. "That was the most fun I've had in a month!" He wiped gore from his arms and chest.

Another dog bayed in the distance. The wolfhound raised his head, lifted his ears, stood, shook, and trotted over to Heather, who gave him and appreciative scratch behind the ear.

"These aren't the only ones who were after me," she said. "More will arrive soon."

"Then I shall take you both to Cathbad's Henge," Scot said.

"Who's Cathbad?" Alanbart asked.

"A druid and my mentor. He'll know what to do. You'll be safe there."

Though debate might have been expected, another hound bayed to the west, and Alanbart and Heather shrugged at each other. She mounted Taffy, and with the wolfhound trotting at their heels, the three unlikely heroes departed north, into the heath.

7

NOON, CATHBAD'S HENGE

"There it is," Scot said, gesturing to a clutch of dark trees settled on a low knob of rocky hill that stuck up, green and gray, from the mottled purple and brown of the heath. A strong south wind gusted warm air across the plain, tossing clusters of heather.

"What kind of trees are those?" Heather asked. "They seem awfully dark."

"Holly," Scot answered. "They're hundreds of years old, and have living intelligence. I can almost feel them thinking when I'm walking within the stone circle and the wind whispers between the boughs. They gossip and groan and creak like old men. Cathbad claims that he can comprehend their conversation."

The reddish clay path upon which they traveled, just visible on the hillside in the noontime light, wound up to the grove. As they followed it, a human form began to take shape against the trees, but much larger than a man. Alanbart halted. "Is that a…."

"Giant?" Heather finished.

"No," Scot answered, though Gonoth did help to construct it. It is a wicker warrior, for the ceremony."

"Who's Gonoth?" Heather asked.

"What ceremony?" Alanbart added.

Scot chuckled and increased his pace, leaping over rocks. He moved tirelessly and held long conversations without losing breath, while Heather and Alanbart found themselves sweating and exhausted, despite the fact that they'd taken turns riding Taffy. He addressed Heather as she struggled to keep up.

"Some would say Gonoth is a giant, and some would call him a green man. He stands tall as a tree and is built like a bear. Cathbad calls him a 'warden of the forest,' and says his fathers are these holly trees. His skin is green-gray like their bark and his hair is as dark and deep a shade as their boughs. His eyes, even, are red as holly berries. He's attractive for all that, too, well proportioned—like a man, not a monster. He's none too bright, though. He serves Cathbad, as do I."

Alanbart and Heather exchanged looks, and he pulled up on Taffy's reins. The horse slowed.

Scot smiled condescendingly over his shoulder. "Oh, don't worry. He's not perilous, unless provoked or unless Cathbad orders him to violence. As for the ceremony," he continued, advancing up the path, "Cathbad had that wicker man built to celebrate the blue moon. I was to capture or kill one of Arthur's knights, and tomorrow we were to place him, alive or dead, in his full glory of arms and armor, inside its chest cavity and burn him. Cathbad is nearly blind, so to read the omens and make prayers he must have a bright blazing fire and it must be at night."

"You mean," Alanbart said, "you planned to burn *me* inside that thing? *Living* or *dead?*"

"Well, yes." Scot admitted. "Though, you're clear of the cage now, seeing that you aren't one of Arthur's knights."

"That's barbaric," Heather said, wrinkling her nose.

"Oh," Scot replied, "remind me again what Arthur's law decreed for poor Guinevere after she slept with Lancelot?"

"She was to be burned at the stake," Alanbart answered cheerfully. "As I recall, though, that one didn't turn out as planned either."

Scot smirked. "Barbaric," he echoed.

They passed under the faceless gaze of the wicker giant. Piled brush and dried grass surrounded it. The hollow of its empty chest was constructed of crisscrossed and lashed branches. It cast no shadow in the noontime sun. Somewhere near its wicker head, an autumn locust made a long keening call. Scot led them toward the cluster of trees.

They hadn't been able to see it before, but a ring of stone circled the hill under the shadow of the trees, about two feet tall and made from boulders of varying girth. Some were cobbled into a wall while other, larger stones stood alone. Some were balls, some loaves, some flat, and some were hewn into great rectangles and carved with runes. Each trunk in the ancient holly grove had the width of a large millstone with roots that entangled and entwined the rocks, snaking down and around them in all directions. Their boughs swayed and seemed to whisper with the wind. An old crow sat on a dead branch, its head nearly bald and faded from purple to white. Its eyes had once been yellow, but were so clouded with cataracts that the pupils had long since disappeared.

"A pet," Alanbart observed. "There's no way that crippled thing could survive in the wild."

"Perhaps a familiar serving the druid," Heather suggested. "You might want to watch your tongue."

"Caw!" it shouted as they neared, "Caw! Caw! Caw!" Then it dropped from its perch and fluttered into the grove.

A gap in the stone wall loomed before them, dark green against the sunlight. Scot ducked under a holly limb and vanished. The wolfhound followed without hesitation. Alanbart dismounted and draped Taffy's reins over a low-hanging branch. He patted the horse and whispered, "Feel free to worry. If you hear me scream, I expect a rescue."

In response, Taffy blew air out of his nose and lowered his head to the grass.

Alanbart glanced at Heather. "Should we enter?" he asked.

"Well, we've come this far." She led him into the grove.

When Alanbart ducked through the arch, he found worn and wobbly slate steps leading down another four feet into a bowl-shaped shady hollow. The wall of stone sank much deeper inside than out. Spruce-green moss and whitish lichen coated the stones and crawled up the trunks. Also, he noted that the wall was a large circle of stone about thirty yards in diameter matching a circle of holly trees—he counted twelve in all.

Dim green light filtered through the canopy of overhanging branches to illuminate a large pentagonal slab that rested in the center of the ring, obviously an altar of some kind. The place smelled of wet soil, decay, moss, and faintly of woodsmoke. The ground was pebbled, mossy, and littered with broken and rotting twigs. A few strands of pale grass grew here or there where the light broke through, though mainly in large clumps around the stone in the center.

"Caw!" The crow called again, fluttering down from a branch to land on the altar. Alanbart noted that the branch, about the diameter of his fist, had been sliced clean off, the flat of the cut carved into a small, screaming, human face. The scarred wood was gray and spider-webbed with cracks and lines. The image disconcerted him, to say the least.

"Cathbad," Scot began, addressing the bird as it fluttered to a stop. "I have brought strangers here against your wish, I know."

"Caw! Caw!" the crow chastised. Alanbart and Heather raised their eyebrows at each other, as if to say, 'Great, he talks to birds.'

Scot continued, oblivious to their discomfort. "It turns out that the villagers were wrong, and your vision would, ah, seem to be mistaken as well. This man is Alanbart, a knight of Lord Ghent of a place called Kent, not of Arthur's Round Table. The woman is named Heather and was fleeing from the Rookery. She is clearly no friend of the tower. They didn't know where to go and were being perused, so I brought—"

At that moment the crow took to wing, fluttered past Scot's head, and pecked at his face. He neither protested nor defended himself.

"Caw!"

The bird emptied its bowels into a sticky white splotch on Alanbart's shoulder.

"Why you little son of a—" Alanbart began, looking with scorn at his shoulder and then with hate at the bird, but even as he did so, it began to transform. Its wings elongated with each beat, the feathers taking the shape of knuckley, arthritic fingers and hands; its neck stretched obscenely; its head expanded, bubbling out in all directions; and its color began to change from dark to bright. Neither flash nor light, nor puff of smoke accompanied the change, just a strange, almost natural growth into the form of an ancient man, bowed by years.

"Cathbad," Heather whispered.

The druid was tall, but hunched, frail and thin with papery skin hanging in wattle-like folds under his chin. He was covered in brownish liver spots, purple veins, and wrinkles. Long unkempt hair sprouted from his temples under a bald crown. It wound thinly in uneven strands down past his shoulders. At one time it might have been black, but had faded to that odd blue-white that black haired people tend to achieve in extreme age. An intricately braided and drooping moustache of the same hue graced his upper lip. Thick brass beads dangled from it, threaded through each woven end. He wore a robe that at one time may have been white, but had been dyed by sweat and wear to a disquieting mottled creamish-tan. Most striking, though, about him were his eyes. No hint of their original color remained. Gazing upon them felt to Alanbart like staring into milky water, the darkness of the pupils barely discernable beneath layers of age. It made Alanbart's eyes itch just to see them.

Ancient as he might be, Cathbad was one of a handful of true druids remaining on the island, the last living disciple of Glyndwyrd, the final high druid to be elected by the great synod. At one time Cathbad had been a powerful and promising man, but years of bad luck, defeats, broken vows, unanswered prayers, and lost comrades had left him insular and bitter. He'd forgotten his promise to aid the people and use his powers to bring glory to the Faith, and now lived wholly apart from civilization. He had few followers, no plan for the future, and dwindling abilities. The fact that he became a mere crow when transfigured illustrated this point. As you may or may not know, a druid's animal forms are directly linked to his magical prowess. A very powerful druid might take avian form as a condor, albatross, eagle, or even a great owl, and animal form as a bear, lion, or aurochs[7]. At one time Cathbad could become a buzzard and a large fox, but now he could only assume the forms of crow and a squirrel, both of these venerable and blind. Of course none of his guests knew any of this, and because the knowledge troubled him, Cathbad kept it to himself.

Before any of the visitors found their words, the old man spoke. "I am Cathbad," he said in a high-pitched, vacillating tone, tremulous with age, "a druid of the Old Ways, and this is my home." He gestured around him. "As you have been brought here by no fault of your own, I shall treat you as guests. You will eat my food and drink

---

[7] An aurochs, for those that don't know, is a massive wild oxen and the ancestor of all domesticated cattle. Regrettably, wealthy knights and lords hunted the aurochs to extinction for food, trophies, and sport. Nearly six feet tall at the shoulder, weighing over one and a half tons, warmed by a coat of shaggy black hair, and armed with a pair of deadly curving horns as widespread as a man's outstretched arms, it was truly the king of primeval European moors, heather, and scrublands.

my tea—the laws of hospitality will be enforced—once you have done this, no harm will come to you from me, and none to me from you, else a deadly curse will be invoked on the offending party. Scot! Bring us oat cake and tea."

"Yes, Cathbad." Scot answered, and then ducked out the opposite side of the henge.

This left Heather and Alanbart watching Cathbad across the empty circle. Neither felt comfortable enough to converse.

The old druid cleared his throat, as if to speak, but then did not.

Alanbart diverted himself by examining the holly trees, noting that many more of the thick low-hanging inner branches had been cut off, the amputated limbs carved into supremely emotional faces snaked out of the trees and stared disconcertingly into the circle. He fidgeted, avoiding their sightless gazes. When the silence became unbearably awkward, he spoke. "So, um, how do you like, uh… druiding?" Alanbart regretted the question immediately.

"It would please me, *boy*," Cathbad answered in an acid tone, "if you would hold your tongue until hospitality has been achieved." But then he continued talking quietly and absentmindedly, as if having a discussion with himself. "Why does my warrior bring them here? And what does the villain of the tower want with this wench? Where is the great knight that I foresaw? And what am I to do about it all? …There was a day when I was younger and would not have suffered this lord of the tower to blight my land. That day is vanished into the night of the past, as if it never had been. . . D'ah! Where is that boy?" He turned, seemingly seeing through the gap in the trees to Scot's activity beyond.

Alanbart turned his back to Cathbad and faced Heather. "You know, he has a point," he whispered. "I've been meaning to ask, why were those men after you?"

"It's quite the narrative," she replied. "Though, I have a feeling that I'll be relating it soon enough. I escaped from his tower, where I was a prisoner. I was not the only captive there, though. Malestair, the lord of that place, has imprisoned King Arthur."

Alanbart gasped at this news, and Cathbad swiveled nimbly around, breathing audibly through crooked teeth. He began to dance a hideous jig on the spot. "Oh-ho!" He shouted, rubbing papery hands together and cackling, "Cathbad may be old, and Cathbad may be blind, but Cathbad has ears and hears many things. King Arthur, you say? Captured? Imprisoned? Glory to the gods! The omens were good for a reason, it seems, very good for old Cathbad the druid!"

Heather put her hands on her hips. "You gleefully celebrate a great man's ruin?"

"Great he may be," Cathbad answered, "but terrible, too, to me and to my kind. How many of us have his knights slain? How many henges toppled? How many groves put to the axe and torch? You mourn the loss of a benevolent lord, but I rejoice at the misfortune of a mortal foe." And at that he laughed a thin wheezy laugh that ended in a croaking cough.

Alanbart turned back to Heather. "What is your intent? You are planning something: don't deny it."

She said, "Of course I *want* to rescue him, but I don't have a plan, and I don't see how the thing can be accomplished. That place is a fortress full of fighting men, and he has a red wizard." Her throat constricted, as she recalled the conversation she overheard while under the bed. She touched Alanbart's arm. "Tomorrow is the blue moon. If we're going to rescue the king, it has to be before tomorrow. The wizard, Rabordath, is going to conjure a—"

Just then, Scot returned carrying a dented copper tea kettle and a bronze tray stacked with four wooden cups and four thick disks of hearty cake. "Gonoth's outside," he said conversationally. "He says that the men of the tower are scouring the countryside in groups of five and six. Admittedly, though, he isn't much good at counting, so he might be wrong. He encountered two troops, but both fled from him. He wonders what is your command?" Scot handed Cathbad a cup, filled it, then broke off a piece of oat cake for the druid.

"I will be with him presently," Cathbad replied. He accepted the cake and waited for Heather and Alanbart to be served. When they each had food, he raised the cake and drink above his head and said, rather sanctimoniously, "Let us eat together in the sight of these stones and trees and bind us by the law of hospitality."

They ate. Both the tea and the cake pleased Alanbart. The tea tasted uncannily like summer grass; the cake, though dry, was made of a hearty oat paste and was speckled with dried elderberries and little black seeds.

When Cathbad finished a bite and sip, he returned the food to the platter and turned toward Heather. "You were telling your tale, I believe. Do continue." He opened his hands in an eager gesture.

Heather described the capture of Arthur's party on the moors, unfolding details of the combat, the rise of the undead and the arrival of the banshee.

"Asacael," Cathbad said, interrupting her. "A more dreadful demon cannot be found in these lands. I must give a thought tonight to her alliance with the tower. Continue."

She described her capture by tower soldiers, her encounters with Malestair and Rabordath, and their plan to conjure a dragon on the day of the blue moon.

"They need both Arthur's and a virgin's blood to complete the spell," she concluded. "They intend to use the dragon to burn lower Britannia into submission, and then release the beast into the North so that it may decimate crops and quell the rebellious locals."

Scot's eyes lit at the mention of a dragon. He rolled back and forth on the balls of his feet, excited at the prospect of combat with such a creature. To Cathbad, he said, "Perhaps this is for the best. I beg you, allow the beast to be born. Allow it to scorch the South. When it returns, I shall slay it and we shall have peace."

Cathbad shook his head and traced a finger down the grimace of an anguished face that snaked out of a holly limb. His mustache swayed hypnotically. "I believe that you would fight valiantly, my brave warrior, but in the end you would die valiantly, wreathed in dragon-fire. A dragon is beyond any of us. The old days are gone and those with the strength of ancients are buried in the womb of earth. We are not now of the same stock, toil as we may, to achieve feats of that kind. No, we may not let this evil be hatched. However, neither are we strong enough to take the tower alone, nor may we do so without the assistance of the gods and without gathering a few important artifacts. Tonight we must have a sacrifice worthy of this endeavor."

"Hold on, wait just a damn minute!" Alanbart interrupted, leveling a finger at the druid. "I ate your damn bread and drank your damn tea, so you cannot bloody well sacrifice me!"

Cathbad scoffed. "You? I mean to beg the aid of the gods, not insult them. We will have the sacrifice for which we built the wicker giant. A knight of Arthur still lingers in this land—I have seen him in my sleep. My crows have glimpsed him from the wing." He turned to Scot. "Bring him to me."

"But where is he, Cathbad?" Scot asked.

"In my vision I saw him in a forest, hunting. The trees were hemlock."

"Most likely the Gloamwood, then," Scot replied. "It isn't but two leagues distant."

"He has to be Sir Gawain," Heather added excitedly. "He was scouting ahead when we were attacked. It would be better by far to enlist his aid than to waste him in a pagan burning. I know him and can get him to join us."

Cathbad stood tall, inhaled and said in a thrummingly resonant voice, "Better to have the aid of one mortal man than the aid of the gods? Girl, you don't know what you're saying!" Heather didn't reply, but was clearly troubled and thinking deeply.

Cathbad moved toward the far archway. "Come," he commanded.

The noontime light hurt their eyes as they left the grove's shade. Cathbad's home abutted the henge wall, a small hut, cut into the hill and roofed with living grass and moss. Smoke curled from a raised stone chimney into overhanging holly boughs. Casting a short shadow across the hovel, the giant, Gonoth, waited for them. He was exactly as Scot described him, eighteen feet tall, muscular, with gray-green skin, forest-green hair, and ruby eyes. He leaned upon a thick tree trunk cudgel, his muscular body proportioned like a man's, broad of shoulder, trim of waist, and attractive of face. He wore simple woodsman's clothing of a brown-gray hue. A certain look of dullness or slowness around the eyes and malice in the way that he held his mouth marred the perfection of his form, though, leaving both Alanbart and Heather uneasy. Cathbad asked, "You see my giant?"

"Yes," Heather replied.

"You wish to rescue your king?"

"Yes."

"Then choose: you may have the help of this *Sir Gawain*, or you may have the help of Cathbad and of the gods. I can cast spells. I own the allegiance of Gonoth and Scot. I can rally a tribe of a hundred vicious goblins to our cause. I can call the creatures of the forest to my service. What can he do, this knight? Which of us stands you in better stead?"

"It seems obvious to me," Alanbart said. "This same Sir Gawain killed my father, so I for one will be happy to be avenged, though I have no desire to watch him burn." At these words, Heather glared dangerously. Ignoring her, he continued, "Although, in truth, I'd rather head north and wash my hands of this whole unfortunate business, as it doesn't really concern me."

"Let us *capture* Sir Gawain," Heather interrupted. "Scot, I will go with you. Sir Gawain knows me, so maybe I can be of service in his capture. We can talk about what to do with him *after* he is our prisoner." Without waiting for an answer, she strode to Scot's side.

Alanbart glanced at Gonoth. The giant flexed a bicep as big as a beer barrel. Goosebumps ran down Alanbart's spine. He recalled childhood tales of giants grinding bones for bread and drinking fermented blood from cups made of skulls. He shivered. "I'll come too," he volunteered hastily. "Maybe I can help."

8

DUSK, THE GLOAMWOOD

"All I'm saying," Heather continued, hopping over a particularly gnarled root, "is that it would be a waste of a good man and of an excellent warrior to burn him as a sacrifice. He's worth fifty goblins, at least, and probably worth Gonoth as well. He has fought trolls and ogres. He defeated a rabid wolfman, wielding only a flaming brand. He won a beheading contest with a giant and outsmarted Morgana le Fay. He's the third most able knight in Arthur's court, for God's sake—bettered in combat only by Lancelot and Tristan. We *should* use him." She'd been putting forward this same point for the last two leagues.

"Gods! Let it go, woman," Scot complained. "I can see that you admire this man…" he paused, looking shrewdly at her, "…if admire is a strong enough word for it, but my orders are simple: capture him if I can, kill him if I cannot."

"What if he kills you?" She protested.

"What if?" He shrugged his shoulders. "There are worse ways to die than in combat with the third best knight in England."

"Do you smell smoke?" Alanbart interrupted their argument.

"No," Scot answered.

"Yes," said Heather, after a moment.

Tall hemlock trees crowded the damp and dark Gloamwood. Their winding roots poisoned the ground near their trunks so that nothing else could grow. The whole landscape was free of undergrowth, save for a sparse sprinkling of small saplings, but carpeted in twigs and brown and black needle-litter. Bracket fungi clung to every dead and dying tree trunk, and mushrooms sprouted from the forest floor. The air smelled of moist soil and decay. Orange-green moss crept across the ground, muffling the sound of their movements. At this time of day, the amber light of sunset sliced though the needles at an angle, leaving the forest floor patchy, bathed in a warm glow in some places and dark as night in others.

"The breeze is from the south," Scot offered. "If there is a fire, it will be in that direction."

"With a great beak of a nose like that—honestly, it's almost Roman—how is it that *he's* the one who *doesn't* smell the smoke?" Alanbart muttered to his horse. Taffy didn't answer and Scot, who did have hearing to match his large ears, pretended not to hear.

As they headed south, the smell of fire became unmistakable. It seemed to be coming from a rocky dell fifty yards distant. They crept to the edge of the shallow ledge and peered over to observe any activity below.

There, with his back to them, squatted a tall and broad-chested knight wearing full armor, but helmless. His silver-gold hair grew to shoulder length, and he'd close-cropped his platinum beard. He wore a crimson surcoat over his intricately and expensively worked armor, which was inlaid with highlights of gold and studded with garnets. A green sash, sparkling with emeralds, cut crosswise down his body. Nearby, a dappled gray and white warhorse stood, saddled but not tied to any of the trees. It lowered its head, sniffing at the earth and showcasing beautiful barding—red leather armor, embossed with gold. Strapped to its saddle rested an ominous green greataxe of superior craftsmanship with an extravagantly long blade in the Danish style. A triangular red and white striped steel shield reclined against a nearby tree, emblazoned with a golden coat of arms—a pentangle, a five pointed star braided into an unending knot. The knight sliced a knife down the length of a medium sized boar carcass, obviously in the early stages of cleaning it for spitting and cooking on the open flame.

Of course, as you have certainly guessed, the knight in question was in fact Sir Gawain[8], and the three onlookers each observed him in a different way. Scot's eyes shone with admiration, excitement, hope, and determination, sizing up the knight as a famous and worthy

---

[8] For those unfamiliar with his fame, Gawain is probably the most frequently recorded name in Arthurian adventures, aside from Arthur himself. As opposed to many other knights, most notably Percival and Galahad, Gawain has a mixed poetic legacy. English

adversary, yet confident in his own ability to best the aging warrior. Alanbart appraised him with an odd combination of interest, aversion, and fear—much the same way that he might scrutinize a wasps' nest that lay in his path. Oddly, he felt none of the anger or hatred that he'd imagined might fill him when gazing upon his father's killer. In contrast to the others, Heather looked on, feeling unsure. A crescent of teardrop filmed each of her eyes, belying some deeper emotional investment or connection. She sighed.

"Let me talk to him," Heather whispered, standing abruptly. "I may be able to convince him to come with us willingly."

In reply, Scot shook his head, put a finger to his lips, and drew the blade from his back. A light gleamed in his green eyes. Not waiting for another comment, he vaulted over the rock, and rode a wave ofsliding stones down into the dell.

"Sir Gawain!" he shouted as he came to an uneasy halt, "I am Scot, swordsman and sworn servant of Cathbad the Old, and I demand your surrender in his name and in the name of the northern gods, who are far more ancient than the hypocritical one that you serve."

Gawain placed his knife on the ground, rose, and sized up his

---

bards revere him as an almost godlike representation of chivalry and prowess on the field of battle, while French jongleurs gently mock his powers of resistance to the charms of women and place him in the second class of Arthur's knights militant. The French also cast him as melodramatic, emotional, and vengeful in a quarrel. For example, in one poignant tale, a knight killed Gawain's dogs, and—enraged—he decided to take revenge by beheading the knight, despite the man's abject pleas for mercy. Unfortunately, as Gawain's blade arced down, the nameless knight's lady flung herself into harm's way and lost her head instead, leaving Gawain remorseful and dishonored.

This story is true, but the image of Gawain as a man at the mercy of his emotions is not. Clearly he felt emotion, but he was in command of it nearly all of the time. As is the case with most carefully controlled people everywhere, however, from time to time he would experience violent uncontrolled outbursts of emotion—rage, pain, desire, and so forth. But these were so rare that to take them as the rule rather than the exception does our knight a great disservice.

In any case, to make up for the catastrophic failure of beheading a lady, Sir Gawain declared that he would champion women for the rest of his days, and he was as good as his word. This, naturally, created a very positive chain of songs and lays that cast him as a pure and perfect knight, renowned for his courtesy.

As you can see, unlike other legendary knights, Sir Gawain was real and human. He had a heroic heart tempered by flaws, and to many—myself included—he still represents the height of perfection that is attainable to inherently defective humans, but again I digress.

adversary. Scot stood shorter and thinner, unarmored, but fifteen years younger. He carried a long two-handed blade that would give him the edge in reach.

"May I avail myself of sword and shield?" Gawain asked, his voice a masculine baritone, untainted by fear.

"Avail yourself," Scot replied with a curt nod. Gawain pulled a shining steel blade from his scabbard, walked to the tree, and hoisted the shield, strapping it to his forearm.

"I can't let this happen," Heather said, clearly agitated.

"We can't bloody well stop it," Alanbart replied, somewhat callously. "Face the facts, the old man is right—you have no hope without his help. Unless we can find some way to placate Cathbad, give him his sacrifice, and still save the life of my father's murderer, our luck has run out."

"We have luck?" Heather quipped, looking uncertainly between Alanbart and Gawain.

"I'm still alive. I consider that lucky. Consider this optimistically; at least it should be a good show." Alanbart kicked out his legs dramatically and tried to give an impression of comfort.

Truth be told, he'd been wearing his armor for far too long, had walked farther than he ever liked to walk in a week, and had seen more blood than he could stomach. The sight of the butchered boar nauseated him. Flies buzzed around it. But acting came more naturally to him than being natural, and this is what 'Sir Alanbart' would do. He patted a rock next to him and concluded, "Won't you have a seat, my dear?"

At that moment the clash of blades resounded, echoing on the rocks. Heather watched with mounting apprehension. Alanbart watched with detached interest. The two warriors fought a fast and ferocious combat. Scot began on the offensive, landing a flurry of blows on Gawain's shield and sword, but despite the speed and savagery of his assault, he didn't break through. After testing his adversary's ability, Gawain began to advance behind his shield, stabbing and slashing at advantageous moments, and pressing Scot back toward a fallen log that he might get pinned against or trip over. Instead, Scot, unarmored as he was, vaulted over the log, interposing it between himself and Gawain. The sound of battle halted for a moment as the two took stock of the obstacle.

During this lull, Heather made her decision, hiked up her skirt, and started for the slope, determined to interfere. At that instant, however, taking in the scene, and letting his eyes rest distastefully on the dead boar, an idea struck Alanbart. He sat upright and grabbed at her arm before she could get away.

"Heather!" he exclaimed. She stopped. "I have a way to keep him alive."

She turned.

"Cathbad is blind," Alanbart said, "so he won't know if we've captured Gawain or not. Here's what we do: We take Gawain prisoner, then we take off his armor. We chop the snout off that boar and then shove its carcass inside the armor. Then we tell the druid that it is Gawain's corpse and that Scot stabbed him in the face. He may or may not check the body, but it will be in full armor and the head will be a bloody mess, so it shouldn't matter. Then, when he burns it in his wicker statue, it will smell quite like a burning corpse, men and pigs both being thin-skinned and fatty. Cathbad will never be the wiser, and if we can keep Sir Gawain quiet, he can follow us and assist us in freeing the king."

He realized, uneasily, that by using the word *we* he included himself in Heather's plan to save King Arthur. Alanbart wondered if he meant it, but kept his thoughts to himself.

Heather assessed his idea, trying not to be distracted by the sounds of the duel, which had recommenced below.

Scot and Gawain displayed phenomenal speed and skill. The pagan swordsman's movements were lithe and fast. He used a cumbersome blade with a speed that seemed almost inhuman. The knight's movements, by contrast, were careful, practiced, and extremely competent—he never made a mistake or presented an opening to his opponent. Gawain handily parried many strokes that would have easily slain Alanbart on his best day. Scot's arcing overhead assaults kept shedding small boughs from the trees. They fell softly to the ground. Sparks flew when the blades clashed, and occasionally the golden disk of the setting sun reflected, flashing from a mirror-like blade or sparkling off of Gawain's polished armor.

This dramatic action, too, took place during that brief interval that comes on clear autumn evenings, when the sun begins to set and the world glows amber. Everything stops, expectant: no crickets, no birdsong, not even a puff of wind. Pausing to soak up that last ray of sun is practically a rule of nature—but not so to men. The clash of steel tore through the serenity.

Alanbart appreciated the artistry of the scene and absently wondered how the fight would conclude if Heather didn't intervene. Gawain wore full armor and was the elder by many years. He would tire first. But the unarmored swordsman would die a horrible death if Gawain landed but one blow. It was a tossup. 'What if they both killed each other?' he wondered, sitting suddenly more upright. That armor was bound to be worth a lot of money, to say nothing of the horse…

Before he brought that line of reasoning to a conclusion, Heather finished her deliberation.

"Let's do it," she said, resuming her descent into the dell. She paused for a single second and reappraised Alanbart, nodding her approval. "Thanks," she said simply, then hurried down the slope. When she reached the ground, she shouted, "ENOUGH!"

Some women—mainly those involved with rearing children—possess a particular tone of voice, and, in combination with perfect control of both pitch and volume, can utter a shout that might cause even a charging army to stagger and slow for a step or two. Such a woman with such a voice was Heather.

Sure enough, the fighting faltered, and she interjected, "Sirs, I beseech you both to put down your swords."

"Heather?" Gawain started, clearly perplexed. "My lady?"

"Woman, I warned you to stay out of this," Scot snapped.

"Listen, we've solved the problem," she said, "Well, Sir Alanbart has." She softened her tone. "Please, sirs, lower your blades."

Scot and Gawain both obeyed.

"By Mary, what are *you* doing here?" Gawain asked, "Have the king, Kay, and my brother been captured? I found the remains of a battle, but their corpses were absent. I tracked them to the tower at the edge of the marsh, but the place was well defended—"

"One thing at a time, Sir," she interrupted. "King Arthur is a prisoner of Malestair, locked in a damp cell. These two men and I are contriving a rescue attempt. As you know, your opponent is Scot and serves Cathbad, a local druid. This fellow…" she gestured to Alanbart, who, while descending the slope, slipped and slid down on his bottom, "is Sir Alanbart, a servant of Lord Ghent of Kent, or so he tells me."

"My father was Alardane of the Outer Isles," Alanbart stood and brushed dirt from his posterior. "Perhaps you remember him?"

Gawain chewed his bottom lip for a moment. "The name does sound oddly familiar," he admitted. "And I do seem to recall your coat of arms from somewhere."

"You killed him," Alanbart replied, "on the bank of the Wye, in your hunt for the white hart."

"Sorry I am to have done so," Gawain said. After a pause, he added, "If you seek reparation through combat, I am honor bound to oblige—"

"Enough of this," Heather interrupted again. "Here's the point: Malestair has captured our king, holds him in the tower, and plans to do him harm and possibly kill him tomorrow in some type of conjuration attempt during the blue moon. We have no hope to affect a rescue without aid. The tower is surrounded by a stout palisade and is defended by nearly a hundred soldiers and a wizard of unknown power. The druid offered to aid us. He has a giant and a tribe of a hundred goblins in his power and will commit them to our cause on one condition."

"And what is that?" Gawain asked.

"That he burn you as a sacrifice to his pagan gods." Alanbart answered, with some satisfaction.

Heather shot him a withering glance and his smirk faltered. "That is his condition," she admitted, "but I believe that we can save you and get the aid that we so desperately need."

She explained her idea. Gawain listened, uncertain about the prospect of sacrificing his armor, but saw the necessity of aid, weighed the loss of wealth and pride against the death of his uncle and his king, and accepted the proposal with surprising grace, even swearing on his code of chivalry to join with them in all perils, large and small.

Scot, on the other hand, remained unconvinced. He acknowledged his opponent's skill and the benefit of having Gawain fight with them. But he wanted no part of deceiving Cathbad and held a strong desire to defeat Gawain for personal glory and to further his agenda of bringing back the old ways of his people. Probably most significantly, however, he did not want to relinquish the duel with so worthy an opponent. Scot was a man who enjoyed risk and challenge more than anything else in life.

Finally, though, Alanbart convinced him. "Look, Scot," he said. "Your primary goal is to prove the strength of the Old Ways, true?"

"True."

"Well, what if Sir Gawain agreed to take a vow to fight alongside you in the old style until we rescue King Arthur? That would show one of Arthur's knights respecting your ways, and test his ability to succeed in the conditions under which you choose to fight. For the next battle we can even fancy up his hair with grease and lime, and paint him like an ancient Pictish warrior."[9] He paused, then added, "Do you have another pair of those braided pants for him to wear?"

Scot considered Alanbart's proposal. The prospect of fighting alongside Gawain in the old ways appealed to him, but obviously didn't appeal to the knight.

---

[9] If your narrator might break in here for a moment, Pict—a somewhat unfamiliar term that's been tossed about a few times—may benefit from a brief explanation. You see, Pict is a generalization for any pre-Scottish inhabitant of northern Britain. Little is known of their culture or language, except what can be derived from place-names or has been recorded by the biased pens of late Roman historians. However, despite that, three things are clear: they worshipped druids, spoke a forgotten dialect of Celtic, and wore blue body paint into battle.

Some surmise that the Picts had a matriarchal society. And though there certainly were Celtic warrior queens (Boudica, for example) in Britannia at the time, any look at the chronology of Pictish *kings* would dispel this romantic notion. It is simply a gross misinterpretation of the fact that the kings sometimes derived their line of succession in *matrilineal* fashion—through the mother's bloodline. In my opinion, this is both correct and wise. It is correct because all babies share their mother's blood—that is, the same blood runs through *both* mother and child in the womb. The father, in contrast, only supplies the 'seed,' so if 'bloodline' exists, one can only trace it upstream from child to mother. The practice is wise, also, for though much debate may rage over who the father of a particular babe may be, no one would dare question who bore it—maternity is an inescapable fact of birth. Mary, for example, clearly bore the baby Jesus just as Olympias bore Alexander, and Danaë Perseus—despite famous claims and disputes over the paternity of their children.

Regardless, Scot followed the ancient ways and fancied himself to be a Pict warrior, even if he was named by his mother after the tribe that conquered them.

Gawain gaped at Alanbart's suggestion. However, before Arthur's nephew intervened, Heather placed her hand on his arm and whispered, "Your armor will be destroyed, so whether you wear a shirt or not will make no measurable difference in the combat."

Meanwhile, Scot perked up at the prospect of fighting alongside Gawain in the old way, but restrained himself and remained noncommittal.

Alanbart continued, "…and what if Sir Gawain agreed to face you afoot in a tournament melee in Camelot following the rescue to complete this duel of honor with an appropriate audience, and perhaps a monetary reward to the tournament victor?"

That did it. Scot agreed.

Gawain, swore and kicked at a hemlock root, scattering some needle litter. He flashed a grim smile and said, "By Christ, if I hadn't already sworn on my honor as a knight to aid you in this endeavor, I'd challenge this *Sir* Alanbart to a duel. He's so charitably giving of my king's money, *my* equipment, *my* honor, and *my* life that it'll be a wonder if I escape this adventure intact. As a matter of fact, I may challenge him after all this is through. Then we'll see if his sword is a keen and quick as his wit."

Alanbart shrank from the threat of combat and mumbled something about getting his horse. He turned and started to climb the slope, scattering an avalanche of pebbles in his wake.

In the interim, Heather helped Gawain out of his armor; then the two began to stuff it full of raw and bloody boar meat. The golden breastplate reflected their countenances. Heather's was equal parts disgust and determination, while Gawain's reflected a piteous expression that one might expect to see during a eulogy. Once they completed that messy job, they hoisted the armored boar carcass over the back of Gawain's horse, Gringolet.

The party then left the Gloamwood for Cathbad's Henge. As they passed out of the forest, the vermillion glow of the set sun colored the horizon behind them.

9

MIDNIGHT, CATHBAD'S HENGE

The sacrificial fire burned spectacularly, roaring, crackling, popping, and shooting twenty foot plumes of yellow-orange flame into the midnight sky. Brilliant embers blended with the starscape before drifting back to earth. As Heather looked on, the wicker statue began to crumble in on itself. The armor inside blackened and the boar began to roast. It smelled of burning hair, crisping leather, and mouth-watering, succulent pork. Her stomach growled (she'd eaten nothing besides a bite of oat cake, a sip of tea, and a thirst-quenching drink from a forest stream since the morning that she'd been ambushed with Arthur's party), and she felt odd, savoring the scent of boar meat sizzling within the statue, but also realizing that it was meant to be Gawain inside that armor.

She watched Cathbad stare into the flame, head bobbing, moustache swaying, jowls jiggling, a wicked grin on his ancient lips. Next to him, at about half his size with disproportionately long arms, a flat-faced head, and short bandy legs, squatted Bruuzak, a local goblin chieftain to whom Cathbad introduced them after sundown[10]. The goblin chief, exemplified all the traits of his species. He was a vile and vicious little hairless creature with black eyes (goblin eyes have no whites), stone-gray skin, and a black heart. He displayed his disquieting smile altogether too frequently, baring sharpened canine teeth. Neither mirth nor warmth shone from that smile; rather, it left one feeling vaguely ill. Also, the goblin constantly licked his chapped black lips

---

[10] Speaking of Bruuzak, this seems like an ideal moment to highlight a few important details about goblins. Most of you probably imagine goblins to be small, cowardly, brainless, sadistic, and carnivorous creatures, more reptilian than hominid. If you believe these popular perceptions, you are about fifty percent correct. Goblins are a

with a pointed maroon tongue, and enjoyed making up creative atrocities with which he and his fellows would afflict the prisoners of the tower raid. In fact, the release of all prisoners (with the single exception of King Arthur) to his 'care' was one of the two conditions that he demanded before offering his aid. A claim to one hundred percent of the treasure found in the tower vaults was the other.

"I am going to rip all the teeth out of one of them and pry off each of his fingernails and toenails," he growled, "and then lock him in a cage and give him the hardest raw turnips to eat. We'll place bets on how long before he starves." His tongue flicked out to lick his lips.

Cathbad nodded absently, seeming to approve, but then spoke on another subject entirely: "This knight cooks like a pig," he concluded. "He smells of grease and fat. Could it be that the famed knights of King Arthur's Round Table are so indolent and lazy, and live so high off of the fat of the land, that they turn to swine inside—fit for nothing but the fire?" He cackled. "Knights on the outside, pigs on the in—Scot! Perhaps we will forego burning and spit and roast the next one you kill."

---

nocturnal subterranean species of mammalian ape, most closely related to baboons (hence, the oversized canine teeth). Their hairless dry skin (much like that of an elephant) is often mistaken for scales. Contrary to popular belief, they are omnivorous. Like the majority of humans, they eat meat whenever they can get it—unlike most humans, though, this includes sentient beings, even cannibalizing one another when necessary. Though not generally as intelligent as humans and lacking an organized system of education, goblins can be quite clever (especially in high-pressure situations), can master human languages, and can copy certain human technologies.

Despite these obvious differences, goblins match the popular definition in three ways: they are cowardly, small, and sadistic. They are scavengers by nature, and so I find myself likening them to hyenas or vultures. They are scary—certainly disgusting—absolutely, but unlikely to attack in normal circumstances. Goblins range in height (even if they weren't naturally hunched) from three to about four and a half feet, probably an adaptation to their underground habitat. Compared with humans, they have short, bandy legs and long, lanky arms. They tend to hop occasionally when they walk, which seems comical until you notice the flame of hatred burning in their eyes.

Unlike humans, goblins are born evil—of course, many great scholars still debate the balance of the human soul, some claiming human nature is innocent and kind and that exposure to society turns us to evil. They claim, for example, that as we grow, we see those who lie, pander, are insincere, indolent, and selfish achieve more in life than those who value honesty, sincerity, hard work, and self-sacrifice, and as a natural consequence we begin to emulate those traits. Others postulate that human nature is selfish and evil, and that society forces us to be good. These philosophers claim that without laws,

Alanbart stifled a laugh, coughing instead and barely containing his mirth at so deceiving the druid. "Aye," he added, "With an apple stuffed in his mouth!"

"Just so," Cathbad agreed.

Heather grimaced and glanced over her shoulder into the grove. In the shadows hunched the cloaked form of Sir Gawain, the firelight glinting off his smoldering eyes. He glowered at the fire, no doubt stewing over the wound to his pride and the cost of his armor. He didn't notice her immediately, so she let her eyes linger on him until his met hers. He returned her gaze for a few seconds and then shrank farther back into the grove.

She'd never loved him more than at this moment. Perhaps the others didn't know what this choice had cost him, but she did. No doubt, Sir Gawain would have preferred an honorable death, charging under the tower gate on his warhorse, sword, shield, and armor flashing in the sun. He'd have killed many of the soldiers, but eventually Gringolet would have gone down, peppered with crossbow bolts, and Gawain would have been swarmed by soldiers and killed. He would have died valiantly in a vain attempt to save his king—a storybook ending to a storybook life. Instead, he'd chosen to give up

---

the enforced morality of religion (complete with the threat of hell and reward of heaven), and most importantly, our desire for the approval of our fellows, we would be little more than animals, concerned only with our own needs and pleasures. They claim that altruism is a self-serving delusion because it is always enacted while seeking the approval of others, or—even at best—to allow one to indulge in self-congratulation. They may have a point, for every church passes the offering plate and every preacher works for pay, but I digress. It is goblins of which I was speaking, and they, most definitely, are born evil.

Goblins, you see, have no concept of love. For them, procreation is exclusively the product of rape. They keep females in cages. Young are tolerated because the goblins understand the concept of strength in numbers. They must endure the young to have security in the future. They only work together when convinced that they will individually benefit from their efforts, and they often plan betrayal to increase these benefits. I could go on, but I think you grasp my point.

It is primarily for this reason that goblin civilization has not thrived in comparison to that of humans. For a goblin, admiration and jealousy are the same emotion, and assassination is the highest form of approbation—a just reward for a life well-lived. Due to this, all goblins live in fear of all other goblins and the word 'trust' does not exist in their vocabulary (though they're happy to use it when talking to humans).

his pride and compromise his honor in favor of increasing his chances of success, thus proving his love for his king greater than his love for his honor or reputation.

Heather turned back to the fire and sighed, allowing her mind to wander in memory against the mesmerizing backdrop of dancing flame. She'd fallen in love with Gawain by degrees over the course of a year in court. True, he was more than fifteen years her senior, but he exuded charm, courtesy, and honor, and was invariably honest and trustworthy. He also looked intimidatingly massive, tall with rippling musculature across his broad chest and back, dense silvery-blonde hair, bright blue eyes, and a winning smile. Then, there were also stories about how he'd refused the advances of the most beautiful woman in the world, how he'd taken it as his responsibility to champion women whenever they asked it, saving many from ravishings, ransomings, and the like. His unattainability made him irresistible.

He flirted shamelessly with everyone, of course (none more so than with the oldest granddames, which Heather found endearing), but she'd always fancied his flirtation with her more serious than most. His eyes lingered on her a shade too long, and his touch as he helped her dismount from a horse was half a caress.

Eight months earlier, on the frigid night of the New Year's feast, when they'd both drunk too much honey-mead and Christmas-wine, the flirtation burst into consummation. It began under a sprig of mistletoe in the great hall, where Gawain found himself courtesy-bound to kiss her, and then exploded in a fit of passion that concluded hours later in her room. Since that night, through winter snows, budding spring, and early summer thundershowers, Gawain had been awkward and bashful in her presence. He'd stopped flirting with her altogether and took pains to be away from court as often as possible.

Then Guinevere had been condemned to burn at the stake, and Lancelot rescued her, in the process ruthlessly cutting down Sirs Gareth and Gaheris, two of Gawain's younger brothers. She still remembered their bodies, laid out for display in the courtyard—twin pale white corpses. One bore a bloody gash from his shoulder to his navel, cut through muscle, bone, and organs, and in the corpse of the other, a stab wound pierced the chest, puncturing lung and heart. Gawain screamed aloud and rent his hair at the sight. His brothers had been unarmored at the time, easy prey to an armed and armored

Lancelot. Gawain saw it not just as an act of treason but as unchivalrous and dishonorable.

From that day Gawain became hard and bitter, focused on revenge. He returned to court but did not spare her (or any woman) a glance. He spent his time practicing with weapons and poring over maps, planning a siege against Lancelot's castle in Benwick and preparing for a duel with the greatest warrior that England had known in five centuries.

Bruuzak recalled Heather from her musings. "Then I'll tie two of them to stakes facing each other, and I'll let one eat as much smoked meat as he wants, but drink nothing. The other," he barked a horrid high-pitched laugh, "may drink all the water he likes, but will never touch food. Their agony and jealousy will be delicious."

"Interesting allies we've chosen," Alanbart commented dryly, looking slantways at the goblin.

"That *thing* disgusts me," Heather confessed. "Under any other circumstance I would eschew its aid and ask Sir Gawain to kill them all, but—"

"Better to have them for allies than enemies, I say." Alanbart interrupted. "Just listen to it talk. I'd find the courage to die in battle before surrendering to goblins."

"I'll tie one up so he cannot move," Bruuzak muttered, "then I'll pluck out his left eye and fill the socket with maggots. I'll bind it up and let them eat their way out!" He showed his canines, laughed his high-pitched laugh, and licked his lips with a flick of his maroon tongue. Uncontrollably, bile ran up Heather's throat.

Alanbart distracted himself by tracking the haphazard flight of a bat that careened in and out of the flickering shadows as it chased after moths and flies drawn to the light. The flight of the lone bat recalled to his mind a story of a sparrow he'd once heard in church, a story about a king in his hall on a stormy winter night.

The king and his advisors sat warm by the fire in a well-lit hall, making merry, when a sparrow flew in through the door out of the cold stormy night. It passed quickly in, flew directly across the hall— east to west, over the heads of the king and his advisors—back into the darkness, never to be seen again. One of the king's men—a druid, in fact—had said at the time that each human life was like the flight of that sparrow: *Out of cold, darkness, and chaos we come to glide a short one-way path through warmth and light, and back into cold darkness we return. No one knows or can know what lies beyond the doors of our experience—where we came from or where we'll go in the end.*

He recalled that someone named Bede first told the story and that it was a Christian story, contrived no doubt so that some priest could supply answers to the unanswerable, but the Christianity didn't hinder the fundamental truth of the analogy. Alanbart shuddered as he watched the bat vanish into the night and wondered what waited outside the door of his experience. He hoped that his hall was long and that his darkness waited far in the future.

He pondered sharing the thought with Heather, but before he could, Cathbad strode into the firelight, transforming into a featureless black silhouette, backlit against the blaze. Only the brass beads in his moustache remained visible, reflecting light as they swayed with his motion. He stood tall, suddenly unbowed by years, took two handfuls of powder from inside his cloak, and tossed them into the fire. The conflagration erupted into a towering pillar of bright green flame, sending hundreds of embers into the sky. The remains of the wicker giant exploded and collapsed.

Cathbad picked up a burning brand, a hazelwood staff, all aflame at one end. He began to chant in an unknown language, a sonorous, rhythmic refrain that echoed off the henge and blended with the crackling flames. His words built both speed and power over a period of about three minutes, rising to a crescendo. He never took his blind eyes off of the fire. No one dared to interrupt.

As he finished, the flames collapsed in on themselves and faded to the level of a campfire. Cathbad, too, shrank back down to the hunched form of an old man, wearily cast the staff upon the fire, and backed away. There was nothing weary, though, about his voice when he spoke. "The Gods grant us success!" he hollered, with flickering orange light playing demonically upon his face. He waited for everyone to visibly relax, then added, "However, the Gods also say that one who is alive tonight watching this fire will be dead before he, or she, sees this moon begin to wane." The gathered onlookers paused as that news sank in. Cathbad's blind eyes rested on the flames; Scot turned pointedly to Alanbart. Heather turned her gaze covertly toward Gawain, who returned her it and nodded.

Alanbart cleared his throat and spoke with insolent cheer across the somber circle. "Do you suppose," he smirked, "they could mean a *metaphorical* death? 'The old Alanbart is dead. Long live the new Alanbart!'"

Cathbad turned to him. "The Gods hate you, boy, and so do I." Silence returned and the fire crackled.

"Why is it that blind people always think that they can see the future?" Alanbart whispered to Heather, bending to pick up an errant stick of kindling. "It makes it hard to pity them at any rate." He snapped it in two. "And speaking of blind men, a tale of such a prophet once taught me the truth that fate comes true only when one tries to avoid it." Her eyes widened in recognition of the allusion. He tossed the two halves of his stick into the fire and put all the unconcern that he could into his voice. "But even if he is right, you have to believe that this old *geezer* is going to be the one who isn't going to make it another day. How old is he? Ninety?" And Alanbart forced a laugh.

The Final Day

10

DAWN, CATHBAD'S HENGE

After relieving his bladder in the tall grass, Alanbart yawned and walked back toward the henge. He passed the pile of still-warm ash and twisted metal where the wicker giant had been, crunching brittle grass under his feet as he did so. The fire had blackened and crisped a ten-foot circle of vegetation. In its center sat the charred and warped remains of Gawain's once-elegant armor, a sad and pathetic monument to Arthurian knighthood. It cast the faintest amorphous shadow in the predawn light. Alanbart thought of the gold, garnets, and possibly even rubies that might be buried in the ash and made a mental note to revisit the spot after it had sufficiently cooled.

He paused to listen to a thrush trill a beautiful morning song from deep in the heather. Enchanted by the cheerful innocence of the melody, he sat on a rectangular slab of stone and took in his surroundings. His gaze was drawn to the gathering dawn in the east, and remained fastened there for a time as he went over the events of the previous evening in his mind.

After the sacrifice and reading of the omens, the druid had gathered them round the fire and outlined his scheme to recapture the king. First and foremost, he planned to send Scot and Alanbart to defeat the banshee in her bog. He claimed that she guarded a trove of magical treasures that would amplify their powers and improve their chances for success against Rabordath.

Cathbad desired three particular things: The Hammer of Autumn, an ancient weapon that could sunder anything crafted of dead wood with one blow and which would grant them immediate entrance to the palisade and the tower; The Staff of Väinämöinen, which would multiply his magical abilities tenfold; and the Ring of Mudarra, which reputedly held the power to cure blindness.

Alanbart saw this all as more than a little self-serving on Cathbad's part, as he reaped ninety percent of the benefit with no danger to his person, but realized, as did everyone else, that the druid stood a better chance of defeating a wizard if he increased his power and regained his sight. The necessity of the hammer was also obvious. Alanbart would have protested, of course, at being included in the party (if you can call two a party) that would venture into the bog after the banshee, except that Gonoth grinned at him evilly. He'd swallowed his objections for that reason and also because of his confidence that he could convince Sir Gawain to go in his stead—which, of course, he accomplished once Cathbad, Gonoth, and Bruuzak retired for the evening.

The chief danger, according to Cathbad, was the scream of the banshee, which had the power to sever the soul from the body, slaying a person and binding his corpse to the demonic creature in an un-death of eternal servitude.

The solution, Cathbad said, was to deafen oneself by shouting and by loud banging of metal on metal, directly next to the ears, until they began to bleed. At this point, the ear canals would be dried and filled with warm beeswax. The two warriors then could commence their attack, impervious to her scream, but would be unable to use the sense of sound to coordinate their attack.

The druid also warned them that many powerful warriors served as the guards of the banshee's inner sanctum. Each great warrior who faced her over the generations (many of whom originally owned the aforementioned magical artifacts) succumbed to her fatal scream and served her in death with all of the martial ability that he possessed in life. Scot showed excitement at the prospect of combat with ancient heroes, an idea that chilled Alanbart to his bones.

Heather's interactions with Sir Gawain also interested Alanbart. Arthur's knight appeared to be nearly twenty years her senior, but their relationship seemed more romantic than friendly. They shared secret glances and, after the sacrifice, talked in hushed tones. Alanbart felt something rare and unexpected while watching them: a twinge of jealousy.

After Alanbart had solved the two dilemmas in the Gloamwood—how to save Gawain and how to placate Scot—Heather thanked him and complimented him on his intelligence, even placing her hand tenderly on his arm, a gentle and warm touch that, inexplicably, he could still feel. He laid three fingers against the spot; strange, he thought, that she should affect him in this way. He'd always considered himself impervious to the charms of women and sought to keep himself aloof from love and romance.

He mentally rebuked himself. Love was a dangerous emotion and too many knights (all of them better than he) had or would die for it: Paris, Siegmund, Tristan, and probably Lancelot next. To Alanbart, the physical sensations were not worth either the emotional angst or the negative outcomes. Still, he felt the unbidden beginnings of something for Heather, and despite the fact that he could step outside of himself, diagnose those feelings as dangerous and ridiculous, compare himself to Sir Gawain and note his utter deficiency, and judge himself to be the worst possible example of manhood, love, and chivalry, those feelings of affection took root nevertheless.

'That's just one more reason to escape from this absurd situation before it gets more serious.' He sighed and shifted positions on the cold rock. A light breeze ruffled his hair, and his mind returned to Heather.

The climactic moment occurred as Alanbart tried to fall asleep, wrapped in a pair of borrowed blankets, too thin to warm him. He closed his eyes and made an attempt to control his breathing, but found himself unable to nod off, probably because of the cold and because he hadn't a drop to drink. Alcohol was his crutch, of late, in combating chronic insomnia. As he lay there, cold and uncomfortable, he listened to the quiet conversation between Heather and Gawain.

"It can never be," the knight insisted gently.

"I know that's what you believe," she replied, bitterness in her tone. "But you didn't think so once."

"It is difficult to speak of it," he said. "I am a Knight of the Round Table, and I have placed a lifetime of belief in the code of chivalry. What we had was not chivalrous and can never be so now."

She remained silent. He continued, his voice gaining power and speed.

"You loved me because I was forthright and courteous. Your feelings for me were and *are* bound up in who I *was* on that day. That man *was* honorable. He was a man of his word. He kept his vows. He respected himself, and that was why you respected him. When we…" he cleared his throat. "When I betrayed my chivalric values, I betrayed myself and in so doing, I betrayed you. I ceased to be the man you desired—the man who deserved you—and doomed our love from its very inception.

"It is a sad paradox, I confess it," he continued after a pause. "If we admit to a love that is founded on shame and embrace our base desires, we betray ourselves and commit to living a life founded on desire and deceit. And if we do not, we maintain our honor and self-respect by betraying our love. And then we willfully choose to live in agony. What fool chooses the agony?"

'I chose the agony of lying on this damned root,' Alanbart thought bitterly, torn between an overwhelming desire to shift positions and a compulsion to eavesdrop on the rest of the conversation. His curiosity soundly defeated his discomfort, and he remained still.

Gawain paused again, waited. Heather replied with stony silence. The hiss of the dying fire and the droning crickets filled the void. An owl hooted somewhere beyond the henge.

"A knight chooses the agony," he added at last. "A lady chooses the agony. We may have been weak for a moment, but we will not commit to a life of weakness and lies, no matter the physical or emotional reward. I will not, in any event."

"You are morally right, of course," Heather responded finally. Her voice, too, was filled with emotion. "And the irony is that this decision will make you more desirable. And my acceptance of it will amplify your love for me." She sighed. "This is the kind of thing, I suppose, that troubadours sing tragic love songs about. I always thought they were just fiction."

"They are," he sighed. "Love is always a fiction, written in the heart of a man or a woman—only when two fictions align do we call it 'true.'"

"Enough of this," Heather said, cutting him off, turning away, and putting a note of finality in her voice. "If this is to be the way of it, I am content. I will always have my memories—many women don't even have that comfort. At the moment, however, we have a king to rescue and on the morrow you may have two battles to fight. Get your sleep, Sir—I'll take the first watch." She walked away, and the conversation ended.

Alanbart's jealousy returned as he thought of it. Could she be Gawain's Helen, his Dido, Brunhilda, Isolde, or Delilah? There were so many stories from which to choose, yet all ended much the same way. Tragic love couldn't be so uncommon an occurrence as it seemed.

Had he stopped to consider it, he might have noted the irony that Gawain was the romantic one of the pair, and that Heather's calm acceptance of the facts showed that though women are frequently labeled as the more emotional sex, they are perhaps better equipped to handle disappointments in matters of love, certainly less likely to take drastic action, and less apt to repeat the same mistake with a different partner.

He remained seated on the rock as dawn turned the east from amethyst to rose. His gaze focused on a tall thistle. Its spiked leaves and stellated globe topped with purple petals, almost like hair, sparkled with drops of dew. A honey bee buzzed near and landed on one of the blossoms. The stem swayed.

As the bee pollinated the thistle, Alanbart heard a few crackling steps in the scorched grass behind him. He began to rise as Heather sat beside him. He grunted a hello, conflicted. He tried to sound cranky, to send her away, but suddenly it seemed that his tongue swelled and he couldn't speak. He focused back on the flower. The bee flew away. He tried to stand.

"Please, stay," she touched his forearm. "You don't mind some company, do you?"

"In the morning I often do," he replied, "but no—" he cleared his throat "—not this morning."

"The plan is progressing," she said, making conversation, "but I'm worried about this undead woman."

"I agree," Alanbart said. "The whole idea of battling the banshee seems to benefit our druid *friend*. He gets a powerful staff and his sight back, and we get a hammer?"

"Yes," Heather agreed, "but we cannot forget that she is allied with Malestair and helped in the ambush on the moors, so strategically it makes sense to eliminate her before she can join her forces with those of the tower. Otherwise I might have objected."

"True, but I don't trust Cathbad," Alanbart said, lowering his voice and gesturing at the henge. "His goals align with yours until Malestair is defeated and the power of the tower is smashed. At that point, he may very well become a foe."

Heather nodded, but didn't add anything. The silence became strained.

"I'm glad that Sir Gawain is taking my place in that attack," Alanbart admitted. "The plan stands a better chance of success with his presence, since I am not much of a fighter. Indeed, I am pleased to think that at least I will not be dying this morning, which increases my chances of not being the corpse to fulfill Cathbad's prophecy by fifty percent." He forced a chuckle, then changed the subject. "It's funny, is it not, that I was born possessed with the qualities of my mother, and you were born possessed with what I assume are the qualities of your father. By rights, you should be the knight and I should be the lady."

Heather smoothed her dress with her hands, plucking an errant thorn from the brown fabric. "My father was a man by the name of King Pellinore. He wasn't really a king, not in the true sense, but he did fight both for and against Arthur and his knights. I never knew him, but the stories I'm told portray him to be a big confident man with a quick mind and a lucky streak. I like to imagine that I take after him. He's dead now."

Alanbart covered her hand awkwardly with his, and opened his mouth to say something that he hoped would sound comforting.

Heather cut him off, but did not pull away. "No, don't tell me that you're sorry for me. I cannot feel a sense of loss for someone that I never met. I'm not his legitimate daughter. I knew neither my father nor my mother. She died giving birth to me, and he, being good-hearted but ashamed of my birth, sent me to foster in a wealthy house."

Another silence passed between them. Alanbart ventured to break it. "You know Sir Gawain well?" he asked, lamely. 'Fool! Imbecile!' he thought, 'Just change the subject.'

"Too well, I fear," she replied. "A year ago I fell in love with him and he with me." She slid her hand out from beneath his and used it to gesticulate, adding emphasis to her final words. "I don't want to burden you with the details."

"Ah," he managed.

"It's over now," she added quickly.

'Why would you tell me that?' Alanbart wondered.

"It couldn't have ended any other way," Heather continued with artificial cheerfulness. "I'm illegitimate and he is a knight, the nephew of the king, and heir to the throne of Orkney. Save Mordred, Gawain is also first in line for Arthur's throne. Worse, there is bad blood between our families, and his people would never accept me. And—we have more in common than you think—Sir Gawain also killed my father in single combat."

Alanbart laughed out loud, but regretted it immediately. "He killed your father, and you claim to love him?" he asked, incredulous.

"You forget, I never knew my father—I only saw him once, and that was from across a room when I was very young," she replied. "Sir Gawain had honorable motives. How does the proverb go? It is better to avenge a death than to mourn one."

"Then I must say that Sir Gawain is a very fortunate man on four counts," Alanbart concluded. "He has a lordship, powerful relatives, immense wealth, *and* your love." He paused. "As for the impossibility of that relationship, I wish I could find words of comfort for you, but they would ring false, because . . ." 'because I'm actually quite pleased about it,' he thought, ". . . because truth be told, I've never been in love," he said instead.

"Never?" she asked, dubious. "But you must be at least thirty years old."

"Not quite," he answered, and added, "and no—never. Love is dangerous and I have only lived this long though a highly balanced combination of superior intelligence and abject cowardice, neither of which support the concept of passionate love. You see, one has to be both brave and a bit of a fool to fall in love. I am certainly no fool, and I have never been brave—not in the traditional sense. Odd, though, that I should be willing to admit to you so openly something that I have kept carefully hidden from everyone else—perhaps it shows some little courage and foolishness after all." He shook his head slightly and returned to studying the thistle, this time considering the formidable defensive spines lining the stem and leaves.

Heather sighed. "I'd say that love is wonderful and that the lack of it has been a great hole in your life, but at the moment I am not sure if that is true." She stood, then changed the subject. "Would you be willing to ride to Camelot? By your own admission, you are no good to us in a fight, and if we fail, we will need to be rescued. Perhaps you can alert Arthur's knights and try to arrive before Mordred does."

"I might be convinced to do so," Alanbart answered, "but I'll need rations, a map, a letter of introduction, and a plea for aid written by Sir Gawain—someone to whom they would listen—and I'll need to be paid. I've already lost a surcoat, plume, and shield."

"I'll see about getting the letter," she responded. "My influence on payment is rather limited; however, I'm sure that the king would be open-handed to his rescuers. He has a history of giving lavish rewards to those who please him."

"And what are the odds of success?" Alanbart mused. "Not good, I'd wager, pagan omens aside."

At that moment Scot stepped out of the henge, yawned and stretched his arms behind his back, whipping them forward with an audible pop. He patted his belly, smacked his lips, and said, "I hope breakfast will be ready before long. I cannot perform acts of heroic courage on an empty stomach." He grinned at Heather and added, "Come on in and keep your companion company—he isn't one for trivial talk."

"Where's Cathbad?" she asked.

"He left before daybreak with Bruuzak to gather the goblins of the Gloamwood."

"I saw Bruuzak go," Alanbart affirmed, but Cathbad wasn't with him."

"He was. He transformed into a crow and sat on Bruuzak's shoulder. He's an old man and moves much more swiftly that way. Say—" he interrupted himself "—when are we getting painted for the party?"

"Whenever you like," Alanbart responded. "And then we'll get you deafened. There are a few choice words that I've always longed to say to a certain knight, and I'm looking forward to the deafenings almost as much as you're looking forward to the painting." He clapped Scot on the shoulder and turned him toward the henge. They ducked beneath the low-hanging limb and down the slate stairs.

Inside, Gawain tested the blade of his oversized green axe on his thumbnail, whetstone in hand. A blackened copper pot full of simmering water and oatmeal heated over a small cookfire.

"Let's put this plan into action," Gawain said, nodding at Scot. He glanced at Heather but ignored Alanbart. "From what I gathered last night, we have eight leagues to ride, a battle to fight, and eight leagues to ride back, all before mid-afternoon. I'm not one to put off work when there's a job to do."

"Good," Scot agreed. "I'll be back with the paint. You may choose to be blue or yellow."

Gawain grimaced and thought for a moment. "If it's all the same to you, I'll mix them and wear green. I have a certain affinity for that color, and your giant—Gonoth is it?—has recalled to my mind my first real adventure. If this ends up being my last, at least going out in green would bring some continuity to the songs they sing of me."

"Certainly," Scot said, stepping out the far entrance and leaving Gawain, Alanbart, and Heather alone. Gawain returned to sharpening his axe:

Shink, shink, went the whetstone, breaking the silence.

"Does Scot have a horse?" Heather asked.

"Not that I've seen," Gawain replied. "They keep no animals here, aside from that old warhound that follows you everywhere."

"Can he ride Taffy?" Heather asked.

"I thought you wanted me to ride south?" Alanbart replied, somewhat defensively.

"It seems to me that time is of the essence here. You could ride south this afternoon as easily as now, and if Scot cannot ride, it will more than double their travel time."

Alanbart considered her words. "Can't you both ride Gringolet?" he asked Gawain, "He's horse enough for two riders, especially if they are without armor."

"Gringolet's beginning to show his years and will suffer no rider but me," Gawain answered.

Shink, went his whetstone.

Heather sent a pleading look at Alanbart. He hesitated. Taffy was his only friend—silly, he thought to be so attached to a horse, but still…

"If you're willing pay me for his service, certainly an arrangement can be made," Alanbart said at last. "I've already lost a shield and accrued a lot of unnecessary expenses. No one is lining up to reimburse me."

"Please forgive the question, but are you a merchant or a knight?" Gawain scoffed. "By God, I'd never sully my name by bartering service like some Jew tradesman."

"That's because your income has always far exceeded your expenditures," Alanbart responded. "You're the nephew of a king and son of a great lord, not some pauper knight living off of his wits alone. It must be easy to look down on others when you're standing atop a pile of gold."

Shink, went the whetstone.

Alanbart hesitated, looked at the axe, swallowed, and took a step backward, but continued, "Maybe you think I'm crass to speak of it, but I grew up without a father *and* without a lord. We had no lands, no income, and nothing but our family name and coat of arms to rely upon. If you think back on it, you may even realize that we had your sword arm to thank for our condition. However, so that you will stop slandering my surname, I'll solve your little problem by taking my horse off the market." He turned his back on Gawain and walked toward the stairs, suddenly determined to mount Taffy and ride north.

Heather stood between them, indecisive. She glowered in Gawain's direction but made no motion to follow Alanbart. What a contrast the two men made, she thought. Gawain sat unconcerned, a powerful hero, handsome, honorable, confident, yet unyielding and somewhat self-righteous, which though well-meaning could come across as intolerant, even arrogant. And then there walked Alanbart, far less imposing physically, but undeniably intelligent. He was a self-proclaimed coward, yet, she suspected that his cowardice was merely a shield. 'Against what?' she thought. At the very least he intrigued her and could hold up his end of a conversation, and he looked cute, in his own awkward way—nothing compared to Gawain, of course, just somehow new and refreshing after the stifling atmosphere of Camelot, which overflowed with bombast, posturing, and hypocrisy.

"Sir Alanbart," Gawain called after a moment, some hesitation in his voice. "Regardless of my personal distaste for your lack of moral—*ahem*—your personal code of behavior, I find that I do require your horse. Also, you may discover that I am not without sympathy for your widowed mother and fatherless childhood. Indeed, I feel that it is much to blame for your current mistaken attitudes. No true knight should be raised entirely by women." He looked at Heather and added, courteously, "Just as, I'm sure you'd agree, my lady, that no true lady should be brought up by men."

Heather shrugged.

After a pause, Gawain finished, "If you would allow me to do so, I am willing to personally pay you some restitution for your loss. I keep a small amount of money in my saddlebags, and would use it to buy your good opinion so that you would be more inclined to *lend* us your horse."

Alanbart faltered. He swiveled to face Gawain. However, before he could speak, Scot reentered the henge with one large wooden bowl and one small hollowed gourd, both full of pigment. The bowl contained a bright cobalt paste while the gourd sloshed with a more soupy paint of a mustard yellow color. Also, at that moment, the oatmeal started to boil over, steaming, and plopping glops into the flames. It hissed and acrid smoke rose from the cookfire.

Alanbart fixed his blue eyes on the oatmeal and sighed. "Very well. I'll take charge of breakfast then, shall I?" He stepped toward the fire, then added to Heather. "I imagine that I've cooked more oatmeal breakfasts than you have."

She nodded.

Scot began reapplying his war paint, slathering his chest with thick clumps of blue pigment and spreading it in expanding circles with his fingers. "I'll need help with my back," he said, gesturing toward Heather. "Would you honor me?"

"I'll do it," Gawain cut in abruptly, leaping to his feet. He cleared his throat and gave his axe one last self-conscious stroke with the whetstone—s*hink*—then set it down.

Alanbart crouched and, using the hem of his tunic as a buffer, pulled the kettle from the fire by its copper handle. Heather sat gracefully on the stones near Alanbart. She smiled across the circle at the wolfhound, which lay sprawled on his side near the stairs, his moist eyes resting on her. She patted the pebbled earth beside her. The dog stood, stretched arthritically, and lumbered over to where she sat, tongue lolling from his mouth. She gently scratched his curly gray scruff as he curled up on her feet.

Gawain broke the silence, eyeing the blue paint with obvious distaste. "Scot, you're certainly skilled with a sword, and so you have gained some of my respect. Yet, I must ask: why have you dedicated yourself to serving the pagan gods of a druid?"

"Because I disagree with your way of life," Scot responded.

"Is it chivalry with which you disagree?" Gawain asked.

"Not at all. Quite the contrary, I honor those few heroes who uphold the code and, as a guide for a generally honorable lifestyle, I applaud it. Primarily, I protest against the lie perpetrated upon the peasantry by those two-faced tyrants who name themselves noble. They claim to want to bring peace and prosperity to the land and to protect the people, but in reality they starve the serfs and force them to fight, where they are slaughtered by the hundreds and thousands. It is the hypocrisy inherent in your system that enrages me."

"King Arthur isn't like that," Gawain answered.

Scot rounded on him. "Have you waged no wars? Does Arthur not wish to conquer all of Britannia? Whom does Malestair of the Tower serve?"

"I think it is safe to say that Malestair serves either my bastard brother or himself. As for the wars, certainly there have been many, and it *is* the avowed wish of Arthur to hold all Britannia; yet, he wishes only to bring peace to this island—as there once was for hundreds of years under Roman rule. When there is one lord with unquestioned power, there is no dissent, no strife. We would be a nation worthy of the name, not some ragtag quilt of feuding clans."

"Peace," Scot scoffed. "For how long? Until Guinevere bears Lancelot's child? Until Arthur dies? Until Sir Mordred lays claim to the kingdom?"

Gawain chewed his lower lip a long while in response. Finally he offered a reply, "I admit that things haven't gone as planned and are unlikely to return to plan, but since when does failure diminish the grand vision? Besides, I have sworn my fealty to King Arthur, to live and die by his side, fighting his quarrels, be they just or unjust. By God, I am a man of honor and I will keep my vow."

"And I, for my part, will continue to combat to convert the isle back to, as you so beautifully put it, 'a ragtag quilt of feuding clans.' And this is my reason: Unlike a kingdom, a clan is never so large that its leaders cease to care about its individual members. They are family and all of them are important. Certainly, feuds go on—sometimes for generations—but they are small in scope, as is the carnage they cause—"

"And when Childebert, the king of the Francs, sails north with his grand army or when Halfdan the Black and the berserking Northmen sail west, what then? Your day is over, my friend, precisely for the reason that you first mentioned. 'A clan is never big enough,' you said. True. And I will complete the idea: a *clan* is never big enough to defend itself against a *kingdom*. That is why the Romans won. It is why we won. It is why you will always lose." [11]

With no response forthcoming, Gawain scooped up some blue paint, fidgeted for a moment in discomfort, then asked, "Are you

---

[11] If you'll excuse me for butting into my own story again, I might clarify that Gawain's assertion—that chivalrous knights defeated the Britons because of their disunity—is (as is everything said by idealists) a bit misleading. In the actual event, William the Bastard (a fitting moniker for the man) and his 'chivalric' followers defeated a well-organized and *unified* Anglo-Saxon army at Hastings—half a *millennium* after the Britons were expelled from England. As far as William's invasion goes, luck played a much larger role in that than anything else. If some unknown Norman archer had not shot King Harold Godwinson through the eye-slit of his helm (threading the needle, so to speak), history may have turned out quite differently.

Speaking of kings and arrows, though, you might be surprised at how often an absurdly lucky shot altered medieval English history. For example, less than three weeks before Hastings, a Viking king by the name of Harald Haradra (one of the most interesting figures in medieval history—I only wish that I had time to tell his tale) went down to death at Stamford with an arrow through his throat; and for an additional example, let us take the Battle of Shrewsbury. In that conflict, rebel leader Henry Hotspur lifted his visor to issue an order, only to have a fatal encounter with an arrow that flew into his open mouth. Simultaneously, on the other side of the lines, Prince Henry of Monmouth took an arrow to the face (yet he lived through a miracle of medieval surgery and then became the victor at Agincourt, a whole battle won by bowshot).

So, to bring us back to my original point, it seems to me that Gawain's response proves that we always find logical reasons to support the natural occurrence of random events. We call the chronicle of those reasons 'history.' Once established, we retell it again and again until it rings true and becomes, through repetition, accepted fact. Gawain certainly accepted his version of the 'facts,' and as Scot did not argue the point, it seems that he did, too.

ready?"

"Yes," Scot replied. He again turned his back to Gawain. The knight's muscles were taut and his jaw worked beneath his skin. Ignoring his own obvious discomfort, Gawain began to spread the blue dye over Scot's shoulders and back, keeping himself at arm's length, as far from Scot as possible during such an intimate moment.

Heather hid her amusement behind her hand.

After a few tense seconds, Scot said grimly, "You know, of course, that you will have to back your beliefs with your blade once all this is over."

"I will," Gawain agreed, "but regardless of which of us is the victor in that combat, time will prove me right. A duel does not change the world—it only affects the lives of two men and their families."

"Breakfast is ready," Alanbart interrupted, eating a clumpy and steaming bite of oatmeal off the end of a wooden spoon. He set the pot down beside Heather. She nodded, accepted the spoon, and ate, her expression carefully impassive.

Alanbart absently ran a hand along the dog's back. "It would be better with milk, or nuts, or fruit," he said apologetically.

"Thank you," she replied, and her eyes returned to the two warriors. She waited for them to resume their debate, but they seemed to have reached an impasse.

In the interim, Gawain rushed to finish smearing paint on Scot. In his hurry, he slapped a large blue glop on the small of the swordsman's back. It began to run down his spine, beneath the line of his belt.

"Uhmm…" Gawain said.

"What are you doing?" Scot snapped over his shoulder. "Don't stand there like a lump—stop it before it runs down the crack in my ass! –Sorry, my dear," he amended, glancing apologetically at Heather.

Gawain reached out a hand, slid it beneath Scot's beltline, then drew it out quickly, gasping. "By all that's Holy, I'll not touch you there when you can reach yourself!"

"Alright then," Scot sighed, and dug his hand down his pants, dredging up a glob of blue paint. He flicked it into the bowl. "A second longer and I would have been blue down to my nether-eye!" He blushed. "Uh, sorry again," he inclined his head toward Heather. "I forget my manners among so many men." He handed the bowl back to Gawain, who eyed it doubtfully and cleared his throat again.

The knight held the bowl a long while before he could bring himself to dip his fingers in, continuing more slowly and carefully than before.

Alanbart said, "Scot, it's apparent to me that you see some of the problems of knighthood quite clearly, but you miss the fundamental one. The priests tell us that according to the Law of Moses, we should not kill other Christians, and yet we consistently fight amongst ourselves. In fact, the very act of swearing fealty to a lord demands that the knight fight *all* of the lord's enemies in *all* quarrels. The duty to one's lord is thus placed above the duty to *the* Lord, and yet the system would also have us believe that our lords are placed above us by God's will—each has a Divine Right to rule. It is a paradox that I have never been able to reconcile.

"Interestingly," he continued, "your old way neatly solves that little problem. As I understand it, the warrior code of Woden suggests that killing a fellow believer in battle actually sends him directly to Valhalla, so in effect you are doing him a favor and your conscience is clear." He scoffed to add emphasis to his last point. "For a Christian, if you kill a knight in battle and he has already killed another Christian combatant, then you send that knight to judgment with a mortal sin on his soul, and doom him to eternal torment in hell."

Everyone paused to consider his statement. In the end Gawain smirked. "Actually, I prefer to send my king's enemies to hell. I'm done here." He slapped Scot on the shoulder with a powerful blue hand, leaving a spattered print.

Scot dribbled yellow pigment in with the blue and mixed them to a grass-green color. "It's your turn." He handed the bowl back to Gawain.

The knight nodded curtly and after another obvious internal struggle, began to slather his shoulders and chest.

"And if I might change the subject," Scot added, "I've been meaning to ask you, Sir Gawain, why did you first decide to fight for King Arthur?"

The tension faded as Gawain broke into a sad smile, full of

memory. "There were many reasons. Arthur is my uncle, of course, so kinship drew me to him, but more than that, he was doing something *new*. Chivalry was never heard of before—at least not in Britannia—and I fell in love with the ideal. You might say that it has been the one true love of my life." He stumbled there, cleared his throat, but continued. "Before King Arthur, warriors were brutes—oh, certainly many were honorable brutes, I don't deny that—but they had no code to guide their actions. They served no greater good than their own desires—at best the desire to become famous after death, and at worst the twin desires for power and riches. King Arthur serves the chivalric code— faith in God, courtesy toward those who depend on his strength, honor toward his fellow men, courage in battle, and humility—five pillars, five points to the star... a shining star to guide men across the sea of life."

He trailed off and his eyes focused on his shield, which lay against the stone wall under the shade of the trees. "Imagine a world like that!" he said to Scot "—a world where everyone believes in and lives up to the code of chivalry. I would *die* for that vision."

"Now, now, let's face the facts," Alanbart interrupted, some wry amusement in his tone. "Ideals and visions aside, you both fight for the same reason—because you're damn good at it. When you're good at something, doing it is fun. Also, you both value honor because it lends your fighting a moral imperative—you both want to be 'right' or on the 'good' side in battle to keep your consciences clean. But you come at it from completely opposite perspectives. Sir Gawain, you find your moral imperative in what *could be*—you are a romantic who fights for an unattainable and ideal future that is pure and good." He shifted his gaze to Scot. "And you find your imperative in what *once was*—an Edenic vision of a past that never existed. Neither of you like the world as it is, and both of you see each other as the problem."

Alanbart paused, watched the leaves rustle overhead, then concluded, "You know, that's the trouble with humanity—half of the dreamers want to carry us forward, kicking and screaming, into an unrealistic and unattainable future, and the other half want us to fall back into an imaginary 'simpler time' when everything was easy." He sat back, content that he'd summed up the problems of the world in a phrase. Perhaps he had.

Gawain and Scot both fixed him with accusatory and sullen expressions.

Heather seemed amused, but when Gawain shot her a dark look, she pretended to be famished and ate oatmeal, avoiding all of them. 'It's not every day that you see someone outdo Sir Gawain at anything' she thought. 'And Alanbart just cut him down with words, effortlessly. Perhaps there is more to this pauper knight than he lets on.'

"Of course," Alanbart continued, enjoying himself immensely, and conscious for the first time that he was putting on a show for Heather's benefit. It was the closest he dared come to combat. "You both hate me because I speak the truth. I'm a cynic. I see things as they are, adapt myself to them, and make the best of the situation. I know that I lack the power to change the world, so I don't try. If I do ever offer to sacrifice myself for a king or an ideal, just fling me from the top of the nearest tower and be done with me."

Gawain examined the large knuckles of his own balled fist, and Scot shrugged and began spreading green paint on Gawain's shoulders and neck. He did it much more comfortably than Gawain had, rubbing the paint in concentric circles, viewing the knight's back as canvas and himself as a great artist. He spoke as he worked. "Sir Gawain, you truly have the shoulders and back of a great hero—surly Thor himself has similar musculature, or Beowulf, or Siegmund—broad as a bear's back, firm as oak. As a fellow man and aspiring hero myself, I have to admit to some little jealousy." He tenderly squeezed the muscle right over Gawain's shoulder blade, causing the knight to almost leap out of arm's reach.

Eyes wide, he stared back at Scot and cleared his throat again, louder still than before. "I, uh—I thank you for the compliment, man, but—by God—just finish the job, please, with—*ahem*—without further comment, or caress."

"As you will," Scot continued as if nothing had happened. "In answer to you, Sir Alanbart," he said, "I don't dare dream that I'll actually alter the world, but as opposed to you, I'm willing to try. Death comes to us all in this mortal life—even to the great and glorious—and for my part, I would be blessed to be remembered as a hero in a ballad."

He stepped back to see if he'd missed any spots, and seeing one, returned to fill it, continuing as if he had not paused at all. "Personally, I would choose to die attempting some great feat, even die in failure, rather than live in ease and accomplish nothing. Songs reach out of the past and inhabit the hearts and minds of those living in the present, so I wouldn't truly be dead."

"And I," Gawain said, stepping quickly away from Scot and his paint, "would live a life dedicated to my ideal. Perhaps, as you say, *Sir* Alanbart, I cannot change this world, yet I can change myself and be an example to others who would follow my way of life. Avalanches start with small stones, and blizzards begin with the faintest of flakes. I am and will remain of small stature in the history of this land, but perhaps through the grace of God I can accomplish big things."

Alanbart shook his head. "Optimists," he said, but his tone showed that he was a bit moved. He picked up the pot of oatmeal and carried it to them. "Here, eat. Then you can get your hair done and Gawain's face made up so that you can go and die like the heroes that you are. Maybe I'll write your song one day, and we can all get what we want—you each can sacrifice your physical mortality to become literarily immortal, and through your deaths I'll gain a stable income."

11

MIDMORNING, BROKEN CROSS MUIR

Scot and Gawain dismounted. Curling steam rose from the hot skin of their mounts in the cool damp air. They'd cantered south on Gringolet and Taffy into a low-clinging morning fog. Trying to make the best time possible, they crossed the River Clyde at Shepherd's Ford, cutting across the heather and the south moors, and eventually connecting with the forest road.

They galloped south along the road under the shade of both cloud and trees and skirted the little forest hamlet of Hawklund, where Taffy was spooked by three hounds outside of a woodcutter's cottage and nearly threw Scot. Finally, they rode west along the edge of the forest until they came to the place where three standing stones lined the shore of a massive bog. One lay toppled and overgrown with twisting vines of blue and white trumpet flowers, but the other two stood, marking the place where, of old, the wooden causeway crossed a patch of bog-water to the island abbey. They draped their reins over a nearby branch and appraised the swampy terrain.

"Broken Cross Muir," Scot said out of habit, though neither he nor Gawain heard the words—their wax-filled ears rang and throbbed painfully with their heartbeats.

The bog took its name from the ruined abbey that graced its only island. A group of Christian priests constructed Three-Cross Abbey almost four centuries earlier to house some long-forgotten relic, and bad luck plagued it from the start. The abbot and his disciples experienced disease, harassment from the Picts, and eventual slaughter by the banshee and her undead cohorts. Asacael's minions then desecrated its halls and put them to unholy use, eradicating every living creature on the island, uprooting every growing plant, and even scraping the lichen from the rocks. The isle was entirely dead. The name of the bog changed at that time from Three-Cross Muir, to

Broken *Crosses* Muir, and eventually simply to Broken Cross Muir. Be that as it may, the old causeway still represented the safest and shortest crossing from dry land to the island. And Gawain and Scot intended to use it.

The foggy air stank. Where they could see it through the swirling clouds of mist, the water rippled red-brown in a light southerly breeze. A thick mat of peat covered most of the stagnant water, from which grew a great diversity of plants.

Carnivorous sundews and pitcher plants clung to exposed rocks, which grew carpets of moss and were bordered in tall sedge and reeds. Where the peat grew thin and soil broke through the surface, hardy grasses formed exposed hummocks, and on the largest of these, mints, diminutive flowering shrubs, and even small blueberry bushes grew. Bulrushes lined the shore and tall clumps of reeds protruded from gaps in the peat.

After taking in this scene, the two heroes turned toward each other and Scot flashed a dazzling smile. He looked much as he did on the previous day. Sir Gawain, however, was much changed, now appearing as a Pictish warrior. His robust chest and thickly muscled arms were slathered in bright grass-green paint, but his blue eyes and silvery-blonde beard stood out in contrast to the color. On his exposed chest, a field of blonde hair curled out of the dried and crusted pigment. Gawain wore soft brown breeches of the finest supple Spanish leather. Designs displaying shields of varying styles were stitched down the outward seam in gold thread. Sturdy brown riding boots hugged his feet. Gawain's hair was, if anything, more outrageous than Scot's. They'd treated it with grease and lime and formed it into four large spikes, two slanting up from behind his temples, and two angling down from behind his ears, creating a sort of X pattern with his face in the center. If he felt ridiculous, he didn't show it. He gave one terse nod in Scot's direction.

They turned to their business. Gawain unsheathed and resheathed his longsword, its nearly-four-foot blade shining briefly as a stray ray of sunlight cut through the thinning fog. He fastened his red-and-white-striped shield over his shoulder, laying it across his back, and hefted the weight of the green battle-axe in both hands.

Scot hung a pair of one-handed infantry maces from his belt. They were simple weapons—a wooden haft wrapped with a leather grip and capped with an oval studded bronze ball. They wouldn't be overly useful against an armored opponent, but he expected them to do a wealth of damage to any exposed and brittle bones with which they came in contact. Following that, he drew his six-foot greatsword from its place on the saddle and slid it through a brass loop that hung on a strap over his shoulder.

They glanced again at each other, nodded a nonverbal agreement, and began their trek into the bog, moving in a zigzag pattern between raised hummocks and exposed rocks, testing each step. The breeze gusted, clearing out the lowland fog. Often, a patch of blue sky melded out of and back into mist. The sunlight struggled to break through and bathed everything in an optimistic white glow that belied danger.

If Scot and Gawain could have listened to the swamp, they may have been more wary. It was eerily silent, without a bird singing, a frog croaking, or a cricket droning. The sloshing of water, the occasional grunt or hiss of surprise as one of their feet sank through the peat, and the other sounds of their passing carried far across the bog and echoed off of the trees of the forest. [12] They already saw the collapsed abbey ahead. It loomed gray against the thin white fog. The granite building took up a full third of the island. Constructed in the shape of a cross, its chapel occupied the trunk, the abbot's and priests' living quarters were located in the southern half of the crossbar, and the devotional materials, books and artifacts were kept in the room on the northern side. The roofs had collapsed on the central and southern sections, strewing rubble across the ground, but many of the stone pillars of the chapel still stood erect, broken fingers in the fog.

As they approached, Scott and Gawain began to see movement. Fifty yards away from dry land, Scot—who had sharper eyes—made order out of the scene. Skeletal soldiers formed ranks on the shore. With a shock of fear, Scot realized that if they caught him on the peat mat over the water, he was as good as dead. Skeletons weighed much less than a man and didn't need to fear drowning. Even if he only fell through into chest-deep water and knee-deep mud, he'd be

---

[12] Perhaps this point is as good a time as any to explain a few important details about the undead, for a small army of those horrific things waited for our two heroes, not five-hundred yards distant: The first thing to know about the undead is that they can neither

unable to adequately defend himself.

Making a snap decision, he pulled the twin maces off of his belt, bellowed, and leaped from hummock to hummock toward the island. He couldn't hear it, but Gawain followed, green axe in hand.

---

see, hear, nor feel. In fact, all traditional senses fail immediately upon death. The dead have only one sense—for ease of reference and understanding, let us call it *death-vision*—and though in some ways it is akin to human vision, it is not based on a line of sight and is extra-sensory to traditional human understanding.

Imagine for a moment that you are a skeleton. As you sense around yourself, there is a gray and nebulous void. Everything alive registers as a painful bright glare and everything inanimate or dead as a comforting numb darkness. The stronger something's will to live is, the brighter it registers. For example, a pregnant woman, healthy child, or star-crossed lover would be very bright, whereas someone old, terminally ill, or terribly depressed would be dim. Also, mammals are brighter than birds, which are brighter than amphibians (followed by reptiles, fish, insects, trees, moss, lichen, and fungus, generally in the order of the great chain of being).

Another thing to know is that dead objects (say a wool shirt, a suit of armor, or a wall, floor, or ceiling) interposed between the undead and the living do not block this sense at all. Finally, the more powerful the strength of will possessed by the undead being, the wider the range of this sense will be. A simple skeleton may sense ten feet, but a banshee like Asacael might sense around three hundred yards.

While it may seem infallible, this death-vision can be overloaded. When many living things are crowded in the same area, they compound their life forces, becoming indistinguishable and 'blinding' the undead. It is no surprise, then, that the undead prefer to act at night or in winter because the life force of plants dims with the vanishing sun, and a forest of living trees or a field of vibrant grass, sucking in sunlight, blurs their perception—like a bright background masking a white silhouette.

The second important fact to know about the undead is that they aren't slow and pathetic fighters that rely on mob strength, as so many storytellers would have you believe. They retain the strength, speed, and skill that they possessed at the moment of their deaths. That said, their bodies do decay and eventually all of the fleshy padding around their bones rots and sloughs off. Then, after a century or two, the bones become brittle and easy to snap or smash. Therein lies their greatest weakness. Like grandmothers, they break easily. However, a warrior should never count a shattered skeleton out of the fight. They can be just as tenacious as a grandmother, too. Legless or armless skeletons will continue to press the attack until they are released.

Released, you are asking, how might that be accomplished? There are only two ways: decapitation or the staving in of the skull. And once an undead being loses its physical presence the spirit within faces an intriguing decision. Most will vanish immediately, winking out of existence in this world and simultaneously into existence in the next (just like most of us upon our deaths). A very few of the stronger-willed, however, will choose to remain, and will become ghosts—beings utterly invincible to physical attack. This is nothing for a wandering warrior to worry about, though. Ghosts are as powerless against the living as we are against them (unless a person chooses to reside in close proximity to said ghost for an extended period of time, which may result in demonic possession or dream-haunting—but those do not come into this tale).

One final thing to consider is the undead's generally solitary nature. Given the rarity and extreme circumstances that are required to create them, usually only one (or rarely a pair) of undead will be in any single location. However, when a particularly powerful will is involved—like Asacael's—it can dominate the souls of the dying, binding them to this world, as occurred with nearly all of her followers. If that will were to be vanquished, its grip on subordinate undead would be released, and the vast majority would quit existence, their bones falling lifeless to the earth. However, neither Scot nor Gawain was aware of that fact, and they progressed toward the island intent on eradicating every last skeleton.

12

THE GLOAMWOOD CAVERNS

Cathbad sat on a rough stone slab in the middle of the largest grotto in the network of caverns spider-webbing through the limestone beneath the Gloamwood. The stale air felt cool and damp, smelling of bat droppings, mildew, and goblin (goblin, for those who have never had the pleasure, is a sort of understated and musky combination of wet dog, boiled cabbage, and spoiled milk). Thankfully a fire burned nearby and thick wood smoke clinging to the cavern roof mitigated the other odors.

Unseen to Cathbad's blind eyes, scores of goblins milled about in the flickering shadows. Many lined the irregular walls and many more knelt on the stone floor around the druid and their chief, an uneasily silent group of gray-faced savages who fingered chipped scimitars, knives, and hatchets.

The fire crackled and popped, and somewhere nearby water dripped from a stalactite into a stagnant pool.

Cathbad gave a vague smile in the direction of Bruuzak. He was as confidant as a man could be in this situation, for he and the chief had already discussed the details of their bargain in private—now, they were required to playact it in front of the tribe so that it would gain public approval.

"I am more than willing to acquiesce to any demand that you make," Cathbad said, "providing that you fulfill my two conditions. They are that you storm the tower, and that you deliver to me—*alive*—the old king who is imprisoned within. I intend to make a sacrifice of him to my gods, a sacrifice that your tribe is welcome to attend."

An old goblin translated as Cathbad talked, barking out words in their doglike language.

"We may keep *all* of the treasure?" Bruuzak hissed with

pleasure. The translation continued.

"Certainly. What use have I for gold?"

"And we may do what we please with *all* of the other prisoners?"

"Yes."

"And the woman from the fire last night?"

"Her fate is no concern of mine."

"What about your giant and warrior?"

"The giant is under my complete control. He is no threat to you, for he would never disobey me. The warrior, though, may value his honor above his loyalty to the gods—this would be a grave fault indeed, but he is proud and it is not to be unexpected. He may turn on us when the moment arrives."

At the translation of this, a low yapping murmur filled the cavern.

"And what are we to do about this? Bruuzak asked.

"Assign your best archer to shadow my warrior. He wears no armor. If he betrays us, finish him quickly. Yet, if he remains loyal, he shall live."

"And you are sure that your magic will break down the gate?"

"A wise man is sure of nothing." Again, a murmur spread through the crowd. Cathbad raised his voice. "Yet, if my hammer fails, my giant will not. Remember, too, that we outnumber them three-to-one."

"Then are we agreed?" Bruuzak shouted, standing tall.

The other goblins stood and roared their approval. It echoed inside the chamber, washing about the walls in a cacophonous echo. After a few seconds, Bruuzak slapped his bare feet against the floor until the uproar began to settle down.

"We will drink to this in blood."

Cathbad sighed heavily. "If we must."

He waited for the cup, thinking through his strategy. It all hinged on success against Asacael. Therein lay the great gamble. If his warrior came back victorious from that encounter, then he would regain both his power and sight. With those, anything could be

104

attained. He need only achieve two goals: the capture of Arthur and the defeat of Rabordath. At the moment, both seemed to be likely outcomes. Certainly the fools who were even now carrying out his plans against the banshee would do everything in their power to free their king—it would be but a simple matter to ambush them outside the tower and take what he wanted through the elements of surprise and overwhelming numbers.

As for Rabordath, Cathbad had already convinced himself that he would be more than a match for any 'wizard' weak enough to attach himself the lord of the tower. In fact, he didn't see how any petty warlock could hope to conjure anything larger than—at most—some kind of serpentine familiar or lizard man. Perhaps with time and effort he might have constructed a golem, but a dragon? An absurd idea.

Bruuzak's cold claw touched his arm, interrupting his thoughts.

"Drink," the goblin said in a gravelly voice.

Cathbad lifted the cup above his head. "To victory," he said, taking a long sip of the cool and bitter iron-tainted alcohol.

"To victory!" Bruuzak echoed, lifting his cup as well.

The crowd stamped their feet and cheered. Bruuzak dashed his bronze cup against the ground and drew his sword. He began to bark in Goblin, and this is roughly what he said: "Goblins! we have been dormant for far too long—hiding underground, living off of stolen sheep, pilfered pigs, and captured children—but tonight that changes. Tonight we march to *battle*!" A great cheer rose again and the goblins' feet slapped the stone to crescendo.

While Bruuzak yapped and growled out his premature victory speech, Cathbad's mind strayed. Could druidism ever be brought back? 'Impossible,' he thought. So many druids with so much knowledge of the faith died before their times—before they could pass on their wisdom. He'd become too old, had forgotten too much, and he was alone. Never again would the Yule log burn in the holly grove on the longest night of the year. Never again would the priestess of Esther dance naked and make love with virgins on the stone alter during the equinox. Those days would not be seen again except fleetingly in the minds of old men and women as they passed from this life to the next.

'The river of time,' he mused, 'flows in but one direction— downhill to the ocean: eternity. Smoke and ashes cannot be called against the wind or formed again into trees. Vanished knowledge cannot be remembered.' Teardrops trailed down Cathbad's cheeks. 'No, the world wears on and wears down like a mountain range. The old, no matter how strong their bedrock, grind to dust in wind, rain, surf, and ice—always in ice. The young rise, jagged, burning, and bare, and all eyes dwell on them.'

'Yet,' he thought, 'something might still be done—not to halt the inevitable change, not to bring back the past, but to avenge it.' He'd squandered half a lifetime feeling sorry for himself. He'd done nothing worth a breath of memory, and that realization had festered in his mind of late. Tonight would redeem all.

'Yes,' he mused, 'tonight every outcome will be to my benefit. If the goblins take the tower without much loss and deliver Arthur to me, then the local power of the Christians will be crushed, the sacrifice of the Christian King will further amplify my abilities, and any avenging army will move against the goblins and not against me. If, on the other hand, the Christians earn a victory, then the unpredictable danger posed by these goblins will be at an end, the banshee will still be dead, and the threat of the tower will be diminished. I could travel between Hazleton, Lanark, Hawklund, and Boghead, and initiate a rebellion that would certainly topple the tower and bring me victory. The local people feel no love for their *lord*. However,' he thought, 'perhaps the best of all outcomes would be if the goblins and the Christians annihilate one another. I would be the only remaining power.' Cathbad dwelled with pleasure on the thought.

Yes, a rebirth of druidism might be impossible, but if he couldn't bring it back, at least he could be sure that it wouldn't die quietly and that it wouldn't die alone. He would spend himself like a sacrificial fire, licking the flesh from his victims as he blazed, bright and brief, against the encroaching night.

13

BROKEN CROSS ABBEY

'Well, this is going better than expected,' Scot thought as he smashed the yellowed skull of a charging skeleton. Beside him, his war paint shining green and hair spiking wildly, Gawain reaped the undead with wide swings of his greataxe. A shower of loose ribs pelted Scot.

Already, the two heroes had smashed nearly fifty skeletons, and the greatest danger was past. The undead almost overwhelmed them as they made landfall, but the duo battered through the first line of defense and made for the nearest freestanding corner of the collapsed abbey. There, placing their backs to the inside angle of an L-shaped wall, it became impossible to flank them. In a precise and deadly side-by-side dance, Gawain and Scot rained destruction on their assailants.

Scot dispatched two legless skeletons left behind by Gawain's axe. He laughed, thinking that they could hold this position forever, but just as he smote another foe, the rest of their undead assailants backed out of range to form a semicircular shield-wall, trapping the two heroes in their corner.

Scot paused for breath and took stock of the situation. Already, he bled from two cuts on his chest, a scratch above his left nipple and a ragged gash inflicted as a spear point glanced off of his ribcage. The latter bled liberally, a crimson streak on his blue war paint. In comparison, he noted, Sir Gawain had sustained only a few minor scratches and showed no acknowledgement of injury. He wasn't even breathing hard.[13]

---

[13] This was, of course, a reflection of varying styles and attitudes toward combat. Gawain was an experienced veteran. The joy of combat and the desire for fame were afterthoughts for the legendary knight. Every parry and slash was careful, controlled, and effective, a transaction to be completed. He was in no real danger, for he had no enemies behind him and faced no opponents of substantial ability. Despite his workmanlike approach,

Regaining his wind, Scot wiped sweat from his eyes (and some blue paint) and squinted at the skeletal shield-wall, considering their tactical situation. Two immediate and terrible possibilities occurred to him. First, the undead might stay in a defensive ring and dare them to attack, waiting for sleep to become a necessity and then pressing the attack. Second, he had a wild and horrifying vision of skeletal archers, spear-throwers, or even rock-throwers pelting them with missiles from behind the ring of shields. Never having fought a legion of undead, Scot realized that he had no idea what their tactical approach might entail. This frightened him more than the skeletons' initial assault.

What actually happened was far more terrifying.

The banshee staggered from around a section of collapsed wall, her lurching gait highlighting the unsettling angles of her deformed body. Asacael's damp skin was rust-brown, her figure emaciated. Her naked chest rose and fell like a bellows. The remains of ancient ropes trailed from her wrists and dragged behind her ankles. Lank bog-bleached orange hair stuck to and matted against one side of her skull; the other had been stripped bald over years submerged in peat and mud.

Flanking her on both sides marched seven undead warriors—clearly her elite bodyguard. Five were skeletons, but two had died recently and wore shining steel armor, still spattered with dried blood and mud—Arthur's knights.

One had his visor down, but the other wore his upraised, and his sickly-pale, yet still comely face stared blankly forward. His close-

---

though, Gawain was capable of a level of skill that he rarely attained—only when provoked to rage or facing an opponent of such talent or fame that it became necessary—and when he reached his full potential, no one alive (save, perhaps, Lancelot) could stand against him.

In contrast, Scot was a talented and passionate amateur. He fought for the pure joy of fighting. Still young, still reckless, he laughed out loud in combat, relishing the sensations, drinking the adrenaline like liquor, testing his limits, and viewing each encounter as a contest—not only of skill, but of style. He was competitive, and (like any great athlete) he sought only the elation of victory.

Often, he would imagine himself in the third person, seeing his choreography in his mind's eye, putting it to poetry, and cheering for himself as if he were a hero of a great lay or ballad. This reckless style, and his relative inexperience, exposed him to more injury than his partner.

cropped blonde beard and facial features showed a marked resemblance to Sir Gawain, though he seemed slighter in the shoulders than his brother. His plume, surcoat, and shield were purple, and his shield bore the symbol of Orkney, a two-headed golden eagle looking simultaneously left and right. The other corpse-knight was thick-set and wore a royal blue cape. The solid blue of his shield bore a pair of interlocking silver keys as its only embellishment. Both knights stood a full head higher than the other skeletons and directly flanked the banshee.

Of the other three skeletal champions, the first had been a Scandinavian sea-king, a gold-enameled open-faced helm on its head, its goggle-like eye guard covering the sockets of its yellowing skull. A warhorn hung over its shoulder against a coat of intricately worked chain mail. It carried a round shield and a wicked Danish battle-axe.

The second wore only shredded leather pants hanging in fluttering brown ribbons from a braided belt. Its pearl-white knuckles clutched two single-edged cleavers.[14] Its hair, brittle and white with age, still clung to its skull in ratty patches. Scraps of blue-painted skin peeled and curled from its cheekbones and forehead—a Pict.

The third skeleton was a Roman centurion, armored in rusted banded mail and helmed with an open-faced legionnaire's helmet with its empty plume-socket affixed crosswise instead of lengthwise—a sign of rank. A tattered crimson cape fluttered behind it.

As the banshee and her bodyguards advanced, the air chilled. Ice crept across helmets and blades, and Scot felt the very mud beneath his feet begin to harden with frost. His breath came in puffs of steam; the hair on his arms and neck bristled. His muscles tensed, and he struggled with a strange sensation inside as he watched Asacael approach. It seemed to Scot as if his conscious mind retreated, attempting to separate from his body. His motion became sluggish and time slowed.

The banshee walked to within twenty paces, then opened her mouth, filled her lungs, and wailed. A devastating and deafening scream

---

[14] The locals called these primitive blades "saex," but the general category of sword became known to posterity as the falchion. More like a butcher's knife or a brush clearing blade than one designed for battle, these heavy single-edged cleavers were a preferred weapon in Scandinavia and the British Isles until around the year 600 AD.

erupted, simultaneously vicious and plaintive.

Peasants heard a faint echo leagues away in Boghead Village and Hawklund Town. As one, they stopped work, shivered, and crossed themselves. A sentry atop the Devil's Rookery heard the cry and fumbled his spear. It clattered to the stone floor of the parapet. At the same moment all of the ravens roosting on the tower's battlements took flight in a storm of dark wings and bickering noise, as did clouds of waterfowl and songbirds rising from the muir and out of Hawkfeather Forest.

At its epicenter, the wave of sound broke against Scot with almost tangible force. He swayed and sagged against the abbey wall. Beyond the ringing inside his ears and the *lub-dub* of his heartbeat, he heard a sort of high-pitched tinny whine that coiled around his mind like a constricting snake. Listening to it, his consciousness reeled and retreated. He willed his mind to swim uphill against the current of Asacael's hate. His body slumped, and he felt an incalculable weariness. Then, the shockwave passed. He leaned against the wall for a moment, stunned, shook his head back and forth, and waited for his mind to clear. Beside him, Gawain let go of his axe, cradled his forehead in the palm of his hand, and pressed his fingers against his eye sockets, trying to clear his vision.

Asacael studied them, leaning forward, poised and expectant, but when Scot shook his head, she shrieked in rage. This shriek was of a different intensity and tenor than the previous blast: short and angry, without a touch of sorrow or pathos. Her lungs inflated again, wider— if possible—than last time, and she leaned back to howl out a second and more powerful wail.

Before she unleashed it, Scot threw his mace.

He watched it hurtle through the air, whirling end-over-end until its bronze head connected low on the banshee's shoulder, above a pendulous red-brown breast. No one heard the wet slap and a bone-crushing snap, but Asacael lurched backwards, the air left her lungs, and her arm went limp. Scot hurled the second mace only seconds later, but the corpse-knight with the keys on his shield, lunged in to deflect the blow.

Scot unsheathed his sword.

Asacael hissed an order in a long-forgotten tongue, but the

undead, more oblivious to sound than even Scot and Gawain, responded to her power of will before she uttered the words. The three skeletal champions advanced through an opening in the shield-wall. The corpses of Sirs Kay and Agravain raised their shields, interposing themselves between the banshee and her enemies, and covered her slow lurching retreat.

The skeletal sea-king advanced, lifted its shield, and dropped into a combat stance. It moved toward Gawain. The Pictish-looking skeleton turned toward Scot. Its twin cleavers gleamed. The centurion hung back, filled the gap in the shield-wall, and waited.

Scot's assailant lunged and dropped into a roll, springing to its feet at such close range that Scot couldn't wield his greatsword. One of the Pict's blades whizzed over the swordsman's head, so close that it shaved off a spike of red hair. The other came in sideways at his guts, but he smashed down with the hilt of his useless sword, deflecting it. Scot ducked its next swing, which scraped against the abbey stones, sending sparks flying into the murky half-light.

Adrenaline coursing through his veins, Scot dropped his sword and did the only thing that came to mind: he grabbed at the skeleton's arms.

The two opponents grappled for a few moments, engaging in a contest of strength. Scot was losing. His enemy whipped him violently around and drove him toward the shield wall and certain death. His feet dug twin trails in the pebbled ground.

In desperation, Scot threw himself backward and dropped to the ground, using momentum to unbalance his foe. He released one of his enemy's arms and kicked upward with all his strength. He felt a satisfying snap as one skeletal wrist disintegrated in his hand.

The joy of combat returned and Scot laughed, but the swordsman's elation turned to fear, and his mirth evaporated as he saw the skeleton's blade arcing toward him. He exerted every effort to avoid the oncoming attack, but this time his reaction was too slow.

Time seemed to protract. The falchion glittered in a stray sunbeam. Then, at the last instant, Gawain's axe, with a heavy Viking shield immovably lodged on its head, swept through the air, deflecting the blow, and crashing, full-force, into the skeleton, splintering it into a shower of bones that ricocheted and clattered about the abbey wall.

Scot studied the scattered remnants of the sea king that had attacked Gawain. He groped for the handle of his two-handed sword, and took the famous knight's calloused hand. Gawain helped Scot to his feet.

The two shared a small smile. Gawain's was a teasing grin, chiding Scot for his failure, and Scot's was equal parts embarrassment, affection, and relief.

They looked back toward the banshee, only to see her escape around a scatter of collapsed rubble.

The centurion formed the remaining score of skeletons into a line, ten wide and two deep, shields overlapping and swords drawn. They advanced behind their shields like a trained military unit. Gawain nodded grimly at Scot, discarded his axe, and started to unsling his shield.

Frantic, Scot considered the wall of the abbey, the rough-hewn stones of which stood about twelve feet high, and then he slapped Gawain on the shoulder. The knight checked his movement, followed his eyes, nodding assent.

The swordsman sheathed his sword in a fluid motion and made a stirrup with his hands. Gawain placed his foot inside, and Scot launched him onto the slippery wall. He grabbed hold, scrambled up, and dropped a hand to Scot—none-too-soon.

Gawain lifted the young warrior clear at the same moment that the skeletons came into range. A spear stabbed into the swordsman's sandal as he went up, nicking his foot and leaving Scot barefoot. The skeleton's empty-eyes gaped up and its spear shook, the Pict's sandal affixed to its point.

Scot and Gawain scrambled precariously along the freestanding wall until they came to the decaying roof above the single intact room of the abbey. There, more secure in their footing, they crouched and began to disinter brick-sized stones from the crumbling mortar, remove wide slate shingles from the roof, and pelt them down at the undead legion.

The first few stones hit home, shattering bones and collapsing skeletons, but the rest of the legion raised interlocked shields, forming what the Romans called a 'tortoise,' and began to back out of range. The stones and slate bounced ineffectively to the ground.

However, danger fast approached from the opposite side of the building. Unknown to Scot and Gawain, who remained insensible to sound, the corpses of Sirs Kay and Agravain had already clambered up the wall and slunk along the edge of the roof, one from either direction, attempting to flank them.

They might have both been killed there, had Scot not detected the movement of a shadow in his peripheral vision and glanced toward Gawain seconds before his assailant, the corpse of Sir Kay, brought its sword down. He saw the advancing knight and, without pausing to think, leapt over Gawain, colliding with the creature and grasping its sword-arm with both hands.

The undead-knight staggered, bracing one foot high on slate roof.

For an agonizing moment, it looked like Kay's corpse would regain its footing, but just as it caught its weight, the roof buckled; its leg crashed through cracked slate, up to the knee. Sir Kay's corpse toppled backwards, Scot still on top of it. The ancient dry-rotted timers splintered under the shock, and the two passed through the roof, out of the sunlight and into the room below, a trickle of slate shingles following them.

Gawain watched as Scot leapt over him, barely managing to duck beneath the Pict's passing body. Beyond Scot, though, he saw the advancing corpse of his brother, Agravain, purple shield raised and sword in hand. Dead insensible eyes stared through and past him. Gawain stood, shrugged his shield from his shoulder, and strapped it to his forearm. He drew his sword.

'My God,' he thought, 'not my brother—my last living brother. Mary have mercy.' But Agravain was dead; his corpse advanced without pity. Gawain fell into a fighting stance, checking his balance on the loose stones and crumbling mortar.

He knew that he was always the quicker, the stronger, and the better fighter, but Agravain wore full armor. He did not. Additionally, Gawain thought, if his brother's corpse behaved anything like the other undead, he'd have to decapitate it or crush its skull.

He decided that his best bet would be to knock Agravain off the roof and hope for a broken leg, arm, or damage to its armor that would hamper its movements. He calculated the distance to the ground and to his horror saw the skeletal legion advance. Some discarded their shields and began to climb, spider-like, up its rough surface.

And then Agravain was upon him.

Gawain parried the first two slashes with his sword and blocked a third with his shield, retreating along the wall. Stones wobbled under his feet and some mortar gave way, but the wall didn't collapse and Agravain didn't stumble. Gawain blocked a fourth slash with his shield, and then launched an offensive.[15]

So powerful and so ruthless was Gawain's onslaught that the corpse-knight fell back, battered by its brother's blade, which scored three stunning hits on its helmet, sliced through the inside of its elbow (a crippling blow to a living man), stabbed into the armor around its knee, and slashed it across the face. The cut opened a diagonal gash, burst the left eye, ran across the nose down to the side of its gaping mouth, and knocked out three teeth. However, none of these injuries affected the corpse. Perhaps worst of all, the gash didn't even bleed, for all of Sir Agravain's blood had long congealed in the lower extremities.

After his attack, which forced Agravain back into the skeletons that now stood atop the wall (and knocked two of them from it to shatter on the pebbled earth below), Gawain found himself winded and trembling with exertion. This gave Agravain's tireless corpse a brief opening. It advanced behind its shield, slashing and hacking at Gawain, who scrambled backward, crouched as small as he could make himself

---

[15] It is likely, reader, that you have never seen trained warriors in sword-to-sword combat, and even if you have, it is impossible to imagine the speed and skill with which Arthur's knights fought. They had no peers; they were culled from the elite of a whole country that had been constantly at war for over two centuries. Both Gawain and Agravain were blindingly fast, incredibly strong, and utterly lethal, and their duel was nothing short of spectacular.

That said, it is important to know, also, that as opposed to the narratives in many romances—which relate longwinded tales of evenly matched warriors meeting and fighting for hours or a day (so equal in skill that neither can find advantage over the other)—a true contest of legendary swordsmanship is almost always over quickly (unless both parties want it to last). The first slight error on the part of one participant means the first severe wound. And the first severe wound means that one of the warriors becomes instantly handicapped, slower, and distracted by pain, which means – almost always – that he dies.

Well, if this were a contest like that, Agravain would have found himself dead three times over in a period of ten seconds.

behind his now dented and scarred shield, and hard-pressed to defend himself.

Worse, some of the skeletons now scrambled up and across the angled roof, getting in position to flank him. They were much lighter than he, so the ancient beams and slates held their weight easily.

Gawain glanced down and did a quick count. Nine skeletons remained, some already beginning their ascent. His odds would be much better on the ground than atop the wall.

Skeletons could climb up and down, but they certainly couldn't risk a jump. Also, he thought, if he moved quickly, he might get a swing at that banshee before Agravain could catch him.

With his undead brother bearing down again, Gawain rolled sideways off the wall, spun in the air and continued his roll once the ground rushed to meet him. He sprang to his feet in a smooth motion, sword and shield raised.

The nearby undead turned to offer a disorganized charge. He shield-rushed one, cut the head from a second, and brought his blade crashing down on a third, cleaving its helmet. More skeletons advanced; behind them closed the centurion, whose skull somehow grinned more broadly than the rest from inside its Roman helmet.

14

CATHBAD'S HENGE

Alanbart combed through the lukewarm ash of the previous night's fire with a forked stick. He'd already disinterred a small mound of gold blobs, melted out of the inlaying on Gawain's once-proud armor, and he'd found twelve large garnets, but as of yet, no rubies. Heather watched him, fiddling with the jeweled and sequined silk belt that Gawain left for her as a keepsake. As he was leaving, the famous knight drew it from around his waist, handed it to her, and said, "Wear this belt to ward off evil and stay safe from harm in my absence," which seemed odd statement to Alanbart.

He wiped sweat off of his brow and exhaled, then looked up at the green-skinned form of Gonoth, who stood behind him, his vacant red eyes upon Heather and a huge hand scratching absentmindedly at his belly. Alanbart shook his head and returned his attention to the pile of ash. 'This insane venture is finally beginning to pay off,' he thought. Gawain had given him a *small* sum in restitution, which turned out to be more coin than he'd planned to ask for from Ghent. Adding the trove produced by Gawain's armor would allow Alanbart to repair his equipment and live a life of frugal luxury for at least half a year. He'd make it through the winter at the very least. And if Heather sent him south and he got paid handsomely for that service, he would earn the twin victories of escaping the frigid north and doubling his wealth.

"I've been wondering, why did you decide to become a knight?" Heather asked, breaking the silence and ignoring Gonoth's persistent stare. She fastened the green belt about her waist, wrapping it twice. Its ends still dangled down in front of her skirt, almost reaching her feet. "What I mean is, if you knew that you were not fit for it, why didn't you try a life in the church? You seem quick of mind and good with sums, and you can read."

"How do you know that I read?" Alanbart asked, surprised.

"You mentioned Dido and Oedipus—both characters from stories that I've only read in books."

"Pardon me, but the fact that you read, my dear, is more surprising than the fact that I do."

"My mistress enjoys correspondence and does not trust her servants to deliver memorized messages. However, sealed written messages are more secure. Her castle has six books—Sophocles, Virgil, Marcus Aurelius, Ovid, Boethius, and a copy of *The Romance of the Rose*.

"Interesting. I've never read Boethius—perhaps I can visit your library one day, but never mind," Alanbart replied. "I didn't mean to stray from the topic at hand. The fact is that I did think of joining the church, and I even briefly flirted with the idea," he admitted, still poking through the ashes, "but the major difficulty is that I'm an infidel."

"Surely not!" She asked, aghast.

"Surely so," was his blunt reply. "I'd like to tell you that I lost my faith when my father died, but that would be a lie. My faith was never strong, and I lost what there was of it by degrees over the course of my childhood—mainly because I thought too much." He sighed, "The world is much kinder to fools than it is to thinkers. Fools can accept lies as truth and rest secure in their armor of ignorance. Take our new acquaintance, Scot, for example. His old ways *are* the new ways—on a basic level nothing has changed except the names we call things and *who* has the power." He smiled sourly and lunged at a promising clump of ash with his stick, crumbling it.

"I've had my bitter days," Heather confessed, "and I've seen my share of human weakness and vice, but I've never completely lost my faith."

"That's likely because you've never taken the time to really *think* about faith. Here is the crux of the matter in my mind: if God loves each of us, why are so few of us rich and powerful, and so many poor and abject? The usual answer is that the hierarchy on earth mirrors the Divine Hierarchy of Heaven, but if so, why aren't the powerful good and the abject evil? So many of the highly ranked ones, like Mordred and Malestair for example, are terrible people. Watch how it works—the politics, betrayals, corruption, and stupidity—there is nothing divine about it." He paused for effect. "Yet, I admit that I prefer my spot near the top to those at the bottom, and that I'll do what I can—and be as corrupt as I have to—to keep it."

She continued to stare at him in disbelief, and then opened her mouth to speak, but Alanbart shushed her: "I know. You are about to say that Satan lifts up the evil lords to thwart God's power (that's the standard argument, I believe) but you can't have it both ways. If there is an all-powerful God who created everything, then He *must have* created Lucifer to *become* Satan. If He has a Divine Plan, then Satan is *part* of that plan—evil, hatred, misery, disease, squalor, death—these must *all* be part of the plan. Mordred and Malestair and their ilk are *part of God's plan.* The other option is that Satan was a mistake. But if God made a mistake—especially one of that magnitude, one *Hell* of a mistake—how can you believe that He is all-knowing and all-powerful? It calls into question the supposedly 'inevitable' outcome of the cosmic battle between good and evil."

He gazed at her with intensity, waiting for a response, but Heather, like so many of us, was a person who became silent when something bothered her deeply. She replayed Alanbart's words in her head, considering them and mentally testing potential answers against his logic. Alanbart let the silence hang in the air for a few seconds before continuing: "Oh, certainly I pay lip service to the *idea* of God on holy days, I give my tithe in church when I must, and I admit that I do occasionally get caught up in the grandeur of the ceremony and feel what you consider 'the Holy Spirit' calling me to judgment, but the feeling always passes."

At this moment, the giant (who though he'd tried manfully to follow the conversation, was becoming increasingly less interested) let loose a thunderous fart that rent the clear morning air. He turned to look behind himself, as if surprised, then cleared his throat, and without saying a word, lumbered away behind the henge, his hand fiddling with his oversized brass belt buckle.

Heather and Alanbart both watched him go—speechless. Alanbart thought, 'Well, at least we know what *he* thinks of this God debate.' But before he could turn the thought into a wisecrack, Heather cleared her throat.

"So you truly believe in nothing?" she asked, pointedly ignoring the lingering stench that burned her nostrils. Her eyes watered.

"No," he coughed, bending over the ash pile as a breeze cleared the air. "I don't believe in *anything*—which isn't the same as believing in *nothing*. Belief in nothing, it seems to me, takes quite as much faith as belief in something. I am utterly incapable of that kind of commitment."

"I see," Heather responded, the first true hint of scorn in her tone.

"And though you might think that I am a hypocrite and a liar (which I am), for masquerading as one of Arthur's knights, and willfully playing at a role that I am incapable of enacting, it somehow seems much better to fake being a knight and so risk inglorious exposure as a fraud and death in combat than to pretend to be a priest—and counterfeit a belief in an infallible and divine God that I do not think exists, memorize a text about Him, advise parishioners in ways to get to a nonexistent Heaven, and collect offerings meant for Him, only to line my pockets. The hypocrisy of that existence would be staggering. Even I, with my prodigious capacity for self-delusion, and somewhat lax moral code, would have trouble leading such a life." He paused, lifting his eyebrows apologetically. "Realistically, though," he admitted, "I recognize that I am too sarcastic and pessimistic to successfully keep up a priestly façade for long."

Heather studied him for a long moment, sighed, and replied, "I think you're wrong. Most of us don't *choose* to believe. We believe because we *have* to. Heaven represents hope. In this harsh, short, and brutal existence, people have to have something to which to cling. Instead of living lives of abject despair, heads hung in defeat, and watering the soil with our tears, we live lives of hope, heads upraised to the sun, cheerful through impossible hardships—lending our hands to our neighbors. Even if, as you seem to argue, God is simply an idea in the human mind and Heaven is only a fiction, isn't a life strengthened by faith better than one focused on the inescapable despair of mortality?"

Alanbart crinkled his eyes and broke into a genuine smile. "I admire you," he replied, "and I do love a good fiction, but I prefer my reality to your dreams. I cannot eat or drink dreams and I like to know that my feet are on solid ground. Besides, lost faith was never revived through conversation. If you want to convert me, you'd better pray for a miracle." He suddenly drove his hand into the ash and came out with a stone the size of a large housefly. He spit on it, wiped it off, and held it to the sun. "A ruby!" he exclaimed.

"A miracle?" she asked.

He laughed. "Perhaps, but I warn you, my cynicism is so strong that it borders on optimism."

She laughed at this in her turn.

"Now," he continued, "if you don't mind, I think it is my turn to ask a question of you."

She shrugged, still grinning. "Alright."

"It appears to me that by most measures, you are an ideal woman—and I don't mean that as flattery. That being the case, what do you see as your future?"

Heather sat down on the stone slab where they'd watched the sunrise, let her eyes fall to the pile of ash, and thought for a moment, fiddling absently with the green belt. "First, thank you, Sir, for the flattery." She shifted her gaze and let her eyes linger on him for a couple seconds, considering his face.

Alanbart pretended not to notice and combed through the ash pile, though his heart increased its pace. He prayed that he wasn't blushing, then realized that he didn't believe in prayer, and finally damned himself for bothering with such pointless introspection.

"And in answer to your question," she continued, "I suppose that my rank and station entitle me to marry a knight from a minor house and raise his children, marry a bastard son from a high house and raise his children, or become an abbess or nun. The Lady Elaine has promised to help me find a match when I wish it, and because she had no love in her marriage bed, she has also vowed that I shall marry for love, rather than rank or station. But…" she trailed off.

"But?" Alanbart prompted.

"Well, admittedly, I have no love for the court, so marrying a lower-ranking knight suits me well. And I really *would* like to be a mother—of young boys, especially—I can imagine them running about the manor-house banging wooden swords together in mock-combat, galloping across the grounds, trying their hands at archery, always dirty and always in trouble. I dream about that sometimes and I always wake happy. I know that raising children would be difficult work and worthy of both my time and energy; yet, I have not sought marriage because I cannot help but feel that there should be *something* more. I want to have value in myself and not just in my offspring. When my children are grown, I don't want to be left, wrinkled and wizen in some dusty disused room, there to while away the waning years of my life in pointless needlework with arthritic fingers." She exhaled and continued: "I do see marriage and children as my future, but I'm not ready to embrace it—not yet. I may sound like our friend Scot (whom you characterize as a fool) but I want to do something of note, some noble deed of heroic tenor that will strengthen my heart with courage in my latter years. I have doubts and fears and sorrows, just like any woman, but sometimes I feel that there is a greatness in me waiting to be let out—*needing* release. Other times, I feel like it is all just vanity and I am trying to play a part that wasn't meant for me..."

She hesitated again, her almond-brown eyes resting on Alanbart's blue ones. He held her gaze for a long time, rolling the ruby around in his fingers and biting his bottom lip. "You are an idealist, and you are strong-hearted," he said at last. "Unfortunately, I am neither, and I only see into my future as far as my money will carry me." He stood, brushing the dirt from his pants. "I admit" he said, "that I asked that question to bolster my argument against the class structure and the idea of any 'Divine Plan.' To me you seem fit to be a queen—don't argue; you do—but doomed to bear a bastard knight's bastard children and to spend a lifetime being looked down upon by your inferiors because of your low birth. It struck me as supremely unfair, but your response has shaken my cynicism. In answer I will say but this: I hope that one day our new friend, Scot, will find that he has made his mark and been sung about in an epic tale of courage—but it is my hope that the tale will be told primarily about you, and that he will be but a side character in a greater—hey!" His eyes widened and he snapped his fingers.

"What?"

"I just solved our problem, and it's so easy! I can't believe it didn't occur to me before."

"Which of our problems did you solve?" she asked, amused at what he was saying and his sudden change of topic. "We have quite a few. If you like I can list them for you."

"Well, Malestair is going to use your blood—the blood of a virgin—to conjure that dragon, right?"

"Yes. . ." she hesitated, already suspecting his 'solution' to her problem, "So?"

"Well, don't you see? It's so thunderingly simple—just lose your virginity."

"What?" Heather's face flushed blotchy pink. "If you think that you can use this to get me to—"

"Oh," Alanbart said, realizing for the first time what his statement entailed, "Oh!" and then he cleared his throat. "Oh, well, I, ah, didn't mean. . ." he trailed off and then his tone changed, "I didn't know that you blushed—" he smiled, "or that you could be embarrassed, for that matter. Don't worry, you're pretty when you blush." He took a breath and straightened up. "Well, it *would* work, wouldn't it? Even if Malestair captured you, he couldn't conjure the dragon, I mean if you weren't a virgin. And—and—" he took the plunge, "Look, you already love Gawain; you admitted it to me this morning, so it wouldn't even be all that, um, *unwanted* on your part. And—hear me out—" he was getting excited.

Heather avoided his eyes, focusing instead on a nearby thistle plant. If anything, her color deepened.

"And Gawain," Alanbart continued, "wouldn't be as likely to refuse, if he knew that, uh, doing it—you know, taking it, I mean taking you—meant saving your life, and maybe even saving England. You could entrap him through his chivalric code. He couldn't say no."

"I, no—I couldn't," Heather stammered. "I mean, I—"

"Okay, I'll find an excuse to take Scot away from the henge for ten minutes . . ."

"No," Heather repeated, louder this time.

"Why not?" Alanbart demanded. "The worst outcome is that you bear Gawain's child—whether you marry him or not, it would still be a mark of distinction and he'd take care of your future—he's too honorable not to." A part of him wondered how he could talk about this so coolly, as if he wasn't invested and didn't feel anything for this girl, but ironically the virtue of the idea trumped his emotional attachment to her virtue.

"No," Heather said again, this time in a tone that halted all argument. "No, I refuse. I won't do that with him, not now, and probably not ever." She looked straight at Alanbart. He could see that she wouldn't budge.

"Well," Alanbart replied, this time averting his eyes, "then that leaves me and Scot." Now *he* started to color. His heart beat was insistent. He heard her cough and he kicked absently at a charred bit of deadwood. "Um," he stumbled, "it does seem that we're alone for the moment. No one else would ever have to know." Now he forced himself meet her eyes.

"You can't be serious," she replied, rising to her feet and turning her back in an attempt to hide an outraged . . . smile? She wasn't blushing.

"It might save the kingdom," he offered, lamely—was she laughing at him? "Hey," he continued, sounding wounded, "you make it sound like I'm a terrible option. You have *no idea* how incredibly discerning I am in my choice of wome—"

Heather gasped in horror. The wolfhound stood and barked, facing south.

Alanbart cut himself off; his hand moved to his sword hilt.

A dozen or more horseman rode north toward the henge, about half a league distant. Sunlight sparkled off of their helmets and spear points and their vibrant colors clashed with the muted purple-brown of the heath. Heather retreated toward him, took his hand.

"There's nowhere to run," she whispered, fear apparent in her voice.

Alanbart snorted. "They have *impeccable* timing." Despite the sarcastic tone, his voice trembled more than hers.

"Let's get under the trees," she pulled him toward the henge.

He groped for his gemstones, scattering them into the grass and swearing.

"Do you have time to put on your armor?" she asked.

"Barely," Alanbart replied, now running beside her. "Gonoth!" he roared.

"Gonoth!" Heather repeated in a frantic scream.

The giant came lumbering around the henge, club in hand. He saw the riders and his eyes flashed a deeper red. He lifted the cudgel and scowled.

"Not yet," Heather instructed. "Wait beneath the trees until you can get to them easily. They're mounted and will evade you in the open field. They'll take you from behind if they can. Sir Alanbart will arm himself and we'll join you in a moment."

Gonoth nodded slowly.

"Come on!" she said, dragging Alanbart into the henge. The wolfhound followed.

"Have you ever armed a knight before?" Alanbart asked as he pulled on his smudged and sweat-stained padded hauberk.

"Never," Heather responded, "but there's a first time for everything."

After five minutes of bungling, bumping, pulling, pushing, and yelling, they'd effectively assembled Alanbart's armor. He pulled his now-plumeless helm onto his head (it still smelled of clayish mud) and grabbed his sword. His mind struggled to find a way out. According to Cathbad's prophecy, one of them would die. Malestair needed Heather, but he didn't need Alanbart. 'I'm a dead man,' Alanbart thought, 'and these are my last moments on earth.' The thought chilled his blood.

"Let's go," he said nervously, and started for the back entrance.

Heather grabbed his arm. "You're going to run out the back? What about Gonoth?"

"What about him? He may hold them long enough for us to escape, a sacrifice for which I will be eternally grateful."

"There's nowhere to go. They're all mounted and we're afoot. There's no cover for leagues. They'll certainly have hounds. Our chances, however small, are better if we face them."

"I'd hate dying on any day, but to be the one destined to fulfill that old bastard's prophecy? That fact bothers me more than anything." He paused, then added, "I wish Taffy were here."

He realized, as he said it, that if his horse were there, he would have made a run for it, but it wasn't exactly what he meant. Somehow he always thought that if it came to death in combat, they'd go together. Here he stood, facing the end without his only real friend.

They crept to the stairs and peered through the branched archway. The riders formed a line, thirteen men long, and cantered toward the henge. The three riders on each outer edge of the line wore light armor and wielded spears, but the seven in the middle were clearly knights, armored in steel and carrying lances with pennants streaming out behind them. The one in the middle wore the most modern and expensive armor and his lance bore a royal blue pennant, sporting a diagonal white stripe and a gray hound's head.

"Malestair," Heather whispered.

The riders reined in and Malestair lifted his visor. As he scanned the area and began to shout out an order, the wolfhound leapt, snarling, from beneath the trees, barking and spooking the less-poised horses.

Simultaneously, a thunderous battle cry broke from their right and Gonoth sprang around the henge, wielding his tree-trunk cudgel. His first swing took the outer two riders off guard. The cudgel came in at an angle, shattering the head of the first and crashing into the ribcage of the second, flinging him from his horse.

At the smell of blood, the sounds of the dog's barking, and Gonoth's approach, the next two horses reared. The third rider pulled up on the reins, but only managed to topple his panicking horse. Gonoth's club came down before the fourth rider, a knight clad in cornflower blue, could calm his mount. It crashed down on his shoulder with such force that it buckled the armor and crushed him into the horse, killing him and snapping its back. The horse screamed horribly and writhed on the ground.

The fifth rider, a knight wearing violet, turned his horse to run, but Gonoth's long reach took him full in the back. His horse galloped a few paces more before the broken knight clattered to the ground, unmoving. The riderless horse bolted into the heath.

Though this has taken some moments to relate, it all happened so quickly that no one moved, least of all Alanbart and Heather. Now she grabbed a stone from the ground.

"Those knights are going to charge Gonoth," she said. "Grab a stone and try to distract one or spook his horse."

Alanbart joined her, picking up a stone.

As if he'd heard her, the next knight in line shifted in the saddle. His horse sidestepped, reared, and charged, clumps of grass flying from behind its hooves. He couched his lance and shifted his shield, which was painted yellow with an angled blue stripe.

As he neared, Gonoth dropped his cudgel and bent into a crouch. Heather waited until the critical moment and launched her stone. Alanbart followed suit. Heather's clanked off the knight's shield, causing an almost imperceptible shift in the angle of his lance as he turned his head. Alanbart's landed almost three feet from the target.

When the knight's head turned, Gonoth attacked. He sidestepped, lunged, and grabbed the lance in both hands. Using it as a lever, he ripped the knight from his saddle and, with all the strength in his shoulders and arms, flung him through the air. The knight screamed as he sailed more than twenty yards and landed, neck first, in a sickening crunch of metal and bone.

While that took place, however, Malestair lowered his own lance and made a quick pass at the wolfhound.

It fled from the charging horse, but stood no chance. Looking back over its shoulder, it realized that it couldn't outrun the charger, and tried to elude the oncoming blow to no avail. Malestair's combat reflexes were well-honed, and he speared it through the flank, pinning it to the ground and snapping his lance. It struggled once to free itself and uttered a final yelp before collapsing and falling silent.

Malestair reined in his charger. He considered the dog, emotionlessly, for a moment, then swished his yellow moustache and wheeled his horse toward the giant.

Heather saw it happen, but had no words. All color drained from her cheeks and she trembled from head to toe. Her fists clenched at her sides.

Already, the next knight began his charge against the giant. This one wore red, and his crimson shield bore a diagonal slash and six small crosses, all in white. He was upon the giant before it could prepare.

Gonoth batted wildly at the lance a second before impact. He managed to deflect it from his chest to his thigh, but the sound of the impact was sickening and the wound was terrible. The red and white striped lance rent the cloth of his pants and sank deep into his gray-green skin before it snapped, leaving a splintered rod of wood protruding from a ghastly wound.

Gonoth sank to one knee, and the knight rode on, out of range of the crippled giant.

As a third knight began to move into position, Malestair stopped him.

"It's mine," he said, and lowered his visor. He tossed the butt end of his broken lance aside and drew his sword.

Heather gasped. Even from a distance of forty feet, it shined spectacularly. Its four-foot silver-steel blade reflected and amplified the sunlight. It was forged with a rounded tip and a trench up the middle. Golden runes glistened, running down that trench straight to the sword's gilded and obviously Christian crossguard, which also sparkled with diamonds.

"Excalibur," Alanbart said with a tone of hushed reverence.

Malestair spurred his horse forward while Gonoth groped for his cudgel.

The horse came in fast, but Gonoth managed to swing, nonetheless. He swung wildly, though, and Malestair took it on his shield, deflecting it over his head.

As the giant's arm passed overhead, he slashed with Excalibur, connected, and sliced clean through halfway between the giant's wrist and elbow. The cudgel rolled into the heather, still gripped by a green hand and forearm. Red blood spurted from the wound, spattering Malestair's shield.

Bellowing in rage and pain, the giant made a final lunge against its opponent. Its hand grabbed Malestair by the neck and began to crush his armor and rip him from the saddle. For an agonizing second, as the armor protested with a metallic creak, it looked like Gonoth might win, but Excalibur penetrated his bicep, and with a flick of the wrist, Malestair slashed the muscle free from bone and tendon. The giant's grip loosened.

Malestair backed his horse adeptly away and rode around the crippled and bleeding giant. When he got behind Gonoth, he drove his horse in and with calm precision slashed behind the knee on his remaining functional limb.

And at that moment, all of the fight left Gonoth, and he began to sob. The torrent of sorrow and agony was simultaneously terrifying and heartrendingly pathetic.

Many things in this world are fearful to behold and horrifying to hear, but the wracking wail of a dying giant is possibly the worst— far worse even than the panicked neighing of still-writhing horse with the broken back or the silent corpse of the loyal dog, pinned to the earth.

Perhaps it is because there is something inside each of us that rejects the greatest of changes, and to see something so powerful turn into something so wretched, so weak, and in such pain was more than Heather could bear. She felt burning nausea in her chest; unbidden tears streamed down her face, and she screamed.

"NO! NO! No! No." Her voice cracked. She charged from the henge, catching up a rock and letting it fly at Malestair. It missed, but her cries drew his attention. His helmed head swiveled toward her.

Alanbart grabbed her arm and pulled her back—it took all his might and weight to do so—still crying and screaming, into the shadows.

Malestair lifted his visor. "Leave the giant to its misery," he ordered. "There is nothing left for it but death, but it may suffer more, before the end." He spurred his horse toward the archway.

Inside the henge, Alanbart dragged Heather, still sobbing, behind the altar and placed it between himself and the entryway. "Stay behind me," he ordered, shifting his grip on his sword to both hands.

Malestair rode boldly into the circle of stone, ducking low under the arch and guiding his charger skillfully down the slate steps. His mount pranced at the foot of the stairs, but he yanked at the reins, halting the horse. Its russet coat shone in the half-light through the holly leaves; his polished silver armor glistened in dancing patterns as the boughs swayed in the wind. The horse's breath came in snorts.

Malestair scanned the henge, distaste apparent in his expression, his brown eyes lingering on the faces carved upon the holly branches. His gaze then returned to Heather. He lifted Excalibur aloft, let go of the reins, and shifted his menacing glare to Alanbart.

Visibly quailing, Alanbart raised his sword in response, but the blade quivered.

"Give her to me," Malestair ordered, gesturing to Heather, "and I'll let you live."

From where he sat, he sized Alanbart up, noting his shoddy armor, trembling blade, and watery eyes. He read fear, weakness, and lack of will in the cowering man's facial expression, in the downturn of his shoulders, and in his limp two-handed grip on his blade. A sudden flame of contempt lit the villain's eyes. He spurred his horse and vaulted over the altar.

Alanbart and Heather ducked out of the way to avoid being trampled. As they stood, Malestair dismounted in a fluid motion and grabbed Heather by the wrist.

She reached for Alanbart.

He lifted a hand halfheartedly, then dropped it back to his side.

Her eyes pleaded wildly.

His were expressionless.

In response, a flicker of contempt flashed across her features, so that for an agonizing instant she and Malestair were looking at Alanbart with similar disappointment. He recoiled as if he'd been slapped, withdrew a few paces, and dropped his sword onto the pebbled ground.

Malestair thrust Heather onto his horse, and mounted behind her. He wheeled around, poised to gallop away.

As it sometimes seems to do in moments of high drama, time protracted for Heather and Alanbart. They gazed into each other's eyes.

As you know, it has often been said that the eyes are the window to the soul, and I sometimes believe that to be true, but like any window, I find that they conceal what is inside behind a reflection of the onlooker as often as, if not more often than, they reveal any useful or deep secrets. In this case, however, Heather saw Alanbart's soul in his tear-rimmed coward's eyes.

He was thinking: 'He is too strong for me. I see it in his stance, and hear it in his voice—he is powerful and he wields Excalibur. Fight? He'd kill me and take you anyway. I'd be throwing my life away, and for what? For an empty ideal? For beauty? For lust? It would be simple vanity—a vain attempt to show myself a knight, to play at having the heart of a lover and the soul of a warrior.'

Heather saw that he had neither, and she felt neither hatred nor contempt; she felt pity. Her eyes softened seconds before Malestair spurred his charger up the stairs. She forgave him.

Overwhelmed, Alanbart fell to his knees beside his discarded sword, and wept—not in relief for his escape, nor in thankfulness for her pity, but because he knew that he didn't deserve either, and because Heather's forgiveness cut him far more deeply than her contempt ever could.

He could have lived with hatred; he thought that he deserved hatred, but then, he realized—and the realization killed something inside of him—that he was too weak to inspire hate, for hatred must be inspired. A person can only hate things that are strong, large, or immutable. He saw himself, for the first time, for what he was: weak and insignificant with a soul made of liquid, always running downhill from fear.

Dimly conscious of his surroundings, Alanbart heard Malestair bark gruff orders outside: "This is an unholy place. Cut the limbs from these trees, pile them around the trunks, and burn them. Oh, and there's a coward inside that I promised to leave alive. Bind him to the altar, and when you're finished, *leave* him here—alive."

15

BROKEN CROSS ABBEY

Scot and the undead Sir Kay crashed through the roof into a dusty, musty room filled with weapons and treasure that smelled like a combination of an abandoned cellar and a library. The corpse-knight fell onto a half-full rack of Roman pilums. A second before impact, Scot saw danger and managed to roll off the knight, upending a table covered with offering plates, platters, crosses, and devotional materials. Still deaf, Scot felt their interlacing vibrations through the flagstone floor.

He lurched to his feet and saw his enemy, too, struggle to rise. The knight was pierced by half a dozen iron spear points, specially designed to puncture plate armor. Four stuck from its chest, poking through at different angles, two had bent from the impact. No blood dripped from the injuries.

Because his greatsword wouldn't be much use in the confined space, Scot drew it, leveled it forward like a spear, and charged. Kay's corpse was still on its knees when Scot struck. He drove the sword through its breastplate. Its tip penetrated four inches into a thick load-bearing pillar, pinning the corpse to it.

Scot searched wildly about for a smaller weapon; Kay's corpse discarded its sword and shield and began pulling at Scot's blade with both hands. It slid its body forward and threw its weight against the hilt, but the sword didn't budge.

At last, Scot's eyes came to rest on a large granite-headed warhammer resting on a shelf. He ran to it, hefted its ponderous weight and turned back to Kay.

The corpse now threw its weight from left to right, attempting to widen the hole in the beam and loosen the blade. On its third attempt, the sword snapped, and Kay lurched sideways.

Scot took three swift steps, planted his foot, lifted the hammer, and—with all his strength—brought it down on the knight's helmed head.

The helmet imploded, the skull shattered, and bloodless gray brain spat out of it, slopping onto the dusty stone floor. The room filled with the rank, sickly-sweet stench of the dead. Scot turned his head, averted his eyes, and swallowed back his need to wretch.

With his sword gone, he thought, he needed to re-arm himself quickly. The hammer was too clumsy. He dropped it and scanned the room. It contained many scattered weapons and valuables. It took him only moments to choose an impressively well-forged longsword with a jeweled hilt and to pull an ornate round Viking shield from a rack.

He ran to the door and kicked it open.

Scot stepped through the archway into what once was the inside of the ruined abbey. The mid-morning sun had burned away all of the fog and shined down on heaps of rubble and worn flagstone paving. No enemies faced him.

If Scot could sense, he would have heard Gawain's desperate battle on the far side of the wall, and things might have turned out otherwise. However, seeing no immediate threat, he searched the area more carefully, and spotted Asacael retreating toward the bog on the far side of the island.

She lurched along, only ten paces from the water's edge, obviously intending to slip beneath the peat mat and escape immediate danger. Scot broke into a sprint, leaping over rough rectangular-cut stones and skidding across piles of fallen shingle, hoping to cover two hundred yards of broken ground before the banshee could splash twenty paces into the bog and vanish beneath the stagnant water.

Meanwhile, Gawain retreated behind his scratched and battered shield. He offered a prayer for salvation to the Virgin Mary (whom he'd had painted inside of the shield for just such an occasion) and glanced above its rim. Another undead legionary slashed in with its short Roman gladius. He reacted, slicing the arm clean off.

A thump to his shield sent him backpedaling toward the shore.

As Gawain delivered another crushing blow, he noted that without sound to accompany action, his mind compensated for silence. When his sword hit a skull, for example, it faltered before the bone cracked and then shattered like a breaking bottle. The feeling of those stages—resistance, crack, shatter—as they progressed, became heightened and took the place of sound, sometimes even fooling his mind into believing that he may have heard something.

This, of course, is a common illusion created by a stubborn brain attempting to maintain expected reality, not unlike that of an amputee who feels the need to scratch a missing limb or a widower who hears the creak his dead wife's tread on the hallway floor.

Gawain wondered that he could ponder these things while engaged in combat, especially when the outcome seemed so grim, but he often found that he fought better when his mind was occupied with other things—fought on instinct, registered danger, parried, deflected, and attacked, all without conscious will or mental effort.

He broke from his reverie in a momentary lull. The bones of nine skeletons littered the ground in a ragged line that marked his retreat, but the undead centurion continued its attacks. Gawain couldn't get a swing at it. It stayed to his shield-side, generally out of reach of his long blade, and waited until he faced other enemies before it attacked. Thankfully, its shorter weapon hadn't yet scored a crippling blow, though it'd sliced a red gash against the green paint on Gawain's sword arm.

More skeletons advanced.

As he fought, Gawain assessed his wounds. Each blazed with agony, so he knew that none of them was serious. Long ago, he'd come to realize that truly horrible wounds—those that were maiming or mortal—didn't hurt initially because they overloaded the heart and mind with sensation. When one experiences too much pain to process, either physical or emotional, a body simply feels nothing at all.

Yet, despite his relatively sound physical condition, things looked hopeless.

Including the centurion, eight skeletons remained, the last three climbing down the wall, and the others running to attack. To make matters worse, the corpse of his brother joined them.

With Gringolet and his armor, Gawain thought, he'd stand a chance, but not like this, winded and wounded, unarmored and overwhelmed.

Two skeletons came in on his right. He dispatched them. Then, he felt the centurion closing from behind. He dropped to his belly and rolled, ending up on his back with his shield above his chest. Its shortsword plunged into the earth, inches from where he stopped his roll. He kicked out, slamming against the centurion's shield and forcing it back at an angle into its shinbones. The sharp gladius stabbed in again, but the centurion had been thrown off balance, and this time Gawain batted the sword away with a swipe of his shield. He then brought his sword down on the exposed arm, snapping it at the elbow.

He swung again at the unarmed centurion and jabbed his blade into the skeleton's eye socket. Once it lodged in the creature's skull, Gawain flicked up and away with his wrist, and dislodged the head. It launched from the sword tip and sailed into the bog. The rest of the bones collapsed into a pile.

But more skeletons were on him before he could stand. He rolled, abandoning his shield for the sake of mobility. At the end of his second roll, he rose to his knee and swung his sword in a wide arc, forcing each of them back. He stood, retreated a step farther, and felt his boot plunge into the bog. He'd run out of room.

Sir Gawain parried two sword thrusts and flung himself clear of a third, slamming into a tall shield and knocking a skeleton prone. He arced his sword up, snapping three ribs off of the nearest enemy, but then Agravain's blade deflected his sword to the ground.

He looked up, only to be greeted by his brother's purple shield. It punched his family crest square into his face, sending him splashing into the bog, dazed and bleeding from a broken nose.

He braced for the killing blow, but instead, the skeletons lost all cohesion. Their bones cascaded to the ground like so much discarded kindling, and Agravain's body tripped, fell to its knees, then toppled forward to a final rest, its helmed head submerged between Gawain's splayed shins.

Across the island, Scot won the footrace of his life. It was the most bizarre confrontation between sprinting speed and sluggish stumbling that has probably ever occurred, and might have been comical under different circumstances.

Asacael managed to take seventeen halting and lurching steps across the island and into the water, sloshing to waist-depth before she realized that she wouldn't be able to escape.

Scot tore across the chapel grounds, leaping stones, dancing across bricks and rubble, and breaking free of the building.

He was closing the final distance with his sword upraised, when she filled her lungs, swiveled, and screamed. The sound hit him like a gale, staggering his stride, slowing his mind, and very nearly killing him on the spot. He fumbled his sword, lowered his shield, and took three faltering steps toward her, the last of which reached the shore. Then, as his unshod foot cracked the thin skin of ice that formed between them, he regained his focus.

She filled her lungs again.

He brought his shield across in a powerful backhand and slammed it full into her chest, bursting a breast, crushing her ribs, expelling the air from her lungs, and felling her into a curled crippled ball on the peat-mat. He grabbed her foot—it felt terribly cold to the touch—and dragged her writhing body back to shore. She was preposterously light, emaciated and hollow, and put up little resistance. He flung her onto the rocky ground, placed his sandaled foot on her chest, and bent to retrieve his blade.

Three quick strokes later, she was finished. He punctured each of her lungs in turn, and then opened her skull, cutting it neatly in two with one powerful slice.

She uttered a last whimper and fell silent, but the air remained chill; her ghost refused to find final repose in death. It resides there still, making the island an ill-boded and hateful place, free from all human habitation.

Scot dug the wax plugs from his ears so that he could hear himself let out a victory cry, then kicked off his remaining sandal and dashed around the abbey, prepared to help Gawain fight off whatever skeletons remained.

When he rounded the corner, his eyes found the knight bent over Agravain's corpse, dragging it up the shoreline toward the abbey. Beyond Gawain, at the corner where they made their stand, bones carpeted the ground like snow.

Scot shook his head in wonder at the sheer enormity of the task that they'd accomplished. In under an hour, they'd defeated an army of skeletons, two of Arthur's greatest knights, and a banshee, and best of all: they were both alive and relatively unhurt—well, he thought, at least uncrippled.

He smiled broadly and laughed aloud, walking toward Gawain to congratulate him, but faltered when Gawain looked tearfully up. He was lugging his brother's corpse from under the shoulders. Its feet dragged on the pebbled earth. Gawain stopped, lowered Agravain to the ground, gathered his composure, and dug the plugs from his ears.

"Well done," he said, holding out his hand. Scot took it.

They considered one another for along moment, hands still clasped. Scot's green eyes glittered out of his blue face, and Gawain's blue ones, still sad, shone through smeared, dripping green paint with newfound affection and respect. They held that gaze for a pair of heartbeats; then Scot released Gawain's hand, lurched forward, and enfolded the knight in a tight embrace.

Taken aback, Gawain stiffened for a second, then accepted the gesture. He nodded, thumped Scot's back, and placed both of his hands on the swordsman's shoulders.

Scot took his eyes from Gawain's and noted that the knight's fall into the bog had ruined his hair and paint. He looked down past the knight's drooping hair to his chest, which was now a mottled and smeared blue-green, bearing witness to their embrace. He grinned.

"Well done," Gawain said again.

"WHAT?" Scot shouted.

"I SAID, WELL DONE!"

Scot nodded, then set his sword and shield aside and took hold of Agravain's feet.

"Thank you, Sir," said Gawain, genuinely moved. He regained his grip under his slain brother's shoulders.

"WHAT?" Scot shouted.

"I SAID, THANK YOU!"

"OH!" Scot replied.

They carried his body into the center of the ruined abbey.

"I should say," Scot said as they neared their destination, his eyes shining, "that I've been blessed to battle beside you today. I always had my doubts about the songs sung of Sir Gawain and of the Knights of the Round Table, but I've never met a mightier or more flawless man, and I doubt I ever will again."

"WHAT?" Gawain asked as he set his brother down on the stone. He wasn't watching while Scot spoke, so he missed the glow in his cheeks and the tone of worship in the swordsman's words. Gawain shook his head and pointed to his ear. "I MISSED ALL OF THAT."

"NEVER MIND!" Scot replied. He mumbled, "I'll tell you later."

After folding Agravain's arms over his chest, putting a blade in his hands, and placing his legs together, they went into the storage room and moved Sir Kay's body out, laying it beside Agravain in a similar position.

"If you don't mind," Gawain said, turning to Scot, "I'm going to—"

"WHAT?" Scot shouted.

"I WAS GOING TO SAY!" Gawain said loudly and slowly, "THAT I FOUGHT ONE BATTLE BY YOUR RULES AND I'M STILL ALIVE. I DON'T THINK THAT I COULD BE SO LUCKY AGAIN." He looked down at Agravain's body. "I BEG YOUR LEAVE TO CONSIDER MY OATH FULFILLED SO THAT I MAY HONOR MY BROTHER'S MEMORY BY WEARING HIS MAIL IN THE NEXT COMBAT."

Scot thought for a moment and nodded.

"I SUGGEST THAT YOU DO LIKEWISE!" Gawain shouted, his voice cracking. He looked Scot up and down, noting his many slight and not-so-slight wounds. "I'D HATE TO LOSE YOU."

Scot hesitated, his face coloring a bit. He took mental stock of his own physical condition: a slice on his forearm, two on his chest, one in his foot, and the innumerable bruises and welts that he knew would develop, and finally shook his head in a negative reply.

Gawain shook his head too—in astonishment and perhaps a little admiration—a wry but sad smile creasing his green and bloody face. Then he crossed himself, bent to Agravain's corpse, and started to strip off the armor. Scot stepped into the storeroom to begin the search for artifacts.

An hour later, they had buried Sirs Agravain and Kay under cairns of piled rubble-stone. Agravain's corpse bore Gawain's shield and sword on its chest.

While Gawain prepared and held a brief burial service, Scot removed the most promising artifacts from the storage room. These included the granite-headed warhammer; a long wooden staff banded with two ivory rings; a stunningly well-forged sword covered in ancient and obscure runes; a small square silver box full of gemstones, gold chains, and rings; an assortment of bejeweled crosses, golden offering plates, platters, and candlesticks; an illuminated Vulgate bible (slightly mildewed) with gem-studded hinges; and a locked bronze treasure chest the size of a horse trough and remarkably heavy. This last item he could not move alone, and so enlisted the help of Gawain.

The heroes' hearing had been recovering as the morning wore on toward noon, and they no longer needed to shout to be understood, though they still spoke with unnatural volume. They'd piled the artifacts and treasure on the shore next to the crossing, and had just finished dragging the chest to that spot. Scot wiped sweat from his brow and drew a massive breath, exhaling loudly.

"How many trips do you figure it will take to get all this across?" he asked.

Gawain shook his head. "One thing I know is that we're never going to get this across," he replied, sitting on the chest and rapping its side with his calloused hand. It responded with a hollow metal clunk. "And I don't think it is worth our time to move these plates and crosses today. I think we should open the chest, take the small valuables, then fill it with the best of what we have left and sink it in the bog where we can find it again."

"That seems a sound scheme," Scot responded. "How do you propose to open it?"

Gawain rose painfully and sighed before replying: "I'll go and get my axe." He limped off in the direction of their initial confrontation.

In the interim, Scot examined his new sword and shield. The steel blade was sharp, angular, and much shorter than his previous one. It was dagger-sharp at the end. Scot felt both awe at the skill of its craftsmanship and a strange and cold sense of disquiet. The steel shimmered darkly and displayed a red tint. Forged of folded steel, the ill-boded patterns of folding could be seen weaving up and down the blade like serpent scales. The sword's cross guard, coated in silver and inset with a line of diamond-cut garnets, met the blade in the shape of a widened V. The diamond-shaped and silver coated pommel, too, was inset with garnets. The haft had perfect balance, likely because it contained lead, and the grip was made of yellowed whalebone, inscribed with dark, illegible runes.

When he shifted his gaze to the round shield, he felt similarly impressed with its detail and craftsmanship. The clasps on the back-facing side were made of gilded steel, each forged in the shape of a different animal: a snake, a hawk, a squirrel, and a dragon. They'd been affixed directly to the backing of the shield, which was made of a pure white wood, a type he'd never seen before. In fact, rather than being made of separate, parallel boards, as were most shields, the whole thing seemed to be cut from a cross-section of a single trunk, complete with growth rings. It also felt impossibly light, given its thickness and hardness. The wood was rimmed with forged steel that still held its polish and sheen. In the center sat a carved image of a large mead-hall, presumably Valhalla.

The outward facing side of the shield was painted midnight-blue, and all along the rim writhed an intricately wrought brass image of Jörmungand,[16] It the center of the outward face rested a steel orb. The many cuts and scrapes on this painted surface showed through, white against the blue. They looked, Scot thought, like the caps of waves on a round ocean. He ran his finger across the surface, feeling the trenches where it had warded off countless blades and axes, and imagined it being carried by a king into the press of a melee, hearing in his mind the shouts and cries of warriors fighting, the clash of steel, the thunk of wood, the crack of bone, and the cries of the dying.

The sound of Gawain returning called Scott from of his reverie. The knight stopped beside him and dropped a long coat of chainmail rings.

---

[16] For those of you unfamiliar with Jörmungand, it is the name of the world-serpent of Norse mythology—a great and hideous snake that encircles the limitless ocean of the flat earth. It is so long, in fact, that it is invariably portrayed eating its own tail. It often wriggles its body in hunger or anger, creating the vast undulations in the water that we see as waves. Jörmungand is, of course, the reason that ships that venture too far from shore do not return and is represented on the borders of many a medieval map or chart.

One more interesting tidbit about Jörmungand: it is the offspring of Loki, the Norse god of mischief, and an evil giantess. Sadly, I must admit to once trying to fathom the logistics of the monster's conception (Loki being only the size of a man), only to remember that Loki, a shape-shifter, could easily accomplish the deed. Even more horrifying, though, is to imagine the birth process of such an endless snake. . .

"This is about your size," he said, "and it comes with a helm and a horn."

Scot set down his shield and wordlessly accepted the proffered gifts.

"They were lying there on the ground next to my axe," Gawain added, "and are in such good shape that I thought there might be some magic in them. In any case, I know your views on armor, but I've also seen your quality as a fighter. I'd hate to lose you." He paused for a second, cleared his throat, and then continued gruffly: "I'd also remind you that you didn't purchase this armor off of the sweat of the peasantry, but won it fairly in combat, which is likely the case for its former owner as well."

Scot opened his mouth to respond, but before he could, Gawain continued: "Look here, this morning I hated you and thought of you as my enemy and rival, but I have since revised my opinion and I feel badly that I ever held it. I lost my last true brother today, and now all I have left is Mordred, and those brothers who have shared the womb of warfare with me. Though she is a cruel mother, we two have been reborn today through combat. Our blood is comingled on this ground."

"Like our paint," Scot added, pointing to his chest.

Gawain sighed, shrugged, and leveled a thick finger at Scot's face. "Just wear the damn armor."

Scot stood, and without a word picked up the mail shirt and began to pull it over his head. As he did so, he heard a loud *CLANG*. Gawain brought his axe down on the lock. Scot's head emerged just in time to see the knight crouch in front of the chest and lift the lid.

"This thing is full of brittle straw," he said, digging his hand around inside. He disinterred an old linen shroud, a skull and jawbone, a scrap of cedar wood, and a chipped terracotta cup.

"I imagine those are religious artifacts," Scot said while fastening a sword belt around his waist and slinging the warhorn over his shoulder. He scoffed. "No doubt that is a gobbet of the sail of St. Peter from his boat on the Sea of Galilee, or perhaps it is the veil of the Virgin Mary. That bit of cedar wood is either from Solomon's Temple or the True Rood. The skull clearly belongs to St. George, and the cup, unquestionably, is the Holy Grail." He laughed aloud.

Gawain bit his lip. "I don't doubt that these *artifacts* had value to the holy fathers who lived here, but if any of these were truly powerful relics, the banshee wouldn't have been successful in conquering this place. Besides, one of my fellows, Sir Percival, has seen the Cup of Kings in a vision sent to him directly by Christ, and it was nothing like this clay mug."

Power filled Gawain's voice as he recounted the vision of his brother-knight: "The Grail is a golden chalice that emits pure white light, unwavering and warm as sunshine. Three are the number of handles coming from the sides. Five are the number of diamonds adorning the neck, representing the value of Christ and his humanity. Five are the number of rubies, representing the five wounds of Christ. Eleven are the pearls around the base, representing the disciples. One space for a twelfth pearl sits empty, lost by Judas and for the finder to fill." He paused and set down the dirty cup.

Scot cleared his throat in discomfort.

"As for the others," Gawain continued, "we'll bury the skull and say a few words. We needn't worry about the scrap of wood. I've travelled far through Europe, and I assure you that there are enough pieces of 'the true cross' that we could build Solomon's Temple or Hrothgar's Hall anew from them and still have enough left over to celebrate Yule." He picked up the linen cloth, tearing a long strip from the side, and added, "With this, at least we can bind our wounds."

About fifteen minutes later, bandaged, armed and armored, the two warriors stood ready to depart. They'd filled the bronze box with all of the treasure that it could hold, including gemstones, gold coins, devotional materials, plates, and a crucifix. They sank it in the shallows and built a small cairn of stones on it to mark their return. They buried the skull in a shallow hole and used the scrap of wood as a grave marker. The cup remained discarded on the shoreline at Gawain's feet.

The sun shone bright as they readied to set off across the muir.

Arthur's nephew stood in Agravain's armor and had both his brother's purple shield and the green axe slung across his back. His new sword rested in its sheath. He carried the Vulgate Bible in his right hand and a small silver box of precious stones and rings in his left.

Beside him, Scot, helmed and wearing mail for the first time, looked across the bog. He slung the blue shield over his shoulder, sheathed the longsword on his hip, and held the hammer in one hand

and the staff in the other. He scanned the island one last time, his eyes coming to rest on the terracotta cup.

"You know," he said, "Sir Alanbart told me that he was searching for The Holy Grail. Perhaps I should bring that cup to him and let him carry it back to his lord. What could be the harm?"

"By Jesus!" Gawain replied. "It's bad enough that the abbot of this place preformed rites with a false artifact—it would be far worse to add the blasphemy of Alanbart to it. At least the abbot earnestly believed this to be some kind of relic, and sometimes even misplaced faith can produce a small miracle. *Sir* Alanbart believes only in personal profit and would use this piece of clay to do the Devil's work."

He set down the box and picked up the cup, hefting its weight in his hand.

"Let us not tempt anyone else to wrongfully use this cup. Certainly no blood should be shed over it."

He wound up and pitched it far out over the bog. It splashed into the water fifty yards away. Gawain bent to retrieve the box.

"Come on," he said to Scot, "let's get back to the henge."

16

NOON, CATHBAD'S HENGE

Alanbart lay atop the altar in Cathbad's thinning henge, watching a white wisp of cloud wander across the swath of turquoise sky. His hands were bound behind his back, and his feet tied together. The sound of axes biting into wood, cracking and tumbling branches, and the weakening moans of Gonoth filled his ears.

The gap above his head expanded as the branches crashed, hacked loose by the four men Malestair left behind. They worked under the charge of a pompous overweight knight who was outside, no doubt gathering whatever plunder might be found. He'd almost certainly found Alanbart's cache of gemstones. While that thought should have made him feel something . . . Resentment? Jealousy? Frustration? He instead felt an aching emptiness.

Gonoth sobbed again. A crow cawed beyond his range of vision.

"For the love of God!" Alanbart exclaimed, "Your lord is long gone over the horizon—will someone please put that giant out of his misery?"

One of the axes stopped chopping. "You don't know the lord. He'd find out, and we'd suffer," a voice responded from Alanbart's left. "Now shut your mouth or I'll cuff you."

The chopping resumed. Alanbart held in a sarcastic reply—he never much enjoyed being cuffed.

The pentagonal stone slab of the altar was hard, flat, and cold. He couldn't get comfortable. If he rested and lay back, the weight of his body fell on his arms and leveraged his shoulders painfully apart, as if to dislocate them. He could flex his arms, lifting himself up and relaxing that pressure, but then his elbows held all of his weight and became fulcrums grinding against the stone. That hurt too much to withstand for long. Alternately, he could lift his torso with his (poorly-developed) stomach muscles, but that would only give him thirty seconds of comfort before they gave out and he collapsed back into one of the two former positions.

'How like life this is,' he thought. 'Every outcome is uncomfortable, unsustainable, and ineffective against the sacrificial altar of . . . of what?' he asked himself. 'Experience,' he decided. 'Experience is a cold hard stone upon which one could squirm in infinite discomfort, waiting for the inevitable. It all ends with sacrifice at the finish, early or late, willing or unwilling.'

He'd been philosophizing more than usual since his capture. *Capture*, that was the preferable word—it implied better things than *surrender*. Besides, he couldn't do much else in his current predicament but think. And he didn't like his thoughts—they were no less uncomfortable than the altar upon which he lay.

Alanbart shifted from his back to his elbows and sighed. The chopping continued and a limb arched downward. The air churned as it fell, wafting the smell of freshly-cut timber across the altar. A crow circled above, backlit against the bright sky. The lone cloud passed listlessly across the sun, casting a wispy, ephemeral shadow upon him. Out of the holly trees, the faces carved into the snaking limbs stared back. One smiled in ecstasy, one shrieked in soundless torment, and a third burned with smokeless rage.[17]

'Two days ago, none of this would have bothered me,' Alanbart thought. 'Hell, two days ago I wouldn't have gotten involved in this mess.' His cynicism and jaded outlook toward everything had seemed so mature. Like the narrator of a story rather than a character, nothing touched him, until today. All of those things that he'd dismissed as desperate hysterical fantasy—love, courage, honor, faith— were they?

'Watch it, you're getting religious,' Alanbart warned himself. 'Religious? And why not? This is the place for it—lying on an altar,

---

[17] The holly grove, carved a century ago by the druids, was designed to amplify emotion to a cathartic crescendo. You see, druidism (as did most early religions) realized the essential truth that *faith* is an emotional, rather than a logical, response to the world. They designed their places of worship around this fact. Love, fear, guilt, rapture, these are religious words. Believers *feel* their belief. Skeptics *contemplate* their doubt.

surrounded by admonishing faces and falling symbols of a dying faith,' he mused. Certainly, Christianity focused around the idea that innocence and experience were two poles of existence: humanity before and after the fall. He'd always thought of the second as annihilating the first. Fools and martyrs were innocent, the former doomed to become the latter. The goal of life, obviously, was experience, and experience inevitably led to cynicism, atheism, selfishness, and disillusionment. Because those were the inexorable outcomes of living, Alanbart had embraced them as truths.

Yet, at this moment he wished that he'd died defending Heather against Malestair. Oh, he was aware of the futility and pointless stupidity of such a gesture, but now that he'd survived, he didn't want to live with his decision and its outcome. He kept reliving the moment, seeing Heather's pleading eyes turn to disgust and then to pity, feeling his own internal shift from fear to self-loathing. He turned his head and closed his eyes as if she slapped him.

How could it be that experience, which always led to the real, the sad, and the disillusioning, now led him in the opposite direction? Who can fall into innocence? Perhaps it happened because things had become so utterly hopeless that he was giving in to honor, faith, and love in the desperation of despair.

'Can despair generate hope?' Like so many paradoxes, that made some strange, unexpected sense.

Try as he might to outthink it, he couldn't be nonchalant and cynical about the fact that Heather would die tonight. He *knew* that it would be smart simply to shrug, laugh at her foolishness, and move on, but that seemed impossible. Something had indeed altered inside him as he lay there.

In truth, he wasn't any more honorable or religious than when he woke on the previous morning. He'd simply ceased to value himself more than these things. He'd gone from loving himself to loathing himself—and therein resided the great change.

He no longer saw the significance in his own continued existence. He didn't become courageous; he experienced the opposite shift. He didn't mind dying because he saw himself as utterly valueless. But as he lay there contemplating his own death, he thought that he might as well die in such a way that he at least tried to do some good for someone who deserved it.

'Heather.' He smirked. 'And if you sacrifice yourself for her, will it return enough value to your life that you'll regret the sacrifice at the last minute?' An ironic phrase that he'd flung into the firelight last night returned to him then: 'The old Alanbart is dead. Long live the new Alanbart.'

He chuckled painfully, then groaned and tensed his stomach muscles, relieving pressure on his elbows. Gonoth emitted a long low whimper from outside the henge.

Alanbart winced. Yes, this was indeed the perfect setting to think painful thoughts. But more to the point, what should he do? He knew what yesterday's Alanbart would have done: wait for Gawain and Scot to return. They'd be sure to liberate him, then he'd tell them that he planned to ride south for help as Heather had requested. He knew full-well that if help did come, it would arrive too late, so instead of going, he'd ride away and wait for them to leave the henge. Once they'd gone, he'd sneak back, collect his gems and whatever could be looted from all of the dead knights, and then cut the head off Gonoth's corpse.

Head in hand, he'd ride back to Lanark town, accept their monetary thanks for his giant-slaying, pawn any heavy objects, and ride north to Glasgow town. Once there, he could repair his equipment and wait for a response from Lord Ghent. He would no longer have to concern himself with the others or their fates, and he'd be back on his chosen path. It was an admirable and intelligent plan, and he hated it almost as much as he hated himself.

His stomach muscles gave out and he collapsed back on the altar in pain.

But what else could he do?

'Join the attack? And what, die?' He was of no practical use but as a target. Besides, he thought, without Gonoth, what chance of success was there? He could give himself up and try to infiltrate the castle. 'Why? To see Heather again, obviously.' But what good could he pretend there?

Shouts woke him from his contemplation.

"Lads! Grab your swords! Arm yourselves!" a raspy voice called from the direction of the stairs. "Two knights arrive from the south and we'd best give them a proper welcome."

17

THE RED ROAD

Heather sat uncomfortably atop a dead man's horse, her cold and numb hands bound tightly in front of her. Malestair rode beside her and the three remaining knights followed, strung out behind them in single-file. They'd already forded the river through knee-deep water and cantered down the Red Road toward the Devil's Rookery. The noon sun warmed her skin and a light south wind rustled brown grass and purple heather on either side of the path, stroking her hair in an unwelcome manner.

The road bore an apt name. When she'd first heard it mentioned, Heather assumed that it might be symbolic of the tower's bloody history or of Malestair himself, but upon closer inspection, it was simply a beaten dusty trail in red clay soil, broken occasionally by white limestone rocks and dead grass.

She studied the path while they rode. As she sat, she worked on a plan. Escape seemed impossible, bound and outnumbered as she was. If she tried, they'd catch up and bind her tighter. She knew that an attack would come—at least she hoped it would—that night, and she must be ready to assist the king. Perhaps this capture could be turned to advantage: she'd be in the dungeon when the attack came, and if she could somehow free her hands and get to Arthur . . .

She considered the tower's layout. Four floors rose aboveground, crowned with battlements and supported by two cellars below. The first subterranean level was a storeroom lined with large bins heaped with root vegetables, hung with bags of salted meat, and stacked with casks of water and barrels of ale. In the bottom level lay the dungeon, a single cramped chamber, rough-cut into the bedrock. The other four levels, from the ground up, were the greathall, the knights' quarters, the lord's rooms, and . . . well, she'd never been above that point.

But what if Scot and Gawain died on the banshee's isle? Gonoth was as good as dead. Alanbart could be. Would Cathbad still move against the tower without them? If not, it might be up to her to save the king. An attempt must be made, somehow.

Malestair interrupted her thoughts. "You know," he stroked one side of his moustache absentmindedly, "it wasn't easy to do that."

"What?" She asked.

"Kill that dog. Jotun was his name."

"He hated your men—they obviously cared for him well."

"Coddle a dog and it goes soft. That's what happened to that one. It may surprise you, but I do have feelings, on occasion. Jotun was too old to be useful. I should have killed him a year ago to save the expense of feeding him and to free him from the uselessness and pain of age, but I couldn't bring myself to do it. I was weak."

Heather said nothing.

"My competence, you see," Malestair continued, "comes from my willingness to take difficult actions, especially to earn the obedience my subordinates. I am willing to kill a thing that I love. Fear and respect—these are necessary to maintain."

"Justify it any way you want. You're a pig. Had I any hope left of escape or revenge, I'd be eagerly awaiting your fall, but as I have none, I am numb and care not. I hope you choke on a chicken bone or catch the ague and perspire to death in an unbroken fever."

"I'm glad you are starting to see things my way," he chuckled. "And from this moment, I'll take chicken off of the menu—one can never be too careful."

"How did you find me?" Heather changed the subject.

"Oh, it wasn't easy. You evaded my men and eluded my dogs. If I didn't have a wizard, you might have escaped entirely. You see, you made the mistake of leaving your cloak behind. Rabordath took a cutting from it and cast a spell. I have here," he said, pulling something from his saddlebag, "a wizard's tool with magic in it. There is a sliver of iron imprisoned in this glass, and it floats on a pool of quicksilver. See?"

He held it out for her inspection. In his long fingers rested a round bubble of blue glass. It was the size of an apple, half full of a silver liquid with a black wedge floating atop it. The iron splinter, not quite an inch long, pointed directly at her chest. He moved it left to right, and the wedge turned, always facing toward her.

"It is a seeking spell. Wherever you go, as long as you live, this will aim at your heart. Romantic, is it not?" He smirked. "Of course, this bauble is worth far more than you are, and it will be reset and useful again once you are dead, so I imagine I'll have a hard time convincing Rabordath that we shouldn't kill you tonight."

Heather didn't reply.

"Speaking of death," Malestair continued after a pause, "I'm sure it was a pity to watch Sir Gawain burn on that pagan pyre. Did he scream? —No, never mind. I want to remember him as glorious as he was, not screaming in druid-fire. Yes, we found his armor and charred bones. Truth be told, it saddened me to see that sight. The memory of it will linger inside my heart as a monument to human frailty. He seemed invincible; indeed, he was one of a very few warriors who might have had the skill to best me in combat. In truth, I hoped to encounter him, now that I wield Excalibur, and establish a greater reputation. Alas, it is not to be." He sighed, then continued, "You must admit though that with the death of Sir Gawain—the only other survivor of Arthur's party—the sun of your hope has set."

"He was dead before they burned him," she said, "speared through the shoulder and slit across the throat in the Gloamwood. He didn't scream." She paused to let that sink in. "I admit, now," she concluded, "that I have nowhere to run and no one to run to."

Malestair smiled thinly under his moustache and patted her hand. "There, there," he said in mock comfort. "It won't last long. Once we're done with you, I'll give you a choice between life as a whore to my men (at least until we have need of the seeking spell again), or a quick and honorable death. Oh, I know what you'll choose, but think on it just to be sure. I learned at an early age that women perform better when you give them the illusion of power and choice." Amused at his own observation, he drew up his horse. "Ah," Malestair said, gesturing south where the outline of a tower could be seen against the sky, "home at last."

He inhaled deeply and wrinkled his nose in distaste.

18

CATHBAD'S HENGE

From Alanbart's limited vantage point, the ensuing conflict sounded short, lopsided, and bloody. He heard clashing steel, a couple of compelling screams, and a retreat out the rear archway.

Gawain's voice called: "I'll to horse and after them. You untie Sir Alanbart and find out what happened here and how long ago. Perhaps it's not too late to overtake them."

Immediately, Alanbart felt Scot's rough hands working the knots at his wrists and ankles. He stood, unstable on cramped legs, and took in the scene of desecration and carnage.

Many of the holly limbs were lopped off and lay scattered among the woodchips. Soldiers had chopped one tree almost halfway through at the base, exposing the heartwood. It would surely die. Three bodies lay upon the ground, two soldiers dead at the archway and a slain knight not three feet from the altar, his chunky headless form draped across a bough over which he could not scramble in time to escape. His head had rolled out of sight.

"What happened here?" Scot asked.

"We were attacked by Malestair and a dozen men. They took Heather. Gonoth's dying outside—he's been bleeding to death for hours. I beg you, go and put him out of his misery. I'll—" he paused and gripped the altar for support. "I guess I'll get to work cleaning up in here."

Scot shook his head and turned toward the door. "I must give Gawain aid to take the two who escaped, lest one travel to the tower and tell the lord. I'll be back before long." He took the stairs two at a time, instinctively ducked under the low-hanging limb that was no longer present, and turned the corner.

Alanbart regained his composure, grabbed the headless knight by the feet, and began to drag his corpse in the same direction.

Five minutes later, Gawain and Scot returned. Cathbad, in the form of a crow, sat perched on Scot's shoulder. The three younger men put everything in order. Because Alanbart lacked the strength to complete the deed, it fell to Gawain to put Gonoth out of his misery. After a moment of dour silence and an exchange of eye contact, Gawain beheaded the giant with one smooth and perfect cut of his axe. They dragged the holly boughs out and amassed them into a great pile around the giant, then collected all of the bodies (including the portly knight's missing head), laid them flat, and stacked their weapons and armor to the side.

Alanbart went to Taffy and patted him affectionately on the shoulder. "I'm glad to see you, old friend," he said, running his fingers through the horse's mane.

Taffy bent his head and began to nibble the grass.

"Well, don't get overexcited at our reunion," Alanbart added in a hurt tone. "It may be short-lived."

Meanwhile, Cathbad, now in human form, waited inside the henge. He bent over the altar, still and silent. When Scot went to tell him that they were ready to bring forth the treasures of Asacael, Cathbad did not even look up, and uttered these words in a cold and abstracted tone: "A hunting hawk will choose a dead tree from which to gaze upon the world because there is no life obstructing his view, bending whatever way the wind wills. A dead tree stands firm and prefers to snap, rather than bend, when the air gusts too strong or the snow piles on a load that is too heavy to bear. It falls piecemeal to earth while it rots from the inside out. Perhaps the hawk chooses the dead tree because the view is more precious, for once the tree collapses, that perch is lost to the world forever."

"What?" Scot asked.

"It is nothing—just an old man's musings," Cathbad drew himself up and turned from the altar. "These trees thirst for vengeance, and they shall have it. Bring me the artifacts."

They brought forward the treasures and heaped them on the altar, the staff, the hammer, and the box of jewelry. The Bible lay hidden in Gawain's saddlebag. To all of them, Cathbad said, "First, there should be a ring that is made of braided yellow-gold. It has neither stone nor rune, but has one discernible feature. It is said to be almost imperceptibly scarred on both sides, as if it had been split with a cleaver and re-fused in the fire. And so it was once sundered, half belonging to father and half to son. It is called the ring of Mudarra, and it will restore my sight."

Scot dug through the box, finally holding up a glittering gold ring. "I've found it."

Cathbad slipped it onto his middle finger and closed his milky eyes tight. Five seconds passed in silence while an odd azure illumination slipped in pulses from the slits of Cathbad's eyes, and then the druid opened his lids to reveal keen crystal-blue irises rimmed and flecked with highlights of lapis. His gaze pierced them.

"I thought never to see again," he smiled. He scrutinized the henge and his happiness dribbled away. He spun slowly, taking in the damage. Tears crept down his wrinkled cheeks. "And this is the sight with which I am greeted." His tone modulated from sorrow to bitterness. "Yes, these trees thirst for vengeance and they shall have it." He turned to Scot, "What are you wearing and who," his unnaturally bright eyes flicked to Sir Gawain, "is this warrior wearing purple and bearing an eagle on his breast?"

"I," Scot faltered, "I—"

"If you knew anything about coats of arms, or had the civility to address me politely," Gawain interrupted, "you wouldn't have to ask that question. I wear the arms of Agravain of Orkney, and I am the last living son of King Lot and Queen Morgause. I helped your warrior fight the banshee, won you that ring—your sight—and will rescue my king (or die trying) with or without your help."

Cathbad scowled, about to make a caustic comment, but Gawain continued before he could do so. "I also just fought and killed a Christian knight to save this pagan place from the axe, a deed that even now weighs on my eternal soul (God forgive me), so I might be owed a measure of courtesy by you."

"That explains him," Cathbad said, turning back to Scot, "but it does not explain you. What is this? Armor?"

"It is—it's the spoils of victory. I have made a pact with Sir—uh—with this knight who saved my life. He battled the banshee in our old way, painted and without armor. He did well and proved himself worthy of Woden's gilded hall. He asked me to fight the next battle his way. How could I, in good faith, refuse to do honorably for him what he has already done for me? Am I to prove my faith the weaker and less honorable?"

Cathbad scowled. "Perhaps he already proved his faith the weaker for giving it up to fight in the old way, and perhaps you will dishonor yours by returning, as you say, the favor. To me, this decision smacks of cowardice and the love of life, which is always a good soul's downfall."

"Oh, get down off of your pulpit, you old hypocrite," Alanbart cut in. "He's told you his motive, and let's say you choose not to believe him—let's say you believe that he's trying to increase his chances of living through the next battle—can you blame him? Especially after you croaked out that prophecy that one of us is going to die?"

"Yes," Cathbad said, his voice full of indignation, "I can blame him for that, and I will do so, and so will the gods."

Scot withered a bit, shrinking back beside Gawain and shifting his weight self-consciously from foot to foot.

"If you want him to take off his armor, then take off your magic ring and don't pick up that staff that they brought you, but be sure that you lead the attack, just the same," Alanbart continued. "I called you a hypocrite, and I mean it. Maybe you aren't wearing armor, but you're enhancing your power and chances of survival just the same as him, and if your gods frown on one, they'll frown on the other, or they're not just gods at all—not that any god is."

Gawain and Scot gaped at Alanbart in disbelief. Scot's mouth hung slack, and Gawain's eyes twinkled with something—was it mirth or the beginning of respect?

"Boy, you disrespect the gods amidst this sacred grove, and for that I should kill you." The leaves rustled ominously without a breath of wind and a shadow crossed the sun.

Alanbart was genuinely unconcerned, an odd and empowering feeling. In fact, it was downright liberating. He lifted his hands in an open gesture. "At this particular moment in time, I don't give a damn what you do to me."

Cathbad raised a knuckled hand to the sky. There followed a slight flicker and an almost imperceptible rumble.

Gawain stepped forward. "When you threaten him, you threaten me. Hear this: By God, I will not stand idly by and watch this happen. If I must, I will kill you, old man, whether it ruins my chances of rescuing my king or not. No man's life—not even a king's—is worth betraying my chivalry and compromising my honor. I will not stand by and see a helpless ally threatened with death."

Insolent, Alanbart added, "And let's not forget the laws of hospitality, the fact that we broke bread together in this very grove, and the curse that you, yourself, invoked upon the breaker of that vow."

Scot, standing between them, said nothing.

At last Cathbad sighed and relaxed his shoulders, lowering his arm. His voice, though, still threatened retribution, "I am one of—perhaps the last of—the gods' instruments on this plane of existence, but each man's fate is already written. Your life's string is not to be cut upon this instant, but every man is born to die, and in death each will meet the gods. The gods neither forget nor lightly forgive insult."

Cathbad considered the altar, then reached for the staff. Holding it over his head, he said, "The Staff of Väinämöinen, at last!" It shone in the midday sun. "And now, the test." Cathbad held out his arms. He mumbled some incantations, waited a moment, and then began to flap them up and down—a ridiculous posture for an old man, and at the sight of it Alanbart didn't quite stifle a scoffing sound—and as he did, the druid began to change.

Cathbad's head collapsed in on itself, his hair turned from white to red-gold, his nose grew hard and yellow, his legs retracted into spindles, his mottled white robe shaded to tan, gold, red, and brown, and bloomed into feathery plumage. He flapped majestically aloft.

"Aeeeck!" shrieked the golden eagle as it lifted into the holly trees and perched on a freshly-cut branch, grasping with bright yellow feet and wickedly-sharp talons. The eagle gazed out with ice-blue eyes and pruned itself placidly, then shrieked again and beat its wings, taking flight and passing over Alanbart's head, rising in expanding upward-curling circles.

"You son of a bitch!" Alanbart shouted, shaking his fist into the sky. A large white and brown splotch oozed down his shirt. "Twice!

I can't believe that bastard hit me twice."

Scot shook his head. "Well, that sure beats a blind blackbird. Should we presume that his powers increased in proportion to that change?"

"That seems like a reasonable assumption," Gawain agreed. "But more to the point, do you suppose that he'll come back?"

"Still more to the point, does anyone have a crossbow?" Alanbart asked, only half in jest.

"He'll be back," Scot ignored Alanbart. "The trees must be avenged."

"In the meantime," Alanbart removed his shirt and scraped off what he could on the altar's stone edge. "Let's work on our plan."

"Our plan?" Gawain asked. "You now intend to fight with us?"

"Honestly? I think so." Alanbart shrugged. "My intelligence is telling me 'no,' but I'm in the midst of one of those cliché struggles between mind and soul—if there is such a thing as a soul. What I feel that I must do and what I know that I should do are at odds—and, frankly, I'm not sure if it matters that I recognize what's happening to me if I still don't have control of either my thoughts or my emotions." He pulled himself up, sitting bare-chested and cross-legged atop the altar. "Oh, don't think that I've somehow swelled with sudden courage. No, no, certainly not. If anything, I've gone insane."

Scot and Gawain exchanged surprised and confused glances.

"You two are brave," Alanbart continued. "Each of you has your ideal—a powerful dream that you fight for and for which you are more than willing to lay down your own lives. Scot, you'd gladly die for honor because it is more important to you than your life."

"That is true," Scot confirmed.

"And Gawain," Alanbart added, "you'd merrily martyr yourself for the code of chivalry."

Gawain nodded.

"The fact that you love and respect yourselves amplifies the value of the sacrifice and makes it more poignant. That is true bravery." Alanbart smirked. "Me? I have no ideal for which to die. The only thing I've ever held of value is my own life—my future, my comfort, and my security. The change that has happened to me is that I no longer value myself, and so I'm careless about what fate befalls me."

Gawain gaped, but Scot cleared his throat, still shifting awkwardly from foot to foot. "And to what, or whom, do you owe this sudden change of heart?" he asked.

"Experience," Alanbart patted the cold stone altar.

"What?"

"I've never before understood—experienced—the outcome of my cowardice. It never affected me before now."

"And today it did?" Gawain studied Alanbart's face. He saw the conflict and hesitation, and then supplied the answer: "Heather."

"Indeed," Alanbart admitted. "Here I am, unharmed, and she is a prisoner being dragged to the tower. You may ask how this situation came about. It is exactly as you imagine. I surrendered her, unfought."

"Malestair would have killed you." Gawain answered with matter-of-fact bluntness. He dismissed Alanbart's cowardice as a thing of custom, common and to be expected.

"That's it?" Alanbart asked. "No reprimand? No righteous indignation or statement about my moral and physical inadequacy?"

"Well," Gawain said, "Of course, I would have preferred death to dishonor, but you had none to lose, and you aren't one to go seeking death."

Instead of being insulted, Alanbart laughed. "That, sir knight, was true, but I'm ready to die now, if it matters." He pulled his shirt back over his head. "The amusing thing is that my mind keeps insisting that this feeling—this lack of fear—is only temporary and that I will inevitably revert to my 'true' self, but I am not yet convinced that that is so. So, shall we get to planning our attack on the tower?"

Gawain looked to Scot, who was staring off into the Holly trees. He cleared his throat to regain the swordsman's attention and said, "Maybe the first thing that we should do while we wait for Cathbad's return is consider our resources. We've lost the strength of Gonoth, but we've brought back a trove of treasures from the banshee." He gestured at the altar. "We have the hammer that is supposed to sunder the gates of the tower, and we have a pair of perfectly worked swords bearing runic letters."

"Perhaps I can read them," Alanbart offered, sliding from the altar to his feet.

Gawain considered him skeptically. "Reading is a difficult skill. Even of the sons of the wealthy and powerful, few are learned in its secrets."

"Nevertheless, I am proficient in all of the many languages that I speak. Fluency is a far less useful skill than you imagine it to be, let me assure you. Hand me your blade," he ordered, holding out his hand.

The knight unsheathed his shining sword, flipped it, and handed it hilt first to Alanbart, who gazed at the engravings on the blade.

"These runes are Gothic," he said after a moment's scrutiny. "And this sword's name is Mimung."

"Mimung?" Scot echoed. He stopped fidgeting and examined Gawain's sparkling blade, awe in his voice, "The sword of Wudga?"

"Or a replica," Alanbart closely considered the place where the blade met the pommel.

"Mimung, the sword that defeated Langben Rese? The sword that clashed in combat with Attila's own dark steel?"

"Mimung, wrought by Wayland," Alanbart read. "—that is all that the runes say, in any case." He handed it carefully and somewhat reluctantly back to Gawain, who held it more reverently than before.

"By Christ, how is that even possible?" Gawain asked. "That sword was lost to eternity."

"Apparently not," Alanbart responded. "In my rather large literary experience, I've noticed that these things tend to vanish for centuries and then turn up in the hands of heroes at the opportune moment of crisis—what better hero than you and what better moment than now? It all seems quite fitting."

"Nevertheless, a work of Wayland in my possession, it is difficult to digest. God's hand must be in this."

Alanbart studied the bright blade and its flawless cutting edge. "I cannot guess about the hand of God, or if He even has hands for that matter, but let's not be modest. That isn't just a work of Wayland, it is the best work of that famous smith's hands. He made it for himself, and Wudga was his son."

Gawain nodded, "I did not take you for one who appreciated

the songs of battle and heroes, nor for one of such a fine . . . learning. Perhaps you would care to explain more of your history." He resheathed the blade.

"Why not?" Alanbart said. "I never had much of a knightly education; that much is true. You killed my father when I was quite young, but that doesn't mean that I had no education, nor that I was without a father figure. The facts of the matter are not entirely mysterious. I told you that I grew up lordless, travelling from castle to castle with my mother, eking out a living however possible. All of that is true, but there is more to the story. The missing fragment involves a famous bard by the name of Aelfric, of whom you may have heard." He leaned against the altar and sighed, ready to continue with his story at length.

"Pardon me," Scot interrupted. "I am quite captivated by your tale, of course, but in all today's trials and travels, I've neglected to answer the, um, call of duty, and believe me, my duty is calling." He grunted. "I'll be right over here," he said, gesturing to the edge of the henge. "Don't delay for me," he called over his shoulder as he shambled off.

"By all means," Alanbart laughed, "go right ahead—apparently even legendary heroes are not immune from necessities. I suppose that Achilles, on occasion, had to squeeze demigodly nuggets out of his invincible ass. I'm sure they were as long and epic as Homer's poem," he added, mostly to himself.

"So, this Aelfric?" prompted Gawain, trying to avoid the awkward turn in conversation.

"Indeed," Alanbart continued, "less than a year after my father's death, my mother and I were in a desperate state. Our money was spent, our goods nearly all pawned, and we'd traveled to three courts looking for succor and finding none. We would certainly have fallen on hard times, and truly we might have died, had not luck thrust Aelfric into our path. At the fourth castle, that of King Mark in Cornwall, we met him.

"Aelfric was a potbellied but lithe little man with a white beard and long gray hair circling a bald crown. He had twinkling green eyes— much like yours, Scot," Alanbart said in the direction of the swordsman, who was unclasping his belt atop the henge wall, "—and a surprisingly deep voice for such a thin frame. He ended his stay as musical entertainer to that court, and he took pity on us where Mark would not. We shared Aelfric's travels all around Britannia, and though I didn't understand it then, now I am quite sure that my mother shared Aelfric's bed."

At this juncture the rending sound of flatulence and of splattering viscous liquid came from the wall. Both Alanbart and Gawain turned nervously in the direction of the sound, only to lock eyes with Scot, who was crouching just beyond the wall and visible from the chest up. His face was straining.

Both knights murmured with embarrassment and averted their eyes.

Scot sighed contentedly: "Ohh, that needed release."

Gawain shielded his vision.

"Sorry!" Scot called, unapologetically. "There was a small grove of elderberries under the oak yesterday, and I'm afraid that I ate them all—they were so ripe, plenteous, and tasty. Speaking of ripe . . ." he groaned.

Alanbart and Gawain winced again as another cascade erupted.

"I don't want to miss your story," Scot grunted. "Please go on."

"And now we know why people call the north uncivilized," Gawain muttered under his breath. "If he wasn't such a skilled swordsman and honorable warrior . . ." he trailed off.[18]

---

[18] If I may interrupt myself at this, ah, pungent juncture to make an observation, it is an interesting aspect of human nature that we ritualize, label as obscene, and obsessively seek to disguise those human urges that overlap with animal behaviors. 'Civilized' society, as Gawain characterizes it, would have us believe that we are wholly unnatural beings and goes to great lengths to nurture and support that illusion.

Take eating, for example. How many inexplicable rules dictate the proper way to present and consume food? It is a repeated ritual that is designed to disguise the fact that we murder and then devour our fellow creatures. Then, of course, there is 'romance' and reproduction. Half of obscenity is (dare I say) couched in the erogenous, and all of it refers to the act of mating in animal terms. Instead of letting the animal romp in polite society, we prefer to cloak it in words like 'love' and pretend that both sexual attraction and action are expressions of some deeper elements of an immaculate soul, not just sweaty animal urges that growl for consummation.

Finally, of course, there is excrement, the place where the other half of obscenity lingers. When actively engaged in empting our bladders or bowels, we must hide ourselves, be morbidly silent, and seek to give the general impression that nothing impolite is occurring, even taking measures to mask unseemly odors. Surely, the living

Alanbart cleared his throat and struggled to return to the topic at hand. His speech was punctuated by a series of unpleasantly resonant blasts from Scot's direction.

"Um, well, as I said, my mother paid Aelfric for our continued existence with her virtue (such as it was), though for that matter we both came to love him, so it wasn't much of a sacrifice. He it was who educated me—and he knew everything. I learned songs of heroes, genealogies of famous families, chronicles, annals, histories, mythologies, and languages. In truth, Aelfric wanted me to follow him in his profession, but mother wouldn't hear of it. I was born a knight, and a knight I would stay."

Gawain's facial expression betrayed his feelings (or possibly reacted to the rancid and oddly fruity odor that now wafted over them).

"I know—I know," Alanbart winced. "Obviously, you think that I'm a terrible example of knighthood, and you're right. But I wouldn't have been much of an entertainer either. As Aelfric once told me, you cannot be a great bard unless you've had at least one great experience, and you cannot sing of valor, villainy, heroism, loss, love, or betrayal unless you've experienced them firsthand. I had not and still have not (though today has already begun to rectify that). Certainly up through this moment I've had no great appreciation of heroism, which I've always considered to be the first step to martyrdom."

Gawain interrupted the narrative: "How old is Aelfric? And does his still live? My father used to tell tales of hearing Aelfric the Entertainer sing in Orkney as a child, and he died a decade ago—an old man."

"Aelfric lives, a prosperous gentleman of around seventy years—threescore and ten, as he puts it."

"Impossible. He'd be at least a hundred by now."

Alanbart smiled. "Fortunately, Aelfric is immortal."

---

embodiment of an immortal soul should not squat and defecate ingloriously upon the dusty ground, for we are made (or so I have been told) in the divine image of God.

If you don't believe me, try to find a classic tale that makes mention of excrement. They are few and far between. We like our fiction, too, to be immaculate. Woe be to those, like Scot (and myself), who flout this social rule and ignorantly remind us of that loathsome truth: we are animals.

"Blasphemy!" Gawain gasped.

"Oh, not immortal by strict definition, no—he has in fact died two times already. He told me the story once. Would you care to hear?"

Gawain nodded.

"I know you both to be men of honor," Alanbart turned hesitantly to Scot, "and I must swear you to secrecy on this point. Aelfric would demand it."

"As long as it reveals no devilry, I swear secrecy," Gawain agreed.

"I swear it, too," Scot added, pants still down around his ankles, and then (for the first time) he blushed, abashed. "But before you share your great secret, I must confess that I planned this badly." He gestured to his behind.

"Now he admits it." Gawain said with a smirk.

"You see," Scot said, plucking a small sprig from the nearest tree. "Holly leaves are covered in sharp spines . . ." he poked his finger on one and grimaced. "So, could one of you lovely lads kindly see fit to fetch me a scrap of cloth?"

Alanbart shook his head, "Not a chance, my friend."

Gawain paced out into the sunlight, returning a moment later with the slain knight's surcoat. He tossed it to Scot, who proceeded to clean himself.

Again, Gawain and Alanbart averted their eyes. The latter attempted a joke to lighten the mood. "Sir Gawain, you are ever the courteous hero. You can extricate anyone from any excrement."

Scot chuckled at the wordplay. Gawain did not.

"A prickly predicament?" Alanbart ventured.

Nothing.

"A defecation situation?"

The only sound was the gentle clinking of Scot's belt as he shifted positions.

"No?" Alanbart cleared his throat.

Scot's laugh broke the tension. "He sure saved my ass," the swordsman added.

Gawain still didn't crack a smile. He put his hand on his sword hilt and gazed to the south. "We should not linger here overlong. Arthur and Heather await our aid."

Scot nodded, searching the sky, then hopped back over the wall. "But as we cannot commence their rescue without Cathbad—and he is likely overflying the tower to offer us intelligence, I, for one, would like to hear Alanbart's secret."

"Well, then, as I was saying," Alanbart nodded, "Aelfric—the original Aelfric that is—took a lesson from the druids. They pass everything—poems, stories, spells, and knowledge—on by word of mouth, never writing down their secrets on the historical page. It is their greatest strength and weakness. No one may know their secrets who is not worthy, for how would he learn? Yet, when the last druid passes, his faith passes with him, lost to eternity. And so it might happen that when Cathbad dies, his faith dies too. So too is it with Aelfric.

"When the first Aelfric felt his strength waning, he selected a worthy protégée and taught him all that he knew—every story, song, lay, ballad, and poem. When the boy—Thorvald by name—became a young man, the two boarded a boat to Denmark, an old entertainer and a young apprentice, and they disembarked as Aelfric, the young entertainer, and Thorvald, his elderly servant. Fifty years later, on the return voyage, the transition happened again, This time ending with a young Aelfric and an old Helmet, and so Aelfric has lived through three generations, and may yet survive many more."

Gawain nodded. "That's not anything unnatural—just a master-apprentice relationship, with the one addition that the apprentice literally becomes the master."

"Apparently Aelfric got the idea from your sword-smith, Wayland, or so his descendant told me. One day he was calculating a chronology of heroes and he found that the famous smith 'lived' for nearly five centuries. Of course, he assumed that it was just literary license for such a useful side character, but then he got to thinking how such an inhuman 'lifespan' might be accomplished, and the idea was born. In fact—"

"Ahem" Scot interrupted, walking back over to them while rubbing his hands on his braided pants. "Speaking of Wayland, I've been waiting to ask. Would you please tell me what my blade says?" Scot held out his dark and angular sword for inspection.

"Certainly," Alanbart took the blade, careful not to handle it where Scot had. "These runes are different from those on Gawain's blade." He considered the engravings for a long time. "They're Dwarf runes," he said finally, "the kind adopted by the Norse. This sword is not of Wayland's manufacture."

Scot's looked down, deflated.

Alanbart examined the blade again. "It is called Hrunting."

"Hrunting?" Gawain and Scot echoed together, the latter latching greedy eyes on the blade.

"The Hrunting, held by Beowulf, borne in battle against the mother of Grendel?" Scot asked.

"So it would seem. If true, this blade was forged by Regin, brother of Fafnir, cooled in a bucket of blood, laced with dragon-poison, and wielded by Unferth. I, obviously, have heard the tales." He handed it back to Scot and then began to chant from memory:

Matchless in melee,   it never failed in fighting.
Its wielder in war,   warrior or warlord,
Defender or destroyer,   had glory dealt him by destiny.
Wretched Unferth wouldn't   bother about the blade.
No, he drank down his days,   drowned his
Courage, swallowed the seeds   of cowardice,
And gladly granted it to   a hero higher than
Himself. He would not   dive down into danger,
Far from friends,   to face a fearsome fiend.
Gone was his glory,   sunk was his sun.
The new hand that   held Hrunting would
Soar so far skyward   that its story should
Never sink, a ceaseless star,   alight in everlasting night.

"And now you are a part of that tale," he concluded.

"May I only prove worthy of my part," Scot sheathed the blade.

"You will," Gawain said, placing his big hand affectionately upon Scot's shoulder. "I am convinced of it." He cleared his throat and removed his hand, dropping it to his side; yet, his eyes lingered on Scot's face. "Say what we will about your colloquial mannerisms, you were meant to be here. You were meant to meet me, and you were meant to have that blade. I see the hand of God at work in all of this, and it steadies my belief in our ultimate victory."

"It will certainly make for an interesting story," Alanbart said. "If I get out of this alive, I may visit with Aelfric and see if it might be recorded in song. In any case, Scot, you are no longer an unlucky bandit, and you finally have a weapon of a high enough quality to match your braided pants."

"Are you mocking my pants?" Scot rubbed a hand down his yellow and green woven leather breeches. "This is the second time you've mentioned them."

"We all mock the things of which we're the most jealous" Alanbart replied through a half smirk. "And now, I believe we were going to plan our assault on the tower?"

"Quite right," Gawain agreed. "Firstly, what are the odds?"

"Well," Alanbart said, "we've got a druid, an excellent swordsman, a knight of the Round Table, me, and somewhere around one hundred lightly armed and armored but bloodthirsty goblins. Not a bad army. What are we up against?"

"According to Heather, Malestair said that he had nearly one hundred men. Allowing for exaggeration, let's say that he had eighty-five. Well, there were twenty-eight dead at the ambush site when I got there. I defeated a party of four later that day, which makes thirty-two."

"We killed five at the oak," Scot added helpfully.

"Ok," Alanbart said, "Five at the oak, then, and there are nine bodies outside at the moment. So, eighty-five subtracting thirty-two is fifty three, minus five is forty-eight, less nine is thirty-nine. He can't have many more than forty men at the moment."

"And some of them are likely not in fighting condition," added Gawain.

"So how many will be on the walls when we attack?" Scot asked.

"We'll figure that five of them are knights," Gawain answered.

"One will be in charge of the gate, but the others won't be occupied with such menial tasks. So we're looking at around thirty-six men."

"Yes," Alanbart agreed, "but there will have to be a minimum of three shifts, so we're realistically talking about only thirteen men at one time."

"Right, and of those thirteen, one will be on the tower—that brings us to twelve, two will be guarding the tower gate—ten—and one will be outside of Arthur's cell, which leaves us with nine men on the wall."

Scot laughed aloud. "Nine! You make the odds almost sound in our favor."

"If we surprise them, they will be," Gawain said, "but if they can get forty men on the walls or even twenty-five in the tower with the door barred, then our hundred goblins won't be able to storm the place. They're weak in physical strength and horribly disorganized—and they're all insufferable cowards and backstabbers at heart."

"But if we can find a way to breach the gate and take the tower door before they know what's happening . . ." Alanbart said.

"Then it will be a slaughter, and our only worries will be getting both Arthur and Heather out of there alive."

Scot hefted the hammer. "Then we'd better hope that this thing works."

"Why not test it?" Alanbart asked. "Is there a door on Cathbad's hovel? Even a wooden table might be sufficient."

"There is one more thing to consider," Gawain added, his expression grim.

"And what is that," Alanbart asked.

"If Malestair has Excalibur," Gawain said, "then he probably has the sword's sheath as well."

"And?" Scot prompted.

"The sheath of Excalibur is enchanted with a powerful magic and prevents the bearer from coming to any mortal harm from a physical attack. Malestair would be invincible."

"So, we cut it off his belt?" Scot asked.

Before Gawain answered, they heard a fluttering of wings.

Cathbad flew into the circle and landed near the altar, transforming into his human form just in time for his feet to touch the earth.

"Have a nice flight?" Alanbart asked, some hostility in his voice.

"Pleasant," was the icy answer. "The wind is warm today, and it was rewarding to see the world again." He paused and then wrinkled his large nose. "The air is much cleaner up there. What, in the name of the gods, is that stench?"

Scot studied a spindle of brownish weeds at his feet.

Alanbart stepped forward. "Surely you know that dead men's bowls leak with no living will to hold the muscle closed. There are many dead men outside, and a giant."

"Indeed," Cathbad nodded. "We can add that to the list of defilements of this holy site." He cleared his throat. "The eyes of an eagle are extremely sharp. I bring tidings. High, I circled over the river valley and saw much that may be of interest. For instance, four knights and a woman just entered the tower fortress on horseback. Also, there is one hidden soldier watching at each of the two southern fords, both with small and swift mounts."

"Does Malestair suspect our move?" Scot asked. He shot Alanbart a thankful look.

"I don't see how he could," Alanbart answered, winking at Scot. "He believes that you're dead," he gestured to Gawain. "He crippled Gonoth, and he thinks I'm finished. I can't suppose that he fears what he imagines to be an old blind druid. There must be something else afoot."

"Perhaps he is waiting for reinforcements?" Scot asked.

"Then why hide the observers?" Cathbad returned.

"I'd say he is waiting for an uncertain friend," Gawain said, his eyes narrowed in thought. "He has Arthur in his dungeon. It would stand to reason that he informed Sir Mordred, but this puts him in an awkward spot because on the surface my brother still serves Arthur, and so there is a chance—however slight—that he would take Arthur's side and storm the tower."

"I agree," Alanbart nodded. "But I think it's more than that. He's hedging his bets. He's conjuring a dragon tonight. I think he means to destroy both Mordred and Arthur in one quick pounce, and then claim the throne for himself. Heather hinted something to that effect when she first told me the story. If the dragon summoning is a success, then Malestair wins it all. If it is not, then he turns Arthur over to Mordred and becomes his chief vassal. Either way, he wins. I don't think that Mordred's possible betrayal has even crossed Malestair's mind. I think he's just being cautious in case Mordred moved more swiftly than he anticipated."

"That doesn't change the fact that we have to get past them somehow," Scot said. "Cathbad, you could fly overhead and take them from behind."

"We can't risk that," Alanbart interrupted. "If he dies, our only link to the goblin force is gone. Without their assistance, the attack would certainly fail."

"Agreed," said Gawain. "I would offer to chase him down, but a small and swift riding pony would outrun Gringolet or Taffy."

"We need a ford to move the Goblins across," Alanbart pointed out. "They cannot move in plain sight or we'd lose the element of surprise. If they came in from the north, they'd have to circle the wall in the open to get to the gate in the south. The whole force would be on the walls before we could get halfway to the gate. We've got to get them across the heath and under the cover of the forest."

"The chieftain, Bruuzak," Cathbad cut in, "has already agreed to move his goblins across Shepherd's Ford and then over the heath. Indeed, they should be on their way to meet me now. You have no idea the pain that it took me to convince them to march in daylight."

Alanbart drew a deep breath. "Then I'll go and get captured. The watcher at the ford will have to escort me back to the tower before returning, and then you'll have your opportunity. I'm not much use in combat, so this is the best I can do."

"That might work," said Gawain, "but we should find a way to use your capture to our benefit."

"I have a magic," Cathbad said, "that may be useful in this. I can draw runes on your wrists that emit flame. If you are bound with rope, it will burn to a cinder and you shall be free."

"And if he's bound with iron?" Gawain prompted.

"Then the magic will heat it to a red-hot glow."

"Delightful," Scot shook his head.

Alanbart grimaced. "That sounds uncomfortable. How would I ignite the flames?"

"You would use the power word, 'cynnau.' Can you remember that?"

"I'll write it down," Alanbart replied, only half jesting.

19

AFTERNOON: THE DEVIL'S ROOKERY

Malestair escorted Heather into his chamber and shut the heavy oaken door behind her. The bar scraped against iron as he locked it in place. His room had been returned to precisely its former state. The wolf-skin rugs had been re-lain and the faded and mildewed tapestry rehung on the inner wall. Grit and small clumps of dried mud littered the floor. A sunbeam filtered in through the narrow archway and dust motes drifted aimlessly through it. The embers in the fireplace had faded to cold ash. Malestair gestured to the straw mattress of his bed.

"Take a seat, my lady."

Heather complied. She looked searchingly at him, trying to discern his purpose.

"Oh, don't worry," he said. "Nothing terrible will happen to you here, but my men expect certain behaviors from their lord and might be disappointed if they were not carried out. Right now, for example, they assume that I will take you against your will and ravish you, then fling you, bleeding and bruised, back to the dungeon." He adjusted a heavy, crimson drape. "Who am I to disillusion them? And besides, I quite enjoy their jealousy and ribald jokes."

Heather cocked an eyebrow.

Malestair turned to the fireplace, picked up a pine log from a stack along the wall, and placed it atop the pile of ash. Heather tensed. His back was toward her.

"You see," he moved another log, "I am not particularly given to vice. I have no need for female company, I do not over-indulge in spirits, and I am Spartan in my appetite. These are qualities that make me strong, for in many they are weaknesses that may be exploited." He finished piling the wood and turned back to her, leaving the fire unlit.

"Why?" Heather asked, she'd wasted the opportunity, "if you are so predisposed against vice, do you choose to do evil?"

Malestair considered this, then straightened and looked into her almond eyes. Something in them—he couldn't tell what—led him to answer honestly. She would be killed in any case, he mused, so why not tell her the truth? "I choose to do evil because I desire to be remembered in history and song."

"But—"

"Why not do good?" he scoffed. "When I was a youth, my lady, I realized that I was intelligent, strong, and swift. I was also ambitious—a trait that has never left me. I thought, in my youthful ignorance, that I might be the next Achilles, Alexander, or Archimedes. I studied, thought, planned, and trained every single hour of every single day to achieve my ambition.

"But," he continued, brushing long fingers over his short blonde hair, "as I aged, I realized that though I am smarter than most men, I am not and never will be Archimedes. There are many who are brighter, more intuitive thinkers, and more inventive than I. I also found that though I had great gifts in swiftness and strength (and length of arm—a most useful trait), and though my training propelled me above nearly all, I was no Achilles. By the eve of adulthood I already knew two knights who were faster, stronger, and instinctually better at combat than I. If I knew two such men, I reasoned, how many more might there be?

"I was intelligent enough, too, to make another realization. Though I mastered combat tactics and learned the fundamental rules of leadership, I discovered that I could not be a leader. When I said to a group of men, 'Follow me!' they did not follow. Upon making this discovery, I impartially observed and made a study of myself, and I found that people have a natural distaste for me—it is something unalterable in my appearance and demeanor from which most men recoil. Meeting me is akin to seeing a snake or a spider. Try as I might—and I did try, mightily—I could not alter this outward perception and so I could not and still cannot lead armies of righteous men. Oh, I have since filled that gap with respect and fear, but it is not the same. I could never be Alexander."

Heather opened her mouth to reply, but Malestair leveled a finger at her. "Be silent, woman, and listen." He leaned back against the hearth. "Realizing that I would never live up to my ambitions and considering myself in a disinterested way as a whole being, I created a picture of myself and my future: competent mediocrity. I was taller than most, stronger than most, swifter than most, smarter than most, crafty, and ambitious, but I also was disliked by my superiors and peers. By birth I was entitled to almost nothing—I am the bastard son of a powerful knight, but he too was generally disliked. How, then, was I to achieve fame? The answer is astoundingly simple:

"I have become a villain, a role for which I am astonishingly well suited. You see, I show a marked absence of emotion—I have very little spleen, it seems. This is the reason why, while most would be brought to spasms of tears and feel a crushing sense of grief when faced with my various revelations, I was unaffected. This, too, was an advantage that would place me beyond most calculations and free me from the crippling cowardice of conscience."

He paused and studied Heather.

"I see," she said at length, looking away from him at a poorly made tapestry. On it, a crowned man rode a horse that was far too small for him. He had some kind of oversized hawk on his outstretched arm. "And are you satisfied with your choice?"

"I will be," Malestair said, and offered her an empty laugh. "I intend to be the man who kills King Arthur, usurps the throne, beggars a nation to build an army—an army that follows not through leadership, but through fear, respect, and a desire for plunder—and who ravages Europe. I may not be the next Alexander, but I can be the next Attila."

"I see," she said again, but she did not really see.

"Now, if you will," he advanced toward her. "Please scream as if you're if fear and pain."

"What?" She turned her eyes from the tapestry.

"Do as I say, woman."

"Why?" The word left her mouth before she'd considered it, and his backhand hit her so fast that she couldn't recoil. The slap resounded in the empty room.

"Scream," he ordered again.

"I—" she began but Malestair slapped her a second time. She fell back on the bed, her eye already beginning to swell.

"This will become increasingly more violent," he said. "I suggest that you do as I say." He marched back to the fireplace and disinterred a club-sized piece of pinewood, spoked with the stubs of concentric braches, and cradled it in his thick-knuckled hands.

Heather screamed.

"There," he said, almost soothingly. "That's better. Now scream for me one more time, and then begin to moan with pleasure—not pleasure precisely, but with a pleasurable sort of pain. You know what I mean, and make it loud enough to be heard."

He tapped the pinewood cudgel against his thigh.

Heather thought about refusing, but saw the hard edge in his eyes, the absence of conscience or concern for her, and complied. She screamed loudly, and then began to sob. They were little sobs at first, but they turned into moans and got more powerful and more spasmodic with time.

Malestair smoothed his moustache. "If I was a man who enjoyed such things," he observed between her gasps, "I don't think that anything you could do would keep me from you at this moment. That's quite enough, however. You may stand."

She rose from the bed, her chin set and pride in her eyes. He reached out, stroked her cheek, then took hold of the V in the neck of her shirt and tore it open with one vicious yank. Her breasts fell free and she reached to cover them.

"Now you look more the part," he muttered.

She shied away, using both her arms to cover her nakedness. He advanced two steps, waited for her back to hit the wall and then brought his brown leather boot up in a swift kick that caught her, with enough force to lift her off the ground, right between her legs. She fell to the floor, gasping in pain. After a few moments she croaked, "Why?"

"A woman who has been bedded by me cannot go walking about the tower as if nothing has happened. She should feel it, there, between her thighs."

She began to rise, and he clubbed her across the shoulder blades with the cudgel, dropping her to the stone floor again and tearing the skin with the protruding ring of snapped branch stubs.

"You will rise when I tell you to rise," he said, then tossed the cudgel in the general direction of the fireplace, went to the door, lifted the bar, flung it open, and called out: "Guard!"

A young man at arms entered, his eyes wide as he scanned the room, noting Heather's crumpled form, bleeding back, and the way she covered her breasts. He looked at her greedily. As Malestair rotated to face the young man, he was buckling his belt.

"Find her a new shirt," he ordered. "Then take her down to the dungeon." He paused, as if considering something. "I am not finished with her yet," he added with malice. "If you or anyone else touches her before I am finished, I will see that man made a eunuch, then hung naked from the tower wall and left for the ravens. Do you hear?"

The guard swallowed. "Yes, lord." He bent to help Heather to her feet. As she hobbled from the room, she made eye contact with Malestair. His brown eyes were triumphant. Hers were no longer full of loathing—yes, she still hated the man, but what had been an over-boiling emotion was now spiced with understanding, and for the moment, her hate merely simmered.

"I suppose that I should thank you for this," she said over her shoulder in a begrudgingly grateful voice that held a tinge of bitterness.

She didn't see his face, but she heard his amused reply, "Most women do."

20

MIDAFTERNOON: THE HEATH

"So," Alanbart said to Taffy as he led the horse through the heather south of Cathbad's Henge, "how was your morning? Don't skimp on the details."

Unsurprisingly, the horse made no response. Their legs swished through the vegetation. A thrush trilled in the distance. Bees buzzed nearby. Alanbart could hear the low rumble of Scot and Gawain conversing twenty paces ahead as the two heroes walked their horses beside Cathbad, who was riding a captured mare.

"Oh, don't be coy with me," Alanbart chided, rumpling Taffy's coarse mane. "I saw what you and that filly were up to earlier."

That much was true. When Alanbart and the others had left the henge, they'd found Taffy draped across the back of the dappled brown and white mare which Cathbad now rode. Taffy didn't even have the decency to look embarrassed about it. In fact, sensing danger, he'd increased the pace of his consummation.

"That mare," Alanbart continued, gesturing ahead, "is no doubt young and charming, but there is more to a potential partner than age, hair color, bone structure, and scent. What do you know about her? Who is her father? What are her beliefs? How many riders has she had? Have you even glanced past her doe-like eyes at her teeth? Do you want to be—forgive the pun—saddled with her when she becomes a nag?"

Taffy bared his broad teeth in what might have been a bold smile, but was probably just a yawn. A fly landed near his eye and he shook his head.

"And then there are the obvious problems of race and class," Alanbart continued. "You're Welsh and she's English. Can you reconcile that? You're a charger, a knight's steed, and she's a mare belonging to some lowly man at arms. It could degrade your station."

The fly landed on his lip and Taffy blew air out.

"Fine, but I warn you, you don't know anything about her. You haven't even known her long enough to have a basis for opinion."

Alanbart's step faltered and he thought, for a moment, about Heather. His eyes crinkled and his face lit with a crooked, sheepish grin.

Taffy didn't break stride and lurched Alanbart forward. The young mare walked just ahead, her posterior jiggling with every step, and the old warhorse eagerly followed her scent.

As Cathbad crested the low hill that they'd been climbing, he raised a bony arm into the air. Gawain and Scot drew up beside him. As Alanbart belatedly neared the top, he gazed down upon a large gathering of goblins. Their raiment was dark, but the polished blades of axes, spears, knives, and swords glittered in the sunlight. The creatures crouched, winced, and waddled slowly across the open heather, grumbling and yapping in their filthy language.

Alanbart's eye was drawn to several horrible battle standards that shook and flapped in daylight. Cow, bear, and human skulls bobbed atop twisted wood poles, two to a banner, as the goblins advanced. The largest battle standard displayed the screaming head of an old woman in an advanced state of decomposition. Worms wriggled out of her eye-sockets. A second banner framed an image of a ravening wolf, bloody-jawed, goblin eyed, and wreathed in fire. A third depicted an oversized raven perched upon a bone-white ribcage, but the raven's eye was a brilliant and cold blue. In its mouth it held a human . . . what was that? Oh, Alanbart cringed, realizing.

"Don't worry too much about them," Gawain said in a low tone. "They're vultures. They look scary, they are vile and disgusting, and they eat the dead, but they're cowards—all of them. Charge, and they'll scatter."

"At least, for a time," Scot added.

"For a time," Gawain nodded.

Indeed, as the goblins clambered up the hill, they did resemble vultures, all bedecked in dark leather, fur, and feathers. Few had proper armor. Their dry, gray, and scaly skin showed on protruding arms, legs and heads. Black beady eyes squinted in the sunlight. They all lurched and hopped on short bandy legs, yammering and whining in the midday sun. They kept their heads and eyes averted, and when one did lift its head, it shaded itself with an arm or hand.

'Vultures in the day,' Alanbart thought, 'but probably owls at night.'

As Cathbad met Bruuzak with a formal greeting, Alanbart turned to Scot, who held the reigns of one of the captured horses. "I'll have to go and get imprisoned in a few minutes," he acknowledged. "I'd rather not see Taffy taken, too, if I can help it. Would you be willing to switch mounts with me?"

Scot raised an eyebrow. "Certainly," he answered. "I'm fond of Taffy, and I feel that he fancies me as well."

"He does," Alanbart hesitated, "and if I don't, um, return from the tower, will you kindly care for him? He's my best—my only—friend."

Scot held out a hand for Taffy's reins. "You may call me friend, too, if you like," he said.

Alanbart rumpled the horse's mane again. "Thank you, I will. And watch out, friend," he added, "because this horse loves the mares. He's probably mounted more females than you or I have, combined."

Scot appraised the horse. "That's a certainty."

21

THE DEVIL'S ROOKERY

The plan, such as it was, had gone perfectly. Alanbart rode across the shallow stony ford, stopped conspicuously on the far side to water his horse, turned and bent to get some water himself, and then Malestair's watchman confronted him and took him prisoner. The watchman tied Alanbart's hands with a leather strap, forced him onto his horse, and led him south to the tower at a quick trot. Presumably, the goblins began to cross the river as soon as he was out of sight.

The two riders then traveled uninterrupted to the Devil's Rookery, were ushered through the main gate of the palisade, dismounted, and were led into the tower by a red-faced knight with an oversized blonde moustache (obviously in emulation of his lord's) and a weak chin, but burly biceps. Once inside the greathall of the keep, Malestair confronted Alanbart about his escape. The conversation was short and brutal.

"How did you get away and where are my men?" Malestair demanded, sitting tall in the creaking black armchair, the single piece of furniture set on six-by-six foot stone dais.

"I could lie and say that I killed them," Alanbart responded, his natural sarcasm taking a turn toward impudence in his newfound self-contempt. He looked defiantly up at Malestair from the gritty flagstone floor. The chair creaked as the lord of the tower shifted his weight. He nodded at the knight, who cuffed Alanbart across the mouth with a mailed fist. He staggered back three steps and tasted blood.

"You will say 'my lord' when addressing me," Malestair commanded, "and you will give me my answers quickly and honestly."

"Yes, my lord," Alanbart replied, sucking his bleeding lip between words. "Cathbad—the druid—returned, confronted your knight, and killed him."

"And the other four?"

"Them too."

"Explain to me exactly how it is possible for a blind old man to defeat a knight and four men at arms?"

"A tongue of blue light leapt from his hand into the belly of your knight, my lord. He dropped his sword and his arms shot out to the sides, quivering. His eyeballs burst. It was awful, my lord. Then, the light jumped from both of his outstretched arms to the two nearest soldiers. They, too, went rigid and died. The others turned to run, but found that vines grew from the ground to tangle their feet and they could not move. The vines continued to grow with terrible speed, twined around them, dragged them down, and constricted. I can still hear their screams and the snapping of bones and the popping of joints." He shuddered, grimacing convincingly. "Then the druid let me go."

Malestair fingered the hilt of Excalibur. "Had I known of this druid's power, I would not have suffered him to live so long. He stood abruptly. "No matter; I shall deal with him soon enough."

"My lord," Alanbart began, "what will you do with me? I beg you, my lord, not to forget that you promised me that I might live."

"Did I? I suppose I did." Malestair fingered the golden hilt of Excalibur, protruding from a worn black leather scabbard, and then he turned to the knight who stood beside Alanbart. "I like to think that I'm a man of my word. Beat him until he cannot stand up, but don't *kill* him, and then toss him in the pit with our other *guests*. Don't free his hands and don't feed him, however. He can live as long as he likes."

His beating was merciless, but Alanbart made it through with nothing broken aside from his nose, and he only lost one tooth—a canine. He suffered the soundest thrashing he'd ever experienced in his life, and despite the fact that he was in agony, he found himself enjoying it in a sort of detached way.

He'd wondered if pain would snap him back to his old self, or the fear of being captured and having his life threatened, but he'd found that neither had a measurable effect on his state of mind. In fact, after thirty seconds of brutality—just about the time when he hit the floor and got a hard boot to the nose—he stopped feeling the pain altogether and took a mental step outside of his body, imagining to himself how it would seem to see the scene in the third person, as if he were a spectator instead of a participant.

The illusion was quite effective. As he became less and less visibly affected by the violence, his attacker grew bored, dragged him by the collar to a spiral stairwell, flung him down, opened a trap door, and dropped him through.

Alanbart hit the ground so hard that he vomited, then rolled onto his back. His eyes couldn't focus. The trap door (or rather *doors*, for he saw three of them circling above his head) closed with a thud; then all the light vanished. His ears buzzed and he could barely hear. He lay there a moment, going over the events of the past quarter hour in his mind, when he felt a soft caress on his forehead.

"Alanbart," a woman said; her voice sounded far off. "Alanbart, what are you doing here? Is Gawain…?"

An exhausted groan was all that Alanbart could muster for a few seconds. He spat a mouthful of blood and tried to chuckle, but gurgled indecorously instead. His dislodged tooth clattered meekly on the flagstones. "*I'm* fine," he croaked. "Thanks for asking. And it's good to see, or rather, hear you as well." He coughed again. "The attack is coming, and Gawain is in far better health than I am at the moment." He stuck his tongue into the bleeding socket of his missing tooth. "He beat the banshee. Is the king here?"

"That I am," a rich baritone voice, gravelly with age, sounded from his left. "To whom do I have the honor of speaking?"

"It is no honor, believe me my liege, to speak to me, but my name is Alanbart and my father was called Alardane. I am a knight in the service of Lord Ghent." He coughed painfully and spat more blood.

"Ghent?" the king scoffed, "I might make a disparaging remark about that upstart lord, but after all, he is the *lord* of Kent, and all that I am currently king of is this cell, and even then, I don't believe that one of the inhabitants considers me to be his rightful sovereign."

"Bloody right I don't!" a heavily accented Scottish voice barked from Alanbart's right, followed by clinking chains and a dry hacking cough.

"Who's that?" Alanbart asked the king.

"The Thane of Glamis, he tells me, wherever that is," Arthur said. "Though as for that, he's as much Thane of Glamis as I am King of Britannia at the moment."

"Nevertheless, my name is Sinel, and I am Thane[19] of Glamis!" Impetuous rage filled in his voice. "I was captured—I don't know how long ago—by the lord of this dismal place—in combat." He coughed, wheezy and dry again. "I should be dead—or insane—after so long a stay in this rat-hole, but I'm too hateful to die and I was already crazy when they dropped me in here." He laughed, his insanity perfectly audible to everyone in the room.

Alanbart cleared his throat.

"I'll get out one day," the thane said into the silence. "Then I'll kill them all!"

"Don't worry about him," Heather said. "He's on our side—or at least, he'll fight with us when the time comes."

"That I will," Sinel said, "providing that none of you gives me a reason to kill you." He chuckled madly and stifled another cough. "I suppose, *Arthur*, that I may have a reason to kill you—this tower-lord is your clansman after all—but unless you are man enough to face me in single combat, or until you meet me in the field at the head of an army and with harness on your back, you're safe from my blade. I swear it."

Arthur chuckled almost good-naturedly in reply, but a slight edge backed his voice when he responded, "I'm afraid, Sinel my friend, that my days of single combat are all but behind me. I'm an old man now, much as I hate to admit it. My next duel will doubtless result in my death, though I may still have one or two campaigns left in these bones. But surely none to such an unpleasantly cold and damp a place as this, so I believe that far northern Glamis will be spared from my wrath."

"Alanbart," Heather broke in, "what news?"

"Well," Alanbart sat up with a groan, "can you lean me against the wall? Thanks. Well," he spoke slowly, as it took effort to organize

---

19 Oh, and 'thane,' for those who are unaware, is a rather antiquated term for a powerful landholder, like an earl, duke, or baron, but dating to the Anglo-Saxon period, rather than the one that followed the Norman conquest. Sinel's insistent use of the term both insulted the King of England and challenged his authority, but as the word was so passé, it also flung insult back at Glamis, identifying him as an outlying yokel from an uncivilized land.

his thoughts. "As I said, Gawain and Scot defeated the banshee…uh, Gonoth died, and…um, Cathbad successfully rallied the goblins. My capture isn't quite a setback—actually, it is an essential part of the attack. Malestair had men watching the fords, so my capture was necessary to provide a distraction, luring the watcher away so that the goblins could cross undetected and reach the woods. They're closing on the tower as we speak. A pair of archers will finish the scout on his return to the ford—I imagine that the signs of the passage of a hundred goblins couldn't be missed—trampled grass and all that."

"Goblins?" Arthur interrupted. "Am I to stake my life on the assistance of such vermin?" He sighed. "Has it come to this?"

Heather recognized the rhetorical question and didn't respond. After a moment, she asked, "When will the attack begin?"

"According to Cathbad," Alanbart replied, "the goblins refuse to embark on an attack until after sunset. Gawain and Scot have the hammer and they plan to try it on the gate at sundown. Then the goblins will charge and under cover of that distraction, Scot and Gawain will make for the tower, use the hammer again, and force their way directly down here. Once we're all free, we'll fight our way up and out." He squinted into the darkness, trying to no avail to make out the lines in her face. "If nothing else, it has the virtues of being uncomplicated and of depending on the goblins for nothing but a diversion."

"What of Malestair and Excalibur?" she asked.

"They're more worried about the sword's scabbard than the blade itself. It's said that it makes the wearer impervious to injury."

"Then they can ease their minds," Arthur said. "My scabbard was smashed by the banshee's scream. It seems to me that the act of saving my life destroyed its magic."

Alanbart stared into the gloom, his eyes adjusting enough to see the faint outlines of light around the trapdoor above. "I'm glad to hear that. In any case, Scot and Gawain are arguing about who should have the honor of the combat. Personally, I think that Gawain stands a better chance—oh, and they brought back a pair of legendary blades from the banshee's horde, so either way they'll be well matched. Whoever clashes with Malestair, the swords alone will make it a duel worthy of song."

Heather sighed and fidgeted uncomfortably, smoothing the fabric of her dress in the darkness. "Can we do anything besides sit here and wait?

"I'm afraid not."

"I've been doing nothing else for two days," Arthur cut in. "At first it was terrible, for work and worry have been such constant companions to me that I couldn't stop myself from imagining every calamitous outcome of my capture, but yesterday afternoon I resolved myself to my fate, and now—but for the near constant wheezing and hacking of dear Sinel—the cell feels almost like a hermitage."

On cue, the Thane of Glamis coughed, cleared his dry throat, and tried to spit. Still trying to make out his companions in the darkness, Alanbart said,

"Yes, my liege, this is quite a pleasant spot for an escape from reality, especially given the rank stench of what I assume to be the communal chamber pot." Never in his life had the young knight imagined meeting Britain's king in such a ghastly place.

"I do seem to have exchanged one chamber pot for another, but I think I prefer the literal one's odor to the figurative one with which I used to live," Arthur replied, clearly exhausted. "Perhaps you don't understand the burden of leadership. Every decision that a king makes—every single one—has consequences. Who lives and who dies? Who receives honor at my hands and who shame? Who is to be punished and who is to be forgiven? Will they react with good will or ill? How will their retainers, friends, and relations react? How will I plan for those reactions? I assure you that being king has given me some sympathy for God. He sits alone upon his eternal throne—no one is His equal, no one wields His responsibility, and *everyone* is jealous of His power. And when that power is not used directly to benefit an individual, then that individual invariably blames God for his own failure."

"Maybe the crown *is* just a golden pisspot," Alanbart mused. "I suppose I never took the time to look down into its circle to see what lay inside."

"Few do," Arthur replied. "Most look only up, and to them the crown glitters with gold, glory, and power, but that's just an outward impression. The result of each of those things is isolation, jealousy, and conflict. Worst of all, with my wife, Merlin, and Lancelot gone, and with Gawain's mind consumed with the poison of revenge, I have no one left with whom I can converse as an equal. My every action and every utterance must be carefully scripted and planned. Believe me, kind sir, this is the first truly open discussion that I've held since the Feast of the Transfiguration, and before I could even have this, I had to be made powerless and shrouded in the darkness of a cell." He paused, waiting for a reply. None came.

"Even so," he continued at length, "I assure you that it has been a weight off my shoulders to believe for a day that it was all over and done with, or at least beyond my power to put right. I felt just as I imagine mighty Atlas must have felt when Hercules took on his burden for a day, but then Atlas had to go back and bow beneath the weight once again, and so must I. It already begins to gather above me and press upon my shoulders. Ironic, isn't it, that the idea of escape from this stinking hole seems to me a return to the prison of my life? But forgive an old man his moment of weakness."

"Perhaps, my liege, if you will allow me an observation," Alanbart began timidly. He groaned as he shifted positions. "This is an excellent example of the law of moderation. Too much of anything can be crippling—from the comical: too many lovers (most men can't keep even *one* woman happy), too much dinner (it can make one feel worse than hunger and the long term consequences of corpulence are worse than those of near-starvation), or too much wine (which has obvious consequences), for example; to the serious: too much wealth or power (both bring enemies—the more one has, the worse they are) or too much land, which brought down both Alexander and Rome. It is true with anything: we never know when we've had enough until we've had too much. And then, how can one go back? Time moves only forward, and it takes a rare man to freely give up what was earned through effort, self-denial, and determination."

"Indeed," Arthur agreed, "I'll think on your words. But enough of this depressing chatter. We can have complaints whenever we like. Because this cell is my earthly escape from life's burden, and because that escape ends tonight (one way or another), why not pass the time in grand fashion? It has often been my custom when waiting for an event, to fill the time with tales of magic, chivalry, and heroes. What about it, lads—and dear Heather, of course—who will regale me with a tale? Who is the greatest hero of history or legend? Share the name and the tale if you like." He clapped his hands twice as if to signal a start.

"If it's heroism you want," Alanbart began, "then it's likely you wish to hear of Hector, Leonidas, Roland, Beowulf, or Beorhtnoth."

"Everyone on that list died in battle," Arthur noted.

"So they did."

"Is that, then, a necessary factor of true heroism?"

"No, certainly not—at least, I hope not—but it increases the impact and lasting power of a heroic deed, don't you agree?"

"Why, do you think, does it so raise the honor of a hero?"

Alanbart shrugged: "Because those who die in combat cannot outlive their reputations or ruin them through subsequent misdeeds."

"Hear, hear!" Sinel said, clapping slowly from his side of the cell. His chains clanked and rattled. "This man has known a few 'heroes,' I'd wager. I, myself have seen many a heroic deed done in battle by a man who later that year murdered his brother, got drunk, and raped his neighbor's wife."

Arthur sighed heavily but ignored the bait. "Of your list," he began, speaking again to Alanbart, "which I note includes *none* of *my* knights, which man do you feel is the most heroic, and why?"

Alanbart considered this a moment. "Well, because I'm talking to a king and because I already slighted him by not selecting his knights (an oversight for which I blame the blinding pain in my skull), I should in all politeness probably select Leonidas. He was a king who sacrificed himself for his people. Before he even marched from Sparta, he knew that he'd lost, that he and his men were walking into the maw of Hades, yet he fought nonetheless. So, too, did Beowulf and Hector fight with foreknowledge of defeat. Roland and Beorhtnoth, however, both died for pride and vanity, and so I strike them from my list."

"Yet," Arthur prompted, "despite your careful homage to kings and crown princes, you still haven't answered my question."

"That is because I do not believe that any of them is the most heroic," Alanbart admitted. "All three were responsible to their people and fulfilled their obligations with the loss of their lives. They were admirable and acted in a way that encourages admiration—why else would history immortalize their stories? Yet, could they have done otherwise? Had Beowulf or Leonidas fled from their foes or sought terms with their enemies to save their own skins, they would not be counted as heroes, but as villains of the highest order. They were *expected* to be heroic and merely lived up to those expectations."

"Wait," Heather interrupted, "you believe that higher expectations lower the value of heroism?"

"Certainly," Alanbart replied, unfazed. "Each time a great hero faces danger, it has to be greater than the previous time, or he earns no glory."

"That seems supremely unfair."

"And so it is—the chamber pot of kingship and glory, as your majesty indicated—but the greater the initial expectation, the less the triumph. It's a fundamental truth of humanity. If Goliath beat David, no one would remember the giant's name (to say nothing of David's). But, when there is little expectation and the hero has a choice to either live and be a coward with *no* foreseeable consequence, or be heroic and die, *then* that person has the greatest potential for heroism. And that is the reason why out of all of the many men of bravery in songs of battle and heroes, I believe that Wiglaf is the greatest."

"Wiglaf?" Heather asked. "I've never even heard of him."

"Wiglaf, son of Wexstan," Glamis said from across the room, "was the only one of Beowulf's followers to stand with him in battle against the flaming dragon."

"Very good," Alanbart confirmed. "His part in the tale is small, but to my mind he casts a shadow longer than even Beowulf himself."

"Tell it," Arthur prompted with enthusiasm, "and explain."

"Yes, do tell it," Sinel echoed. "It's been long years since I heard that tale."

"I will do so," Alanbart said, then closed his eyes and welcomed the ancient verses to his throbbing mind.

Still strong, Beowulf   stood with sturdy shield.
Magnificent was his mail,   high was his helm.
Courageous, he called out   that creature under cliffs,
Daring that dragon   to creep from its cave,

Its hallway to hell,   and face him with fire.
His cry rang clear   near the crags and cliffs,
And the hell-snake heard   his human voice.

Its back arched in anger.   It uncoiled upward.
The bitter breath of   the burning beast burst

Forth from the fissure,   but Beowulf bore the blast.

His stout shield withstood   the foe's fierce flames.

The rocks resounded   with his warlike wail.

The strong old soldier   swung his sword,

A killing cut   that could have

Damned that dragon   down to death,

But the blade broke,   split, was sundered,

And Beowulf began   his first fight against fate

As well as foe.   The brutal blow and the

Broken blade bid   the beast to battle.

Enraged, wrathful red   fire filled its chest

And flowed forth,   surging at that soldier's shield

Heating it so hellish hot   that metal melted,

Bent and buckled,   while Beowulf burned,

Wretched and writhing   in red-glowing mail.

Here, the Thane of Glamis endured a prolonged coughing fit. After he finished, Heather said, "And where is this Wiglaf? You haven't even mentioned his name."

"Patience, my dear," Alanbart responded. "Beowulf's shield melted, his sword broke, biting flames surrounded him, and he bellowed with rage and pain. The old king was defeated and dying, and he *knew* it. And what's more, anyone who heard his scream *knew* it as well; yet, Beowulf chose to fight on, even to his inevitable end. But his men—twelve hand-picked soldiers—ran for their lives and hid in the woods, all except for one, and his name was Wiglaf. As the poet says:

Their leader losing,   life leaving that lord of men,
His comrades cowered,   fled to the forest,
Earned eternal shame,   but a single soldier
Stood strong and silent,   weighed down with worry

Drowning in doubts,   fearing fire and fate,
But remembering kindness,   kinship, kingship, and rightness.
Wiglaf wouldn't wait   to wade into warfare.
He unslung his yellow   pine-wood shield,
Unsheathed his sire's sword,   and fared forth into the fray.
Never had he known   the clashing of combat,
But courage coursed   through his stout soul
And the serpent was stung   by his strong steel.

"Wait," Heather interrupted again, "so, Beowulf faces the dragon alone, to save his people, a *king* who is too old to win, realizes that he's dying, and fights on, and this Wiglaf is the braver?"

Alanbart smiled. "Allow me to finish, my lady."

She settled back against the wall, skepticism audible in her sigh.

"Wiglaf," Alanbart continued, "charged down that path, into the fire. He discarded his burning shield and crouched behind Beowulf's melting iron. Then he rose up and lunged. His sword bit deep into the dragon's chest, puncturing what might be termed its 'fire bladder'—the vital organ that was the source of the creature's burning breath. The inferno blew out in a spout from the dragon's wound, shearing the flesh from Wiglaf's hand, which was ever-after utterly useless, and when the dragon turned to attack the young warrior, Beowulf leapt out, dagger ready, and slit it down the middle—"

"All right, now I have a different problem," Heather cut in. "Beowulf broke his sword on this dragon and now he cuts it in *half* with a *dagger*? I'm not—no—it just doesn't make sense."

Sinel came to Alanbart's rescue this time. "Actually, woman, it does make sense. Obviously you've never gone hunting. No one guts a deer with a sword. It doesn't work. Gutting is knife-work."

"Uncourteously said, but correct," Arthur agreed. "The center—the power—of a dagger is near the handle, my lady," he politely explained. "On a sword it is halfway down the blade, or sometimes even near the tip. Especially with a man of uncommon strength, like Beowulf, the dagger would be a much better close-quarters weapon, and ideal, as the thane says, for gutting an enemy.

Please proceed with your tale, Sir Alanbart."

Alanbart removed his tongue from the empty tooth socket and spat. His mouth wasn't bleeding much anymore. He continued, "So it was that two kinsmen killed the dragon—a primeval spirit of pagan fire. Of course, Beowulf died from his wounds, but Wiglaf lived to lead his people's brief doomed resistance to the swift Swedish invasion." He sighed. The room fell silent, but for a slight clink of Sinel's chains.

"And I suppose that now you'll explain to me," Heather said, "why this Wiglaf is so much braver than any other person who comes to the aid of his—or *her*—king in a seemingly hopeless situation?"

"Because," Alanbart replied, "in that fight, Wiglaf was a boy— untested in combat. His weapons and armor were new to his hands. He had no weight of expectation on his shoulders. In fact, all of the 'great' warriors fled around him, leaving him to make his decision alone. He, too, could have run and no one would have faulted him. He had an excuse beyond reproach. The greatest warrior anyone had ever known—Beowulf, slayer of Grendel, champion of a thousand combats—was dying before his eyes. What could *he*—a mere boy in ill-fitting armor with a yellow wooden shield that was little better than a torch against dragon-fire—what could *he* hope to accomplish?

"Still more, Beowulf was super-human. He had the strength of thirty men and by his own admission had never faced fear. There stood Wiglaf, youngest, weakest, most inexperienced and ill-equipped of the old king's followers, terrified, and perfectly *normal* in every way, facing a dragon. And he *alone* had the courage to help his lord. Together they defeated that dragon. Because of that he represents true heroism."

An odd passion that Heather never heard before filled his voice, something high, noble, and incongruous with what she'd seen of him in the past. She said nothing in response, but this new facet of Alanbart's personality captured her interest.

"I must say," Arthur began, clapping three times in approval, "You have more than convinced me of young Wiglaf's place among heroes. It is interesting, though, to consider the men you chose. One can tell a great deal about a man by his choice of heroes. You picked six: Leonidas and Beowulf died for their people; Roland and Beorhtnoth died for pride, and Hector and Wiglaf fought for their families. You value family above all else, it seems. Why?"

"Perhaps because I never really had one," Alanbart answered.

"Though as for people and pride, I've never had those either." He smiled to himself. "Maybe we all value most what we don't have or couldn't accomplish, and so we imagine it to be perfect for those who have it. I recently missed a chance to die in combat—it weighs on my mind."

Heather felt a bitter mix of contempt, pity, and righteous anger at his words, and even though she could barely discern his outline in the gloom, she looked away, setting her jaw in defiance. Arthur, beside her, closed his eyes and nodded into the darkness in Alanbart's direction. After a pause he asked with artificial cheer, "What about you, Glamis? Do you have a favorite hero?"

"Aye, of course I do," the thane bit back. "But he is not like this 'Wiglaf,' and he hasn't died yet. Thor—Thor the thunderous is stronger than any man, giant, or god. He can boast better, drink deeper, love longer, hit harder, and shite stronger—" Here Arthur cleared his throat disapprovingly, but Sinel ignored it. "—than any mere *man*, living or dead, and he is the father of my line, dating to the earliest beginnings of the world. To choose another would be blasphemy."

"And he too," Arthur acknowledged, "according to legend, will die one day in a battle that he cannot win. Fighting, I believe, Jörmungand, the world-serpent, during the battle of Ragnarök. Yes, Sir Alanbart, maybe you've made a great discovery here. It may be that self-sacrificial death is a prerequisite to eternal heroism. I should give a thought to my death—perhaps I, too, should die in combat." He paused, then asked of Heather, "What of you, my dear lady? Who is your ideal hero?"

"I will honor you, my liege, by selecting one of your knights," she said, "though not a dead one, so it may muddle this theory that you've been debating." She sighed. "When Sir Gawain—"

"Of course, you would pick *him*," Alanbart grumbled.

Heather ignored him. "When *Sir* Gawain," she repeated, "an untried youth, took up the Green Knight's game to save your life, he earned my admiration and," she paused, struggling for a word, "*respect*, and when he held true to his word and bowed down to receive the axe stroke that would surely decapitate him—not once, but three times— he proved that he possessed courage that was a match for the bravest in the world. And when he resisted the charms of Lady Bercilak (who was said to be more beautiful than Guinevere) on three successive winter mornings, he showed his strength of will. Those feats alone would rank him among the greatest heroes of legend, but you have seen his other adventures with your own eyes and heard them sung in your own hall. I do not need to sing his praise to you."

"What about the story, in frequent circulation, that he cut the head from a helpless woman?" Alanbart asked.

"It is too true, and was a sad accident, though almost entirely her fault, and he made amends for it. He punished himself far more severely than anyone ever could punish him, just like he did for taking the belt from Bercilak's wife." She ran the green belt through her fingers, then turned back to Alanbart through the darkness. "Like your Wiglaf, Gawain is human—flawed as we all are, perhaps more deeply flawed because of his unyielding nature—and yet, he struggles and strives, and succeeds, despite those flaws."

Heather rose and began pacing the length of their cell. "I think that as a woman it is hard to admire a man unless he has obvious defects. Perhaps it is more important for us to pick a man with flaws that we can respect and accept than it is to pick a man with attributes we admire."

Aware that a silence had descended on the room, Heather paced another lap, then added, "But before I turn this heroic discussion too feminine, I should end it by asking you, King Arthur, who you believe is the greatest hero of legend or song."

"Well," Arthur began "we have seen heroes who fight for family, for their people, for pride, and we know that Gawain fights for an idea—and maybe fighting for an idea is more pure somehow—but as far as I am concerned, the greatest hero never even swung a sword. If He died in battle, it was in battle with the weakness of His own human form. Of course I speak of Jesus, the Christ, Servant of servants and King of kings. And, interestingly, he is another man who sacrificed his life for a greater good. How could I choose anyone else?"

He cleared his throat and continued: "But, as you can see plainly from my politic choice, I am once again carefully selecting my words and assessing outcomes. The weight of rule has returned unbidden, and so the door to my mind must swing closed. I have enjoyed our conversation more than you know—you have given me much to think about, and now—"

The trap door opened, and backlit by firelight, two silhouettes appeared over the pit. "All right, you down there—all but you, *great* Glamis—come on up. Rabordath has need of you!"

22

HAWKFEATHER FOREST

"This is a pleasant forest, compared to that Gloamwood,"
Gawain noted as he and Scot walked under the rustling maple and oak
foliage.

The ground was covered in a litter of leaves, peppered with
moss and lichen-splotched rocks and boulders, and full of soft bracken
that swayed in the afternoon breeze. Rays of sunlight poking through
the canopy danced in the movement of bough and bush. The air
smelled pleasantly of fern fronds and leaf decay. A brook burbled
nearby, south along the slope of the ground, just loud enough to be
audible. The two warriors led their horses and directed the force of
goblins within the edge of the forest.

"I agree," Scot replied. "It reminds me of the fair forest behind
my family's farmhouse. When we were boys, my brothers and I built
log castles and defended them with quarterstaffs and clubs. I say my
brothers and I built them, but both were much older than I, so they
always did the thinking and building, and they also badly beat me at any
games of craft or combat."

They paused and goblins passed beside them, yapping and
grumbling in doglike voices.

"I, too, had brothers," Gawain said, ignoring the noisy
creatures as best he could, "three of them, and now all are dead. It
seems appropriate to me that you mention times long past though," he
added, reaching out and stripping the leaflets off of a fern frond with
his calloused hand. "I find my mind returning to the long past more
and more often as I age. Moments that I thought nothing of as they
passed are now some of the most visited landscapes in my memory."

Scot nodded then stared forward, ignoring the muted yapping
of goblin conversation and focusing on the knight's words.

"I was always closest to Gareth," Gawain said, "which is odd considering that I am the eldest and he the youngest." He turned, checked the progress of the goblin hoard. "Do you mind a tale?"

"Please," Scot replied.

"Well," Gawain continued, "one day the two of us—Gareth and I, he was nine and I, fifteen—sneaked away from training and from chores and rode across the rocky hills to a lake that lay on my father's land. This was an odd sort of lake, ancient, rocky-bottomed, very deep for its narrowness, and ice-cold. They used to tell tales of water spirits and ancient creatures living in its depths, but they didn't concern us—we were young and immortal, and death had not yet enjoyed any bite. We took an abandoned boat that some local peasants used and spent that warm May afternoon on the water. The boat had poorly splinted oars and a slow leak in the caulking, yet these flaws somehow heightened the perfection of the day.

"Gareth and I talked little, but I remember sleeping in the sunshine, the boat bobbing in the blue water under the blue sky, a loon calling from the east, and a burbling bittern wading the reedy shallows on stilt-like legs. When I closed my eyes, I saw orange from sunshine on my lids and a light breeze wafted from time to time, barely a breath on my cheeks.

"On that day, perhaps more than any other of my life," Gawain continued, "I felt perfectly content with the world and my place in it, and I am certain that Gareth did too. Perhaps it was this mutual understanding and the need to say or do nothing, but that moment is branded upon my memory. And what is it weighed against the grandeur of my life? I assure you it is nothing compared to the highs and lows that I've experienced through action and loss, and it was nothing to me while I was living it, and even afterward, when we were being whipped for shirking our chores, it had little value. But now I wouldn't trade it for any opportunity or treasure." He shook his head.

Unfortunately, the poignancy of the moment was destroyed by coarse guttural laughter as a group of five gray-skinned goblins tromped past them. The goblins, overcome with mirth, gasped and guffawed in hyena-like fashion, tears streaming from their black eyes. One, unable to stand, leaned to the side and braced himself against the flank of Gringolet. The horse whinnied and shied away toward Taffy. Gawain advanced on the goblin and pulled his sword an inch from its scabbard.

"Get back, there, or by-God, I'll run you through!" He whispered through clenched teeth.

The goblin paused, looked at Gawain, and burst out in another peal of laughter, staggering away in the process.

The monsters were, in fact, reacting to a particularly hilarious joke. Goblin humor is not, as a rule, funny to (or appropriate for) humans, and certainly their jokes don't translate well from Goblin to English, but nonetheless I will make the attempt.

As they walked, the goblins amused themselves with various familiar jokes—usually involving rape, feces, incest, sodomy, or all four. Because they already knew the punch lines, these didn't do much more than set the mood, but as it turned out, one of the largest and most vulgar goblins had been holding his latest comic invention back.

"Explain to me," he said, sensing the opportune moment to unleash his creation, "the difference between a cartload of quarry-stone, and a cartload of human infants."

"Uh," his fellow stammered, trying to think of a proper response. "The stones don't stink?"

"No, idiot," another cut in, "it's that the stones aren't delicious."

"I know, I know!" a third—smaller than the rest—yipped. "You can't sodomize the stones!"

An outburst of laugher rolled through the group.

"Well, you can, but it *hurts,*" the second added with an obscene gesture.

"You can't, imbecile," the third retorted. "Stones don't have a front or back."

"You're all half-wits," the original teller said. His smile widened and his eyes filled with satanic mirth. "The difference, fools, between a cartload of quarry-stone and a cartload of human babies is simply this: you *cannot* unload the quarry-stone with . . . a pitchfork!"

After that, the goblins couldn't regain their composure for nearly five minutes[20].

In any case, neither Gawain nor Scot could understand Goblin, so their 'joke' passed unnoticed. The two warriors watched with distaste as the group of monsters passed on into the forest, then resumed their walk, footfalls in step with each other.

"My brothers," Scot continued the previous conversation, "too, are dead. They were killed in combat, fighting for their clan against one of your king's Lords of the Northern Marches. My father, who was a freeman land owner, died with them at the same battle. The soldiers came soon after. They beat me until I was no longer conscious, then they . . . killed my mother and burned the farm. I awoke alone."

Gawain looked blankly at Scot and could think of nothing to say. Year-old leaves crunched under their feet.

"Oh," Scot added, "we were in rebellion against your king's 'righteous' rule, and so you'd say that we deserved death, but I was a twelve-year old boy with a dead family and a burned farm. If it wasn't for a crippled clansman named Courtney, I probably would have perished that winter. He lived through the slaughter of that battle, but had an arrow through the meat of his calf and was missing three fingers on one hand. He hobbled to the farm, where I cared for him and he for me. Together we rebuilt the house, farmed the fields, and found a reason for living. He taught me to fight—he was a surpassingly strong swordsman. We went on that way for five winters, until Courtney fell into a fever and died. I gave the farm to my cousin and walked away— nothing remained to tie me to the place."

"Believe me or not—that is up to you—but I am sorry for you," Gawain replied. "I rarely hate my enemies. More often I pity

---

20 Now, if you just laughed at that vile and disturbing exchange, you may be feeling sudden guilt. Don't. I, myself, laughed at that joke the first time that I had the misfortune of hearing it, and I spent an evening in disquietude, wondering if I was evil because of it. I am not any more evil than you are. You see, laughter is a natural defense when something is impossible to rationalize, conceptualize, or accept, and a whole branch of humor is based on that unavoidable human response—shock and laughter are linked. That said, though, I think that we all have a little goblin in us, for most jokes, humor, and laughter come at the expense of someone—the man who accidentally sets his clothes on fire, drinks spoiled milk, or says something inexcusable to his wife, for example—and we laugh in the relief that it hasn't (yet) happened to us.

them. And though I believe in and try with all my might to uphold the code of chivalry myself, I have no illusions about what happens with men after a battle—even if I myself never partake in it."

"I didn't intend to tell you the tale, and am certainly not seeking your sympathy, but what you said made me yearn for my youth," Scot said. "That time is as gone as my brothers are, and neither it nor they will ever return. It doesn't do to dwell on it though, because it makes me long for a feeling of family that no longer exists."

"That's the tragedy of memory," Gawain said with a sigh. "Sometimes I wish that I was born as a bird or a mouse. How long, do you think, do small creatures remember, and what do they know of life and death, honor and dishonor? That squirrel there, for example," he gestured to a small gray leaping fearlessly from the branch of one tree to another, over the heads of a line of marching goblins, "do you think it knows that it will die or feels one pang of sorrow for the death of its neighbors? If its nest-tree fell in a storm or was consumed by fire, how much grief would it spend on the occurrence?"

"Perhaps we should take a lesson," Scot said.

"Perhaps we should," Gawain agreed. "Speaking of forgetting the past, though, how are your wounds feeling? I've never felt an injury heal more swiftly than the one on my arm."

"Now that you mention it," Scot said, "I don't feel injured at all. Hold up." They stopped and Scot removed his helmet, pulled his chainmail hauberk over his head, and took off his shirt. He unwound the bloody linen strips from around his chest. They both stared incredulously at his perfectly healed and scar-free skin.

"Heavenly Father!" Gawain exclaimed.

"It's as if I wasn't slashed," Scot said, running his fingers where the wound used to be. "Are these magic?" He lifted the cloth strips and inspected them with wonder.

"Were those, then, real artifacts in that chest?" Gawain asked, "Or is this a miracle made to help us rescue the king?"

"All I know is that you'd have done better to bandage your face," Scot quipped, gently touching the long line of crusted blood on Gawain's cheek.

"So I should have," Gawain agreed, brushing Scot's hand away and feeling the tender wound on his cheek for himself. "But then the

Bible and the bones? And the . . ." his eyes widened.

"The cup!" Scot laughed out loud. "You flung it into the fen."

"Once my king is rescued and my vows are fulfilled, I must go back," Gawain said. "It couldn't possibly be the Grail—I'm not worthy of such a quest—but it must have been something of import."

"Why not?" Scot asked. "We have Hrunting and Mimung, the ring and the staff, and now wrappings that heal wounds as if they hardly happened. What else might not have been on that island?"

Gawain removed his helmet.

"Here, help me off with this cuirass. I'd like to check on my wounds as well. Besides, we're far enough into the woods now. We'll let Cathbad catch up and travel with him to the point of attack."

23

LATE AFTERNOON, THE DEVIL'S ROOKERY

.The guard prodded Heather, Arthur, and Alanbart up the staircase, a cramped well of stone that spiraled up the northwest edge of the tower. A large tree-trunk pole with iron fasteners rested in the middle of the stairwell and heavy pine-wood steps rose in clockwise circles around it. The passage wound so tightly that they had to move in single file, and Arthur, the tallest and broadest of them, had to duck, twist his body, and lead with his shoulder.

"Getting down these was the most terrifying part of my escape," Heather said from behind Alanbart as they climbed.

"No talking." the guard directed, and thumped her with the butt-end of a torch that provided the only light in the enclosed space. They proceeded in silence until they reached the fourth floor, where a second guard barred their assent and redirected them to spill out of a small archway into an open semi-circular chamber.

It had a low wooden ceiling of about six and a half feet and was dominated by a long table, strewn with papers, books, and burned out candles protruding clumsily from wax-dribbled earthenware bottles. The table was cut to fit into the rounded wall under the single small window. A large wicker and willow birdcage hung from the ceiling beside the table, the inmate of which was a regal-looking kestrel. He shuffled on his perch and bent his head to preen his feathers.

In the center of the room within a raised circle of stone, heaped-up coals smoked. Over them, hanging from an iron framework, rested a copper cauldron, four feet across the mouth. A round hole in the wooden ceiling revealed blue sky above and allowed smoke to escape in a fragrant billow. The full moon peeked into the room through the opening, visible in broad daylight. The coals emitted so much heat that the change in temperature was noticeable and uncomfortable.

Two figures stood at the table, one short in stature and wearing crimson robes, and the other tall and thin, draped in a royal blue cloak. They turned as the prisoners entered the room. Both glistened with sweat.

The tall figure was, of course, Malestair. He smirked with characteristic cruelty at the prisoners, but he didn't draw their glances. The shorter man demanded their rapt attention.

He had a high forehead and a long nose. No hair grew from his face, save his reddish eyebrows, and he was clean-shaven down to his jaw line. He held a crooked staff topped by an iron sphere, but none of them even noted those details, because their eyes were affixed to his hair and beard, which were composed impossibly of blazing flame.

The man's entire skull seemed wreathed in a lion's mane of red-orange fire. The style of his beard, perhaps, had something to do with this effect. It would probably be more properly termed a 'neard' because it grew from under his jaw and on his neck, rather than from his cheeks and chin. In any case, he was Rabordath, and he looked like a demon straight out of hell. The prisoners were suitably impressed.

Malestair stepped forward and confronted the guard who'd brought them up.

"Why did you bring *him*?" he gestured to Alanbart.

"My lord, the wizard said to bring up the prisoners, except for Glamis."

"I did," Rabordath admitted. "I was unaware that you had another *guest* downstairs, but it makes no matter. I might enjoy an audience and the dragon may be hungry after it is conjured."

"Very well," Malestair said, then gestured to the flat stone wall that that spanned the diameter of the tower. "Tie them there," he ordered.

The guard prodded Alanbart and Heather along the wall, through the center of which passed a low arched doorway. An oaken door, ajar, revealed an armory beyond. A horizontal spear rack and shield stand could be seen inside.

The stone wall that divided Rabordath's study from the keep's armory sported four large iron rings, two on either side of the doorway. The guards affixed each of the prisoners to the wall by untying their leather bonds, running them through a ring, and binding them tighter than before. Alanbart and Heather were lashed to the wall on the south side of the archway, farthest from the stairs. They tied Arthur apart from the others, on the stair side.

For the first time, Alanbart had a chance to inspect the legendary king in daylight. He was a tall and broad man, old, but unbent by his years. He had kind blue eyes under thick eyebrows in a weathered face. His wavy white hair still showed tints and highlights of pale flaxen yellow and had not yet receded from his head. He wore it at shoulder length. His curling white-blonde beard fell to midway down his chest, where he'd cropped it straight across. A combination of exhaustion and resolve showed in the king's expression. He set his jaw and turned his face toward Malestair.

"Now," Malestair began once they'd all been tied in place, "shall we commence the summoning?" He avoided Arthur's gaze by picking up and examining a stray kestrel feather.

"Indeed," Rabordath agreed, obviously excited. "It should take about a third of an hour to complete. I have all of the ingredients ready, save two."

"Proceed, then," Malestair commanded, discarding the feather. He plowed some papers aside to sit upon the tabletop, crossing his legs.

Rabordath cracked a knuckle with contained annoyance, his eyes upon the scattered papers on his workbench. "Are you going to watch the whole conjuration, my lord?" he asked uneasily.

"Why not?" Malestair fingered his moustache. "I wouldn't miss it. An event like this is a once in a lifetime occurrence."

"Wait!" Heather exclaimed. "How can you complete the ceremony *now*? I thought you had to wait for the night of the blue moon."

"Look at the sky," Rabordath replied with an offhand gesture. "The blue moon is up and visible through the smoke-hole. We can begin the ceremony whenever we like—surely you don't think that the moon only shines upon us at night?"

"Hold," Malestair held up a hand. His brown eyes narrowed at Heather. "How do you know about the ceremony?"

"I…" she faltered, realizing her misstep. "I was hiding under your bed when you talked of it to Rabordath." She figured that the truth couldn't hurt now.

"You mean to say, that when we were all searching for you, you were under the bed in my chamber?" He glowered at her in anger, but after a long second he laughed—artificially—until he shook. "You are a still smarter and braver woman than I gave you credit for, and you already owned considerable credit in the court of my opinion. I won't make that mistake again."

"She makes you look like a fool," Alanbart interjected. Malestair discarded his mirth instantly, and Alanbart—as he so often did—regretted the statement. "Hell, she makes me look like a fool… my lord," he added weakly, searching unsuccessfully for a way to retract his comment, "which, admittedly, isn't hard to do, because, obviously, I am one," he trailed off.

Malestair yanked an iron poker from the wall and shoved it into the coals. He looked Alanbart in the eyes for a silent three seconds, and then returned to the table. He then addressed Heather, opening his long arms in an inclusive gesture that swept the room. "Who have you told about this?"

"I told Sir Alanbart here," she said, "and Cathbad the druid. Alanbart was going to ride south to get word to Camelot, but he was *captured* by your man." She emphasized the word with a tone of bitter disappointment.

Alanbart lowered his head in mock embarrassment.

"And Cathbad laughed in my face when I asked for his aid and said that he hoped your dragon would kill King Arthur and burn down all the churches of the South."

"Is that so?" Malestair asked, then lowered his voice with suspicion. "Yet, you thought we couldn't perform the ceremony until tonight, and you seemed upset and unnerved by the realization that we would complete it now. You've outwitted me once. Never again. I think that I'll double the guard. A druid—even a powerful one—is only one man, but we can't be too careful." He turned to the wizard. "We've already waited long enough, though. Rabordath, proceed with the summoning."

"Well," Rabordath began in his nasal voice, running his fingers through the flames atop his head, "my lord, first I will need to momentarily borrow your sword. We must, after all, take the king's blood with his own blade."

Malestair drew Excalibur from a battered black leather sheath. The room became brighter as the adamantine blade reflected and multiplied both the sunlight from the window and the torchlight from the walls. Rabordath took the sword and picked up a mid-sized silver goblet, banded in bright gold and set with amethysts. He walked over to the king and hesitated under Arthur's unflinching gaze, fidgeting with Excalibur's bejeweled hilt.

"Your highness," Rabordath began. "I require a cup of your blood."

"Oh, just dispense with the formalities and *cut* him," Malestair urged from the table. His hands curled around the wood in anticipation.

"Yes, my lord," Rabordath replied. He looked up at Arthur, who did not alter his stony gaze. A guard unbound the king from the wall. "I apologize for the necessity," Rabordath continued, "but I have decided that it would be most effective and least affecting to you to remove your left little finger at the topmost joint. Please hold your hand wide open. I wouldn't want to maim you."

Arthur did as he was told.

Rabordath raised Excalibur and brought the flashing blade down swiftly on the finger, which he sliced off with the ease that a sharp knife cuts the end off of a perfectly cooked and plump sausage. The fingertip fell uselessly to the floor, but Arthur made neither sound nor motion. The wound bled profusely and Rabordath caught the dark dripping blood in the shining silver goblet. However, the wizard, obviously nervous, talked effusively as the blood dripped: "You'll note that the cup in which I am collecting this blood reflects the nature of the man from whom the blood is taken. A king deserves a jeweled goblet, and such a receptacle I have prepared. The amethysts even show the purple of royalty and empire.

"Now," he continued when Arthur didn't comment, "many fools believe that magic is brought about through words, and many an amateur wizard would be chanting foolish nonsense at a moment such as this. Indeed, even the tome from which I work is filled with nonsensical drivel designed to mislead fools and confuse natural philosophy with religion."

He paused; Arthur remained silent. "The truth is that magic is mostly mathematics—that and deep understanding of the natural philosophy of the world. In the present case, this conjuration has everything to do with comprehending and being able to manipulate the four humors, the four elements, the four planes of existence, the annual cycle of the moon, the two genders, the alchemical formulas of Avicenna and Magnus, the astrological progressions of Jupiter, Venus, the sun and moon, and the latent powers within the blood of both royalty and virginity."

Again, he paused. Arthur still ignored him, but Malestair seemed quite interested, so the wizard continued, sycophantically directing his discourse at his master. "In the present case, there is a coalescence of many of these forces and numerals around an astrological event that opens a gateway to the plane of fire and . . ."

As he prattled on, Alanbart turned his head to Heather and whispered, "I'm sorry."

"For what?" she asked, keeping her eyes on Arthur and her words hushed.

"For abandoning you to this," he replied.

"You're here now." Her almond eyes found his. "And don't pretend that I'm some foolish lady who needs to be rescued. Had you resisted Malestair, you'd be dead and I'd be right here without you. True, I might have appreciated the show of bravado—until you died— and then I would have felt guilt for the rest of my life, knowing that you'd died for me. I realized almost immediately that you did what had to be done—the clever thing. You are clever, Alanbart; it is your chief characteristic and best trait. Unchecked bravery may be admirable in a man like Lancelot or Gawain, but it can be wasteful as well. No, I wouldn't see you change the past, even if you could. Don't be sorry. In any case," she dropped her voice even lower "just as Gawain saved you at the henge, he will save us here. Have faith in *him* and all will be right in the end."

"You worship him like a religion," Alanbart said. He shook the ring to which he was bound, testing its strength. It was strong. "You still love him, don't you?" he asked, but it wasn't really a question.

"Of course I do," she responded, "but it's doomed. He is idealistic, so he's easy to fall in love with, easy to forgive, and hard to get over, but the problem with idealistic men is that they're righteous and judgmental. This would be unpardonable in a man who didn't hold himself to the standards that he claims to believe in, but our knight does hold himself to his standards—in fact, he holds himself to far higher standards than he expects out of most other people. He sees the world with a moral code that registers only good and evil, and I've found that in his judgments and decisions he's mostly correct."

"Is here and now the time and place to be having this discussion?" Alanbart asked, feeling sickeningly hopeless sorrow rise up from his stomach.

"No, it isn't," Heather admitted, but we're not likely to get another and I'd rather not focus on what is happening to our king."

She glanced at Arthur, winced, and then returned to Alanbart. "The problem with a man like Sir Gawain," she continued in a low whisper, "and love is that he holds his lover to the same unattainable standard to which he holds himself. If either she or he fails to live up to his expectations, then the relationship fails as well. In this case, it is not I who is failing Gawain; it is he who is failing himself. It is, of course, a personal matter that I won't get into now, but it's for the best because I certainly would fail him sooner or later, given enough time."

She looked back at Rabordath who'd now embarked upon a detailed explanation of the means by which he calculated the lunar calendar, and then returned to her subject. "Alanbart, Gawain doesn't love me for who I am. He loves me as an extension of himself. He sees me as an ideal version of what a woman should be. He doesn't really know *me*, and has simply filled in what he doesn't know with creative assumptions and wishful thinking that is drawn out of *himself*. It is partially my own fault that he does this because, when I met him, I set about becoming the perfect woman to attract him. I wanted his love, and I would have become anyone to get it. Ironically, he probably sees me as a far better person than himself because of it, and no doubt he would be crushed to find out that I am not better—"

Alanbart opened his mouth to disagree, but she shook her head: "—no, you don't need to join in the conversation. Just let me talk. It's good for me. At my age," she said, "I fully realize that all men and women who are in love lie to themselves to one degree or another. Love, I've found, whitewashes its object. Any blemishes, crevices, or cracks are filled with pure and bright illusion, the root of which is vanity. Only over time does this brightness wear off."

Alanbart studied the masonry of the wall. It's dark, grainy granite stones bore marks of the chisel. He imagined how they were lifted to this height, by serfs up the staircase, or by rope and pulley system, he wondered.

"I, myself," Heather continued, "am guilty as well. I first fell for Gawain because of the challenge. He was unattainable. I liked that. I thought it was because he hadn't met the right woman, and I set about the task of becoming that woman with great energy and determination. I almost succeeded, except that my ultimate success was my ultimate failure. I tarnished his self-image and so he retreated from me, seeing himself as unworthy of the ideal woman he believed me to be."

By this point, Rabordath had moved on to the theory of astrology in Magnus' *Speculum Astronomiae*. He expressed his understanding that the positions of the planets, stars, and moon have a primary effect on the physical (rather than spiritual) world through the strengthening and weakening of the connections between planes of existence, central elements, and bodily humors. Interestingly, he noted, not only was that very day the blue moon, but it was also the day that the moon would come closest to Earth on that particular year—an event that occurs once every five centuries.

Arthur's blood nearly filled the tall goblet.

Heather continued to ignore the scene as best she could and distracted herself by helping Alanbart understand her ideas on love. "As you can see, the whitewash with which I covered Sir Gawain is starting to chip and crack." She shook her head. "But don't think that I'm out of love with him or that I'll ever truly be so. A woman cannot ever stop caring for a *good* man whom she has loved, as long as he still cares for her and remains good."

"Why," Alanbart asked, though the words caught briefly in his throat, "do you suppose that is the case?"

"A woman loves a man for his mind and for his soul. She may be attracted to him for other reasons—physical, financial, or practical—but that is why she loves (if she loves), and discovering those two things is what a relationship is for her. I'm not in a position to say with certainty why a man loves a woman, seeing how I'm not one."

"Nor am I," Alanbart added, "since I never have."

"That should be enough," Rabordath said, realizing suddenly that he'd collected far more blood than he needed. "My lord," he turned to Malestair, "would you be willing to...?"

"With pleasure," Malestair replied. He walked to the fire and removed the iron poker, which now glowed red. He took the long way around the room, passing by Alanbart. As he did so, he ran the poker across Alanbart's upper thigh. His brown breeches burned away in a wide gash, and he hollered in pain, tears welling in his eyes.

Malestair brandished the poker before Arthur's grim face, and said, "This will hurt."

He grabbed the king's left hand and pushed the poker against the bleeding stub of his finger. Arthur groaned through clenched teeth, but remained conscious. The smell of burning flesh wafted about the room. The guard then reaffixed the king to the iron ring on the wall.

In the interim, Rabordath set the blood-filled goblet on the table and turned back to Malestair. "Your sword, my lord," he offered Excalibur. Malestair returned the poker to the coals and sheathed the king's blade.

"And now," Malestair said, "I must go see to my walls. Do not finish the summoning without me. I shall return shortly." He ducked through the archway into the spiral stair.

Rabordath took up a second cup, this one made of thin white porcelain without blemish or adornment. He then fished among the litter of papers, books, and bottles on the table until his hand found a knife. He walked over to the prisoners and held the two objects up for their inspection. The knife glimmered, formed of one large piece of metal, blade, hilt, and all. The cutting edge gleamed thin and sharp.

"A silver knife that has never tasted blood," Rabordath said, "and a porcelain cup of purest white in which to catch the blood of a virgin. The significance of these objects can hardly be lost on you. The knife itself is virginal—never before completing the task for which it was designed, and the cup is pure, perfect, and fragile—just like a maiden before she is broken..."

He moved close to Heather.

"My lady," he said, "I must now collect your blood. As with your king, I shall remove the tip of your little finger. It will cause the least long-term damage. However sharp my knife may be, inevitably

213

this cut will be harder to make and will hurt more than the last. A knife lacks the heft of a sword, and silver is not steel."

He paused, awaiting any response.

Heather nodded, seeing no way out.

Alanbart tensed. He considered trying the magic words to ignite his bonds. 'And then what?' he thought. Two armed guards were in the room and he had no weapon. In a best-case scenario he might take Rabordath's knife and kill him with it, scramble to the armory to get a spear and shield. 'And then? Then the guards will threaten to kill Arthur and Heather if I don't surrender,' he thought. 'Checkmate.' No, he couldn't act yet—he needed to wait for the attack, for a distraction that would give him some hope of success.

A guard unbound Heather, clasped her wrist, and held out her arm. Heather opened her fingers wide. Rabordath set down the porcelain cup and went to work. Alanbart turned away, fixing his eyes on the willow cage by the table and mentally mapping every detail of the kestrel's plumage.

The bird had an eye like a tiny polished onyx bead. Yellow skin surrounded the eye and it sat in a fine dusty-gray colored head. The feathers on its back were a shimmering auburn, spotted with dark brown diamonds, bordered in white, and its tail was a brown-tipped gray. It was a beautiful creature. As he watched, it fluttered its wings, adjusted its position on its perch, and twisted its head to prune its back.

In truth, I have often noted that we focus on unimportant details when we're trying to avoid a reckoning with reality, and Alanbart now did just that. His ears heard Heather's strangled gasps and Rabordath's grunts as he completed his task with difficulty. Certainly it was a botched job, and much more painful for the botching. However, Rabordath did manage the cut and began to collect her blood in the pristine white cup.

Alanbart shifted his gaze from the bird to the wizard's flaming face, avoiding Heather's eyes, and said, "Even if this spell works, how are you going to control a dragon?"

Rabordath shrugged in response. "It might be that I won't be able to control it at all. The spell doesn't say any more than that it will conjure a dragon."

"Well then, isn't this ludicrously dangerous?"

"Of course it is," Rabordath answered with impatience, "but to *see* a dragon with my own eyes, and more, to be responsible for the conjuration of such a glorious and legendary beast, is too great an opportunity to pass up. When was the last dragon seen in Britannia? The one killed by St. George? What if that was the *last* one in Europe? Even if the conjuration does end badly and the dragon kills me or all of us, it would still be a legacy worth having. I would be a wizard worthy of fame. But if we can control the dragon, teach him, or maybe *ride* him… think of it!" He paused, his eyes focused on the smoke-hole.

"You, I suppose," Alanbart said, "are imagining riding a giant winged beast, shooting lightning bolts from your hands as it emits torrents of flame from its mouth. You'd burn everyone who stood in your way and control the island. I congratulate you on your grand, albeit misguided, imagination."

"No," Rabordath said, bending to pick up fallen parchments and put right the mess that Malestair had made of his table. "I have no desire for power. I only desire the dragon—the future beyond today, if I am successful, is immaterial. Conjuring such a beast is all the fame and power that I hope to achieve. Tomorrow I shall be content to die."

Heather, who had been biting her lower lip, asked in a faint voice, "Don't you have enough of my blood yet?"

Rabordath cleared his throat. "Close to enough, my lady, just another five or six drops." He walked back to her began counting, "Four, five, six. There." He placed the cup on the floor and drew the poker from the fire. It was unwieldy and he held it badly. "This is going burn terribly. You may scream or go unconscious."

He moved close to her and pressed the scalding metal against her wound, holding her hand fast in his. She did scream. She thrashed about, freeing herself prematurely, and Rabordath had to cauterize it a second time.

To avoid watching her torture, Alanbart met Arthur's murderous expression. The king plainly wanted swift and bloody vengeance.

Rabordath tossed the poker aside, retrieved the cup of Heather's blood, and carefully aligned an assortment of bottles, oils, feathers, and other oddments in the empty area of his workbench.

"Reaffix her bonds," he commanded, scanning a mold-stained

parchment.

Alanbart turned to Heather as the guard bound her hands through the ring. "Are you all right, my lady," he asked, using the phrase in reference to her for the first time.

"Yes," she replied. "It might have been better, but it might have been much worse. I'll live."

"Have you given a thought to our escape from these bonds and from this room?" he asked, hoping that he might distract her from the pain with questions. "I'm having some trouble working out the finer details of my strategy."

"Nothing has come to mind," she replied with a weak smile. "My current plan is to pray. When I've done everything that I can and life looks hopeless, I always do that. I know some psalms that would be good to hear now, but it seems right to fall back on the Lord's Prayer. I've memorized it in Latin. She began slowly chanting under her breath:

Pater noster, qui es in caelis:
sanctificetur Nomen Tuum;
adveniat Regnum Tuum;

At this point, Arthur joined her, his voice deep and resonant. Hers, too, increased in volume. Rabordath stopped and turned toward them. The two guards studied the ground; one crossed himself surreptitiously.

Alanbart pretended to listen, but instead thought about how ironic it was that people who tried to be religious and curry the favor of God went immediately to the Latin version, as if it carried a magic power that their dialects lacked. The people who killed the Son of God spoke Latin, for Christ's sake. Not to mention the fact that He was God, and if He did exist, he understood *every* language. 'Besides,' he thought, 'I bet it sounds better in Hebrew. Everything is best in its original.'

Together Arthur and Heather finished the prayer:

fiat voluntas Tua,

sicut in caelo, et in terra.

Panem nostrum cotidianum da nobis hodie;

et dimitte nobis debita nostra,

sicut et nos dimittimus debitoribus nostris;

et ne nos inducas in tentationem;

sed libera nos a Malo.

After a respectful silence, Rabordath cleared his throat. "That was lovely," he half mocked them. "Thank you." He turned his flaming head back to the table. "And now, I think I am ready to begin. "You," he summoned the nearest guard, "come with me to the storeroom. I must fetch the final ingredient."

Rabordath disappeared through the entranceway.

Alanbart whispered to Heather, "As soon as the attack begins and I have an opportunity, I think that I can slip my bonds."

"How?" she asked.

He winked, "Magic. If I do escape, though, I'll try to surprise Rabordath and overpower him. He certainly is smaller and weaker than I am. If I win, I'll cut you two free. Then we'll go straight to the armory and try and fight our way downstairs. Scot and Gawain will be headed for the dungeon, so we can't count on their help."

"What about the guards?" she asked.

"Once the attack begins," I'm guessing that Malestair will lead those two down to join the defense. That will leave the odds in my favor . . . assuming that I don't have to face a dragon."

"You won't," she said; an ironic smile lit her lips.

"Why not?" he asked, but before Heather could answer, Malestair and a guard entered, hefting a large wineskin made from a whole deer hide, tanned, oiled, and expertly sewn together. Rabordath followed, the old wizard's cane clunking on the wooden stairs and then tapping on the stone floor. He turned to the guard who had been overseeing the prisoners. "Take your master's place." The guard leaned his spear against the wall and relieved Malestair at the wineskin. "Now, fill the cauldron three quarters full."

Together, the guards lifted the skin over their heads and carried it to the cauldron. They uncorked the spout, which was in one of the front legs, and let the liquid pour into the heated metal. It burst into hissing steam. They turned their heads away and continued to pour out until the steam subsided.

"Enough," Rabordath said. "Recork that skin and lay it under the table."

Alanbart's eyes watered and the hairs curled in his nose.

"Vinegar?!" he coughed. "You just poured vinegar into that scalding cauldron?"

They all coughed now, their eyes crying and noses dripping.

"I am simply following instructions," Rabordath snapped through the acrid mist. He pulled a small bellows from the wall and began to work the fire. "We must wait until it boils."

It didn't take long for the vinegar to bubble avidly, filling the room with the horrible pungent stench that comes each year at pickling time. Content with his work so far, Rabordath consulted a piece of yellowing parchment.

He read, "Start with boiling vinegar in a copper kettle, spiced with a dust of precious metals."

He took up a soft leather pouch and pulled out a small handful of glittering dust, sprinkling it into the pot. He returned to the list: "Add acid ash from thundering Etna, powdered rock from rumbling Hekla, charcoal made from Ironwood, then from a virgin pour the blood."

He shook a measure of black ash from a glass container into his hands and dumped it in. He then used a mortar and pestle to ground up a nugget of rock, and tipped these grains into the broth as well. The wizard pulled two chunks of blazing charcoal from the fire with tongs and dropped them, sizzling, into the pot, and finally took up the porcelain cup of Heather's blood and drained it in, shaking it gently to ensure he'd added the last drop . Peering over the lip of the massive kettle, Rabordath returned to his list. "Now stir it with witch-hazel wand, and add to it three red fern fronds, a salamander preserved in wine, then from an urchin, remove the spines."

He did so, stirring with his cane. "Drop in a fang pulled from a viper, add five legs from different spiders, add to it a cockatrice feather, then watch the mixture blend together."

At this, he and Malestair stood back, watching the vinegar churn and boil.

"How long do we watch?" Malestair's brow watered from the heat and stench.

"It doesn't say," Rabordath replied. "I imagine that we have watched long enough." He returned to the list. "Drop now in a sprig of heather, dug from a defile in stormy weather. Add in an
eyeball of a cat, ten small wings from ten small bats, skin of a snake and talon of an eagle, then a lord's blood to make it regal."

He followed the instructions, concluding by pouring in about half of Arthur's blood and
setting the goblet carefully down.

"Next?" Malestair asked.

"Patience, my lord," Rabordath answered. "I cannot afford to make a mistake. We'd have no idea what the consequences of an error might be." He turned the parchment over in his hands. "Let me see. Ah, yes: drop in a rock fallen from the sky and an ivory-cut six-sided die. Let it boil for three minutes, and then plunge the victim in it."

"The victim?" Alanbart asked as Rabordath dropped a shining dark stone and a white ivory cube into the cauldron.

"Oh don't worry, yet," the wizard said over his shoulder. "The idea of the spell is that the dragon will have many of the physical and instinctive characteristics of the animal sacrificed. For this I have selected a kestrel—flight, regality, trainability, killer instinct[21]. A kestrel is an ideal choice. Also, the sacrifice must be fully submerged in the liquid, so a small animal was necessary."

He crossed to the cage, opened the door, and grabbed the bird before it spread its wings. He carried it tentatively, held it above the pot, and said, "Arise, eternal dragon from the plane of fire, take this sacrifice, use its fleeting life as a gateway, and crawl forth into this world!"

He slit the bird's throat with the silver knife and dropped it,

---

[21] A delightful idea Rabordath has here, conjuring a dragon that mimics the victim in its physical form, but a foolish one. As most people now know, dragons are a unique species with specific, predictable, and unalterable physical traits and behaviors born into them. Presuming to manipulate a dragon's characteristics in this way is akin to removing the tails of two dogs, breeding them, and expecting them to bear tailless puppies. Foolishness.

with a splash, into the pot.

24

DUSK, HAWKFEATHER FOREST

"Nearly everyone that I know who has achieved power—at least, those who are not born to it—has done so through an overabundance of evil character traits," Gawain explained. "They lie, cheat, manipulate, equivocate, and sometimes even murder. King Arthur is the only ruler I have ever met who is genuinely kind, honest, and generous of nature."

He spoke in hushed but earnest tones to Scot as they crept through Hawkfeather Forest, about a hundred yards from the western edge. They could see light from the waning sun on mixed fields of dead grass, thistle, and heather beyond the forest's edge, but it was shady and cool under the branches. Cathbad and Bruuzak led the group and walked about twenty paces ahead. The goblins followed as quietly as they could. Still, a low yapping of whispered conversation, a swishing through bracken and undergrowth, the muffled clink of weapons and armor, and the frequent snap of a stick breaking underfoot could be heard. The birds had stopped singing, but Gawain wasn't concerned with that; he was attempting to reconcile Scot to acceptance of King Arthur and chivalry. He'd been pressing the conversation for some time and didn't intend to fail.

"In some ways," he continued, "these good character traits make Arthur vulnerable and at times might even make him a less effective ruler—goodness always assumes that every statement is true and meant with right-intent, so evil always has that advantage—but they are also the reason that I (and many like me) follow Arthur and the reason that the Round Table and the code of chivalry work. Perhaps Clarent, the sword in the stone[22], chose him specifically for his

---

[22] 'Wait, what's that?' you ask, 'I thought Excalibur *was* the sword from the stone.' If you made that error, you aren't alone in your assumption, but think about it: Excalibur was a

good qualities."

"I have a blister," Scot responded, displaying one sandaled foot.

"What? What has that got to do with Arthur?"

"It hurts," Scot explained, pointing to where the leather strap rubbed against a raised redness on his ankle.

"But, you fought a Banshee and had many and worse injuries-"

"Yes, but they're healed and a blister is bothersome. Changing sandals is always annoying. Don't you agree?"

Gawain sighed. "Try to think about something else. King Arthur, for example. There isn't an ounce of hypocrisy in him. He is beyond reproach."

"I suppose he never gets blisters, then," Scot murmured, then looked up and said, "And in truth, one of the reasons that I'd rather retain my code and my religion is that my gods are flawed and hypocritical. They get blisters—metaphorically. Thor wrangles with rage and Loki with jealousy. The only perfect god, Baldr, was killed for his perfection, which of course proves that pure perfection is an imperfection, or . . ." Scot hesitated, "something like that." Even he felt that he could have summed that up better.

"There's pagan wisdom for you," Gawain scoffed in derision. "Perfection is imperfect and imperfection is preferable. It's circular logic."

Scot rolled his eyes, rubbing his ankle. "Paganism (as you condescendingly call my faith) *is* circular. Your Christianity tries to make everything into a straight line... in order for your world to make sense, everything must have a start and an end. In any case, your king is cut from the same cloth as your Christ—both are like Baldr, too good to last for long—either you are blind or he is a liar. *Real* people and gods struggle to be their best and *fail.*"

"Then you choose to live a life based on the inevitability of failure?" Gawain asked. Feeling his argument slipping away, the knight

---

gift from the Lady in the Lake. How, then, could it also be from the stone? Less feared for its keen edge and reputation in battle, Clarent became Arthur's secondary sword, but it remained a symbol of status, power, and the right to rule (that is, until it was 'acquired' and shamed by Sir Mordred).

started to get rather frustrated with himself and with Scot for his stubbornness. "That's just hopelessness and depression."

"Quite the opposite," Scot replied. "Life ends with death for each of us—for kings, and slaves, and gods—we are tied together by the final knot of death and failure, so there is no reason to look down on any other or for the gods to be patronizing or judgmental. We all lose. We all fail. We all die. But we all fight, and struggle, and defeat is not refutation."

"But where is your ideal to live up to? That is what you are missing. Christ wasn't made perfect to make me or you feel small. He wasn't perfect so that He can sit in judgment of our failures, or so that we can judge the failures of others. He was perfect so that we can see and emulate His perfection. And so it is with chivalry, and so it is with Arthur. They are *ideals*—and even if you or I cannot become an ideal, we can follow one, and through the simple act of emulation—*even when we fail*—we become better."

"Assuming that you are aright in all that you say, that Arthur is an ideal," Scot said, sensing a weak point in Gawain's argument, "then his kingdom should copy his example, but it doesn't, so what went wrong?"

"Guinevere—a woman."

Cathbad turned at this with a twinkle in his eye and said to Gawain, just loud enough to carry through the forest, "Ah, Christianity's classic excuse: *A woman made me do it.* You see, I've been listening to you prattle on about ideals, your king, and his kingdom." He smiled a crooked smile, waiting for the two warriors to catch up.

Surprisingly, Gawain laughed. "Yet, I'll continue to 'prattle,'" he said, "as long as I'm able. I suppose you're correct that blaming a woman lacks proper humility and is discourteous. Woman is in fact not the problem with man. Man's lack of ability to control himself around woman is at the root of the problem. Just as wine is not the drunkard's problem—lack of self-control is—women are not the downfall of great men, but their own insatiable desire for women is. Consider history. The weakness begins with the first man and his mate, Eve, but there are countless examples: David and Bathsheba, Sampson and Delilah, Paris and Helen, Sigmund and Brunhilda, Tristan and Isolde, and now Arthur and Guinevere." He held out his hands in apology.

"Everything always comes back to women, it seems," Scot

interjected. He kicked over a tall tan-capped mushroom, noting the soft texture of its brown under-folds. "I'd rather have this blister than a wife."

Cathbad cleared his throat imperiously. "The three great mysteries of the world are the gods, death, and love." He spoke with the tone of a teacher.

Scot shrugged in response. "And you need a woman for love?"

"The simple fact is," Gawain interrupted, "that women rule the men who rule the world—they wield the power of influence whether they want to or not. They are our true monarchs and have most of the power with little responsibility. The code of chivalry accurately reflects that truth."

"Little responsibility, but all of the blame," Cathbad cut in.

"It amazes me that humans are the more plentiful race," Bruuzak added in his doglike voice, grinning his vicious grin and liking black lips with a maroon tongue. "Goblin women are kept to be used for pleasure and childbirth. They belong to the tribe. No male has his own female and no female has power."

"Heh, sounds sublime," Scot winced.

"Maybe that is why your race is a failure," Gawain responded coldly, not deigning to make eye contact with the goblin. "Your males lack proper inspiration. Yet," he looked to Scot and ignored the goblin's hissing intake of breath, "I admit that if the Round Table falls, it will be at Guinevere's feet. Arthur and Lancelot will *blame* her, just like Adam blamed Eve, but they should bear the blame themselves. They fought for her, even if she didn't ask it."

"So you admit, then, that it isn't the Queen's fault," Cathbad observed.

"It is Lancelot's fault for not being man enough—or for being too much of a man, I cannot decide—to resist her, and it is Arthur's fault for being so blinded by his own goodness and his love for both of them that he could neither predict nor plan for the event, nor even believe it to be possible. And yet, if a woman caused all of this trouble, a woman may repair it."

"What do you mean?" Scot asked, perking up from a state of contemplative boredom.

"Heather," he replied. "I ask you, who organized us and

brought us to this juncture?"

"Well, Alanbart had the idea to—"

"Fie! *Sir* Alanbart would certainly have ridden north, given half the chance. Without Heather, I would have attacked the tower alone and died, and you would be safe and bored, whiling away the afternoon at your henge."

"Yes, but how did she—?"

"She rallied us, motivated us, and joined us. It doesn't matter *how*. By Mary, she's *led* us all to this point. We march by her will and on her orders—all of us—Cathbad and Bruuzak," here he addressed the goblin for the first time, "even you."

Scot smirked, and Bruuzak mumbled: "I march on the orders of only one woman; my goddess is *opportunity*, and I have made her my whore. I'll ride her where I will. Your weakness may have prodded you to this point, but I saw an opportunity for profit, bloodshed, and amusement with little risk compared to the greatness of the reward, and I snatched it."

Gawain ignored him again and resumed his conversation with Cathbad, though he directed his remarks to Scot: "Women rule the world because most men want to be ruled. It's easier that way. Unlike women, we grow tired of the details of life and become content with the mere illusion of control. They have no need of such illusions—that is one of the many reasons that I've tried (and failed) to remain aloof from romance. Yet here am I, being led by a woman."

Scot cast his eyes back to the ground and studied the jagged forms of fallen maple leaves as he walked, favoring his left foot. He caught sight of an armored millipede, nudged it, and watched with satisfaction as it curled into a tight circle.

"Perhaps," Cathbad observed, "that is the reason that so many priesthoods are celibate. It is hard to serve two masters, especially if one of them possesses the gateway to all of the pleasures of this world and the other only promises to hold the key to pleasure in the next."

"Possibly," Gawain conceded, "though I have never thought of myself as priest-like. Yet, think on this, both of you: Men fight much harder when they fight for a mother, a sister, or a lover than they do for a father, brother, or friend—they even fight harder for those things than for religion. Most say it is because women are not able or allowed to defend themselves, but to me it seems more than that."

"I for one," Scot interrupted, "find it foolish to waste all these words on women without a single woman present. And in any case, being a lone man with neither desire for nor prospect of love, the topic doesn't interest me overmuch. Besides, we are nearing our destination. The tower waits just through those trees." He pointed to the west. "When will we attack?"

"When the sun dips below the horizon, and not minute before," barked Bruuzak.

25

RABORDATH'S CHAMBER

Rabordath and Malestair stared at the dead kestrel as it leaked 'magic' broth all over the stone floor. They'd fished it out with tongs and waited a few minutes for the spell to take effect. It hadn't.

"It didn't work," Malestair said, stating the obvious. He ran a hand across his balding scalp.

"I know; I fail to understand why. I followed the instructions precisely." Rabordath picked up the parchment. "Boiling vinegar, precious metal dust, ash from Etna, rock from Hekla, ironwood charcoal, virgin's blood…"

Alanbart's mind raced. 'Heather knew that it wouldn't work,' he thought, 'How?'

"I stirred it with witch hazel, added red fern fronds, a salamander preserved in wine, spines from an urchin, a viper's fang, five legs from different spiders, a cockatrice feather… everything was in its proper order."

"You're not a virgin!" Alanbart exclaimed, looking at Heather. "It was Gawain! No wonder he's such a miserable sod, what with all of that guilt melting over his chivalry!"

Rabordath and Malestair both turned to listen.

Heather blushed. "And you have room to make accusations," she retorted. "Men! You always place so much emphasis on virginity, but none of you ever are virgins yourselves. I'm sure *you're* a still virginal at your age" Her defense modulated to sarcasm.

"Well, actually I… I," Alanbart trailed off. He, in his turn, began to redden, which made the cuts and bruises on his face burn with heat.

"You are!" she gasped.

A feverish light shown in Rabordath's eyes as he consulted the parchment.

"I... I never wanted female entanglements," Alanbart began. "Physical love is just another form of weakness to be exploited by a lover or an enemy. How many men have died for it?"

"I've double checked!" Rabordath interrupted with urgency, putting his black-nailed hand on Malestair's sleeve. "Nowhere does the spell say that the virgin must be a woman."

"Then we take *his* blood and start again?" Malestair asked.

"I believe that it could work, my lord."

"Hold on! You can't—" Alanbart began, frantic. "There's no possible way that you have the ingredients to do it a second time."

Rabordath bent over his workbench, rattling bottles and pawing through envelopes. "I think I do have enough of almost everything." He turned and picked up the tongs. "I'll need to retrieve the fallen star and the ivory die, but most of the ingredients were singles of a pair. I have extra fern fronds, cockatrice feathers, salamanders, urchins, and spider-legs a-plenty. I even have enough of his majesty's blood. I need a new sacrificial animal, that much is true and presents a minor problem, but it should work." After fishing out his two ingredients, he addressed the guards.

"Take this cauldron by the chains—they're quite cool—empty it over the side of the tower, and return it to me. Once you've replaced it, one of you run downstairs and bring up a load of small lumber and the other find me an animal—raven, cat, or wolfhound pup (I think there is a new litter in the kennel), something small."

They turned to Malestair for approval, he nodded, and they left, carefully balancing the cauldron between them. Rabordath turned to Alanbart and wiped his silver knife clean on the hem of his robe. "Now," he said, curling a lip in either disgust or amusement, "I must take your blood."

"Wait!" Alanbart exclaimed, backing flush against the rough stone of the wall. "You can't—not with that knife. The silver blade has to be a virgin too."

"Damn!" Rabordath spat. "He's right."

"Are you *trying* to help them?" Heather hissed in his ear. "Stop solving their problems."

"I can resolve your dilemma," Malestair said to Rabordath. He picked up the goblet that was still half full of Arthur's blood, took a sip and made a face. The tips of his moustache hair glinted with royal blood. Everyone, including Rabordath, winced and looked away.

"I had to," Malestair explained. "Who else gets that kind of opportunity?" He cleared his throat. "This cup is pure silver?"

"Um, yes," Rabordath answered, still avoiding eye contact. "But it, too, has tasted blood."

"Not its base," Malestair responded. He pulled the stub of a candle out of an earthenware jar and carefully poured the king's blood inside. He set the goblet down, drew Excalibur with a flourish, and cut the stem and base of the goblet off in one clean swipe. He started for the armory. "There's a grindstone in there that will put a good edge on this." He grinned at Alanbart as he passed.

Alanbart listened, sweating through his tunic, as the grindstone spun and scraped against the edge of that silver base. Funny, he thought, that death or incidental injury should no longer scare him, but that anticipating inevitable pain still awakened unavoidable terror in his heart. 'Maybe anticipation is what makes torture torturous,' he thought.

26

HAWKFEATHER FOREST

"Well," Gawain turned to Scot, "are you ready?"

"Yes. Are we riding or walking?"

"I'd as soon ride," Gawain said, stroking Gringolet's mane, "but what will we do with our mounts once we reach the gate? Abandon them to the crossbow bolts of Malestair's archers?" The horse nuzzled its huge head against the knight's hand. "No," Gawain said at last, "we'll advance afoot."

"It may be more difficult to retreat out of range if their archers attack," Scot replied.

"If they decide to shoot us, we'll have to go in at a run and trust that the hammer will work. If we flee, Heather and Arthur die— I'd die first."

"Speaking of Heather," Scot began, "I've been meaning to ask you something." He glanced at Cathbad and Bruuzak, then pulled his shield from Taffy's saddle (the horse was *still* staring at the mare) and slung it over his shoulder. He resheathed Hrunting and then hefted the hammer.

"What is that?" Gawain reaffixed his helm, lifted the visor, and armed himself with shield and sword. Leaving his axe hanging from Gringolet's saddle, he turned to his companion.

"Shall we go?" Scot asked, leaving the question unstated and taking a stride toward the forest edge. Gawain nodded, drawing even with Scot under the brightly lit leaves lining the clearing.

They fought their way through brush and bracken into amber twilight. The blazing ball of the sun was still visible, sinking behind the tower, and the full moon shown from a blue sky. A half-mile of open scrub lay in front of them before they'd make it onto the dusty red-dirt path that led to the gate.

Scot said, "I didn't want to ask in front of Cathbad and Bruuzak, but I will ask now. You talked a lot of women just now and ended with Heather. Do you love her?"

Gawain grimaced. "Is it so obvious?"

"No, not at all. I wondered with the way she watched you and her tone when the two of you talked. I've gleaned little from you until just now, unless silence can be seen as an admission—it seems to be with some."

Gawain kept his eyes locked on the gate ahead, but answered without hesitation. "Yes, I do love her, but God knows that I cannot afford to. I am a man, and to remain one in my own eyes, I must make necessary sacrifices, and love is one of them. I have an oath to Arthur that supersedes my feelings for Heather. He is trapped in that tower and must be freed ere I can breathe a word of love. Also, I have a vow of vengeance—sworn to a bishop in a cathedral, my eternal soul as collateral—against Lancelot, who killed my brothers. To dwell happily on love would be a profanation of their memories until they are avenged. I have banished my heart and will live as a loveless exile until my vow is fulfilled."

"Honor always comes before affection, then," Scot said glumly. "Might end up being a tedious and tiresome existence."

The clink and creak of their armor and the swish of the heather against their legs filled the pause in conversation for a pair of restless seconds. Gawain sighed. "A man must have his priorities. In any case, if I betrayed myself, I would be betraying her. Now, I'm going to sound like a priest in his pulpit, but you've begun to listen and I've begun to talk—why not finish it?" He held his hand low, trailing it across the purple tips of the tallest heather.

"A man's soul, you see," he said, "isn't shared between man and *wife*. It is shared between man and *God*. Only these two can see it and judge it; only these two can know of its rightness or wrongness, and only these two need approve or disapprove. Many a man has wealth, power, strength, reputation, the respect of his fellows, the love of a woman, the blessing of the church, and still bears a hidden hatred for himself. You or I may see a man and wish to switch places with him, not knowing his secret shame—a shame that becomes more burdensome the more secret he keeps it. I've seen it with Lancelot, with Agravain, and with Mordred."

Here he stopped despite their exposure to any keen-eyed archers on Malestair's battlements. "Scot, I say this now as a lesson, for this may be the last time that we talk: Each man must approve of his own his soul and must feel God's implicit approval before he *can* love, or—by Christ—that love itself becomes a mockery and reflection—a lie that can only take two paths and can only end one way, with heartbreak. But I have a long tongue, and will not bore you more with explanations."

He resumed his march toward the tower.

"Please," Scot said earnestly, "we're getting into crossbow range, so I desire a distraction—I can't imagine a worse way to die than to be killed by a coward from afar."

"No," Gawain shook his head. "I've said enough for one day, but know this: I would not compromise my soul—not even for Heather—and I pray to Mary that she understands that."

They stepped out of the fallow field and onto the dusty red clay. The wooden palisade and tower loomed ahead, backlit against the smeared pink of the sunset. Ravens circled the tallest battlements. Beneath them, the palisade had been built from tree trunks and sat upon the crown of a low rocky hill with a small cliff on the south side. A gatehouse faced that direction, easily defensible because there were about ten yards of grassy space between the doors and the cliff itself, a fifteen foot near-vertical drop. They'd closed to about seventy yards from the gate now, within crossbow range, and though no one hailed them, silhouettes moved atop the palisade walls, watching their advance. Scot counted them.

"There are nine guards up there," he said.

"I know," Gawain returned.

"But I thought you said that there would be nine on the walls altogether, not just the one facing us."

"Either I miscalculated, or Alanbart talked," Gawain responded.

"What do we do?"

"What we planned to do. What other option is there?"

They advanced steadily on the wall. When they reached the

eastern corner of the palisade, a voice called from above, "State your name and business or we shoot."

"I'm going to try to use this armor and some bravado," Gawain whispered to Scot, then shouted to the guards, "As anyone can plainly see, my arms and armor declare me to be Agravain of Orkney. This is my squire." He gestured to Scot. "My business is with Sir Malestair alone. We will wait at the gate until you fetch him."

They continued to walk, uninterrupted. Mumbled conversation, incoherent, spilled down on them from above. "We need to know more of your business before we disturb the lord," a voice finally called.

"Judging by the number of men up there, I'd say you already know my business," he shouted back. "And since I know you've already sent for your lord, further conversation has become pointless. You may either shoot us and then explain to Malestair why we're dead, or wait for him to issue his own orders."

At this point, Scot added a nervous shout of his own. "I always wait for my master's orders. It's safer that way." After ten more seconds, they reached the gate, unimpeded. Scot glanced over at Gawain. "Now?"

"Now," Gawain agreed.

Scot drew back the hammer, braced his feet, and swung the granite headed weapon against the thick oak door with all his might.
BOOM!

The impact was so loud and so deep that both Scot and Gawain felt it in their stomachs and bones. The forest echoed with the thudding sound; the ground shook, and all of the ravens took flight in a cacophony of irritated cawing. Into the woods in a perfect circle for a half-league around the tower, like a ripple in a pond, all of the leaves and needles fell from the trees.

This, of course, exposed the goblins, who took it as their cue to charge. On they came, yipping, yapping, and yammering like dogs and monkeys in their hobbling, jumping runs, knuckles often grazing the ground, bloodlust clear in their twisted faces

Scot and Gawain were as stunned as anyone inside the walls; Scot nearly vomited from the cataclysmic shock wave that swallowed the surrounding forest, decimating the trees. It took both men a few seconds to gather their wits. The door was simply gone, shattered into thousands of woodchips and fibrous bits of woolen-looking material that mulched the area in a sort of blast-cone.

Still queasy, Scot turned slowly, taking in the defoliated woods. He just had time to think to himself, 'Now we know why it's called The Hammer of Autumn,' when Gawain tugged at his elbow. Side by side, the two of them sprinted through the archway, trying to cover the short distance between the gate and the tower door without being cut down by crossbow fire from above.

27

RABORDATH'S CHAMBER

The vinegar boiled a second time; the porcelain cup of Alanbart's blood rested on the table, and the spell was being cast when they heard and felt the hammer's blast on the gate. The tower trembled beneath their feet:

BOOM!

Everyone took a breath. The bird cage (which now contained a wild raven that cawed constantly) and cauldron swung from their hooks. Even Alanbart, who'd thought about nothing but the searing and throbbing pain in the missing tip of his stunted and cauterized finger, was stunned out of his stupor.

"You two, follow me!" Malestair directed the guards as he headed for the door, but ducking under the archway, he nearly collided with two more soldiers, one racing down the stairs and one up.

"My lord!" The one from the battlements stammered, "The front gate is gone!"

"What?"

"It's just… gone." he replied, still dumbstruck. "Something's smashed it into splinters."

"The Druid," Malestair said under his breath and turned to the other soldier. "Report."

"I was sent to tell you, lord, that Agravain of Orkney is at the gate with words for you," the second guard stammered.

"Impossible. He's slain. You four," Malestair began, unsheathing his sword, "follow—"

BOOM!

A second blast rocked the tower. The four guards staggered

and Malestair put one hand against the wall to regain his balance. An alarm bell rang from above.

"You," Malestair pointed at the guard from the battlements, "run up, see what's happening, find me, and report. You three, follow me!" He led the way down the stairway at a run, leaving the prisoners alone with the wizard, whose red-cloaked back and inferno of hair was turned to them as he attended to his spell.

"Let me see," Rabordath said to himself, "I've added the ash and rock, charcoal, virgin blood, fern fronds, salamander, and urchin spines. Where was I? Ah!" He read aloud and proceeded to follow each of the instructions in turn: "Drop in a fang pulled from a viper, add five legs from different spiders, add to it a cockatrice feather, then watch the mixture blend together."

He waited.

"Caw!" the raven cried and flapped wildly against the cage. A purplish black feather floated between the wicker bars and onto the wizard's table.

Alanbart focused through the pain, 'Now's your moment. No—wait until that guard from above goes by to find Malestair. If you make your move now, he'll see.'

A minute passed. The raven cawed three more times. Rabordath resumed: "Drop now in a sprig of heather, dug from a defile in stormy weather. Add in an eyeball of a cat, ten small wings from ten small bats, skin of snake and talon of eagle, then a king's blood to make it regal."

He followed the instructions perfectly. The guard rushed by, clearly in a panic.

"Caw!" cried the raven.

"Drop in a rock fallen from the sky," Rabordath said, and picked up the rock from the table. *Plunk*, it sank in.

Alanbart was trying to recall the magic word. "Sinew?" he said aloud.

Nothing happened.

"And an ivory-cut, six-sided die," Rabordath read. *Plop*, it sank to the bottom.

"Kin-now?" Alanbart tried next.

"What are you doing?" Heather whispered.

"Trying to break free," Alanbart responded. "Cathbad put a spell on me, if I can only remember the magic word. Choir-now."

"Caw! Caw!"

"Let it boil for three minutes," Rabordath said, and began counting aloud, "One, two, three, four…"

"Cayenne?"

"…ten, eleven, twelve…"

"That sounds French," Heather said. "Cathbad's a druid. His words would be Celtic."

"…twenty-one, twenty-two, twenty-three…"

"Great," Alanbart said, "one of the languages that I don't know. I wrote the word down, but it's in my pocket, and I can't reach it. Can you?" He twisted his body toward her; she did the same, trying with all her might to reach the pocket in his breeches. She twisted painfully to turn her back to him. Her fingers skimmed the fabric's edge.

"…fifty-nine, sixty, sixty-one…"

"Caw!"

"Can you… get… any… closer?" she asked straining as hard as she could.

"I'm trying!" Alanbart whispered between ragged breaths.

"I've reached it," Heather said at last, then, dejected, "There's nothing here."

"…ninety-four… ninety five… ninety six…" Rabordath continued to count.

"It's in the far pocket then," Alanbart sighed.

"You've got to be able to remember. What did Cathbad say?"

The raven cawed.

"Well, the spell is supposed to start a small fire, so maybe the magic is the Celtic word for fire."

"I don't know Celtic," Heather said apologetically.

"…one hundred and twenty-six…"

"My liege," Alanbart asked in a loud whisper. "Do you know

Celtic?"

"Certainly," Arthur replied. "I was raised in Cornwall."

"What is the Celtic word for fire?"

"There are many Welsh words for fire," Arthur replied. "Noun or verb? Great or small? Wild or cooking? It depends on the type being used," and he began listing them off:

"Fflamio?"

"No," Alanbart said.

Rabordath turned, shushed them, then said,

"…one hundred thirty-six… I can't afford to lose count. …one hundred and thirty-eight… and between your jabbering and the cawing of that infernal bird, I'm almost at my wit's end."

He turned his attention back to the cauldron.

"Ffaglu?" Arthur said, more quietly so as not to draw attention.

"No."

"Ennyn?"

"Not it."

"…one hundred and forty-two"

"Llosgiad?"

"Not even close."

"Christ's blood! How many words are there?" Heather interjected, her frustration evident.

"Well," Alanbart replied with a smirk, "when you contemplate the complexity of language, the number of words isn't surprising. Consider English, for example. We have: fire, flame, inferno, blaze, burn, conflagration, combust—"

"Are we having this conversation right now, Professor? Are we?" she interrupted.

"Cinder, ember, smolder," he continued, ignoring her, "spark, ignite, incendiary—"

Heather released an exasperated sigh. "Incendiary, indeed," she warned. "Be thankful that my hands are bound."

Alanbart chuckled.

"Coelcerth?" Arthur asked.

"No." Alanbart said. "It sounds something like ka-new"

"...one hundred and fifty-five"

"Cynnau?"

"That's it!" Alanbart said, and then spoke the word in a loud, clear voice. In seconds, bright orange flames ignited in circular coronas from his wrists, incinerating his leather bonds and setting him free.

He didn't hesitate. He charged Rabordath, who was turning to discover where the flash of light had originated.

Alanbart slammed his knee into the wizard's chest, doubling him over. Then he grabbed him by the shoulders, spun him, and plunged his head into the boiling vinegar. The hot acid—mild thought it was—splashed up, coating Alanbart's left hand and soaking his wound, which hurt so much that he released Rabordath and staggered dumbly, blinded by pain. The cauldron tilted, spilling into the coals and sending up a scalding cloud of acrid steam that surrounded the red wizard.

Rabordath's head emerged from the liquid and steaming fog, still ablaze with illusory fire. He emitted a gurgling scream and grabbed at his face with both hands. Alanbart opened his eyes, took firm hold of the back of Rabordath's flaming head with his right hand, and forced it down into the pot, badly burning himself in the boiling vinegar.

Rabordath reached for purchase with his hands. One grabbed hold of the scalding copper cauldron, scrabbling against its smooth surface, while the other plunged into the white-hot coals, knocking some to the floor. He must have screamed into the boiling vinegar, because bubbles erupted from the brew. The second-rate wizard lurched twice, spilling more broth into the coals, then ceased to move, his flesh crisping and burning as Alanbart held him fast above the flames.

Finally, Alanbart staggered backwards, doubled over in pain and nausea. He cradled his scalded right hand in his wounded left, closed his eyes, shook his head violently to clear it, then straightened up.

He stumbled to the table and retrieved Rabordath's silver knife. Slicing through the king's bonds, he passed the knife to Arthur, who freed Heather.

"Well done, my boy," Arthur tossed the knife away. It rattled on the flagstones beside Rabordath's inert form.

"Thank you, your highness," Alanbart cradled his hands gingerly against his stomach. Struggling to gather his wits and catch his breath, he looked to Arthur to take charge.

Surprising to neither of the men in the chamber, Heather spoke up. "Let's get into that armory and outfit ourselves as best we can," she said, throwing one of Alanbart's arms over her shoulder and pulling him through the archway.

Impressed, Arthur followed.

28

THE GREATHALL

The hammer shattered the keep door in the same way that it did the gate, except that this time Gawain and Scot were not stunned. The two men were through the opening before the wooden shards hit the ground. Two guards stood inside, but the blast caught them flatfooted, and they were dispatched with ease.

Together in the greathall, Gawain scanned the area for threats, while Scot tried to locate the stairs. As he found them, three knights in full armor came clattering down. Each drew a sword, unslung a shield, and advanced, two toward Gawain and one toward Scot.

Ready for a fight, the Pict dropped the hammer and drew Hrunting. He pulled the blue shield from his back and fell into step beside Gawain.

"There may be more coming," Gawain observed. "Shall we fight back to back?"

"Feel no fear from your rear," Scot replied with a grand gesture and a chuckle. "No sword will stick in your ass with me covering it."

"Somehow," Gawain shook his head, "despite your way with words, I find that comforting." He dropped into a combat stance.

A plank table occupied the center of the room, making it impossible to fight three armed knights, so Scot and Gawain drew up near the smashed door and waited. Their opponents closed the gap.

The man facing Scot seemed larger than his fellows, but he halted, just out of sword-range, hesitant to make the first move. He was either cautious, Scot thought, or afraid. They weren't the same thing. As the two sized each other up, Scot heard a clash of steel. Gawain had engaged his opponents.

While weapons clashed behind him, Scot's opponent feinted

twice, but the swordsman refused to take the bait. He held his position behind Gawain. Though he was sorely tempted, he didn't turn to see how his friend fared.

At last, the big knight attacked.

He brought down a swift overhead swing that Scot blocked with his shield. The swordsman slashed with Hrunting, but it was deflected. The combatants exchanged a series of blows, testing one another for weaknesses.

Behind him, Scot heard the shriek of tearing metal followed by a clang, and suddenly in his peripheral vision, a helmet rolled clumsily into view, leaking blood. A heavy thud confirmed a body hitting the floor.

"It's even!" Gawain shouted. "Let's finish them!" And Scot broke formation, now on the offensive.

He swung three times as his opponent backed away, two of his strokes were blocked, but the third clanked off his the larger man's helm, a dazing blow. Scot took advantage of his enemy's momentary disorientation and delivered a powerful thrust that drove straight through the man's steel cuirass. The knight dropped his weapons made a burbling noise inside his helmet, slid backward off Hrunting, and swiveled just enough to crash and clatter onto the table.

Scot turned to see Gawain bring down an overhead stroke on his remaining opponent, using all of his considerable strength.

His enemy, a knight clad in white, tried to parry with his blade, but Mimung snapped it off. The white knight sagged back, dropped his shield, raised his visor, and shouted,

"I yield!"

Scot thought that the man looked old for a knight, probably in his forties, with a splash of gray in his carefully trimmed goatee.

Gawain leveled his sword at the man's face, then raised his own visor and said, "Your name, that of your father, and your word before God that you will join with us for the remainder of this combat."

"My name is Cathair; my father's was Carew, called the Wild. You have my oath."

"You are now the servant of Sir Gawain of house Orkney, and you'd do well not forget it. Take us to the dungeon."

The man nodded. "It is this way, Sir."

He led Gawain down the spiral staircase; Scot followed.

Neither group knew it but, as the two heroes and their guide vanished around the corner of the stairs, Malestair and his three men at arms appeared, rushing from the floor above.

Malestair stopped, scanned the area, noting the smashed door and four corpses, and then gave orders: "You three," he said, "guard this door." He pointed." Flip over that table and slide it to about two feet from the entranceway. Stand behind it and use your spears overhand. You *must* secure the tower. Allow no one but my men entrance to this room. The door has been breached and the tower infiltrated. Attackers have obviously taken the stairs down to the dungeon. I will deal with them myself."

He turned toward the stairs as a fourth man at arms entered the room from above.

"My lord," he stammered, "we're under siege. Hundreds of goblins are charging from the woods. They're already at the gate."

"Get back up, quick as you can, and blow the horn twice for retreat. We need as many men as we can in the tower. Without the gate, the palisade is indefensible. Go!"

The guard sprinted up the stairs. Malestair drew Excalibur and ducked into the archway that headed down to the storeroom, walking slowly and cautiously, alert for any noise.

Cathair led Gawain and Scot into the storeroom. As they entered, a lone guard, obviously nervous and pacing back and forth, raised his weapon, a sturdy mace with an iron head, to offer a challenge. Before he could do so, Cathair spoke. "Drop it," he ordered.

The guard hesitated, and Gawain added in a commanding voice. "Do as you're told, fellow, or we will have no choice but to kill you."

The guard let his mace clatter to the dusty floor. "What's happening?"

"That's no concern of yours," Gawain replied. He turned to Scot, "Guard the archway. We may be followed," and then back to Cathair, "Tie this soldier up and leave him unharmed in the cell. We'll come back for him later." Cathair and Scot both complied.

The guard backed away a few paces and said, "But —"

"You'll thank me, fellow, for this kindness later," Gawain said. "Trust me on that." He sheathed Mimung and bent down to grasp the iron ring of the trapdoor that led to dungeon's lone cell. He pulled.

Malestair rounded the corner, Excalibur pale and shimmering in his hand. He quickly counted and sized up his three opponents, then backed into the protection of the stairwell. "I am Malestair, Lord of the Northern Marches, and I rule in this tower. You are intruding on my domain. I give you the option of surrender."

Scot grinned at Gawain who smiled in return. "Rescue your king. I'll handle this," Scot said. He noted that Malestair didn't have a shield and slung his own over his shoulder to even the odds.

"I am Scot, swordsman and servant of Cathbad the Old, High Druid of the North, and I am here to exact restitution for the harm that you have caused. If you will not pay, I shall take that restitution from your body." He scanned the lord of the tower up and down, locating the black leather sword sheath hanging from his belt. His grin broadened.

Malestair scoffed. "I am a trained knight and wield Excalibur, the greatest weapon in the world. You are welcome to try your luck against me, *swordsman*." He fell into a defensive posture.

Scot showed his teeth, raised his blade in a mock-salute, and charged to the attack. He brought down a hail of blows at a stunning speed. Hrunting and Excalibur clashed, dark blade and bright battling in the gloom. Malestair underestimated both the skill of his opponent and the quality of his sword. He was hard pressed to match the moves of wild Northman, and Scot forced his retreat up the stairwell.

Despite the fact that the cramped stairway wound upwards in a clockwise spiral, giving the defender more sword-room, Scot landed two hits, removing the gardbrace over Malestair's right shoulder, and cutting a trench down his breastplate that rent his royal blue surcoat.

The lord of the tower, however, recovered. He continued his retreat, carefully now, hoping to back into the greathall where he would have more room to wield his longer sword, and where the numbers would be to his advantage.

While that went on, Gawain lifted the trap and called into the gloom, "Arthur? My liege?"

"I'm not your *liege*," a heavily accented voice shouted up, "but I would appreciate your help."

"Where's the king?" Gawain demanded, lowering a wooden ladder into the cell and climbing down, "and who are you?"

"*King* Arthur was taken upstairs with the strong-spoken lass and the chatty knight over an hour ago." He coughed dryly. "And my name is Sinel. I am Thane of Glamis."

"Well met, Sinel," Gawain said. He brought Mimung down on the man's chains. Sparks flashed and the dungeon echoed with a clang. "I am Sir Gawain of the Round Table, and I am here to rescue my king. I would appreciate your help. Every able man is a boon at a time like this." He swung again; this time the blade broke the chains.

"You have my help, Sir, and my gratitude—at least until we escape from the tower," Sinel replied. The two of them climbed the ladder and Gawain rushed to the stairwell. Sinel bent to pick up the discarded mace then followed him upstairs.

Meanwhile, Scot continued to advance on Malestair; their swords clashed as the taller man retreated into the greathall. Scot's swordsmanship stunned the over-confident lord of the tower. Even with the advantages of a longer blade, longer reach, and the high ground, Malestair couldn't get a good thrust in against him, failed even to scratch the mad northerner's skin. The villain grew unsure of himself; a small cistern of fear started to fill in his mind.

As Malestair backed into the hall, Scot stopped and assessed the tactical situation.

A dozen men stood in the room. They'd upended the table and slid it forward, nearly against the door. Five healthy men at arms defended the entryway with spears under the direction of a knight in a green and yellow striped surcoat. Goblins surged through the door and were slaughtered by the defenders, who stabbed spear points into their shoulders and faces.

Four men at arms leaned against the wall in different states of injury, two punctured by Goblin arrows and the others nursing stab and slash wounds. One cranked a heavy crossbow to the loaded position the middle of the room. He held a quarrel in his teeth, ready to load onto the string.

Numerous bodies littered the ground around the entrance, a

few knights and a handful of men at arms, but these were overtopped by at least a score of slain goblins. Even as Scot stood watching, the wave of goblins subsided.

The striped knight called out, "Down!" just as a volley of arrows sliced through the opening, many sticking into or bouncing off of the plank table, but a few flying overhead and into the room. They skittered across the stone floor. No one was hit.

Scot made eye-contact with the men who had their backs against the table, but they didn't move. Scot, too, remained where he was—to advance against so many would be suicide. Another wave of goblin arrows came through the door, as ineffective against Malestair's men as the last.

Malestair backed to the center of the room, sheathed Excalibur, and took the loaded crossbow from the man at arms. In response, Scot dove for the stairwell.

A moment later, Gawain, Sinel, and Cathair came trooping up, the latter still unarmed. Scot unslung his shield from his back.

"What's the situation?" Gawain asked, all business.

"They have about eight healthy men in there, Malestair, a knight wearing green and yellow stripes—"

"That would be Sir Guthric," Cathair cut in. "He's good with a blade, but young and reckless."

"Alright—well, Malestair and Guthric, then, and six men at arms with spears, but they're under attack by the goblins. Malestair has a crossbow pointed at this archway."

Gawain, also, adjusted his shield. "Do you think the goblins will break through?"

"Not likely," Scot replied.

"Then, there's nothing for it but to attack, before the goblins are broken."

"First, describe the sheath of Excalibur to me," Scot said.

Gawain raised his eyebrows. "It was a hard scabbard made of gold-plated steel and covered all over with runes and ornament. Why"

"Malestair doesn't wear it," he replied.

"Are you sure? Gawain asked.

"He's got on a simple sheath of black leather," Scot explained.

Gawain nodded grimly at that news. "You two," he said over his shoulder, "follow us."

Scot lifted his shield and led the charge.

29

THE ARMORY

"You do realize that you just single-handedly defeated a red wizard?" Heather said, pulling a chainmail hauberk over her head.

The three prisoners stood inside the armory, which was a smallish semicircular room crammed with a poorly organized mass of weapons and armor. Boxes of crossbow bolts and buckets of arrows were stacked on the floor beside a couple of horizontal spear racks, an empty beer barrel filled with swords, a rack of heavy wooden shields, three shelves of helmets, and a pegboard hung with chainmail shirts and leather jerkins with metal studs.

Alanbart managed to grin, despite searing pain in his scalded hand. "Yes," he said, "and I badly burned myself in the process—it already begins to blister, and the skin is going to ooze. Can I at least tell people that the burn came from a wizard's spell?" He, too, had found a chainmail shirt and pulled it on, struggling to keep the metal from contacting his hands.

Nothing in the room fit Arthur well—he was too large for the chainmail, and it didn't adjust. He tried to squirm in an undignified way into the largest leathern jerkin, which was both too short and too narrow, but the leather stretched some and had ties under each arm, so he could adjust it to fit (almost). He took an open-faced helmet from a shelf and placed it on his head.

"It *was* a spell," Heather replied happily—she was free and reveling in that fact; things were looking up. "Or did you forget that the broth you drowned him in was magic?"

"It does not feel correct for me to stand here and see a lady arming for battle," Arthur interjected. "It would please me, my lady Heather, if you would stay here, safe, until the battle is won."

Heather smiled kindly at the king and then refused, albeit

politely. "My liege," she said, "I could not wait here, unsure of the outcome, until someone came for me. It would be torture. And," she continued, "as Malestair has already told me that he plans to either kill me or turn me into a whore for his men, I think I prefer to die on my own terms. Besides, I'm bigger than some men and strong for a woman. I may be able to assist you. Three is stronger than two."

She, too, chose an open faced helm and moved for the sword barrel, but as she did so they heard an unsettling sound from the adjoining room.

Everyone froze. The raven began to scream and flutter in its cage. Then followed a metallic crash, the hiss of vinegar on coals, a blast of hot wind, and—most disturbingly—a loud wet rending and cracking noise like a man being drawn and quartered. A throaty growl, far deeper and more ominous than that of the largest bear, emanated from the room. The raven continued its frantic cawing.

They looked at each other in terror.

"Let it boil for three minutes and then plunge the victim in it," Alanbart whispered, recalling the final words of the spell. "You don't think...?"

Another loud crashing noise, this time of wood splintering, came through the archway. The raven went silent.

"There's only one way to know," Heather said, and inched toward the door. She poked her head around the frame and her almond eyes went wide with terror.

Heather found herself staring straight into the yellow cat-like eye of a thirty-foot-long, glistening red dragon that somehow coiled into Rabordath's chamber. It had a face like a crocodile: a long thin snout ending in pronounced nostrils, lined with many, many dark shining teeth. Large snakelike fangs protruded from the roof of its mouth. Four charcoal-black horns grew from behind the ear-holes, two curving up and two coiling down. A snakelike neck joined the head to the body, which was long and thin, but muscled like a boar.

It's short, thick, and clawed, legs and arms protruded like those of a monitor lizard or salamander, but ended in talons, sharp as an eagle's. Two bat-like wings folded along its back, the membranes of which were brownish-pink with bright red veins. A powerful tail coiled out behind it, forking a foot from the end. Parallel rows of black spikes ran down its spinal cord from the tip of its horned head to the ends of its forked tail. Its scales were the color of freshly spilled blood, except under the belly where they grew longer, almost banded instead of scaled, and transitioned to a creamy yellow.

Seeing it sprawled across the floor of the adjoining room, basking in the heat of the coals, Heather sucked breath in between her closed teeth in an involuntary thrill of terror. At the noise, the dragon's slitted pupils narrowed in recognition.

She whipped around the doorframe, slammed her back against the stone wall, counted to two to regain her courage, and then grabbed the heavy oaken door and swung it closed, searching frantically about for a bar or a fastener. There was none[23].

---

[23] Now, at this point, you may be musing to yourself, 'I wish that I knew more about dragons,' or are certainly having some such thought. And right you would be to enquire. Dragons, you see, are exceptionally rare, exceptionally powerful, and exceptionally interesting. They are, by definition, rather monsters than beasts. The distinction between the two, I think, has to do with human qualities. A monster possesses human traits, while a beast is entirely inhuman. Goblins, ogres, trolls, giants, and the like are monsters because they are both *human* and creature, and so is a dragon. Indeed, dragons possess many human qualities. Physically, of course, we have little in common, but mentally we are equals, or nearly so. A dragon lives far longer than a man, and so is able over the course of years to become far wiser.
Dragons can speak in human tongues, if they bother learn them, and inherently embody the sins of pride, rage, and avarice. They invent songs, stories, and riddles, and each lives by a code of behavior that it creates for itself. They can fly, dig, and breathe flame, though they fear the cold dampness of water and refuse to swim. They are disproportionately strong for their size, which is already impressive, and thus are probably the single most powerful creatures on this planet—perhaps only equaled by the sperm whale, the leviathan of the deep.
There is a myth, frequently in circulation, that dragons of different colors represent distinct species. That would be as ludicrous as to make the assertion that men of different colors are not men. All dragons have these physical features in common: four clawed legs, two wings, two eyes, four horns, poisonous fangs, parallel rows of back spikes, a forked tail, and fiery breath. They come from what Rabordath called 'the plane of fire,' but what is more properly termed 'the place of fire'—the center of the earth. Most often a dragon is born from a volcanic eruption, but as was the case here, a juvenile dragon could be called forth by a conjuration spell.
We will label this individual dragon as adolescent. It was probably sixty years old. It had lived, at any rate, long enough to become one color—very young dragons are, like chameleons, able to change the color of their scales. Whatever color that they were when they lose this ability is the color that they remain, and thus it is that green dragons tend to be found in the forest (where they matured), blue ones on the shores of the ocean, and black ones in lightless caverns. Red dragons come out of fire, and are the most common, and gold dragons—the most rare—are invariably raised in our world by a parent who has

"Quick," Alanbart said, already in action. "Pile some of this armor and weaponry in front of the door. He toppled over a spear rack and slid a barrel of crossbow bolts in front of it. Arthur dumped a large pile of chainmail shirts and helms there as well and then went back for more. Then Alanbart, with sudden inspiration, grabbed two swords from a barrel, and wedged them under the crack, acting like steel doorstops.

Just in time. The door shuddered with an impact.

"What did you see?!" Alanbart shouted to Heather as they continued to pile arms and armor against the doorway.

"There's a dragon in there, but you already figured that. It's red-scaled and almost fills the whole room, and I think it's getting bigger."

As if it could hear them talking, the dragon hissed and splintered the wooden door with a lash of its tail. They got a glimpse of red scale and shining black spikes as the pile of armor and weapons rattled across the floor, an utterly useless barricade. Flame burst through the opening, setting the weapon racks and shelves alight, and a wave of heat vented across them from that corner of the room. "We're dead," said Heather. There was, for the first time, absolutely no life in her tone. She simply stated fact. Arthur remained silent.

"Can we get by it to the stairs?" Alanbart asked.

"It will surely kill us if we try." Heather said. .

Arthur took up a spear. "There are worse ways to die than in combat with a dragon." The creature's head started to snake through the archway, and the old king stabbed at it, jabbing the spear into the roof of its nostril. The dragon roared in pain, drew back, and blew a second blast of fire into the room. The wooden ceiling and rafters began to burn. The heat was shifting from uncomfortable to unbearable.

"I'll distract it. You two go for the stairs," Alanbart said to Heather. He heaved a heavy yellow shield from the floor and bent to

---

an extensive treasure horde. But our dragon was an adolescent, had no horde, had not yet learned to speak a human language, and was predisposed to anger because it was not used to the comparatively frigid temperature of the surface world.

pick up a spear.

"No, let's all go," she replied.

"Look," Alanbart said. "Those stairs are encased in stone and made of wood. Even if we all did make it to the stairwell—which we all know we wouldn't—the breath of that beast would cook us on our way down and the stairwell would turn into an inferno. Besides, I'm the least valuable. I should make the sacrifice. I'm no good in a fight and my hand is almost useless. He's a king, and you... well, you're the reason I'm here. It would invalidate every foolish thing that I've done if you died."

Heather touched his shoulder gently. Their eyes spoke. Hers weren't pleading or surprised; they were earnest. They glistened. His sodden coward's eyes looked at her, then down at the ground, then immediately back to meet hers, and were changed. They simply said, 'I have to.' He bit his lower lip.

"Honestly, it is not for you," he admitted suddenly and then paused. He didn't say it, but he thought, 'I love you.' Instead, he said, "I must redeem myself to me."

Alanbart's expression morphed quickly from weakness to strength. His jaw clenched, and his eyes possessed a fire that Heather had never seen there before. He searched her face, his very expression stating the unstated. 'I may not have lived like a knight,' he seemed to be saying, 'but I will die like one—I will die doing the right thing for the right reason.'

She nodded, bent forward and kissed his mouth. "Take this," Heather pulled Gawain's green belt from her waist. "You may as well wear a lady's favor into your final battle," she said with mock cheerfulness. She draped it over his shoulder.

"And this," Arthur said, placing a heavy greathelm over his head, only penetrated by two small eyeholes in an unadorned face.

"Go for the stairs," Alanbart said again, his voice muffled. "And go fast. Don't look back." He turned the helm toward the spear in his hand, shrugged, cast it to the floor, and walked slowly, almost dazedly, toward the room with the dragon. The strength in his manner was gone, replaced again by weakness.

Alanbart didn't walk pridefully like a hero, nor purposely like a martyr. He skulked, head slightly down, shoulders hunched, like a boy being forced to church. Bits of flaming bark fell from the ceiling beams between them.

Heather said nothing, only watched him raise his wooden shield, take a deep breath, run around the corner, and disappear through the door.

Arthur watched the scene with the wisdom of a king, and though neither Alanbart nor Heather shed a tear, two trails of moisture coursed down the older man's cheeks and into his beard. He, too, said nothing.

Heather grabbed Arthur's knobbed and rough hand, moved to the door, and waited for her moment.

It came. Alanbart screamed as he entered the room, drawing the attention of the monster, which swatted at him with a forearm, slamming into his shield and flinging him to the southeast corner. There he sat, wedged in the narrow angle. He struck so hard that the wind was knocked from his lungs and he almost lost consciousness.

The dragon then drew back its crimson crocodile head and sprung forward, but not to strike. Three feet from Alanbart, it opened its mouth wide, like a snake disjointing its lower jaw, and vomited forth a blast of white-orange liquid flame that struck against and splashed off of Alanbart's heavy wooden shield with the force of a waterfall. Its flaming ricochet splashed the ceiling, dribbled down the walls, and pooled on the stone floor next to the upended copper cauldron. Everything wooden in the room was ablaze.

As the dragon let forth this blast, Arthur and Heather ran. They hugged the wall behind raised shields and made straight for the staircase, leaping the dragon's tail to reach the safety of the stone arch just as the dragon closed its mouth on the river of white-hot death. Heather's final glimpse of Alanbart was of the knight cowering in the corner, yellow shield ablaze, helmed head shaking—whether in terror, laughter, or pain, she could not tell.

30

THE GREATHALL

Scot charged from the archway, bellowing a battle-cry. Leading with his shoulder, he kept his body sideways to reduce his profile and covered his face with his shield. Gawain followed with Sinel roaring behind him. Cathair waited cautiously in the archway, either to watch for a weapon to become available or to see how the initial confrontation would be decided—likely for both.

Malestair loosed his quarrel and it flew true, colliding with Scot's shield. The arrowhead bit into the wood with a crack, but only penetrated about two inches, and—lucky for Scot—it drove through a mere finger's width above his forearm. In fact, the arrowhead splintered through the beautifully carved doorway of Valhalla, which adorned the inside of the shield. Scot faltered and thought about the inevitable outcome, had he not borne a shield into battle. Gawain passed him by on one side and Sinel on the other.

Malestair called out: "Agravain! I am for you!" He dropped the crossbow, hefted an abandoned shield, and moved toward Gawain, who'd closed his visor.

Certainly, Scot thought, it must have astounded Malestair to see Agravain alive. Clearly, he felt more confident in his ability to best the knight than in his chances against Scot in a duel of swordsmanship. The Pict allowed himself a moment of pride at the thought of Malestair's apprehension—after all, Agravain had been one of Arthur's knights, a formidable force on any field of battle.

The lord of the tower, however, no longer stood alone. In the time that it had taken for Scot to talk to Gawain in the stairwell, Malestair had divided his forces, taking two men at arms and the green striped knight—Guthric, was it?—to join him against the newcomers. Two of the badly injured men stood shakily and awaited a chance to pick off an unwary adversary. One leaned on a spear for support.

Perhaps an overview of the greathall would allow you to picture the scene with more clarity. The central room of the Devil's Rookery was a fifty foot circle of stone, paved with rectangular flagstones and ringed with a fine gravel periphery. The stairwell coiled along the east edge. At the far north squatted a raised dais with Malestair's black armchair. Directly across from this loomed the smashed doorway with the plank table overturned to face it. Four men repelled another massed goblin offensive from outside. To the west, the smooth circle of the wall somewhat flattened to incorporate an oversized fireplace and chimney that ran up the height of the tower. Two long benches still rested in the center of the room, looking oddly misplaced without the table between them.

The benches, however, created three 'lanes' (like jousting lists) in which the fighting would occur. Gawain met Malestair on the west side, Sinel—unarmored and armed only with a short and heavy mace—took the lane to the east, and Scot entered the middle lane where he would face Sir Guthric and one man at arms.

Guthric stood shorter that Scot but had a confident stance and didn't retreat as the Northman advanced. The supporting man at arms was gray-haired and scarred, hunched behind the knight's left shoulder (protected by his shield), and wielded his spear overhand. He watched Scot's advance warily, his eyes assessing the younger man in a cold and calculating manner.

"Remember, lad," the old soldier barked to Guthric, "this isn't a duel of honor. This is battle, and 'tis your responsibility to stay alive and to keep your lord's men alive at all costs. No risks—let him come to you—and when he does, the quicker we make it, the better for us all."

Guthric didn't respond. The single black eye-slit in his Sallet-style helm looked out expressionlessly.

A bellow and thud from Scot's left indicated that Sinel was engaged. Guthric cast a nervous glance in that direction, and the Pict took advantage of the moment to attack.

Their blades clanged twice, and then the old man's spear drove in, forcing Scot back.

"Focus on your enemy," the veteran snapped without turning

his head or changing his posture. He kept his eyes on Scot's eyes.

Cries for mercy and more screams came from Sinel's direction, and ringing steel could be heard from Gawain's, but Scot, heeding his enemy's advice, kept his focus. He drifted to the right but didn't get far before his calf connected with the long wooden bench.

Both the contact and the noise distracted him; when his eyes darted toward the floor, the old man's spear struck again, viper-like. It caught Scot square in his chest. Luckily, the woven-metal rings of his mail shirt held. The thrust shoved him into the bench, which tottered for a moment before toppling.

Scot leapt across the falling bench, but it fell on the toes of his unprotected foot. He winced in pain, would have cried out, but he'd lost his wind and gasped noisily instead. Guthric wasted no time and launched a flurry of blows. As Scot frantically blocked the offensive, half-hopping on his throbbing foot, he thought about how anticlimactic it would be for him to fail here—a warrior who killed a banshee bested by an old man at arms. It couldn't happen. Retreating into Gawain's combat lane, he drew his enemy away from the protection of the spearman.

Guthric moved to follow across the bench. Scot reversed direction and shield-rushed him, sending him clattering and spread-eagled, to the ground. Sensing an unexpected advantage, the Pict went for the quick kill, but as he did, the spear struck again. This time the man at arms aimed for Scot's neck, but missed by just a few inches, slamming into the sweeping neck-guard of Scot's helmet. The resonant clash stunned him, and the helm wrenched clockwise, cutting off vision to his left eye and slicing the bridge of his nose.

Scot's ears rang, his foot throbbed, and he struggled to draw breath, but he was a warrior who knew his business. He ignored the blood running across his cheeks and chin and, with a single swift motion, closed on the old soldier, forcing him to use his oversized weapon at close quarters. The soldier made an ineffective thrust, and Scot struck. He stepped under the spearhead and sliced down through the arm holding the shaft, cutting the hand clean off with a visceral splashing sound. The old man cried out then crumpled, cradling the stump in his remaining hand. Blood spurted between his fingers, the spear clattered across the flagstones, and the severed hand dangled from a shred of skin, its fingers limp and dripping blood.

Scot then rounded on Guthric, who was on his feet and swinging. Because Scot's vision remained partially blocked by the helm, Guthric intentionally drifted into his blind spot. They circled for a few seconds, exchanging halfhearted blows. Scot pivoted to keep his assailant in sight, and Guthric orbited, trying to gain the advantage.

When Guthric swept his blade in from the side, Scot stepped into the swing, his shield raised.

Thunk.

The sword stuck into the wood. Guthric struggled to pull it free, and Scot brought down an overhead stroke.

Clang.

Hrunting sliced the knight deep between his shoulder and neck. The blade sang as it buckled the armor and sank down a finger's length, snapping his collarbone.

Guthric fell back, wrenching his blade free in the process, but Scot kicked it away. He tapped the visor of the fallen knight's helm and said, "Yield or die."

Guthric fumbled with his visor, lifting it to reveal his youthful, sweat-drenched face. Obviously striving to contain both pain and terror, he spoke through clenched teeth: "I yield."

Scot nodded and scanned the room, taking in the carnage around them. To his left, Sinel stood with dripping blade and mace over the bodies of several slain men at arms. He was bending to the tallest of them and stripping his armor. To Scot's right and slightly behind, Gawain was engaged with Malestair.

The lord of the tower certainly fought from the worse position. He was helmless, missing the gardbrace on the shoulder of his sword arm and defending himself with a heavy iron-rimmed kite shield made for his men-at-arms. The assault had come so quickly that he didn't have time to arm effectively for combat. Yet, he remained confident. He wielded Excalibur and had faced Sir Agravain many times in tournament melees and never lost.

Gawain, in his own turn, felt grimly poised. He didn't fear Malestair; he had a sword that equaled Excalibur, and he wore better armor. Gawain also held an advantage in that Malestair assumed that he was his brother, a somewhat less-adept swordsman. The knight however, did feel the strain of today's action. He was older than Scot, and the battle at Broken Cross Abbey had sapped his energy. Following that with a hard ride, a scrimmage at the henge, a march through the forest, and a duel upon entering the tower, Gawain had put his stamina to the test. He found it more difficult to fill his lungs with enough breath. Also, his arms felt heavy and no longer moved with the speed that he depended on to survive.

"I don't know how you lived through that banshee's scream," Malestair said as their blades rang, "but you can't hope to best me."

Gawain remained silent.

"I have Excalibur," Malestair taunted, hoping for some response, and still got none. He began to get nervous at receiving no recognition from Agravain—was the knight still alive, he thought, or did he face some kind of specter?—and so he intensified his attack to cover up his apprehension.

Excalibur and Mimung flashed and clashed again and again. Gawain continued his workmanlike defensive style, matching his adversary's moves and waiting for an opening. He cut, slashed, thrust, parried, and blocked, backing toward the stairs.

Malestair pressed the attack, testing his opponent, but moved with caution as Agravain's skill seemed to him to be much-improved. Twice his opponent's blade nearly caught his face and shoulder. Also, Malestair noted that the knight's sword didn't chip, dull, or bend like others had when pitted against Excalibur.

Up to this point, he'd been assessing his opponent, trying to find weaknesses, and not over-commit himself or reveal his full strength, but Agravain showed no obvious weakness and matched every move that he'd tried.

Malestair decided to give everything that he had in an all-out attack, one he'd often used to win duels. It would require skill, speed, dexterity, and deception. He'd slide toward his opponent's shield, make a feint like he was spinning farther in that direction, but instead plant his foot and pivot clockwise, keeping his shield behind him to offer some protection and bringing his blade around in an arching, spinning strike that increased its power through centripetal force. This often took an unwary opponent off-guard and caught him full in the unprotected sword-arm, crippling him at a blow. It was a dangerous move, one that would leave Malestair open to attack if it were anticipated, but he needed to end this duel.

Malestair drifted, and when Gawain moved predictably to counter, he spun—seeming to go further right, but then twisting suddenly left.

The maneuver fooled Gawain but only for an instant. He recovered in just enough time to leap back and lift Mimung. The two swords connected with a shuddering clash, and the knights pressed against each other.

"Who or *what* are you?" Sweat trickled down Malestair's face and around his flaxen moustache.

Gawain shoved him back and took advantage of the moment's respite to open his visor. "Gawain, son of King Lot of Orkney, nephew of Arthur Pendragon, and slayer of Malestair of the Moors."

Color drained from Malestair's already blanched cheeks. "How?" Malestair asked. "I saw your . . ."

"Armor?" Gawain answered but didn't continue the conversation. Instead, he began his own attack. Gawain thrust and slashed, forcing Malestair back.

The villain parried, all the while considering his options, what he knew of Gawain, and where he might find advantage. While their swords continued to sing their steel song, he settled on taunting Gawain—perhaps if he could enrage him, he thought, the knight's emotion would get the better of him, and he'd make a fatal mistake.

"Today I discovered," Malestair began with a strained smile, still retreating, "that we have something in common." He parried a slash with difficulty. "That serving maid—Heather I believe she is called—was a delightful diversion in my chamber this afternoon."

Gawain halted his attack and fell into a defensive position. "Explain yourself."

"Oh, certainly she resisted," Malestair said, mopping sweat from his forehead with his sleeve, "but—ask any of my men—after a few slaps and screams, she was moaning with pleasure. Afterward, she admitted to me that you were the only other man to have her."

Gawain's expression flitted from anger to confusion. Malestair had to be lying, but why would Heather reveal her—and his—shame? That was a betrayal, one that he could neither fathom nor deny. He slumped back; Mimung quavered in his hand.

Malestair sensed his enemy's weakness and smirked. "Women never know what they want until they get it."

"And men never want what they have," Gawain added, almost to himself, "until—"

"Between sharing your lover and losing your brother," Malestair interrupted, beginning to advance once again, "today has been a memorable day for you, but you know the saying—bad things come in threes. Maybe I can still kill your king before nightfall."

This was, of course, a fatal miscalculation. With that final word, ambivalent sorrow exploded into rage behind Gawain's eyes, and the legendary knight attacked, heedless of his own life.[24]

The attack that Gawain launched stunned and terrified Malestair. He'd never seen such swordplay, to say nothing of facing it with his own blade.

With a cry, Gawain darted in and hacked a corner off of Malestair's shield. Mimung and Excalibur then clashed three times before Gawain delivered an arcing slash that was a shade too fast for Malestair. The tip of Mimung caught him in the jaw of his open mouth, below the skull and the tongue, and sheered it off. A handful of teeth and the severed jaw bounced once then slid to a gruesome stop, splashing the flagstones. Malestair' tongue lolled dumbly against his Adam's-apple amongst a cascade of crimson blood, staining his blue surcoat blackish purple.

Malestair screamed, a sound without modulation, and red-tinted spittle sprayed into his drooping moustache and across Gawain's chest. The wound was not fatal and the fight wasn't over. The lord of the tower, horribly disfigured and breathing audibly (and bloody tongue flapping against his neck) brought down an overhead stroke that Gawain blocked with his shield.[25]

---

[24] Now, you may or may not recall, but I have said that when Gawain was properly inspired, he was one of the (if not *the*) foremost swordsman in Europe. He was cautious by nature and rarely fought to his full potential, but rage was a catalyst that could push him over the edge (as Lancelot would soon discover during the siege of Benwick).

[25] It suddenly occurs to me that a less adept narrator might take advantage of this situation for some poorly placed comic relief, perhaps inserting a comment about how Malestair's plan was finally being *unhinged*, or maybe how that cut was *shaving it too close*, or conceivably that, for the rest of his life Malestair would now only be able to *speak in tongues*. Thankfully, I don't abuse my audience with such tongue-in-cheek nonsense and will proceed apace.

Gawain advanced, offering another punishing forehand that Malestair took on his weakening shield. By this time, though, its wood was chipped and cut from Mimung's heavy blade, and when the sword connected—with the strength of Gawain's fury—a crack sounded, and the shield buckled, its lengthwise boards snapping in half. It hung on Malestair's arm, both useless and cumbersome.

Gawain followed up his advantage with a backhand that Malestair barely blocked with Excalibur. Gawain leaned his weight on the blade, forcing the lord of the tower back, and then punched his steel shield into the man's jawless face. Malestair fell, blinded and nearly unconscious from the pain. Gawain stepped on his arm, pinning Excalibur to the slate floor. He inverted Mimung and placed the tip at Malestair's throat.

Normally, a knight of Arthur's court would have asked his opponent to yield; instead, Gawain made eye-contact with Malestair and waited for the man's eyes to plead. When they did, he thrust the tip of his blade through the taught, blood-smeared flesh of his neck, severing the veins and arteries.

As Malestair's blood pooled on the flagstones and the life drained from his eyes, two things happened. First, Arthur and Heather erupted from the stairwell at a full sprint, followed by smoke and fire, and second, the men at arms at the door defeated the goblins who were pressing wildly to get in. Only two defenders remained. They looked at one another in a combination of joy, relief, and disbelief, and then back into the room in fear and confusion.

Gawain bent to retrieve Excalibur. He passed it, hilt first, to Arthur, saying, "My liege, it is good to rest eyes upon you again." He turned guardedly to Heather and added. "You as well, my lady." He paused to recover his composure. "Sir Alanbart?"

Heather shook her head.

Gawain nodded.

Arthur took quick stock of the situation. His voice boomed in the greathall, "To any who now join us, amnesty will be granted. I here give my word, and that is law in my kingdom."

The men at arms made eye contact with the king and kneeled. Cathair stepped from the stairwell, bent to retrieve a discarded sword, and said, "I am yours, my liege."

Guthric struggled from the floor to his knees and kissed the hem of Arthur's shirt with bloody lips. Sinel leaned against the wall, surrounded by the corpses of the wounded soldiers he'd murdered. Rather than bow, he stooped to clean his blade on the shirt of a dead man.

The king looked imperiously around the chamber. "Good," he said. "Now that that is settled, let's fight our way out of this place." He advanced toward the doorway, but as he did, a high and vacillating voice carried through the archway, echoing off of the circular walls.

"I am Cathbad, High Druid of the North, and I give you one opportunity for surrender. In a moment I will transform into a cave-bear, smash that table like a twig, and lead a hoard of goblins in to kill you all. Alternately, you may surrender and depend upon my mercy to save you."

"Cathbad," Scot called, "there is no need—we've won!"

"Then come out here," Cathbad replied, "and we will divide the spoils of victory."

Scot turned to his fellows, shrugged, and nodded. "Let's go."

"Hold!" Arthur ordered. "Do we trust this Cathbad?" he asked Gawain.

"No, my liege," Gawain responded, "but without his aid we wouldn't be standing here now."

"My king," Heather interrupted, glancing at the ceiling and gesturing to the smoke that billowed out of the stairwell, "I don't see that we have a choice."

"Quite correct," he said, clearing his throat. "Lads, arm yourselves. We shall exit in a body. You there," he gestured to a man at arms and then to Guthric, "help this knight to his feet and allow him to lean over your shoulder. And you," he said to Scot, "since you know this druid, you must lead the way."

Scot slid the table to one side; then he and the rest of the party passed through the doorway.

31

TWILIGHT, THE COURTYARD

Outside grew dark. The moon still shone, but the wind picked up and clouds collected around it. In the dim purple twilight, the scene in the courtyard was one of carnage. Bodies of men at arms, servants, and a few knights littered the ground, five to every one goblin corpse. The battle had been a slaughter, but next to the doors of the keep, goblins lay heaped in a deep pile, at least thirty in various stages of death and dismemberment. A clutch[26] of curious ravens settled into the courtyard and picked at the faces of the human corpses. They preferred man-flesh to that of the goblins.

As Arthur and his party crossed the courtyard, the surviving goblins milled about uneasily, nearly fifty of them, armed with a conglomeration of weapons: bows, spears, hatchets, and short curved blades that were neither long enough to be swords nor short enough to be daggers. They closed behind Arthur's party, surrounding them and cutting off their retreat to the keep. Eventually the king and his followers ceased their advance and clumped themselves into a defensive circle, wary of treachery.

Bruuzak and Cathbad parted the ring of goblins. Cathbad glowed eerily pale in the fading twilight. His white robe shimmered in the moon-glow and both his blue eyes and the brass beads on his moustache glittered. He spoke first, "We have won a great victory over the forces of the Tower! You may put your weapons away."

Bruuzak licked his lips, fingering the hilt of his curved blade.

Scot sheathed his sword and took a few steps toward Cathbad.

---

[26] Interestingly, a group of crows or ravens gathered in one location is referred to a murder—'a murder of crows'—but that particular plurality seemed (ironically) far too apt to use in this circumstance.

The others remained where they stood and did not lower their weapons. As Scot joined his master, he broke the uncomfortable silence. "How went the fight out here?" he asked.

"Obviously, it went well enough," Cathbad answered dismissively, but his eyes fixed on Arthur. He raised his voice again. "If you do not lower your weapons, these goblins *may* take you for enemies," Cathbad cautioned. "My grip on them is not so strong that they will ignore an obvious and insulting threat."

Arthur opened his mouth to respond, but before he could, there was a sudden red-orange light and crackling from above. The crown of the tower blazed. Like a giant torch, it lit the scene in a flickering fiery glow. A pillar of smoke trailed under the gathering clouds and full moon. Wind gusted across the courtyard.

When they returned their attention to one another, Arthur locked Cathbad in his gaze and held it until the old druid broke eye contact. "How do we know that you don't intend to betray us?" the king asked.

"We do!" Bruuzak barked, then yapped an order in his native tongue and brandished his blade, still damp with blood.

Arrows knifed through the dusky air. They weren't sent from very powerful bows and the strings were drawn by the comparatively weak goblin archers, so the arrowheads mostly deflected off the knights' armor. However, two of the men at arms collapsed with injuries and Arthur took an arrow to the shoulder.

Despite his wound, the old king lost no time, "Treachery!" he shouted, gesturing with Excalibur: "Back to the tower!"

Cathbad, too, shouted, but this time at Bruuzak: "Remember, the king lives! He is mine!"

Scot rounded on him. "Treachery? What is this?"

The druid put a paradoxical mixture of kindness and disdain in his tone. "That king is singlehandedly responsible for the destruction of my religion and your society. He *must* be held accountable, and the trees *will* be avenged—not just *my* trees, but the forest of the holy places that were burned in lower Britain. This *we* must do. Defeat the knight—I will do the rest."

"I..." Scot faltered.

"This we *must* do," Cathbad repeated, shifting his stony gaze from Arthur to Scot. "Remember your vow."

The warrior nodded and moved in a daze toward Gawain.

Arthur led a charge at the goblins who stood between him and the tower doorway. He, Heather, and Cathair cut through the yipping creatures. Arthur himself killed four in as many strokes with gleaming Excalibur. Heather stabbed one black-eyed goblin in the face, and slashed another across the chest. Cathair did equally well on his side. The remaining man at arms, however, got shot in the back as he retreated.

Gawain tried to hold the rear, allowing three injured warriors time to crawl to the safety of the keep, but he was overwhelmed. He maimed or killed a dozen goblins in thirty seconds. But though the goblins couldn't cause him harm, they were able to bypass him and fall upon the injured soldiers despite the knight's best efforts to defend them.

A goblin stabbed one man at arms through the lower-back with a scimitar. It protruded, curving up near his navel, and he fell. The other—the old veteran with the severed hand—had arrows through his legs and could do no more than crawl. The goblins gutted him like a deer. Nearer the tower, four goblins leaped on poor injured Sir Guthric, pulling him to the earth, where three sat on his arms and chest, while the fourth repeatedly rammed a bloody dagger through the slit in his visor. The whole group made a cacophonous yapping and laughing noise like a pack of hyenas on the steppe.

The only one who didn't make for the keep was Sinel. He turned toward the smashed palisade gate and charged. Cutting and bludgeoning his way through four surprised goblins, he sprinted, unchallenged, out of the gate and into freedom. None of the goblins pursued him, despite their obvious bloodlust.

Scot unsheathed Hrunting and advanced on Gawain, his dark blade glimmering in the flickering light from the burning tower. The goblins kept a respectful distance from Arthur's knight, and only Scot had the courage to advance on him. He locked eyes with Gawain through the slits of his closed visor.

"I made a vow to Cathbad," Scot said, his voice shaking with emotion. "You said yourself, 'honor comes before affection.'" He paused and fell into a combat stance. "Besides," he offered, "if I

prevail, I promise that you'll have a more honorable end than these—"
he gestured to the goblins "—will give you."

Gawain smiled sadly inside his helm, though Scot could not see.
"Honor before affection," he echoed, then raised his sword in salute—
broadside before his face—nodded his head, and attacked. Mimung
and Hrunting clashed, bright blade and dark.

It was a duel worthy of song, far more impressive, in fact, than
that which Gawain had fought with Malestair. Both he and Scot were
swordsman of rare skill, and as neither really wished for the other's
death, it lasted artificially long, for both fighters chose not to attempt a
maiming or crippling blow. Instead, each waited for an opportunity at a
clean kill, which never came. Gawain used superior size and strength to
force Scot back. As he did, the first drops of rain fell, plinking against
his helm. Thunder rumbled in the distance, and the air seemed charged
with electricity.

While the two swordsmen faced one another, Heather, Arthur,
and Cathair defended the doorway of the tower, fighting back a horde
of goblins, but over the heads of her adversaries and across the bodies
of the fallen, Heather kept half an eye on the ongoing duel. Also,
beyond the circling, slashing, pivoting, parrying, and stabbing forms of
Scot and Gawain, she saw Cathbad, staff upraised and moustache
swaying in the wind.

'If only I had a crossbow,' she thought, but even as she did, she
became conscious that her hair was lifting around her head and
standing up on her arms of its own accord.

There followed a blinding electric light, the stink of ozone, and
a simultaneous crash of thunder, so loud that the earth trembled. A
stone pitched from the tower and split as it hit the ground near her in a
cataclysm of earth and rubble.

The goblins all backed away from the flash like a wave sucked
into the ocean.

Beside her, Arthur stood tall and strong, but beyond him,
Cathair was gone. Where he once stood was a blackened splotch on the
stone doorstep and a twisted mass of smoking metal, torn to curling
and melted ribbons of steel.

Scot and Gawain, too, stopped their combat to turn and stare
at the blasted remains of the knight.

Cathbad's voice echoed across the court, amplified to a godlike level. "Surrender to me, Arthur, son of Uther, or see your knight and your lady suffer the same fate. Behold!" A blinding light shone again and a blue-white bolt struck the ground between Arthur and the goblins. They backed farther away, yipping and yapping like terrified dogs. Thunder shook the ground. "I can call the lighting from the sky and tell it where to strike!"

Rain spattered down, slapping the dusty earth in large drops; the wind gusted.

32

NIGHTFALL

Just at that moment, when the last rays of purple twilight bled from the sky and things looked their very bleakest, help arrived.

Through the smashed gate of the palisade, at a fast trot, rode a dozen knights in full armor and one lady wearing a black oilskin cloak. The knights, all but one, wordlessly formed a wedge, lowered their lances and charged into the mass of goblins, slaughtering and scattering them. Their arrival and attack came so swiftly and silently that they achieved almost total surprise. Goblins fell like plague victims; their combined resources could offer no defense against the knights' onslaught.

Yet, before victory could be attained, a bright bolt of crackling lightning struck the armored knight at the apex of the wedge, lancing through both him and his horse and spooking the rest. Horses screamed and reared, some throwing their riders. Those knights who were not thrown, broke off the charge, dropped their lances, and drew their swords, turning their horses to form a wall against the resurgent goblin mob and to protect their dismounted fellows.

Gawain squinted through the slits of his visor, the now driving rain, and the expanding dark at the knight who remained placidly seated atop a shimmering black charger. The stranger sat tall and broad and another lightning strike revealed that he wore a deep purple surcoat. The color identically matched that worn by Agravain and now by Gawain himself. In gold on his triangular shield was not the double-headed eagle of Orkney, however, but a golden dragon—symbol of the Pendragon family.

"Mordred," Gawain acknowledged under his breath.

Another burst of lightning lanced above the palisade, illuminating a mounted knight. As thunder washed over the scene, the woman pulled back her hood, revealing gold-white hair and a wan wizened face. She scowled, ancient, squat, and ugly. Gawain recognized her with distaste as his aunt, Morgana.

Mordred lifted his visor and uttered a single word: "ENOUGH!"

His command carried such unquestionable authority that the fighting faltered, and all turned to face him. He set his gaze upon Cathbad. "Druid, your cause is now hopeless. Yield to me or die."

"On the contrary, I see much hope," the druid replied, "for I control the skies." As he said this, though, a troop of twenty foot soldiers, all armed with crossbows, filed through the gate behind Mordred. The knight smiled behind a close-cropped goatee. The confidence drained from the druid's expression.

"Very well," Mordred laughed. "We will kill you, then. Aunt," he said turning to the woman beside him, "would you kindly defeat this druid? I shall handle everything else."

Morgana nodded and dismounted painfully from her horse.

"Kill *everyone,* save *only* Arthur and my brother," Mordred ordered.

The knights went back into action against the goblins, and the crossbowmen filed along the wall, trying to get an open field of fire. Lightning slashed again, frying a knight where he stood.

"Get behind me," Arthur forced Heather through the doorway and into the smoky greathall. "They wouldn't dare harm me or go against my orders. You are safe."

From a perch atop the burning tower, the scene might have looked like this: Thirty goblins faced off against nine knights beside the tower. That battle was fierce, bloody, and lopsided. The well-armed and expertly trained knights sliced the goblins apart and their morale seemed on the verge of collapse. Sir Gawain and Scot continued their duel in the center, displaying stunning swordsmanship to all. Arthur, Excalibur held in front of him, occupied the tower doorway with Heather protected in his shadow. Cathbad (with Bruuzak now cowering next to him) advanced toward the new threat in the witch, Morgan le Fay.

"Druid," she said, her voice ice cold.

Cathbad advanced a step toward her, prepared to make reply,

and was assaulted by a flurry of ten green energy discs. They flew, spinning, like sling stones, one from each of her outstretched, arthritic fingers.

Yet, a few feet in front of Cathbad, the shimmering discs slapped an invisible wall, like shimmering glass. There, they crackled, popped, and fizzed into nothingness, leaving concentric rings of brownish energy like those left when a rock is dropped into a muddy pond.

Cathbad twitched his beaded moustache and a bolt of lightning struck from the sky, straight at the witch's head. However, the bolt forked into three prongs a foot above her and each arced ineffectually into the ground.

The crossbowmen continued to move along the wall, attempting to outflank the druid. One broke off the back of the line and, unnoticed, climbed a ladder onto the palisade.

Meanwhile, the witch stretched out her hands, joined them at the thumbs, and unleashed a tongue of red flame that burned across the courtyard and spread in brownish ripples in front of the druid, wicking around the outside of his magic shield, but too far from Cathbad even to singe him.

The old druid closed his eyes and the electricity in the air became palpable and the scent of ozone heady and thick. Five lightning bolts flashed down, one on the heels of another, each breaking around Morgan and forking into the ground. Her hair lifted from her shoulders and she cackled, clearly amused.

Bruuzak, who up to this time chose to stay crouched in Cathbad's shadow, took this moment to flee in abject terror. He backed away about three yards and then turned and ran, hopping and knuckle-dragging into the courtyard in the opposite direction from the fighting. Before he could get more than twenty yards though, the witch pointed a crooked finger at him. Her lip twitched into a smile, and a bright green disc of energy lanced from her fingertip, scything through the dark air on Bruuzak's heels. He saw it coming, screamed, zigged, zagged, leapt, and dodged, but it tracked him, moved as he did, and blasted through his back.

The green light slammed through the layers of armor, leather clothing, flesh, muscle, bone, organs, and back out again in inverse order, finally hitting the ground in front of him, scattering pebbles across the landscape. Bruuzak looked at the cavernous hole through his body, and died.

Morgana retracted her finger, effaced her smile. "Druid," she said, all laughter banished from her face, "I see that you are a skilled and arcane master, and I revel in this encounter."

In response, Cathbad flung an outstretched arm in her direction and pointed his staff. A strong wind gusted down from the sky, roaring past her toward the wall of the palisade. It increased in speed and became constant. The rain bent horizontal, slapping against her cloak and face. Her lank gold-white hair, wet and matted as it was, blew like flapping flags behind her head, along with her cloak and garments. She leaned into it.

Pebbles lifted off the ground as the wind increased in power, small ones at first, but soon round ones as large as sling stones and oblong ones the size of songbirds. Morgana le Fay staggered in the strong blast of wind, but the passing stones did not hit her; instead, they parted around her like running water around a tall rock, leaving a wake of bruised and battered injury behind it. The stones pelted the crossbowmen, wounding many and killing some. They dropped and scattered, and the sound of their screams mixed with the roar of the wind, the dull thump of stones on flesh, and clang and clatter of pebbles hitting metal helmets and the wooden palisade.

The blast subsided and the stones dropped back to earth, piled in a drift against the wall. The witch smiled, and again outstretched her hands, flinging forth a second tongue of flame that connected with the glasslike shield, licked around it, and vanished.

Cathbad laughed. "Is that the best that you can do, witch? You should not have been so insolent as to challenge the gods!"

She, however, continued to smile as if she had some secret of her own, and indeed she did. Behind Cathbad, atop the palisade, the crossbowman who'd separated from the others cranked his bow and lined up a careful shot. The witch took a step toward the druid and doubled the intensity of her flames, which changed in color from red to indigo.

Lightning and thunder rolled and a barrage of bolts fried the crossbowmen who still stirred behind the witch. With the death of their chieftain and without the direct aid of Cathbad, the goblins lost heart, broke, and attempted to flee, pursued by the knights. Scot and

Gawain continued their combat, their swords flashing in the gathering gloom. Gawain's armor reflected the light of electric bolts and magical fire. Arthur relaxed his posture as the battle swung by him. Heather's eyes darted around the deserted greathall and came to rest on the discarded hammer. Mordred sat silent on his ebony charger, eyes focused on Cathbad.

The lone crossbowman behind the druid pulled the trigger on his weapon. Its bolt sailed unimpeded through the dark, wet air and struck Cathbad under the left shoulder blade. The druid arched backward, let go of the staff with one hand, and his magical shield faltered. Two additional crossbow bolts sailed through from the front, striking the old man. He writhed. Tongues of indigo flame began to puncture and eat away at the shield. The Druid's death was only seconds away.

But before Cathbad fell, his muscles swelled, his shoulders lifted, his neck bulged. Coarse gray hair bristled in patches. He opened his mouth and his canine teeth elongated into fangs. He yelled, and his yell became a deep-throated growl. Lightning flashed, undirected by his hand.

In the blaze, Cathbad could be seen in his new form. He'd become a massive cave-bear, eight feet tall at the shoulder. The crossbow bolts stuck out of his hide and blood ran down his sides, but what appeared to be mortal wounds to the old man, were barely scratches to the great bear. It roared again and leapt at Morgana.

Her fire swirled around it, torching its hair and crisping its flesh, but it did not falter. She relaxed her flames, lifted her crooked hands, and shot another salvo of green energy bolts. Ten glowing discs slammed into the bear in quick succession, along with four more crossbow bolts. It staggered and slowed as whole patches of flesh were burned and blasted away, but still it reached the witch, grabbed her in heavy arms, and began to crush her frail body in a horrible hug.

Morgana pulled her head as far from the beast as she could and placed the palm of one hand on its forehead, mumbling some incantation in an arcane tongue.

A pale, shimmering nimbus enveloped the great bear and it shrank back into a man. Cathbad's body was blasted by magic, blackened and burned, punctured by at least five crossbow bolts. Blood poured from his wounds, and the light faded from his eyes. He released his grip on Morgana and fell at her feet.

She cackled, but the laugh had barely begun when a blazing blue light enveloped them both. A broad bolt of lightning, like a pillar of electric air, shot out of the earth into the dark sky.

It took Cathbad's body and Morgana le Fay with it, leaving only two brass beads, a gold ring, and a strong smell of ozone behind. The rain continued to pour down in sheets into the courtyard, but the full moon glowed through a hole that the massive bolt blasted between the clouds.

Scot and Gawain's swords were locked and they pushed against each other, strength versus strength, as Cathbad vanished into the air. In his peripheral vision, Scot saw Mordred's knights, now finished with the goblins, advancing on him behind Gawain, swords upraised and dripping both rain and blood.

"Cathbad is dead, and your vow died with him," Gawain said. "Yield to me now and I'll see that you live."

Scot held his blade, still pushing Hrunting against Mimung.

"Yield, I beg you."

With obvious uncertainty, Scot lowered his blade and kneeled: "I yield to you, Sir Gawain, and to you alone. I am your servant and prisoner."

"I accept your surrender," Gawain said, opening his visor and giving the formal response.

He turned toward the advancing knights. Five remained. The other three chased the fleeing goblins about the empty yard. Arthur and Heather stepped from the archway and moved toward Mordred. The knight sat atop his horse, gaping at the blackened earth where his aunt and mentor once stood.

"I thank you, my son, for the timely rescue," Arthur said.

Mordred turned, seeming to see through his father, and then fixed his eyes on Scot. "I ordered you to kill *everyone* except for my father and brother!"

"This prisoner has yielded to me and I will not see him killed," Gawain returned.

The knights hesitated at this and looked to Mordred for orders.

"Kill him!" Mordred commanded, "And if Sir *Gawain* resists," his eyes narrowed, recognizing for the first time that he was not dealing with Agravain, "slay him too!"

The knights advanced, swords drawn.

Gawain shrugged wearily at Scot. "I gave my word, so shall we?" he asked.

"Thank you," Scot managed, his voice cracked with emotion. They stood side by side, defiant against Mordred's knights.

"Stop this madness at once," Arthur ordered. "We're all on the same side here."

"Are we, *father*?" Mordred asked, a harsh chill in his voice. Four crossbowmen moved into formation behind him.

Scot and Gawain engaged the five knights in a flurry of steel.

"You know," Gawain admitted as he fought two assailants, "I'm tired. I'm not the youth that I once was."

Scot didn't reply as he fought three enemies simultaneously.

The men vied for position, for footing, for a weakness in their opponents' defenses, when a deafening blast thundered through the courtyard.

The fourth story of the tower exploded in a sudden billow of expanding flame, rocks and charred support beams tumbling down amidst a scattering of ruined furniture and blazing tapestries. A six-foot rectangular slab landed on one of Scot's adversaries, crushing him into the gravel with a sickening sound Scot would recall until the day he died. Next to Heather the copper cauldron clanged to earth, cracking with the impact. She ducked back at the sound, and avoided a hail of small stone chips and bits of mortar. Ducking bits of falling rubble, she heard a terrible roar from above.[27]

---

[27] Now, if you've never heard a dragon roar (even a juvenile dragon), you're missing the single most thrilling and terrifying experience of your life. A dragon's roar sounds like that of a lion—a 30-foot 20,000-pound lion—overlaid with the hiss of a similarly sizeable snake, and followed immediately by a chaser of some brief clicking, metallic throaty grinding, and a barely audible crackle like dry wood on an open flame. These latter, though quiet in comparison to the sonic blast of the initial roar, seem amplified because they occur in the moment of perfect stillness that always follows in its wake, right before onlookers start screaming in terror, losing control of their bowels, and fleeing for their lives. For, you see, a dragon's roar has an effect like magic and spreads terror in all those

Everyone looked up to see the silhouetted form of the dragon, backlit against the flames, its head raised, jaws open, and wings spread. It finished its roar and scuttled over the edge of the shattered tower, circling down the rough stone like a lizard on a tree trunk.

The unmounted horses bolted and the remaining crossbowmen dropped their weapons and ran, all but the lone marksman on the palisade, who simply cowered where he stood.

It was a testament to the morale of Mordred's knights and the leadership of the man himself that not one of them fled. They, and all of our heroes, stood stunned and seemed rooted to the spot—until the dragon stood unresisted in the courtyard, blood-red scales shining in the firelight, reflecting and refracting the orange-yellow glow of the burning tower.

Mordred's knights retreated to stand in line with Gawain and Scot, who were, a few seconds ago, their adversaries. Three more knights returned from chasing goblins. They all stared at the dragon as it cocked its crocodile head, considering them like hors d'oeurves at a pre-tournament feast. It was a surreal moment. No one knew quite what to do or how to react.

A terrified scream split the awestruck silence. A man pinwheeled through the sky and landed with a bone-splintering crunch atop the pile of dead goblins beside Heather. He'd been hanging over the edge of the crumbled tower, struggling with his blistered and burned fingers (all nine of his fingers) to keep his grip on the rain-soaked stone, dangling three stories above the courtyard. His feet scrabbled against the wall for purchase, but found none, and he fell.

Unbeknownst to everyone else, Alanbart had managed to stay alive through a combination of extraordinary luck and quick wit. He was being cooked by dragon fire as Heather and Arthur sneaked by. He screamed in agony and tears dried hot on his cheeks, but he laughed too—laughed at himself for becoming the martyr, violating the fundamental rule of his embarrassing existence, and laughed because for the first time in his life he was truly happy. He liked himself—he genuinely did—and at that moment, all would end for him. The irony

who hear it; only the most disciplined warriors can bring themselves to stand against it, and most of those require clean underhose as a result of the encounter.

was too much to bear, and he both laughed and cried about it while waiting for the dragon to roast his very bones.

As he huddled there, the skin blistering and burning on his arms and legs, he watched Arthur and Heather make the stairwell. The dragon heard them and it whipped its long neck around, shoving its head through the doorway, and vomiting fire down the stairs behind them.

As Alanbart watched, waiting to die, his eyes came to rest on the copper cauldron which lay on its side in front of him with a small scum of vinegar-broth pooled in the bottom. He dropped his shield and scurried into the four-foot mouth of the great pot, then grabbed its still-hot edge with blistered fingers, and tipped it down over his head. There he sat in that cramped darkness, afraid to move with the heat increasing every moment, the air thickening.

Outside the cauldron, the room blazed. Even without the presence of the dragon, Alanbart would have burned to death in an instant, and even if he were magically impervious to heat, he would have asphyxiated. The fire hungered for oxygen and ate all of the air. The only breathable supply lay hidden under the cauldron.

Eventually the dragon tried to break free from the room, slamming against the stone walls, shaking the tower, and belching torrents of flames. The wooden ceiling collapsed. Flames billowed out as the inflow of oxygen hit them. The crisscrossing beams went next, and without their aid, the walls began to bow out, the mortar between the stones crumbling in the heat.

Finally, the dragon burst from the tower, collapsing the walls outward and sending the stones crashing down in all directions. The monster roared and lashed its tail, which knocked into the cauldron. It tipped, rolled, and spun over the edge. Alanbart leapt out at the last possible second, grabbed madly at the wall, and was left hanging by bloody, blistered fingertips. He watched the dragon climb away from him and tried, unsuccessfully, to scramble onto the stone platform above. His hands slipped and he fell.

Now Heather gasped and knelt beside him. She removed his dented helmet. Alanbart's lined face dripped with sweat and his hair lay matted to his scalp. His clothing was drenched and his skin badly burned. He'd obviously broken his right arm and both legs in the fall—they twisted to unnatural angles—but he was still alive and the green belt, her favor to him, shimmered in the light of dragon-flame. It was wrapped crosswise over his body, miraculously undamaged despite scorch-marks all over his armor. He grimaced, clinging tenaciously to consciousness.

"Alanbart," she called, "can you hear me?"

His eyes found hers and he responded with a weak smile. "It doesn't even hurt," he murmured, and coughed, bringing up some blood. She tried to hide her concern.

"Oh, it will," Heather said with mock cheerfulness. "Give it time." She pulled two lank strands of sweat-soaked hair off of his face. "Alanbart," she repeated his name, soothingly.

"You can kiss me again, if you want," he said, "though I'm sure I've looked better."

"No," she shook her head slightly, her eyes on his. "You never have."

Again, the dragon roared, shattering the moment. Heather turned toward the sound.

The knights gathered in a ring around it, all save Arthur and Mordred, the latter of whom blocked the gate with his horse and turned back his fleeing crossbowmen. The dragon reared its head back and unleashed a gushing stream of liquid flame against Gawain, Scot, and four of Mordred's knights.

Most of them raised their shields in time, but a knight clad in white and sporting a black unicorn as his heraldic device, took the blast of liquid fire full on his helmet. It splashed through the slits, and he wrenched it off, clawing at his burning face and screaming, "My eyes! My eyes!"

Scot led the remaining knights in a charge, his wooden shield impressively ablaze, but the dragon battered it with its forearm, sending him tumbling to the side. As the swordsman tumbled across the courtyard, the monster's head struck like a snake at the next charging knight, puncturing the plate on his shoulder with its ebony fangs and injecting him with blood-congealing poison. He sat down, groped ineffectively at his wound, and then began to shake and froth from the mouth inside his helm. He slowly collapsed, rocking into a fetal position, and went still.

Gawain and other three knights, however, did survive to close within sword-range of the beast.

The well-forged blades of Mordred's knights were ineffective against the dragon's hide. Like steel against stone, they made a scraping sound on the scales, made visible scratches, and drew sparks, but could not draw blood. They only served to annoy and anger the monster. Mimung, however, slashed down on the seemingly impenetrable skin of the monster's forearm, cracking a red scale and drawing forth an ooze of boiling black blood, drips of which congealed and cooled into stone on the edge of the rain-soaked blade. The great serpent reared in pain, flapping its wings to hold its forearms aloft, and snatched up two knights, one in each hand. It crushed one and bit the head from the other's shoulders.

By this time, Scot regained his feet (his shield had extinguished in a puddle beneath him) and charged. The three knights behind the monster advanced cautiously into range. Arthur, too, turned toward the dragon and advanced at a trot, Excalibur held aloft. In his undersized leather jerkin and open-faced helm, he was far more exposed than the others.

Gawain dodged under the uplifted and exposed bands of the dragon's underbelly and jabbed up, skillfully sticking the blade between cream-colored ribbons of dragon-scale. More black blood erupted from the wound, dripping in sizzling splotches to harden on the pebbled ground.

The three knights behind stabbed and struck at the dragon's tail in desperation.

Scot drove Hrunting deep into its side, causing another oozing wound.

Crossbow bolts, as quickly as the bowmen could draw and fire, clouded the air, bouncing and ricocheting off the armor around the creature's head. One struck close to its eye.

The dragon found itself surrounded by so many threats that it became indecisive, and so tried to handle all of them—or as many as it could—at once. It battered at Gawain with its wing, knocking him prone. It torched three crossbowmen with a long spewing stream of liquid fire. Then it released the lifeless knights in its forearms and fell back toward the ground, pinning Gawain under its right arm. Its tail lashed back and forth, upending all three of the knights attacking from the rear.

Arthur moved in, sword upraised, but the serpent swung its snake-like neck sideways along the ground in a powerful arc (like a giraffe), and whipped it into his shield, sending him sailing through the air, legs kicking, to crash against a two-wheeled cart beside the tower. Damp straw smoked and smoldered around flaming bits of debris.

The dragon then buffeted Scot with its wings, knocking him down again. It flapped vigorously and lifted off the ground, still carrying Gawain in its claw. There it hovered, out of range of swords, rotated, and spewed a rain of flame onto Arthur and the three knights who stood near him.

"Protect the king!" one of them shouted, a man in orange with a white griffon on his surcoat. Two of the warriors managed to cover him with their steel shields as the flames spattered down and lit the darkness, splashing off in a flaming spray. Though Arthur was wholly protected, some drops of the fire hit the knights, and ignited their silken surcoats, enveloping the pair in harmless but impressive halos of flame. Arthur leapt to his feet as the cart of straw ignited in earnest.

Scot assessed the situation and realized that the dragon couldn't be reached by men on the ground. He sprinted toward the nearest palisade tower, scrambling up the ladder, two rungs at a time.

Gawain, trapped in the monster's grip, thanked the Virgin Mary that his shield arm was pinned to his chest and that Agravain's armor was so well crafted. The dragon squeezed, but the claws couldn't dig through the pinned shield and his plate had not yet buckled. He prayed for deliverance as he slashed repeatedly at the dragon's wrist with his sword.

Because of his terrible angle of attack, he couldn't get enough power on his swing. He realized that he needed to invert his blade and stab at the dragon, but dangling in the air without a clear line of sight through the eye-slits of his helm, and without even the comfort of a stable position, he didn't dare try to flip and catch his only weapon. For, if he lost it, he would be defenseless against the serpent's head, should it choose to strike.

Arthur formed the knights on the ground into a defensive cluster with him at the center, overlapped shields upraised. The dragon-breath sprayed against them, but none got through. They were, however, completely impotent against the monster. A lone crossbowman seemed to be their one hope, but it took him almost half a minute to crank and load his bow between shots, his bowstring was soaked, and the dragon so terrified him that his usually flawless aim shook.

The dragon hovered, its back to the palisade, just out of range of the ground attack, and turned its attention to Gawain. The creature struck at him, and he parried with Mimung. Twice he deflected poisonous fangs with his blade, and as the great serpent arched its neck for a third strike, Scot reached the top of the palisade tower.

The wooden structure was rickety and shabbily constructed, but it did soar twenty-five feet in the air, which left him about five feet taller than the airborne dragon, and within striking distance of a running leap.

The mad Pict didn't hesitate. He discarded his shield, inverted his sword, ran to the edge, and leapt, screaming a battle-cry.

His blade slid through the pinkish-brown membrane of the monster's wing, rending it with a tearing noise like canvas on a ship's sail splitting in a storm. He rode the cut all the way to its body. His intention had been to catch hold of a protruding back-spike, but he missed the target and the force of the impact knocked the wind from him. He toppled to the ground, struggling to breathe. Hrunting clattered some distance away.

Scot's attack proved effective. No longer able to stay aloft, the dragon flapped frantically and crashed to the courtyard. It dropped Gawain.

The famous knight took the brunt of the fall on his right hand and arm, and he, too, lost his wind. Heather watched the confrontation with growing apprehension. She could see that her blade would be useless and thought about picking up a discarded crossbow, but an idea struck her. Looking at the injured dragon, coiled on the earth with its back to the palisade tower, she remembered the discarded hammer—the one used to shatter the gate—just inside the door to the tower. She patted Alanbart's cheek and said, "I'll be right back—stay awake!"

She sprinted into the tower, hefted the hammer, and pounded across the courtyard, challenging the dragon face to face.

Meanwhile, Arthur led three remaining knights against the monster. They advanced behind a shield-wall, weapons drawn, but seeking protection in numbers. Flames burst ineffectually against them;

as the torrent lessened, they charged.

The serpent swung nimbly around and its tail lashed across their shields, toppling them in a clumsy, exposed jumble. The tail coiled around one knight, constricting him and crushing his armor. Its head struck, and another of the knights died, foaming at the mouth. The head reared again, catlike eyes fixed on Arthur. His shield got tangled between the legs of one of his slain fellows, leaving him only Excalibur to defend himself.

The dragon's pupils narrowed. Seeing the glittering blade and sensing danger in striking, the serpent unhinged its jaw. The red-glow of false flaming sunrise cloud be seen roiling up its throat.

Scot rose to his knees and scanned round for Hrunting. It lay maybe ten paces off—too distant to reach before the dragon struck. He scrambled to his feet, ran five paces, and dove for it anyway.

Gawain rolled over, tried to rise, and discovered that three fingers had been dislocated in the fall. He swore in pain and fell back to his elbow. He couldn't even hold his sword. Nevertheless, he lurched to his feet and sprang toward Arthur, determined to rescue his uncle by throwing his own body in the dragon's way, but even as he ran, he realized that he wouldn't make it.

The great serpent clearly had Arthur cornered. Wielding Excalibur, the king had maybe ten fleeting seconds left to live.

Heather sprinted across the courtyard, hammer in hand, but ten yards still remained between her and her goal; like Gawain, she was helpless to protect her king.

The dragon's eyes glittered and the flames boiled forth, but at that instant, a purple and gold striped lance crashed into its chest with all the combined force of charging warhorse and armored rider. The lance drove through the dragon hide and snapped off.

The monster flailed its neck in pain, spewing wild flames over Arthur's head. The palisade began to burn. Black blood boiled about the protruding lance, and that, too, ignited.

Mordred drew his famous sword, Clarent, and looked down at his father from atop his glistening charger. "Get back!" he ordered. "Leave this to me!"

Arthur wrenched his shield free, determined to aid his son if he could.

Mordred slashed at the dragon. Ineffectual sparks glittered along his blade and against the stony scales of the creature's shoulder. In response, it lifted a clawed arm and brought down Mordred's great charger in one blow, gouging into its flanks and toppling the knight. The horse screamed as the monster advanced, its weight snapping strong bones. Black blood dripped onto the horse's neck and sizzled into its flesh, kindling its mane to livid flame. Its eyes bulged wide in wild pain and terror.

Mordred rose in the cascading rain, shield upraised, and blocked a strike of the dragon's darting head, the force of which again knocked him off of his feet.

Heather reached the guard tower. The wooden structure, stretching three stories into the air, was resting on four thick tree-trunk pillars. She took aim at the one nearest to her and swung the heavy hammer. Her strike lacked force, but it didn't matter:

BOOM!

The ground shook, the sound echoed, and the tower wobbled unsteadily. She dragged the heavy hammer to the second support that lay on the inside of the palisade, hefted it, and swung again:

BOOM!

The tower swayed. Heather dropped the cumbersome weapon and ran. The supporting columns on the outer wall bent, creaked, and snapped. It toppled, twisting drunkenly as it fell.

The crashing and splintering of wood mixed with the roaring scream of the dragon. Flames erupted from the wreckage and the fire's glow reflected off the cloud of dust that rose, curling with effort, into the rain.

The pile of burning wood shuddered as the dragon tried to rise. The monster's crocodile-head protruded from a heap of splintered wood that rested under two crossed beams. Its baleful eye glared at Arthur. The king dropped his shield, gripped Excalibur in both hands, and placed his left foot forward. He touched a spot atop the dragon's head and between its eyes for aim, lifted his sword and prepared to bring it down. He looked across the dragon to see Mordred standing opposite, his armor dripping but lit by fire, his helm removed, and his sword, Clarent, held tight in his hand. Mordred knitted his dark brows and nodded.

The dragon's pupils narrowed and it shook violently. Wood tumbled and fell; more ignited, shedding a brighter light on the scene. Excalibur rose and chopped down, Clarent rose and came down, and both blades lifted and fell again.

Finally, the dragon's skull shattered. Father and son had joined in the slaying of a legendary serpent.

Gawain stood behind his uncle, cradling his dislocated fingers. Scot joined them, holding both Hrunting and Mimung. He slid the second blade into Gawain's sheath and touched his friend's shoulder gingerly. The knight nodded a curt and simple thanks.

"I am grateful, again, my son, for the timely rescue" Arthur said with warmth, holding his hand out to Mordred.

The dark knight considered his father's hand and then scanned the scene. Of his original fifteen knights, one survived. Morgana was gone, and a lone crossbowman remained of his company. Ranged against Arthur, Gawain, Scot, and Heather, his odds looked slim. Making his decision, he held out his hand and clasped his father's in a firm grip.

The old king pulled his son into a long hug, and then released him, clapping his knobbed hands to Mordred's shoulders and staring earnestly into his face.

"Father," Mordred said, "remember today kindly, for I saved you. Those who claim that I am your enemy, and there are many—do me an injustice and you a disservice. All should know that today if I had hesitated but for a few moments, you would have been melted in dragon fire. Instead, I plunged my lance into its flesh and placed my body between you and your fate. Have I not redeemed my honor in your eyes and earned your good opinion?"

Arthur smiled with genuine affection. "Indeed you have, my son, indeed you have." He then added, almost to himself: "Bring the fattened calf and kill it. Let's have a feast and celebrate. For this son of mine was dead and is alive again; he was lost and is found." He released Mordred, who considered at him with an oddly guarded expression.

"Father?" he asked.

Arthur nodded, "Fear not, my prodigal son, that I shall find some appropriate way to reward your loyalty and devotion, for today you have earned it all."

As the king said this, Mordred's face relaxed. He shot a secret gloating grin over the king's shoulder toward Gawain. It was full of malice. Despite the momentary reconciliation with his father, the rift between Mordred and Gawain clearly remained. Their day of reckoning lay before them; both men understood that.

Heather appeared from around the burning wreckage that hissed in the driving rain. She removed her helmet and her matted hair dripped with perspiration. She smiled sheepishly past the king and his son at Gawain. When the knight returned her gaze, she lowered her eyes to the corpse-ridden ground.

The king, assuming that Heather's embarrassment was directed at him, stepped away from Mordred and held a hand out to her. "I never thought that I would owe my life to any woman other than my own mother, the Holy Virgin, and the Lady of the Lake. Lift your head, Lady Heather, and look upon your King." He touched her chin gently.

"My lady," Mordred interrupted. "I'm not sure whether I should thank you or not. I was in the middle of a melee with the dragon, true, but the tower nearly hit me as it toppled. By almost killing me, you either saved my life or robbed me of what would have been my greatest glory—that of slaying a mythical beast, unaided." He smirked, considering the burning and steaming carcass of the slain dragon, then shifted his gaze to her. "As the event has already occurred, we shall never know."

Heather squirmed uncomfortably under his scrutiny. She didn't know how to respond, so she changed the subject. She looked back at the tower and said, "Forgive me my liege and my lords, but I must tend to Sir Alanbart's wounds."

"Sir Alanbart lives?" Arthur exclaimed. "I should very much like to see him."

Heather led the way to where Alanbart lay, twisted atop the pile of slain Goblins. He clung to consciousness and watched them approach. He tried to grin, but only managed a grimace. "The bed upon which I lie lacks comfort."

Arthur smiled sympathetically. He knelt and rested a combat-calloused hand on the injured knight's chest. In a voice too low for the others to hear through the crackle of flames and hiss of rain, he said, "So, fate has prevented both you and me from dying in battle today— I'm almost sad of it. What better way to die than in combat with a dragon? Now you and I can go on to outlive our heroism and besmirch this day's glory with unfitting deeds." He chuckled, patted Alanbart's hand once, and rose.

Over the king's head Alanbart glimpsed the black shadow of a bat flitting in and out of the firelight. He thought once again of Bede's sparrow. 'And so, five sparrows continue their flights through the hall. Out of the darkness of chaos we came, and into that darkness we shall return.' He hoped that they wouldn't see that darkness for many years to come.

The king turned to the others. "Who is skilled at setting and splinting bones?"

"I am," Gawain offered.

"Take care of Sir Alanbart's wounds," the king commanded. To the others, he ordered, "Scour the courtyard and check for injured men who may yet live. Bring them here. Then collect the horses. Check the stables and—" he paused, remembering something that Rabordath had said, "—the kennels. There may be a litter of newborn hounds to bring with us to Camelot."

"If you find any living, goblins," Mordred added, "finish them."

Arthur nodded his approval and two knights moved off.

"By God, I almost forgot," Gawain exclaimed as he watched them begin to check fallen men for signs of life. He motioned to the lone crossbowman. "Find some way to get into the basement of the tower—get hold of some rope or a ladder. There is a guard tied up in the dungeon. Bring him before the king for judgment."

The man moved off. Gawain looked at Alanbart, but spoke to Heather, "We have to get him off this pile before I can splint those legs." To Alanbart, he added "This is going to hurt."

"What doesn't?" Alanbart asked.

"Earlier today," Heather took Alanbart's shoulders, prepared to lift him, "you said that you needed a miracle to rekindle your faith. Well, you're alive after facing a dragon and falling from the top of that tower. I consider that to be a miracle. What do you believe now?"

"A miracle would have set me down, uninjured, on my feet," he quipped. "If this is a miracle, it is one made through quick thinking and good luck."

"It may be a miracle of magic," Gawain cut in. "I see that you're wearing my belt."

"Heather gave it to me," Alanbart responded defensively. "I—" He groaned and winced as Sir Gawain straightened his broken legs and (grunting in his own pain from his newly relocated fingers) lifted him gently up, laying him as flat as possible on the pebbled, muddy ground.

"Sorry," he said. "I'm going to have to set and splint them in a moment. You know," he changed the subject in hopes of distracting the injured man, "though I gave that belt to Heather, I got it indirectly from Morgan le Fay. I imagine you've heard the tale."

"This is *the* belt, then?" Alanbart asked, trying to feel the silk and emeralds with his left hand, though his blistered and burned fingertips didn't register much sensation.

"Yes, and when Lady Bercilak gave it to me, she said that it would prevent me from sustaining a mortal wound. You, Sir Alanbart are *not* mortally wounded."

"Miracle, wit, luck, magic," King Arthur cut in. "Why not all four? God knows each has played its part in my life over the past three days and two nights." He sat down heavily on a barrel, put his back to the wet cold stone of the tower, and sighed in contented exhaustion.

"Speaking of which," Gawain said, "if I may ask one question, my liege, how is it that you lived through the encounter with the banshee that killed Kay and Agra—and my brother?"

Arthur nodded. While he talked, he unfastened his shield and let it clatter to the ground. "We will have time to talk of it later, but it was the damndest thing. I was knocked off of my feet, unconscious, and when I awoke, I was imprisoned. It seems that my scabbard somehow took the blow for me. The metal was peeled back and curled like a lily flower. The thing was blasted and useless—but it served its purpose. I sit before you living and sound in both mind and body— well, almost. I have a favor to ask." He turned. "Lady Heather?"

"Yes, my liege?"

"Will you kindly pull this goblin arrow from my shoulder?" he sighed. "It begins to pain me." He leaned his head against the tower and closed his eyes. Rain fell on his upturned cheeks.

In the midst of all this, Scot stood next to the dead dragon, unnoticed and unsure. This moment marked the high point of his life as a swordsman, warrior, and hero. In the space of two days, he'd held his own in a fight against Sir Gawain (the third greatest warrior in the history of Britannia), defeated a banshee, earned Hrunting, and wielded the legendary sword against a dragon. He'd also lost a mentor, had his ideals challenged, and made a true friend with whom he would trust his life. He felt more exhausted than he'd ever been and also more fulfilled.

Scot collapsed to his knees and his blue-painted, soot-blackened, and bloodied face broke into a broad lopsided grin. He began to laugh. He laughed with abandon because he didn't know what came next, because he was overjoyed to be alive, and because there was nothing else that he could do but laugh. The sound carried across the silent rain-drenched courtyard and everyone who heard it—yes, even Mordred himself—cracked a genuine smile.

Epilogue

Flags whipped in the wind above the invitingly imposing façade of Camelot. The afternoon sun slanted warmly, illuminating the red and golden leaves of maple and oak. Long yellow strands of willow tossed along the riverbank, and the white stone of Arthur's castle gleamed. The contrast of light and shadow played upon its towers, walls, courtyards, fountains, gardens, and the spectacle of tents, pennants, horses, and men, blooming like a flower around its periphery. Two months had passed since the incident of the dragon, and the king's reputation as a monarch with near supernatural power for good over evil had swelled throughout Britannia.

Arthur had called up his grand army and begun preparations to march and sail and march again, all the way to Benwick to besiege Lancelot and reclaim his queen. The host would depart in three days' time, but today the king decreed an epic feast, and tomorrow, a tournament. It would all begin with a ceremony rewarding the loyalty of his most worthy subjects. Chief among those to be honored were Gawain, Alanbart, Heather, Mordred, and Scot.

The ceremony would take place in the great feasting hall at the center of Camelot. Our heroes and Mordred awaited their recognition in the adjoining room, which housed the famed Round Table. It was a tall, broad, cylindrical chamber, hung with narrow flag-like tapestries that displayed the coats of arms of the Round Table Knights. Natural light filtered generously from a circle of many-paned arching glass windows nestled beneath the dome of the roof.

Heather, Alanbart, and Scot stood at the outer edge of the vast wooden table, while Gawain leaned against the wall behind his chair. Mordred, who wore dramatically polished and enameled black armor of interlocking steel scales, took a seat—Arthur's seat—and leaned back, placing his mailed boots on the table. He wore a smug look that Gawain silently promised to wipe off his face with whatever force of arms might prove necessary. But alas, my friends, that is a tale for another day.

The heroes were all changed in appearance. Gawain wore silver plate, for Arthur had decreed that all knights participating in the morrow's tournament should attend the feast in mail to distinguish intrepid warriors from secure spectators. If anything, this new suit was more impressive than the one Gawain had lost to the fire. Though not inlaid with gold and gems, it sparkled in light from the west-facing windows. Recently forged, it better fit the knight's body and was made of heavier, harder, and more flexible steel in the most advanced style. It was encumbering mail intended for warfare rather than travel. Over it he'd draped a purple silken surcoat with the twin-headed eagle of Orkney woven ornately in gold thread. He had Mimung in his scabbard and both his hair and beard were freshly trimmed and combed. His broken nose had set more or less straight and the healed wound on his cheek left a distinguished-looking scar.

Across the wooden table from Gawain, Scot stood, no longer a Pict painted in blue. He'd washed himself, showing for the first time his pale skin. Instead of sticking out at angles, his bright orange hair now ran down his back in ringlets and curls. He sported a month's growth of auburn stubble on his jaw. Scot still wore the chainmail hauberk, but he also sported a polished steel chest plate and shoulder guards. He'd slung his blue shield, now blackened with burn marks, over his shoulder, and hung Hrunting at his hip. He had a new confidence in his posture but the same old twinkle in his green eyes as he took in the tapestries, deciphering the coats of arms and naming the knights to himself. It was obvious to any who saw him that Scot felt awed to be standing there, in a place where the greatest warriors of the age would gather.

Heather no longer looked plain. She wore a gown of warm brown silk, studded with amber and citrine gems. Cut moderately low in front and back, it modestly revealed her figure—an ideal balance between appropriate and seductive. She wore a net of yellow-gold thread over her auburn hair, also studded with amber and orange gemstones. She had copper bracelets on her wrists, rings on her fingers, and a dangling necklace of stringed uncut topaz about her neck. The scarred and purpled nub of her left little finger, a deformation that she shared with Alanbart and Arthur, was the only thing that marred her perfection. She was, both Alanbart and Gawain separately thought, an incredibly beautiful woman, made more so through contrast because she was so *unlike* her peers in interests, attitudes, personality, and now experience.

It was Alanbart, however, who displayed the most dramatic change. His legs were weak and he walked with a limp, relying on the aid of a willow staff because his bones hadn't set perfectly. He ached all the time. Burn scars bristled across his arms and legs, but mostly on his hands. A sulfur-yellow tunic, adorned with a crimson cockatrice, hung from his shoulders. He'd combed his hair and shaved his chin. The most obvious change in him, though, was not external. The nervous demeanor was gone, replaced by a newfound calm, and the wry cynical wit of his expression and eyes had matured into a sort of knowing wisdom.

"So," Gawain said to Alanbart, "how does it feel, Sir, to be a hero?"

"Maybe you should ask Scot," Alanbart answered. "I don't feel fit for the title. Indeed, when people use it in reference to me, I feel embarrassed and unworthy. I know that the rest of my life will be a long and futile attempt to live up to that one hour of one day. Frankly, it's a burden. Is that what heroism is? It's not at all what I imagined from the songs."

Gawain responded with true affection. "Yes, yes, for the most part it is. They tell me that I am a great hero, but mostly I just feel human, and flawed. What I've accomplished pales in contrast to how I've failed others and mostly myself over the years."

"I don't know," Scot offered. "Being a hero feels fair and fine to me."

Mordred turned to him and looked him up and down under his dark brows. "That's because you're young, inexperienced, and living in the sunrise glow of a moment of glory. Enjoy it, fellow, while it lasts. You've accomplished something that you've longed to achieve and felt was an impossible dream since childhood. You'll have the best half-year of your life (if you're lucky) and then the glory of this moment will set beyond your horizon. You'll be left empty, questioning everything, and wishing for a challenge to equal the old. It is the central cycle of every ambitious man's life—it is the reason he seeks and achieves glory, and the reason that one day his own glory grows too heavy and crushes him, especially as he gets too old to bear its weight."

Scot ran his fingers through his hair and pondered Mordred's words. Gawain stroked his beard, scoffed, and said, "Don't listen to my brother's cynicism—he isn't telling the whole truth. Heroism isn't ambition and you *can* have one without the other." He turned from Scot to Alanbart. "I think you'll find that the heroism of your one hour of one day has its effect on the rest of your life and will never 'set,' as my brother so poetically says, beyond your 'horizon.' When the future is looking grim, you'll now know that it isn't looking *so* grim as it could be. Living through danger breeds optimism because it could always be worse and often has been. It also breeds confidence because you know that you are a man who went alone to face a dragon and lived. No one can take that from you, and everything will seem paltry in comparison."

As he finished, the door opened and the rumbling sound of an expectant crowd spilled in from the hall. A young page entered, bowed graciously to Gawain, and said, "The king is ready to begin the ceremony." He turned, passed back through the door, and our heroes followed him.

The hall was beautifully bedecked in color and splendor. Knights of all ages (some armored, some not, but all dressed in dazzling shades of shimmering silk) and their bejeweled ladies thronged around the dais. Yet, a central aisle did exist in their midst, a pathway of marble flagstone, a bright ribbon beside the gray granite of the rest of the floor, kept open by a handful of strategically placed men at arms. Our heroes advanced along that path and stepped up to face the king.

Arthur sat, regal, upon his gilded throne, a sparkling crown on his brow and a golden scepter in his hand. He rose as they arrived and gazed at each of them in turn. The king wore a heavy purple cloak of fine cloth, bordered with white ermine, and over that an ermine shoulder-cape down to his elbows across front and back. His blue eyes twinkled. Gawain kneeled, and the others followed suit, Alanbart, Heather, and after a moment of hesitation, Mordred—all but Scot, who gave a deep and respectful bow, but remained standing.

"Rise," Arthur commanded.

They rose.

"Each of you has rendered us an invaluable service, and here in Camelot, we reward loyalty and those who put their lives in peril for our sake with open-handed generosity." His old voice rang across the hall. The crowd became silent. Arthur held Gawain's gaze for some seconds, and grinned. "My nephew, for leading a rescue attempt, defeating my foe in a duel to the death, facing a fire-breathing dragon in combat, and countless acts of courage and love—too many in fact to here name—we offer you this reward."

The same young page stepped up from behind the throne and, with lowered head and eyes, handed forward a sash of shining crimson silk. It was wonderfully woven, fringed with tassels of red-gold beads, and set with garnets and rubies. Arthur set down his scepter, lifted the sash, and draped it over Gawain's head.

"This belt," he began, "was brought to me many years ago by your brother, Gareth, after he defeated Sir Ironside, the red knight, and rescued the ladies Lyoness and Linnett. As you leave with me in three days' time to avenge your slain brother, it seems only proper that you wear this, as his token, into combat. Also, here in front of this gathering I openly appoint you as grand general of my army, second in power and command only to myself." He clasped the knight's hand in both of his.

"All of my life," Gawain began, emotion apparent in his voice, "it has been my privilege to serve you, my uncle and my king. I swear before Holy God and this assembly that I shall continue to so do from now until the day of my death—and beyond, if I find myself able— obedient to your laws and with love in my heart."

He knelt and the king laid his hand on Gawain's head.

The rest of the recognitions progressed in a similar manner, with similar ceremony and gestures of appreciation. Alanbart received a knightship and a large manor house with some attached lands in Nottinghamshire. Heather received a thin silver chain bearing a large emerald pendant that once belonged to Queen Guinevere, was elevated to the rank of Lady, and was gifted a small stipend to be paid for her upkeep annually for all of her remaining life.

For his heroism, Mordred received a public statement of love and thanks and as well as command of all Britannia while Arthur and Gawain were away in France—it was not quite the open declaration of legitimacy for which Mordred lusted, but it was enough to satisfy him for the time being, and he thanked his father in appropriate terms, if somewhat coldly.

Scot's reward presented the only difficulty. Arthur, however, recognized the situation when he observed the swordsman's refusal to kneel to him, and both anticipated and controlled the problem. He held Scot to last, and when the warrior stood before him, he said quietly,

"I planned on offering you a knighthood, but I see in your eyes that you would refuse me. What is it that you desire?"

"I... I don't know," Scot admitted. "I can think of nothing that you can give me at this time, great king. All I wish is to be allowed to compete in the tournament."

Arthur shook his head slightly with genuine sadness in his expression. "I am afraid that only knights may do that," he said after a pause. "Even as a king, I am powerless against a traditional law of that magnitude. Yet, I suspect that this, too, can be satisfied. I know that you have friendship and respect for Sir Gawain. He, as well as I, holds the power to knight you. You can become his man. I will absolve you of all duty to me, save only what comes through him. What do you say to that?"

"To be Gawain's man?" Scot asked.

"Once concluded," Arthur said, by way of warning, "the vow cannot be broken until death parts you from his service. Do you accept that?"

Scot took a short breath and held it. He looked away from Arthur at Sir Gawain, his eyes lingering on the man's scarred face. "I do," he said, flushing a little. He cleared his throat and refocused his eyes on the king. "I have already yielded to him in combat and am honor-bound to him."

"Good," Arthur said, "then let us get that done with, and since I cannot let you leave without granting you a boon of some kind, I will offer but this: that the next time that I receive a plea for help from a village or a lady, or the next time that an ogre, troll, or dragon marauds through a part of my great realm, you may have the honor of the quest. This I swear."

The king then turned to Gawain and said loudly, "Sir Gawain, this man has humbly asked nothing from me but to be bound to you as one of your loyal knights. We beg that you will accept him into your service."

Gawain seemed taken aback, but at once recovered from his surprise and made a courteous reply. "By Christ, this was not supposed to be a ceremony wherein I was greatly honored twice-over." He nodded at Scot and drew his sword. "Your service I gladly accept, if it is willingly given with your whole heart."

"It is given with all my heart," Scot replied. He knelt and kissed the blade. Gawain glanced at Arthur.

"You may," the king said, his crown glittering as he nodded his consent.

Gawain shifted his blade to his left hand and then slapped Scot full across the face with particular violence. The sound resounded through the hall. The onlookers inhaled audibly. One woman gasped.

Scot straightened up slowly, a flash of wounded pride in his eyes. He did not raise his hand to his throbbing cheek.

"That," Gawain said with a compassionate sigh, "is the last blow that you shall *ever* receive from *anyone* without defending your honor and mine. Remember it. Brand it into your brain alongside your promise and this ritual."

He held out his hand. Scot took hold of it. When he rose, it was to thundering applause.

The ceremony finished, servants brought out tables, and lords and ladies seated themselves by rank. Mordred and Gawain sat on either side of Arthur at his table on the dais. Scot was shuffled away to meet the men of Orkney and take his place among Gawain's household knights. This left Heather and Alanbart sitting together at the end of a long table full of minor knights and their ladies who sat near the main doorway to hall. A lightly stained white linen tablecloth and copper cutlery rested upon the tabletop. The goblets, too, were of copper. The guests seated with them knew each other intimately and were already engaged in conversation—much of it obviously about recent events.

Alanbart looked at Heather and grinned. When she returned his smile, he turned away, feeling suddenly abashed. A minstrel began to pluck at a lute somewhere nearby and sang a comical French song of a lowborn fool hopelessly in love with a beautiful princess. People listened and laughed. Alanbart recalled Gawain's words about being a man who had faced a dragon, turned to Heather, and cleared his throat.

"My Lady Heather?" he began.

"Yes?"

"This is—uh—an awkward question at an awkward moment, but," he paused to lick his lips, then chuckled at himself. "Christ's blood! This is harder than fighting that dragon. I—" he stuttered, "I know it's sudden and maybe surprising, but I want to formally ask you for the privilege of your hand in marriage. —Hold!" He held up his hand in a frantic gesture, stopping the word—whatever it was—that she opened her mouth to pronounce. "Hold your answer until I tell you my reasons."

She folded her hands in her lap and waited—her lips a thin line.

"First, I... well, I have fallen in love with you. Yes, I have. You are a woman worthy of song—proud, intelligent, self-reliant, radiant, and caring, a rare combination of traits. There, I've said it, and the rest becomes easy. I know this probably seems quite sudden, but the fact is that I've decided to find my surrogate father, Aelfric, and to take my place as his heir—I'd become one of the greatest storytellers in Europe. But in order to do that, I must leave Britannia and not return for at least two score years. So, this is probably the last time that I will have the privilege of seeing you and, thus, the last opportunity that I may ever have to ask.

"Now, besides my ardent feelings for you, there are some other, more pragmatic, reasons: To begin, I have just been granted a small manor house and lands in Nottinghamshire. They require a mistress, and I trust you to be that mistress. As I said, I'll be away, travelling Europe. If you don't wish to be always near me, I can provide you with self-sufficiency and comfort. I'll leave you in complete control of the manor and the entirety of its income will be yours—oh, but you'd be welcome to travel with me, too, of course, if you like."

He paused to lick his lips. Her hands remained in her lap and a hint of a demure smile began to play about her lips. She waited patiently for him to finish.

"I warn you though, that being the wife of a bard—even a famous one—isn't an ideal life, but it has its perks. You'd get to see Paris, Rome, Athens, and Constantinople. I would, ah, adore your company."

He paused again and cleared his throat. He looked miserably uncomfortable. She looked amused.

"God, I'm terrible at this," Alanbart admitted. "There is one more thing, though. If you're still waiting for Sir Gawain," he sputtered, "I understand that as well. He's a legendary knight, and at this point, I'm a just an overly-intelligent cripple, but mine is an open offer. You may come, find me, and accept in the future. I'm convinced that I'll never find someone else—I'll certainly never seek out anyone else. Though, I suppose I crossed paths with you, so it is always possible—"

Heather put her hand to his lips to stop his rambling proposal. "Shh," she shushed him. "I do love Gawain," she said, "and I *always* will, but I also know that he'll never let himself love me as anything more than a remote and semi-fictionalized ideal woman. If you can accept the fact that I love him, then you're closer to accepting me as *me* than he'll ever be..." she trailed off. "And I *do* have an attraction to you. You, Alanbart, may be 'just an overly-intelligent cripple,' but you interest, amuse, and challenge me. Women don't place as much value on what can be seen with the eyes as men do—it fades, you see, and the man who is an attractive fool at twenty becomes simply a fool by fifty—but even so, I cannot yet call it love."

Alanbart took her hand in his and interrupted. "Lady Heather, I think that I can accept your feelings for Gawain. As you once said, it's hard not to love an honest idealist—it's why I fell for you (and it's why Gawain fell for Arthur). But this may ease your mind (and mine) about Gawain a bit: Aelfric once told me that strong passionate loves always destroy themselves. They are kindled of a fire that burns so hot that no amount of fuel can sustain it. Those loves, Aelfric said, either dwindle with contact—unable to burn bright through the dreary intercourse of daily life—or suffocate with distance. Only a small and steady flame, he said, can last a lifetime. Though I haven't loved before now, I've found it to be true of other passions. Those who fall headlong into obsessions do so often, and always quickly move on to new obsessions. Take our passionate friend, Scot, for example—"

"This Aelfric was a wise man," she cut in. "I would like very much to meet him. And you interrupted me. I was about to say that it is time for me, too, to speak pragmatically. At some point in her life, every woman must think of her happiness and her future. My future with Gawain holds only sorrow, my future with Elaine would be only boredom, and my future with you would be tempered with your love and respect, travel, independence, and security." She took a breath, held it in for a moment, and exhaled. "Sir Alanbart," she gently smoothed the fabric of his sleeve, "you have made me a generous offer, and I accept. You already proved that you'd die for me. How many women get that proof of devotion and still have a living lover?"

Alanbart gaped at her in disbelief. "Perhaps *this* is a miracle."

She pretended not to hear. Instead, she touched the stunted end of his little finger with her index finger and smiled. "Alanbart, I want to travel Europe with you, and I'd like to talk to you more. I'd like that most of all, I think. You talk to me like no other man ever has, like an intelligent man talks to another intelligent man whom he respects, not like a man talks to a woman. There is no artifice or condescension, and I like that. I imagine that we will have plenty to say to each other on our travels?"

"Indeed we will," Alanbart responded, still in a daze.

"Good," she replied, and rested her head on his shoulder, trying out the posture. She liked it well enough. "And I would like to see Jerusalem, so add that to our list of destinations."

"I will do so, my lady, but if you think that some old temples and relics are going to convert me, think again."

"Oh no, it isn't relics or buildings that will do that," she replied mysteriously.

At this point fifty trumpets, hung with silken flags in a multitude of colors and designs, blew a long high note, and the feast began.

Waiters brought forth food. Whole cooked geese and pigs, sides of beef, haunches of venison and lamb, soups, stews, chowders, fish, puddings, fruit, turnips, cabbage, breads, and crackers—everything, indeed, that might be imagined or described—was brought in a long train and set upon the tables. Serving women carried pitchers of ale, wine, and mead around and filled goblets, horns, and flagons. Everyone turned to the head table, to the king, waiting for him to bring food or drink to his lips and so begin the feast, but he did not eat or drink; instead, he rose.

"My friends! My lords! My ladies, and my good knights, many of you know that we have a longstanding tradition in Camelot…"

"Here he goes again," Heather whispered into Alanbart's ear. Alanbart smiled knowingly, the crows' feet at the corners his eyes furrowing into happy lines.

"…that we will taste neither food nor drink at a high feast day until we have seen with our own eyes a combat worthy of song, or until we have heard one of our knights recount a true tale of courage, magic,

304

and heroism—a tale to amuse, educate, and inspire us to greater and more glorious feats of chivalry." He held his arms wide in an inclusive gesture.

"His cooks must *hate* him for this," Alanbart noted, looking longingly at the browned and steaming skin of a roast goose. His mouth watered. "I wonder how many wonderful meals he's ruined this way."

After a pause, Arthur continued, "We do not intend to change our tradition now. Who, then, will entertain us on this fine autumn evening?"

He sat heavily on his throne, awaiting an answer.

"I'll accept this challenge," Alanbart whispered to Heather, and he stood, leaning heavily on his staff. She squeezed his hand and released it before he thumped dramatically into the center of the hall. Alanbart halted, facing the king. An expectant hush fell over the gathering. Arthur sat forward in his seat. Alanbart cleared his throat and began:

"Your Majesty, my lords, ladies, knights, and squires: Few tales tell of heroes and dragons, kings and giants, magic, *miracles*, a banshee, and the undead. Fewer still are those told with the skill to evoke tears of sorrow and induce those of laugher. I, Alanbart, son of Alardane, bring to your chairs and benches just such a tale, and what's more, it is a true tale, as I and some knights present here tonight have lived it…"

And so this tale was born…

The End
(Happily Ever After)

APPENDIX

MAGICAL ITEMS

<u>Clarent</u>: This is, of course, the fabled sword in the stone. Often confused with Excalibur, which was given to Arthur by the Lady of the Lake, Clarent was actually pulled from the stone by Arthur as proof of his divine right to kingship. Following this, it was stolen and wielded by Arthur's bastard son, Mordred.

<u>Excalibur</u>: This famous sword was given to Arthur by the Lady of the Lake. It is a silver-steel blade, very reflective, measuring 47 inches in length and weighing only four pounds. The blade is hammered into a fuller pattern, but is forged of interwoven steel wires and is so strong that it has been said to have been made out of the magical metal "adamant." It has reflective golden runes running up the center trench. The crossguard is steel and gold, set with diamonds and gemstones of topaz and jacinth. The sword is perfectly balanced, immensely sharp, and without flaw. Being forged by fairy-smiths in the land of Avalon, it has no equal among mortal weapons.

<u>The Hammer of Autumn</u>: This hammer has a four foot haft of ironwood, heavy and black as pig-iron. It is carved in an intricate scale pattern, like the bark of a red pine tree, and into the carved trenches between the scales, molten red-gold has been poured, outlining the scales in thin golden lines. The grip on the haft is a smoothed portion of the wood, wrapped in orange-dyed supple leather. The head is made of a block of granite, smoothed on the sides and carved with images of leaves. The block is a rectangle, with an arch across the top. Each end of the hammer has a power-rune carved into the stone. The shaft passes clean through the head, and is banded to it on each side with a small ring of iron. It is said to have been wielded by Thorveld, the son of Thor himself. It is the

most ancient relic in Asacael's collection, and her most prized possession, being the favored weapon of her one "true" love, recovered from his heirs an age after his death. It is said to possess the power to shatter dead wood of any size or thickness (not living wood of a tree, though) in one blow, and that when wielded in this manner, the concussion of its contact reverberates for half a league or more, felling every leaf and needle from every living tree.

The Holy Grail: An old terra-cotta colored clay cup, smoothed at the edges, devoid of design. It has no distinguishing characteristics, but is light of weight and pleasant to the touch. A sip from this cup will cure any wound or disease, visibly energize the drinker, and add ten years to his or her lifespan.

Hrunting: A sharp and angular steel blade, shorter than Excalibur at 43 inches in length, this sword is forged in a clear diamond pattern and is dagger-sharp at the end. It weighs about three and a half pounds. Looking at this blade makes one feel cold and disquieted. Its steel is very dark and has a red tint. It is forged of folded steel, and the angular and ill-boded patterns of folding can be seen in the right light, weaving up and down the blade. Its angular crossguard is in the shape of a widened V, made of iron coated in silver and inset with a line of diamond-cut garnets. The diamond-shaped and silver coated pommel, too, is inset with garnets. The haft is balanced with lead and the grip is made of whalebone, inscribed with runes in a forgotten tongue. The only word that is legible is the sword's name, "Hrunting," written in Old Norse. Legend has it that this blade was made by a dwarf, tempered in chilled blood instead of water, and enchanted so that no wound made by it would ever fully close or truly cease to bleed. It was used by Unferth, champion of Denmark under king Hrothgar, and became cursed when he wielded it to kill his own kin. It passed to Beowulf, where it failed its owner for the first time in his fight with Grendel's mother. It later passed from Geatland to England in the dowry of Thrith to King Offa of Mercia, then through his heirs until the Danes invaded England and reclaimed it. Its last wielder, a captain named Hahhan Hardheart met his fate at the hands of Asacael.

<u>Lady Bercilak's Belt</u>: This green silk belt is long enough to wrap around a woman's waist multiple times. It is bordered with gold thread, has gold clasps, and sparkles with small emeralds. According to song, it possesses the ability to protect its wearer from death caused by any physical harm, though its one test—that of *Sir Gawain and the Green Knight*—was problematic. Read the tale and decide for yourself if it is magical or not.

<u>Mimung</u>: This is a long shining steel blade, gold-gray in the light, weighing about four pounds, and about 45 inches long. The blade in a double fuller pattern with two trenches down the center and it is rounded, rather than sharp, at the tip. The crossguard is an inverted semicircle of gray steel. The haft is balanced with lead. The grip is made of yellowed auroch horn and wrapped in supple leather. A polished stone of tiger-eye sits in the pommel, and another, smaller, sits in the rain guard. Glyphs in Gothic and Geatish on the blade announce its name, "Mimung." The blade is so sharp that it cuts to the gentlest touch, and the eyes scratch and water to look at it. Legend says that it was made by Wayland himself for his own use, but was given to his son, Wudga, a follower of Theodric the Great. It fought the famous duel with Langben Rese, was wielded against Attila the Hun, and no one ever lost a battle by fault of its failure. This remains true, for its wielder, a warrior by the name of Catigern, the second to bear the name, son of Vortimer, was slain before unsheathing it in his abortive attempt to redeem the Staff of Väinämöinen from Asacael.

<u>The Ring of Mudarra</u>: This ring is made of very finely braided yellow-gold. The intricate twining of the gold strands is a marvel to behold. The ring is heavy in the hand, and shines brightly in the light. It has neither stone nor rune, but has one interesting feature, being almost imperceptibly scarred on both sides, as if it had been split with a razor-sharp cleaver and refused in the fire. It has various healing powers, the most noteworthy of

which is the ability to cure blindness.

The Shield of Scyld: This is a round shield of framed white wood
(rumored to be cut from a fallen limb of Yggdrasil, the world-
tree), banded with forged steel and rimmed with an intricately
wrought image of Jörmungand, the world-serpent—a great
golden gilded snake, eating its own tail. It is the mythical shield
of Scyld Scefing, founder of the Danish dynasty. It the center
rests a silver orb and the outward facing wood has been painted
midnight blue around it, representing middle-earth, surrounded
by ocean. The many cuts and scrapes on this painted surface
show through white, like the caps of waves. The clasps on the
back-facing side are in the shape of a snake, a hawk, a trout,
and a dragon.

The Staff of Väinämöinen: This thin and light seven-foot staff, made of
warped and winding driftwood, is bleached gray and deeply
furrowed. The wood is warm and smooth to the touch, and at
the top of the staff, the wood curls in an impossibly seamless
ankh-like loop without a break in the grain of the wood. The
only indication that it is more than a regular driftwood cudgel is
a pair of white walrus-ivory bands fused to the wood and
carved with runes, each exactly one foot from either end.

Acknowledgements

If I might, I'd like to thank eight people and an inanimate object. Please bear with me.

Robert Scott, your mentorship, optimism, and enthusiasm have fueled and at times driven[28] this project forward. During the process of writing and publishing this novel, you wore the various hats of boss, mentor, editor, colleague, and friend. This book is as much a product of your encouragement as it is of my imagination.

Kathy Smaltz and Cindy Siira, you made writing groups a joy. I always anticipated our meetings, and I invariably left energized and inspired to continue my work. This alone would be enough to warrant thanks, but you also took the time and energy to beta-read the whole manuscript, and it is a better novel because of your efforts.

Kyle Pratt, you put in uncounted hours on the technical side of this project, with Photoshop, artwork, podcasts, and the website. Your skill and hard work are appreciated.

Milt Johns and Sara Brooks, thank you for selecting *Three Days and Two Knights* to be the initial novel published by *The Piedmont Journal of Poetry & Fiction* and for your efforts leading up to publication. You took a risk on me, and I value that (now let's make it pay off).

Professor Scott Fields, once upon a time, you were my creative writing instructor at Norwich University. You got me started on this enterprise, and as an English teacher myself, I neither undervalue the inspiration of a great educator, nor the ripple-effect of that inspiration.

Caffeine, in the forms of coffee, chocolate, and green and black teas, you, too, made this work possible. At every step in the process and

---

[28] Clarification: *driven*, less like a cheerful sunglassed fellow behind the wheel of a convertible Camaro, and more like a determined cowboy pushing reluctant cattle.

seamlessly working with all of the people involved, you brought focus and energy to our meetings, a laugh where there might have been a yawn, and insight where before dwelled only numbness. Mostly, though, you got me through those 5:00 a.m. writing sessions in the summer of 2013. Please, reader, enjoy this book with a caffeinated beverage—green tea with jasmine, if you wish to replicate the experience of the author.

And finally—and quite seriously—Elizabeth Todd, rather than thank you for all the myriad things that you've done for me (an exhaustive and exhausting list that would dwarf this book), I will just say that you put up with my pretentions, gave me time and space (that I realistically could and possibly should have spent elsewhere)[29] to write, edit, confer, publish, and publicize this novel, helping me make this fantasy into a reality. I love you.

---

[29] I *will* turn over those strawberry patches, fix the sliding door, and get the van in for an inspection, I promise.

Scott Davis Howard holds an MA in British literature from the University of Montana, Missoula (2008), a BS in communications from Norwich University (2000), is an Agnes Meyer Teacher of the Year nominee, and was a semifinalist in the 2014 Norman Mailer Writing Contest for Educators. He spends his days regaling his 12th grade students with thrilling tales about Beowulf, Sir Gawain, Macbeth, and Dorian Gray, and his nights ferrying his offspring between the soccer field and Cub Scout meetings. In his rare moments of quiet (when the children are eating snacks in the van, sprinkling crumbs all over the carpet), he wonders when and how he became a soccer mom. He wrote the original draft of this novel on an outdated laptop, standing in his kitchen with an infant strapped to his chest.